"The world of crows portrayed by the author might not be the way it actually is, but it is indeed very crowish and could easily exist in an alternative universe only slightly different than our own. "
—Michael Westerfield, The Language of the Crows

"Written from the perspective of a group of intelligent crows and ravens, the Corvids, *Corvus Rising* sheds light on the environmental destruction taking place in our world in the name of progress, economic development, jobs and greed."
—Green Living Magazine

"Anyone interested in the preservation of wildlife, the importance of being good stewards of our environment, or just anyone who is captivated by uncommonly good storytelling, will enjoy this novel and look forward to the next book in the [series]"
—K. Hughes, Amazon Top Reviewer

CORVUS RISING

Book One of the Patua' Heresy

a novel of crows

MARY C SIMMONS

Corvus Rising, Book One, the Patua' Heresy

By Mary C Simmons

Copyright © 2013 by Mary C Simmons

Mary C Simmons

TheBookMidwife@gmail.com

www.authormarycsimmons.com

Ordering Information: Quantity sales. Special discounts are available on quantity purchases by corporations, associations, and others. For details, contact the publisher at the address above.

ISBN-13: 978-0-9912245-1-7

1. Main category—[Science Fiction]—Other category—|Fantasy]

Second Edition

Cover Artwork and Design by Mary C Simmons

ECOFANTASY PRESS

IV

Contents

Map of Ledford & Wilder Island

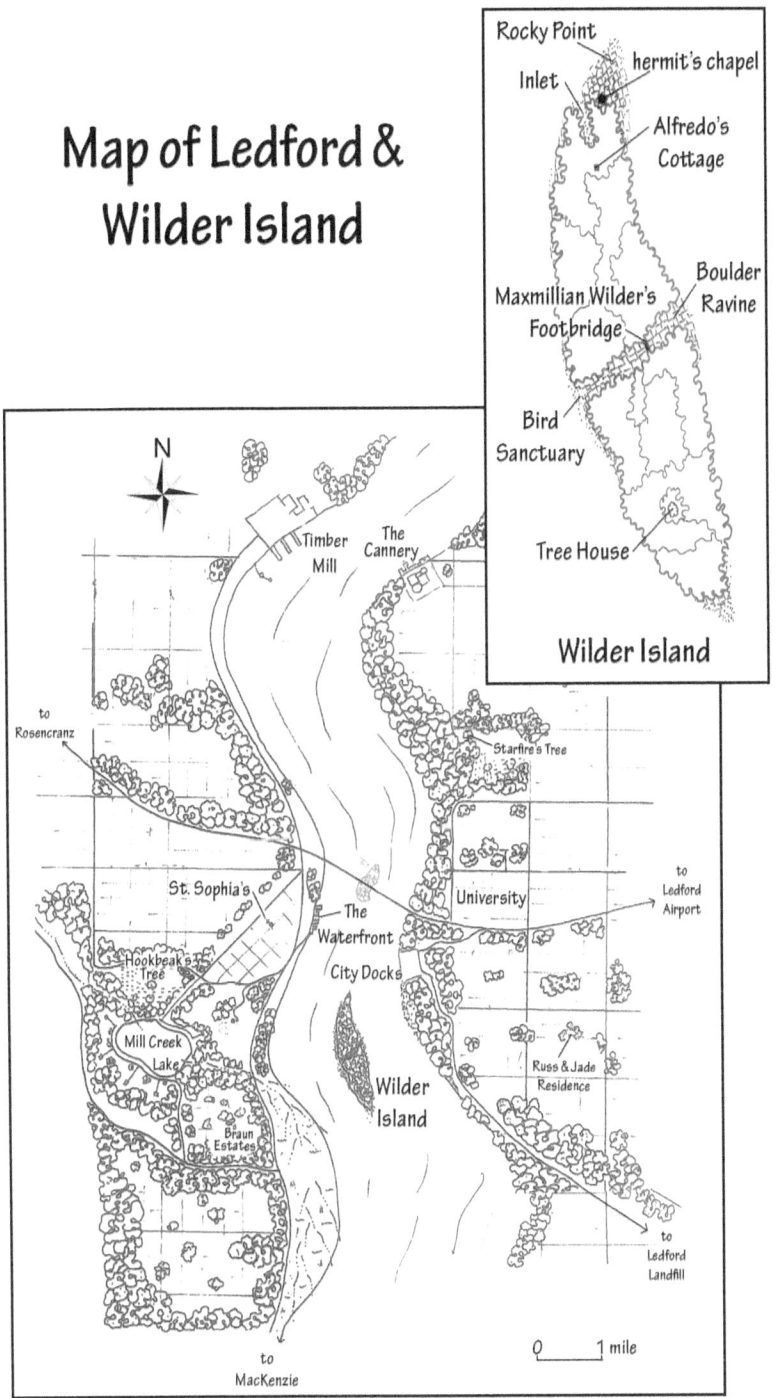

Wilder Island

Rocky Point

hermit's chapel

Inlet

Alfredo's Cottage

Maxmillian Wilder's Footbridge

Boulder Ravine

Bird Sanctuary

Tree House

N

Timber Mill

The Cannery

to Rosencranz

Starfire's Tree

St. Sophia's

The Waterfront

City Docks

University

to Ledford Airport

Hookbeak's Tree

Mill Creek Lake

Wilder Island

Russ & Jade Residence

Braun Estates

to Ledford Landfill

to MacKenzie

0   1 mile

—*1*—

Treasure Island

*T*he birdbath sails through the window, its trajectory a low-amplitude parabola accompanied by a sudden symphony of shattering glass and smacks the floor with a low-decibel endnote. The last slivers of glass fall to the floor, glittering like shooting stars in the midnight sky. The room lay buried in silence, under sparkling shards of glass. An army of black birds explodes through the broken window, screeching and beating the air with enormous wings.

The birds converge into a whirlwind of feather and beak, bringing the cold, dead fragments of glass to life. Swaying and undulating to the rhythm of the beating wings overhead, the dancing shards rip through the fluffy white comforter. Black feathers ooze like blood from gaping fabric wounds.

A single bird falls out of formation and perches on the edge of my slightly open dresser drawer. After staring down upon me with cold blue eyes for a few seconds, the black bird turns its attention to the open drawer and rummages through it with its beak.

Jade bolted out of bed, screaming, "No! Stop! Get out! It's mine! You can't have it!" Eyes wide open, heart racing in the darkness of her dream, she charged across her husband's sleeping body. Knees and elbows flailing as she made her way out from under the covers, she launched herself from the bed and tore open a dresser drawer.

"No, no, no!" she intoned, flinging its contents out into the room. "You can't have it! She gave it to me!" She jerked open another drawer and pawed through its contents, muttering, "Where is it? Where is it? They didn't get it, did they? Oh, please be here!"

"Jade!"

The harsh sound of her name made her look up. The bedside lamp came on. Her husband, Russ, stared at her from the bed. She said nothing as she attacked another drawer, scooping out handfuls of socks and underwear. "Oh, thank God," she gasped. "Here it is." She closed her eyes and clutched a small wooden box to her chest.

Her eyes suddenly focused on Russ, who had appeared beside her, and she grabbed his forearm in panic. "They know where it is now! I've hidden it from them since I was little, but now they broke the window again and came in and tried to take it!" She broke down sobbing. "They know where it is!"

Russ pulled Jade to his chest and held her close. "It's okay," he said, stroking her hair. "Just a dream, hon. Just wake up, and it'll be gone."

She shuddered, clutching him tightly. "It wasn't a dream," she said into his chest. She pulled back and looked him in the eyes. "It really happened. They crashed through the window and—"

"You were dreaming, babe," Russ said, tenderly pushing a lock of hair out of her face. "Just like before. The window isn't broken, and there's no one here but you and me and our fat old cat, Willow B."

It was true. There was no glass. No feathers. Just her and Russ and the pile of clothes she had dumped onto the floor. She dropped her head on his chest. His arms felt so warm and strong around her, and she relaxed slightly. The sound of his heartbeat dissolved her panic, and she gave in to the strong, steady love that bathed her in warmth and safety.

"C'mon," Russ said. He pulled her to her feet. "Here's your robe. I'll make us some hot chocolate, and you can tell me all about your dream."

While Russ banged pots and pans around in the kitchen, Jade sat on the sofa. Willow B aligned himself along her thigh, and she stroked him absent-mindedly as she stared into the darkness beyond the picture window.

The half-moon in the clear night sky dimly illuminated dark creatures as they flitted among the shadows in the small, undeveloped wooded area behind the house. A murder of crows, perhaps? Were they watching her now? Cloaked in feathers black as night, they waited, their black eyes always open, staring into her darkness. Would they come back next time she slept? Would they get it from her then?

She looked down at the small box in her lap and opened it. A strange nostalgia stabbed at her as she gazed upon the spherical object on a leather cord. Black as the shadows in the woods, yet somehow translucent, the medallion had been elegantly crafted. She took it from the box and touched its surface with a finger, feeling its pattern of grooves.

She imagined the unknown artist hunched over a tiny canvas, with a few quick strokes of a sharp blade, evoking a swirling pattern of lines that coalesced somehow into a human hand, from whose palm a fan of feathers emerged. He tossed it aside and began carving another. Then another, throwing each into a growing pile as he carved.

"And here you are, my love," Russ said, his voice bringing her back into the living room. "I took the liberty of adding a dash of chocolate vodka to help you sleep."

Jade took the mug and said, "I don't want to go back to sleep." The dark woods beyond the house gaped ominously, just waiting till she fell asleep. She closed her fingers tightly around the medallion. You'll never get it.

Russ sat down and switched the table lamp on. He nudged her with his elbow. "Okay, now tell me again about this dream that really happened."

The shadows vanished behind the light's reflection in the window. Jade saw herself holding a white cup, a large cat sprawled on her one side, and Russ in his natty old robe on the other.

"The first time when I was about ten, I was asleep in my bed," She set the mug on the table. "Suddenly the window in my room just explodes." She threw her arms up, demonstrating. "And there's glass everywhere," she said, eyes wide in the memory of her fear. "All over my bed, and me, and all over the floor. Except that time, there really was glass everywhere after I woke up."

"Wow!" Russ said, taking her hand and kissing it. "You must have been terrified!" He put his arm around her shoulders. "Did they figure out who or what broke the window?"

She toyed with the collar on his robe. "They didn't believe me about the birds. But I wasn't dreaming. There were crows, Russ." She looked at him earnestly. He nodded, and she fell back against the couch. "I don't know how to explain that night. There was glass everywhere. Smitty thought there must have already been a crack in the window, and when it got really windy that night, a gust just blew it out. Chloe had to help me change my nightie, and then I slept in her and Smitty's room the rest of the night. She had to sing to me so I could fall asleep."

"Well, whatever happened or didn't happen," Russ said, "it must have been really frightening. That dream would give anyone nightmares."

"I was afraid to go to sleep for months," Jade said, oblivious to Russ's pun. "Chloe had to sing to me so I could fall asleep." She let out a long sigh and then sang softly, "All around the purple heather won't you go, Lassie, go?" She reached over Willow B for her mug of hot chocolate. "I've always loved that song. Chloe said my mother sang it to me before she went away."

She gave herself over to childhood memories and her lost mother. "Won't you go, Lassie, go?" she whispered. Willow B purred softly by her side. "But I knew what they wanted that night," she said harshly. "They didn't get it. I hid it after that."

"Hid what?" Russ asked.

"This," Jade said, handing him the medallion on its leather cord. "I've had this my whole life. It's my most treasured possession. Chloe said my mother had made her promise to give it to me when they took her away." She sipped the hot chocolate, feeling its warmth down to her core.

"Pretty cool," Russ said as he scrutinized the medallion. "Fingers and feathers, that's interesting." He tapped it against his teeth. "I wonder what it's made of. Seems really hard, like stone almost, though it isn't heavy enough."

"My mother didn't want to leave me," she said, as if she had not heard him. "And she left me this to remember her."

Russ held the medallion out to her. "I think it's some kind of wood."

She watched it sway back and forth for a few moments. "I used to play with it all the time," she said, taking it into her hand. "But I stopped after that night. I put it in this box and hid it so they'd never find it. It was the only thing I ever had that she touched." She closed her fingers around the medallion and held it tightly in her hand. "I've always been afraid they would come for it someday."

Russ put his arm around her and kissed the top of her head. "Well, it's pretty bizarre that a flock of birds would come through your bedroom window at night and try to steal it. I've heard stories of crows stealing things, but I'm pretty sure they're not out and about at night. I'm curious about why you keep having this dream."

She shrugged and said, "I don't know. Maybe the crows think it's theirs, and they're trying to find it, and somehow they found me in my dreams." She put the cord around her neck and dropped the medallion beneath her nightgown. "It's been hidden in that box for years, buried in my dresser drawer. I haven't even taken it out of the box since before we were married. I don't know how they found it."

Russ twirled a strand of Jade's hair around his finger. She absently stroked the cat. Willow B purred, his eyes like slits.

"Here's what I think," Russ said. "You've had your mother on your mind a lot lately, you know? You're working on a painting of her, and we were talking about it just before we went to bed. Remember? You were complaining about not being able to see her in your mind, and how you always see your paintings in your head before you can paint them."

Jade nodded slowly. A vague image of her unknown mother appeared in the twilight of her perception—a pale face with long black hair, gray eyes the color of dawn.

She touched the medallion on its cord, imagining a dark-haired woman bending over a crib, carefully tucking the medallion under the blankets. *Does she even remember me? How would I know her? How would she know me?*

"I really feel like my mother is out there," Jade said. "Maybe she's trying to tell me something. Maybe she's trying to contact me."

"Honey," Russ said, "it was just a dream. It came from your imagination. It wasn't real. People don't contact people in dreams. That just doesn't happen—except on television."

A sudden fear gripped her. "That's what happened before," she said anxiously. "My paintings invaded my dreams, and my dreams invaded my paintings, and after a while, I couldn't tell which was which, and then I forgot to eat and go to class, and then I got lost, and—"

"Jade," Russ said sharply. "Stop! That's not happening now. It will never happen again. I won't let it. You're right here beside me, and I'm not lost. Willow B is on your other side. He's not lost either."

At the mention of his name, the cat looked up and said, "Mrrrr?"

"Exactly," Russ said. "Even Willow B knows where you are."

Jade stroked the cat and smiled. *Really, what am I afraid of?* She stared into her cup. From the dregs of chocolate at the bottom, the image of a crow slowly took shape—first a wing, then a beak, and then a cold blue eye. Just as it was about to fly out at her, she shut her eyes and said, "Why am I seeing crows everywhere all of a sudden?"

"Probably because I told you about Alfredo Manzi and his plans to make Wilder Island a bird sanctuary," Russ said.

She nodded, remembering. "Seems like the island is already a crow sanctuary; hardly anything else lives there. Maybe this is just a ruse. Maybe this Professor Manzi is there to breed crows."

Russ rolled his eyes. "I would think a Jesuit priest and professor of ornithology would have something more interesting to do than breed crows—especially crows that steal." He tilted his head back, drained his cup, and put it on the coffee table. "In fact, the island is populated by a number of other birds—jays, doves, mockingbirds—the same ones you'd find just about anywhere in the Midwest. And a variety of small mammals—squirrels, rabbits, and the like—live there too."

The island fascinated Jade, as it did everyone in Ledford. The million shades of the mythical green forest beckoned her like sirens.

Strange, fantastic creatures lurked among its shadows. And the crows. She was both attracted and repelled.

"The island was named after Maxmillian Wilder, you know," she said, banishing the crows flapping at the edge of her imagination. "The folk hero of Ledford—I've heard he was a Jesuit too, just like your Alfredo Manzi. Another coincidence, I suppose?" She arched a suspicious eyebrow.

"What, that Alfredo is a Jesuit or that the island is named after Maxmillian Wilder?" Russ asked. "Which part is the coincidence?"

"And," she said, "how'd this Alfredo Manzi, if that's his real name, find you?"

"Oh, stop it!" Russ said. "For God's sake, Jade. There is no plot here, nothing fantastic, no intrigue. He and I work in the same department at MU, remember? He likes birds, I like plants. Manzi's just an ordinary college professor who happens to be a priest."

Jade looked at her husband with raised eyebrows. "Oh, all right, Dr. Matthews," she said, yawning. "Alfredo Manzi is a straight-up guy, even though he's a priest. And nothing sinister is happening on that island of his."

Russ stretched and said, "C'mon, hon," through a yawn. "Let's go back to sleep."

Jade nodded and let him lead her back to their bed. Within moments of his head touching the pillow, Russ was snoring, but for her, sleep lurked far away. She stared at the ceiling, trying to empty her mind.

I wonder if she thinks of me.

Sighing, she turned onto her side and took the black medallion out from under her nightgown. Even in darkness, it seemed to glow from deep within. She closed her fingers around it and shut her eyes.

But sleep would not come. She got up, quietly left the bedroom, and opened the door to her studio. The half-finished painting of her unknown mother rose up and confronted her, begging her for its face. She shook her head and put a blank canvas on her easel.

FATHER PROVINCIAL THOMAS MAJEWSKI'S CAT, Snowbell, knocked a book off the top of a huge bookcase that occupied an entire wall of his office. When it struck the floor with a very un-book-like sound, Majewski rose from his chair to investigate.

"Treasure Island," he said after picking it up and reading the front. It was not a book, but a metal box cleverly disguised as one. He took it back to his desk and sat down. After undoing the small latch, he opened the lid and pulled out a bundle of papers held together by a brittle leather cord, which broke into several pieces when he tried to untie it.

He pulled a folded paper out of the small envelope on the top of the bundle, addressed to a former Father Provincial for the North American Jesuits. "The legendary Antonio de la Torre, my Snowbell," he said, as the pure white cat leaped into his lap. "He sat in this very chair over one hundred years ago." Snowbell sniffed the edge of the letter gingerly. "Do you think he had a cat?"

A hand-colored print of a painting depicting the chapel of the Madonna della Strada at the Jesuit world headquarters in Rome fell out as he unfolded the letter. He read:

> *Greetings, My Dear Brother,*
>
> *The chapel is absolutely gorgeous! Our guide told us that most of the old Roman churches had secret entrances into the labyrinth of passages in which the Church hid the early Christians during times of persecution. And so it was also with the Madonna della Strada! From within the sacristy, we entered the catacombs and went down a steep and dark stone staircase. It was like stepping into a subterranean city, comprised of many streets and alleys that went*

off this way and that. We could hardly contain your
grandnephew!

Wish you were here,

Conchetta

"Wish I was there too," Majewski muttered as he glanced at the stack of work on his desk. But it would have to wait—the faux *Treasure Island* still held a few more papers.

He pulled another letter from the box. The wax seal was still attached to one side of the letter.

6 June 1852

Dear Uncle Antoni, Father in Christ—

Greetings from Cawdaynyalazhadia!

That is the name of this island, as near as I am able to spell it, according to the residents, which are a large family of crows. I have made friends with many of them, especially one named Hozey the Younger. He is a descendant of a very famous crow, Hozey the Great, known for his contributions to nest architecture. I would not have survived this past year without the good Lord Almighty sending these many-feathered companions.

It is my sincere hope that you have been in good health since last we visited. I arrived safely one year ago—how fast this year has gone by!—yet I am quite at home here. I say Mass every day in a humble little chapel, thanking the good Lord Almighty for his gracious providence. My friend Hozey, who helped me build the chapel, brings his wife and kreegans—as the crows call their offspring—who of course squirm and fidget just like human children do in church.

Hozey has shown me many wonders of the island, and he leads me through dense groves of trees so thick and dark I could scarcely manage without an overhead guide.

It is to my wonderful flying friend Hozey that I entrust this letter. He will take it to the Ledford post office across the river and drop it in the post box. Imagine that! A mail crow! I am indeed the most fortunate man on Earth, but for the grace of God and this family of crows.

As you can see, I am well and happy, living piously in God's glory. May God bless you, dear Uncle.

I remain your humble nephew in Christ.

Maxmillian Wilder

"The man's delusional!" Majewski said, shaking his head. Snowbell cocked an ear at the emphatic tone in his voice. He stared at the spidery handwriting. *"I would not have survived this past year without the good Lord Almighty sending these many-feathered companions."*

More than 150 years had passed since Maxmillian Wilder had written this preposterous letter to his uncle. "Why did de la Torre leave this evidence of his nephew's madness in the Father Provincial's office?"

The letter made Majewski extremely uncomfortable, though he tried to brush it off. *The rantings of a madman, nothing more.* But even in the bright morning light of his twenty-first-century office, he could not help but ask if Maxmillian Wilder shared his sister Stella's bizarre sickness. If it was a sickness. "Of course it's a sickness!" he heard his mother's high-pitched voice say.

Memories of Stella surfaced from the depths of the past. It wasn't as if he never thought of her; Stella's face easily popped into his head. He sighed. *I should have saved her from her fate. Or at least I shouldn't have been the one who betrayed her.*

His mother's voice from the past complained inside his head: *"The doctors say Stella has not spoken to anyone in weeks. She just sits there with a blank stare, as if she doesn't notice anyone on the outside anymore. I visited her the other day, but it was as if I was not even there, her own mother. She gives me nothing but that horrible, empty stare."*

Despite the content of his letter, Maxmillian Wilder wrote lucidly and casually of his doings on the island. *But ...* Majewski shook his head. *I cannot believe he or Stella ever actually talked to crows.*

He stood up and wrapped his cardigan close around his chest and stuck his hands in his armpits. The Father Superior's office was notoriously cold, even in midsummer, and the fire his secretary had built in the small fireplace before he arrived had died down. He put another log on the embers and warmed his hands for a few moments as yellow flames rose up and curled around the fresh wood.

He returned to his desk and picked Snowbell up off the pile of papers he had been reading and sat down, cat in lap. He pulled out a hand-drawn map from the box, depicting a small island in the middle of a large river that flowed through a town called Ledford.

"Well, now," he said to Snowbell. "Isn't that interesting? I grew up not twenty miles downriver from Ledford, in a little town called MacKenzie. Look, Snowbell, it's even on this map!"

He flipped the map over and read: *It is hereby certified to the provisions of the act of Congress, approved May 20, 1862, entitled "An act to secure homesteads to actual settlers on public domain," Maxmillian Wilder has made payment in full for—*

"The Homestead Act of 1862," he murmured. "Not bad for a babbling, crazy old hermit." Majewski squinted at the legal description of the property, trying to decipher the hand-written document. "Like a chicken walked through an ink puddle," he grumbled.

He took the last item out of the box—a will, dated May 21, 1862, signed and sworn by Maxmillian Wilder, bequeathing his only worldly possession, the island where he spent his life, to the Jesuit Order upon his death.

Majewski frowned. "Curiouser and curiouser, Could it be the same island?" He rifled through the mail papers on his desk now and pulled the letter out:

Dear Father Provincial Majewski,

My client, Henry Braun, president of Braun Enterprises, wishes to purchase the property known as Wilder Island, a small, uninhabitable, and otherwise useless island within the city limits of Ledford, MN, for the sum of five million dollars. Please see attached map and survey for the island's location.

We understand that the property is owned by your Order. Please contact me at your earliest convenience so that we may discuss this offer.

Sincerely,
Jules R. Sackman, Attorney at Law

"Hmmm," Majewski murmured, as he stroked Snowbell's belly. He put the two maps side by side and compared them. "It is indeed the same island. But why is this obscure island a thousand miles away so important that it attracts my attention twice in the same morning?"

Snowbell attacked his hand with her paws and bit down firmly. "And who is this Maxmillian Wilder, for whom this island is evidently named? Why did he leave his island to the Order?" He wrested his hand free from her fangs and claws. "And why would anyone want to pay five million dollars for a useless island?" He took his glasses off and chewed thoughtfully on the end of one of the temples.

The Father Provincial gave no credence to the superstitious. But when two seemingly unrelated events happened, such as a cat knocking a box of old papers off a shelf and the arrival of a letter from a stranger, each referring to the same tiny deserted island in the middle of one of America's biggest rivers, Father Provincial Majewski detected the hand of the Almighty and the Supreme Order of the Universe.

He put his glasses back on and pushed the intercom button. He spoke into the speaker to his secretary, William Luther, who moments later opened the door and stepped in.

"Draft an answer to this letter, William," Majewski said as he handed it him. "Say I have received his offer and am taking it under advisement. Fluff it up with some meaningless trivia—how grateful we are for his interests, etc., etc."

"Yes, Father," William said, and he closed the door behind him.

An hour later, a knock on the door interrupted Majewski's thoughts and sent Snowbell to the floor under his desk. William Luther opened the door and entered. He handed the Father Provincial the letter he had drafted to Henry Braun.

"Fine," Majewski said after reading it. He signed his name and handed the letter back.

"Oh—one more thing, William. Please check into our archives for a fellow named Maxmillian Wilder, around 1850 or so. And whatever you can find on this Wilder Island."

The other business on Majewski's desk needed his attention, mostly administrative actions requiring his signature. And of course, the matter of the reprobate priests demanded action. Even his beloved Jesuits had not been immune from the scandals plaguing the priesthood. *One of these days I'm going to resign from this lofty hell. Maybe I'll find an island of crows somewhere. No humans or their sordid problems.*

William opened the door after knocking softly and said, "There is nothing in our archives about Maxmillian Wilder."

Majewski frowned, and William continued, "But I did find a bit about two Henry Brauns and an island named Wilder that might be of interest."

Snowbell jumped off Majewski's lap and slithered under the desk. "And?" he said.

"Henry Braun, the fellow who wants to buy the island, is very rich," William said, coming all the way into the room. "And he is the fourth Henry in a row in the Braun family. But it was his ancestor, Henry Braun the First, who is most interesting. Seems he lost the family fortune last century over a trestle bridge he tried to build across the river to Wilder Island, which was uninhabited but for a crazy old hermit."

Majewski gestured for William to sit down. "Really? Wilder Island again. And that crazy old hermit again. Interesting. And what happened to the trestle bridge? Is it still there?"

Snowbell came out from under the desk and leaped into William's lap. "No," he said, pushing her tail away from his face. "It was mysteriously destroyed just before it reached the island."

"Mysteriously, eh?" Majewski said, tapping a pencil on his desk. "As in sabotage or an act of God?"

"They never figured it out," William said. "On the morning it was supposed to reach the island, Henry Braun the First's trestle bridge was gone. Smashed to bits the night before. The thing was, there was no weather that night, and no one heard a thing."

"Interesting," Majewski said, rubbing his chin. "Perhaps this explains our current Mr. Braun's interest."

After a few moments, William stood up and said, "Will there be anything more, Father?"

"No, that will be all. Thank you, William."

After his secretary left, Majewski rose from his desk and put another log on the fire. He sat down in the armchair in front of the hearth and stared into the fireplace. Henry Braun's ancestor receded, and Maxmillian Wilder's letter rose up to trouble him anew.

It just can't be! He shook his head. *An island of talking crows, for God's sake. And the great Antoni de la Torre was in full knowledge?*

He read the letter one more time. Leaning forward, he held it above the flames for a moment. Brother Maxmillian's handwriting seemed to burn through the yellowed paper, searing an indelible imprint in the Father Provincial's brain.

But for the grace of God and this family of crows ...

Slowly withdrawing his hand, Majewski folded the letter and put it in his pocket. De la Torre deliberately hid these papers concerning his nephew and this island in plain sight. As if he wanted someone someday to find them. *But why? Why did he want the truth about his nephew to be discovered?*

He poked at the log in the fire, rolling it over and exposing its unburned side to the flames. He sat back with a long sigh. *Was Brother Wilder mad? Why would de la Torre send his insane family member to live out his days alone on a deserted island? Or did he really talk to crows? The idea is nothing short of heresy—not only to the Vatican, but to the scientific world as well!*

Majewski sighed at his dilemma. Everything in Maxmillian Wilder's letter screamed its impossibility. Yet there it all was, left on a shelf in a fake book waiting for someone to come along and discover it. *Why? What should I do with this island? Five million dollars is not exactly chump change. And if all it has is the remnants of a crazy old Jesuit hermit, why should we not just sell it? Guide me, oh Lord.*

He watched the flames embrace the new wood, hissing, licking, and caressing it with scorching tongues of blue and yellow and orange. A pocket of sap blew up, sending sparks up the chimney and out in the room. *Was that supposed to be an answer?*

Sometimes trying to discern the Lord's will is like trying to see through a brick wall.

The flames danced hypnotically over the wood, and Majewski's eyes fluttered. A flock of black birds erupted from beneath the coals. Up the chimney, and out into the night, a spiral pattern of winged smoke disappeared into the darkness.

The Father Provincial's eyes snapped open, his awareness suddenly focused on a graduate student he'd advised years ago. *Alfredo Manzi.* He hadn't thought of Manzi in a long time. *Bright fellow. Wrote a brilliant thesis on the behavior of crows and ravens. Rather disturbing to some, the birds seemed too ... what was it? Too intelligent? Too sentient?*

But the young priest's dataset was robust, his adherence to the Scientific Method impeccable, and his arguments unassailable. Though Manzi's graduate committee did their level best to roast him alive, Manzi prevailed, cool-headed and full of reason. Majewski chuckled at the memory.

He remembered their conversations fondly; Manzi had deciphered a few of their calls, and as a linguist, Majewski had been fascinated. But a few words don't make a language. He wondered if Manzi had continued his research. *Where is he these days? Teaching somewhere probably. What would he make of our Brother Maxmillian and this island of talking crows? Or my sister?*

Majewski sighed. *I'll ask William to look up Manzi's whereabouts tomorrow.* He settled back into the comfort of his chair. Snowbell dozed on his lap as he scratched her gently behind the ears.

The Priest and the Crow

The Jesuit scholar Alfredo Manzi stood at the window in his office at the Department of Biology at Midwestern University. Wilder Island stood dark and secretive in the morning shadows, beckoning him. He could hardly resist the urge to disappear into its dark forests and its unusually large population of corvids. He had spent his life studying them—crows and ravens in particular.

Six months ago, he had discovered Wilder Island, just after arriving in Ledford. An advertisement for an ornithology professor at the university had brought him, and after a brief round of interviews, he landed the job. He started teaching immediately, taking over mid-semester for a professor who had taken family leave due to his wife's illness.

Alfredo was nothing less than grateful for his position at the university as adjunct professor, however temporary it might be. No tenure possibilities, but no pressure to publish either.

The Order had granted his subsequent request to be assigned to St. Sophia cathedral in Downtown Ledford as its assistant pastor. Between the two part-time jobs, he made a completely adequate income for himself, a man with no obligations—no family, no car, no mortgage.

And there was Wilder Island and its thousands of corvids, right across the river. What incredible luck! In his first few weeks as a Ledford resident, Alfredo had learned everything he could about the island and its namesake, Maxmillian Wilder, the legendary hermit of the last century. He found an old postcard in a used bookshop Downtown—a great many black birds flying above the silhouettes of treetops against a backdrop of a garish sunset.

After turning it over, Alfredo read:

Murder of Crows, 1937
Wilder Island, Halloween Night
Frederick T. Nelson

Later, he had discovered that the original photograph hung in the Ledford city library. "Was this photo really taken on Halloween night?" he asked the librarian.

"Yes, indeedy," the librarian had said, peering over her glasses at Alfredo. "The whole town saw it. There were thousands of them, right at sunset. They started swirling around like a black cyclone, my mother said." The librarian swayed back and forth in her chair with her arms raised high above her head. "They flew around like that till the sun went down, in honor of the old hermit. They say he had died earlier that very day."

The librarian's story had excited him. And then he had met the two brothers, Floyd and Willy, at the duck pond on campus. They weren't from Cadeña-l'jadia, they said. *Cadeña-l'jadia.* The corvid name for Wilder Island. Alfredo had not spoken to a crow in years, out of fear his professional life would be ruined if anyone found out. His graduate committee had very nearly failed him at his PhD defense.

He missed them, the friendly and quite talkative crows of his youth. Floyd and Willy had reminded him of his old friends in the forest behind his boyhood home, but he dared not be seen talking to them on campus. *Perhaps I can sneak off to Cadeña-l'jadia and make a few friends.*

He remembered his first visit to the island, when he walked down the stone steps to the public docks at the Waterfront, and a single outlandish-looking boat that looked like a small island of trees was moored at the for-hire dock.

"Can you take me to Wilder Island, sir?" he asked the Captain, who stood on the dock next to his boat, his great tattooed arms folded across his chest.

The Captain gestured to him. "All aboard for Cadeña-l'jadia."

Startled that the Captain used the crow-speech name for Wild-er Island, Alfredo stepped onto the boat and immediately forgot his surprise as he marveled at the overhead canopy of exquisitely crafted wrought-iron trees. "Thank you, Captain," he said and put out his hand. "Alfredo Manzi. I am a Jesuit and professor at the university."

The Captain nodded and shook his hand. "Pleasure's mine, Padre."

A crow perched on the railing that went all the way around the boat. She studied Alfredo curiously for a few moments, looking at him as if she knew who he was.

Alfredo watched the Captain push the boat off from the dock. His arms were covered in scenes of a rushing river, with fish leaping through its foamy current. He inhaled deeply of the water-scented air, grateful for a day of blue sky and sunshine for his first trip to the island.

"I have heard the river is treacherous between the mainland and the island. I was worried about finding a ride."

The river seemed to rise up at his words and lob a small spray of water, carefully aimed at the Captain's face. But she was not fast enough; the Captain ducked sway, laughing.

"Treacherous she is," the Captain said as he resumed rowing, "for those who don't know her ways. Me, I've been on this river since I was a wee lad. The river, we're friends all these years. She don't give me trouble."

"And that is my good fortune!" Alfredo said. "Not many have made it to the island, they say."

"The river," the Captain said. "She decides who goes and who stays. Few are called."

"Called?" Alfredo asked. "I was not called. I am just curious about the island and its crows."

"Right," the Captain said with a nod, keeping his gaze on the water ahead.

In truth, however, for the entire six months Alfredo had resided in Ledford, he had felt the island pulling him, cajoling him to renounce his life on the mainland and come live among the forests and its crows.

"Yonder's the old hermit's chapel," the Captain said as Wilder Island loomed closer.

Alfredo looked toward the direction where the Captain had pointed. "I see only a tangle of dead branches and vines in the tree-tops. Where is the chapel?"

"That is the chapel, Padre," the Captain said. "The roof, it looks more like a dead tree than anything, what you can see of it through the green. It was pretty fine in its day, I reckon. People forgot it, though, soon as the old hermit died. But the birds, they don't forget. Ravens took it over. They like to build nests and raise their young up in the roof."

Alfredo gazed at the chapel, imagining it full of ravens. "Have you been to the island?" he asked. It had not occurred to him that anyone had visited the island other than the legendary hermit.

The Captain nodded and said, "Yes, sir. I spent some time there, coupla months maybe. The land is too hard. It hurts my feet. This river, she's my home."

The Captain pushed his oar deeper into the water, steering the small boat toward the island. The closer they got, the more turbulent and ill-behaved the river became, though the Captain's boat seemed to float in steady, calm water.

The island was so close Alfredo could see the leaves on the trees that grew near the river's edge. The Captain guided the boat into a small inlet without even a ripple of consternation from the river. When they ground to a stop on the sandy bank, Alfredo leaped off and turned to pay the Captain for the ride, but the man had already shoved back into the current.

"G'day." The Captain tipped his hat. "I'll come back for you at sunset."

Alfredo hoisted his small backpack onto his shoulders, excitement surging through him at the prospect of the unexplored. *An island of crows!* He left the inlet and walked into the dense forest, pushing aside bushes and branches, toward the old chapel he had seen from the river. It seemed as if twilight had fallen, so thick was the tree canopy overhead.

Water dripped from the grayish-white rock layers that poked up occasionally through the vegetation. The geologists at the university had told him about the limestone rock that comprised the island. "It's everywhere around here," he remembered one of them saying. "Underground, too."

He stopped frequently to look up into the leaves and branches overhead. Many birds flew through the treetops; he could hear mockingbirds and cardinals, blue jays, robins, finches, sparrows, and an occasional mourning dove. Everything but crows, it seemed. *Are they hiding from me?*

He stopped at a small pool fed by a curtain of water beads that dripped from between two moss-bedecked layers of gray rock. He squatted next to the pool, filled his cupped hands with water, and drank. He wiped his mouth after he had quenched his thirst with the cool, tasteless water and took out his water bottles. He emptied them on the ground and refilled them with water from the pool.

He stood back up and stepped across the stream that fed the pond. He could see the gray-and-white chapel roof through the green trees. And what marvelous trees! He recognized only a few—basswood, willow, dogwood, and black spruce. Flowering bushes grew between the tall trees, whose exotic scents seemed familiar to Alfredo, but he could not name them. Wildflowers grew everywhere in reckless profusion among the infinite shades of green. He thought of his new colleague at the biology department, Russ Matthews. He was a botanist; this would be his paradise!

Alfredo stepped into a small clearing and beheld the small chapel nestled within a circle of trees. The remains of a door lay intact on the ground; its vine hinges had long ago rotted away. He tore away some vines that had grown across the space between the two trees from which the door had hung and stepped inside. It was quite dark; the old and new vines that covered the roof allowed little light through.

He looked up at the mosaic of blue sky and fluffy white clouds though the interwoven branches and vines of the roof. It seemed for a moment like the stained glass ceiling of the Jesuit chapel in Rome.

"Except this one looks like an upside down bird's nest!" he said. He gaped in wonder for a few moments before noticing two pairs of eyes staring coldly down at him from a nest within the roof. *Ravens.* He could hear faint cheeping sounds from above.

"Greetings," he said, and the eyes vanished. Moments later a large black shape whooshed down from the roof and out the door.

Sunlight filtered through the roof, casting a dappled pattern of light and shadow on a dirt floor littered with forest matter. A crude kneeler hewn from some unknown wood, bleached white by time and weather arose from the center of the roughly circular space.

Illuminated by a patch of sunshine, a human skull on the dirt floor opposite him caught his eye, and with a few steps, he was looking down at a completely picked-over human skeleton. *This must be Brother Wilder's remains. No doubt the island's crows and ravens ate all the flesh off.* Alfredo could not think of a more wonderful way to decompose—giving up one's mortal remains as food for the living. *I will bring a shovel next time and bury his bones. And a marker for his grave.*

"The Patua' has arrived," NoExit said to Charlie. The two birds perched on the railing around the deck at Bruthamax's tree house.

NoExit had flown from the chapel to the tree house where Charlie lived, clear on the other end of the island. Though it was an inconvenience, it was really not so far, only a mile or so by wing. And Charlie had asked him to keep an eye out for this Patua'.

"When?" Charlie asked. "Where is he? How long has he been there? Did you talk to him?"

"About a half hour or so," NoExit said, irritated at being peppered with so many questions. "He is poking around the chapel. And no, I did not talk to him."

"We could use another Patua' on Cadeña-l'jadia," Charlie said.

"Perhaps," NoExit said with a shrug of his wings. "But if he stays on, I reckon we will be moving out of Bruthamax's chapel—soon as the kreegans fledge. We like our privacy."

Alfredo swept the dust off the armrest of the kneeler in the center of the chapel. He knelt on its hard wood, closed his eyes, and clasped his hands together. A withered old man with long gray hair shuffled across the backs of his eyelids. A sudden wind blew a flurry of leaves into a spiral dance all around the kneeler, spoiling his concentration and coating him with dirt. He stood up and brushed the debris from his clothes and hair and left the dark chapel.

"Grawky, Jayzu!" a voice said.

He blinked in the bright sunlight and found a blue-eyed crow looking up at him with a wing outstretched. "Name's Charlie. To what do we owe the honor of a Patua' visit?"

Delighted to find a talkative crow on Wilder Island right away, Alfredo grazed the crow's outstretched wing with his open palm. "Grawky, Charlie!" he said with a big smile. "The honor and pleasure is mine!"

Charlie folded his wing against his side. "Pleasure and honor all around, then. It's not every day we have a Patua' in our midst. But Floyd and Willy told me they had met you. They too were surprised to meet an actual Patua'."

"But I am not a Patua'," Alfredo said. "I am a Jesuit." He stood on one leg and took off a boot and turned it upside down. A pebble fell to the ground. "My name is Alfredo Manzi," he continued, hopping around on one foot as he put his boot back on. "Some call me Father Manzi. At the university, where I am the entire ornithology department, they call me Dr. Manzi. But I prefer Alfredo."

"Yes," Charlie said. "But you are Jayzu to us."

"A good a name as any, I suppose," Alfredo said. He sat down on a log and tied the laces of his boot. "Jayzu it is. But what does Patua' mean? I have heard you use it twice, but otherwise have never heard the word before."

Charlie sprang up to an adjacent rock and sharpened his beak on it. "A Patua' is a human such as yourself," he said as if the priest should know that. "Perhaps it has come to your attention that not all humans have conversations with crows? Those of you who can are the Patua'."

"The Patua'," Alfredo said. "I had no idea there were others like me. I have always thought I am just a freak."

A magpie flew overhead, crying out "Free-eek! Fre-eek!" before disappearing into the branches of a tall basswood tree.

"You are not a freak," Charlie said, shaking his head. "You are Patua'. Back in the day, a millennia or so ago, there were millions of Patua'."

"Millions?" Alfredo could hardly believe it. "I have never heard of them. What happened to them?"

"Hard to say. Extermination by other humans did in a great number of Patua'." Charlie hopped off the rock and beaked a beetle out of the dirt and swallowed it. "Same as what happened to the Neanderthals. But there are other factors and causes. We don't know really."

Alfredo sighed, looking away. An old childhood fantasy surfaced, of living alone on an island with a crow. He smiled sadly at the memory. That was after he had been severely punished by his mother, for "talking like those horrible crows."

"Bruthamax was the most famous Patua' that ever came to the island," Charlie said. "Or anywhere else for that matter. He lived here among the crows, my ancestors, for almost a hundred years."

"Bruthamax?" Alfredo said. "Do you mean Brother Maxmillian Wilder? The old hermit the island was named after?" He leaned down and overturned a rectangular gray rock. A furry brown spider scurried away, leaving behind an egg sac. Alfredo put the rock gently back into place.

"One and the same," Charlie replied. "Though we don't call this place Wilder Island. To us it is Cadeña-l'jadia—'the land of swampy waters amid green forests and mists.' But we don't mind that you humans named it after one of yours we actually admire. In fact"—Charlie shrugged his wings—"we tend to think of Bruthamax as one of ours."

Alfredo felt another pang of homesickness for the crow companions of his boyhood. He saw a younger version of himself playing hide-and-seek with them. Charlie reminded him of his best friend in all the world, a crow named Caleb.

"Much that is written about Bruthamax seems to be folklore and fantasy," Alfredo said, still caught up in memories of his younger self. He was happy to run in the woods with crows, but it was deeply troubling to his family. *My mother sent me to the Jesuits when I was a boy. And within this Order I have disappeared. Like a spider under a rock.*

"We have kept many stories about Bruthamax," Charlie said. "He came because he was Patua', just like you did. My ancestor Hozey the Younger helped him build this chapel, and a house up in a tree down yonder." Charlie gestured with a wing toward the downriver end of the island. "My nest and my wife, Rika, are there in the branches above Bruthamax's tree house. Hozey the Younger lived there too. It's a family tradition."

"A tree house!" Alfredo said. "I had assumed Bruthamax lived here in the chapel."

"Not until his last year," Charlie said. "Bruthamax lived in the tree house until his last year, when he got too old to climb up and down the tree and navigate the way. After that, Hozey and his family took care of him in the chapel until he died."

"I would love to see Bruthamax's tree house sometime," Alfredo said, "if that would not be too much of an intrusion."

Charlie unfolded his wings and flapped a few times, scattering a small pile of leaves. "I will take you there some time, after our kreegans have fledged. You'd be a tremendous distraction, and Rika is already worrying they won't ever leave the nest. All but JoEd, that is. He's an early bird, that one—started trying to fly before he had all his feathers."

Alfredo stood up, brushed the dirt off his pants, and picked up his backpack. "I have been scolded and pecked at enough times by an angry mother bird," he said with a laugh. "The young ones are quite vulnerable during fledging, and I do not wish to interfere. I shall see the tree house another day. Today I will explore the island, with your permission of course."

"Be my guest," Charlie said.

Crow and priest parted, and Alfredo spent the rest of the day wandering through the forest, astounded by the unsullied and abundant growth. He walked, oblivious to the passage of time, gazing in almost stupefied delight at the abundance of creation all around him. Different species of trees each sported their own combinations of gray, brown, or black bark, and the leaves split the color green into a million different shades and hues. Wildflowers grew everywhere grass or shrubs did not, and he felt as if he were walking in the Garden of Eden, wondering if there were snakes on the island.

The scent of flowers, bark, rotten leaves, and mold permeated the air, and he inhaled its fertile essence as a starving man might fill his empty, aching stomach with food. He had spent his boyhood wandering through another forest, and the memory of those happy times infused the present with faith and affirmation.

Springs and tiny streams crisscrossed his path, and he leaped across those he could see. He sloshed through the invisible streams, giving up any hope that he could keep his feet dry. "Perhaps I will come next time with waders," he grumbled.

He picked his way slowly through the dense undergrowth, carefully avoiding what he thought might be poison ivy, though the berries were purple and not the typical green he was familiar with. As he looked around him, everything seemed a bit off. The trees were too tall, or the flowers a strange color.

"I do not think bougainvillea should be growing here," he said, pausing to admire a bush bursting with yellow and apricot-colored blossoms. "If this is indeed bougainvillea."

He stooped down low to study a tiny blue flower with a spotted yellow tongue he had seen growing in profusion along his way. "Now that has to be an orchid."

He picked one and carefully put it in his field notebook to show to his colleague Russ Matthews. "I need to get him out here."

He continued his slow pace though the thick undergrowth until he came to an obstacle he could not pass—a ravine full of gigantic rectangular boulders. The drop was not far, but the landing spot below was a jumbled pile of up-turned, sharp edged rocks. Willow and hawthorn grew in thickets between the rocks, making passage between them impossible. Alfredo decided to not attempt to cross. *I would be ground meat before I could ever get to the other side.*

He felt a rain drop on his arm. Then two, three, four. He looked up. The blue sky was gone, replaced by dark gray clouds streaking hurriedly eastward. Lightning seemed to dart through the trees to his left, and the thunderclap that followed sent him to the ground. The rain started, a sudden downpour, and he was back on his feet scrambling for shelter as he struggled to open his backpack.

He dove beneath the sprawling branches and wide leaves of a catalpa tree and pulled his rain jacket from his pack. After quickly putting it on, he leaned against the trunk and dug again in his pack for his lunch.

The rain stopped as he finished eating, and he looked up at wispy clouds interspersed with blue sky. He glanced at his watch. *It's time to return to the inlet. the Captain will be along soon.* He stuffed his rain jacket into his pack and retraced his steps as best as he could remember. When he stepped out of the forest at the inlet, the Captain and the crow were waiting.

"Greetings, Jayzu!" the crow called out. "All aboard for the Waterfront!"

Alfredo stopped and stared, wondering if he should greet the crow. *But right in front of the Captain? Wouldn't he take me for a babbling fool?*

"Don't just stand there with your mouth hangin' open!" the crow hollered. "Climb aboard!"

"Ease up, Sugarbabe," the Captain said, winking at Alfredo. "Go lightly, remember?"

Sugarbabe looked for a moment at the Captain, tilting her head to one side. "Next time. Maybe." She laughed raucously and held out her wing to Alfredo.

In complete astonishment, Alfredo brushed his fingertips across her wing and stammered, "I uh, that is, my name is Alfredo. At least that is what my mother named me, but—"

The Captain talks to crows?

"And me mum named me Judith," she said. "But everyone around here calls me Sugarbabe. Fits me better than Judith, don't you think?"

Alfredo nodded speechlessly.

"Just like we call you Jayzu," she said. "Much better, don't you think? You don't look like no Alfredo."

"Perhaps not," Alfredo said, laughing at the crow's familiar humor.

So the Captain is Patua'! Surely Charlie knows. Why did he not tell me? It was hard to get used to the idea of others like him, much as he desired companionship.

He wanted to start a conversation with the Captain, but how to start? The Captain's craggy face was hard to read. Alfredo could not guess how old the man was.

"But how do you know anything about me?"

"My beak is sealed," Sugarbabe said, turning her beak toward the direction the caption rowed.

Alfredo watched the Captain's huge tattooed arms push the oar deep into the water, his muscles flexing into fish leaping through curling waves. "Captain," he said after they had passed the rocky point and headed toward the city dock. "I guess you know more about me than I know about you."

"How so?" the Captain said, keeping his eyes on the water. "I know you are a priest, and you know I am a boatman. We both keep company with black birds who talk too much." He winked at Sugarbabe. "What else is there to know?"

Alfredo laughed, his discomfort slipping away with the Captain's humor. A fish leaped out of the water. Or was that the Captain's tattoo? "I was unaware there were others like me until today. I have kept my secret hidden my entire life."

The Captain squinted at him for a moment. "As we all have, Padre."

"As we all have?" Alfredo asked. "Do you know of any Patua' around here, other than you and me?"

The Captain did not reply for a few moments. "A few," he said gruffly, "here and there."

The Captain pulled his boat into one of the docks at the Waterfront. Alfredo tried to pay him, but he just tipped his hat, saying, "G'day, Padre," and shoved his boat back into the current.

Alfredo walked to the rectory at St. Sophia's, reflecting again on the idea that there were others like him. *Shocking, yet fascinating!* He almost longed for what he had never known: close human companionship. At the same time, he had been relieved when Charlie had said there were no other Patua' on Wilder Island. He wanted to be the only one.

HENRY BRAUN POURED TWO GLASSES OF champagne and offered one to his attorney, Jules Sackman, who waved a hand in refusal. "Too early for me, Henry," he said. "But you go ahead."

Even by Henry's standards, champagne before noon was a bit early, but he was in a fabulous mood. He had just closed on a lucrative deal in which he made a healthy profit on a building he had bought for a song. It would provide the seed money he needed for his latest and most grandiose project of them all: Ravenwood Resort.

Henry sat behind his gargantuan desk in his opulent office, which occupied the majority of the second floor of his mansion on a large estate overlooking the river. Ravenwood Resort was destined to be the pièce de résistance of Henry Braun's empire, as well as his personal cash cow. Built on and around the island soon to be formerly known as Wilder Island, the resort would ultimately feature two riverboat casinos, an amusement park, a concert hall, and a shopping mall.

Ravenwood Resort. The irony of the name his marketing agency recommended had amused him. There wouldn't be any ravens left on that island when he was finished, of course. Nor would there be any woods. But the market research people told him the public would spend more money because of the Ravenwood logo, so he went with it. Henry chortled into his glass. He absolutely loved the way the bubbly tickled his nose.

Life was good.

"Ravenwood Resort is going to be fantastic," Henry said after swallowing the fizzy golden liquid. "I'm ready to roll with everything—the architects, engineers—just waiting for the word. Just waiting to sign the check. When will we hear from His Holy Eminence—what's his name again? Majorski?"

"I don't know," Jules said with a shrug. "His name is Majewski, Father Superior Thomas Majewski."

"What do you mean you don't know?" Henry said somewhat irritably as he twirled his glass of champagne.

"It means I don't know," Jules said. "The most recent letter we got from the Father Provincial's office said they've tabled the discussion of a possible sale of Wilder Island until next month."

"Next month?" Henry said with a long-suffering sigh. "What for? What's to discuss? Five million not enough?"

He glanced up at the portraits of his three ancestors, his namesakes, on the wood-paneled walls. Three pairs of eyes stared at him. "Time is money!" he could almost hear Henry the First say as he looked sternly down.

"It's the Catholic Church we're dealing with here, remember?" Jules said. "They're not as lithe and efficient as Braun Enterprises. They probably have to convene a council of cardinals or something to talk about it. I'm surprised it'll only be a month. But relax, Henry. We're offering them a ridiculous price for a swampy bog. I'm sure they'll come around. Just be patient."

"He who hesitates is last!" Henry the First warned.

"Patience is for saints!" Henry said irritably. He got up and strode to the window. Wilder Island, shrouded in a thunderstorm, seemed dark and forbidding. *Soon*, he thought, *I'll drain that stink-*

ing swamp. There'll be lights everywhere. It'll be a sparkling gem. He turned back toward his attorney and glared at him.

"Here's what I'm afraid of, Jules," he said as he sat back down at his desk. "I'm afraid our offer will make them wonder what's so special about this island, and they'll send someone out to look at it. Then they'll want to do an environmental impact study. Then the tree huggers will get involved, and we'll have to worry they'll find some ugly little plant, or a worm, that only lives on this island, and the whole world has to grind to a halt."

"Henry," Jules said, "now you're going off the deep end. Come back. None of that is going to happen. It's just a big bureaucracy, that's all. No need to be paranoid."

"I am not paranoid!" Henry shouted. He glanced up at Henry the First shaking his head.

"I'm worried, Jules," he said, controlling his anger and dropping his voice. "I worry that while you sit on your thumbs, Wilder Island slips through my fingers. I've worked too long and too hard to let that happen. I swear by the blood of my ancestors—" he raised his glass to the portraits on the wall. "I swear that Wilder Island will once again belong to a Braun. As God is my witness."

Henry the First nodded approvingly, with just a hint of a smile curling the edges of his mouth.

—3—

The Tree House

"**I**magine my surprise finding you in Ledford!" Father Provincial Thomas Majewski said to Alfredo over the phone. "It's good to hear your voice after all these years!"

Alfredo was on duty at St. Sophia's, preparing for his shift in the confessional. When the phone rang, he had assumed it would be one of the parishioners, wanting absolution over the phone. Thank the Good Lord Almighty, it was the head of the entire Jesuit operation in North America instead!

Majewski's voice took Alfredo back to his graduate school days and his unfriendly committee. Except for Dr. Thomas, as the students had called Majewski. He was always available and certainly had a more open mind than the other committee members.

"Likewise, Thomas!" Alfredo agreed. "But I'm surprised to hear from you. To what do I owe this pleasant surprise?"

"Well," Majewski's baritone voice boomed, "I don't much believe in synchronicities, but it seems as if this Wilder Island has become the focus of all my attention lately!"

Alfredo looked out the window at the island in the afternoon sun, wishing he were there. He imagined even God would prefer the whispering breezes and his exuberant creation to the cold walls of the cathedral and the laments of rich, lonely women.

"Mine too!" Alfredo laughed. "I can see it out my window as we speak."

"Tell me about this island, Alfredo," Majewski said. "We've gotten an offer from a gentleman named Henry Braun, right there in Ledford, for several million dollars."

Alfredo's blood went cold. *No! You cannot sell it!* "For what purpose?" he said, hoping his voice did not betray his fear. "There

is nothing there, really. It is not considered habitable by humans."
Except by me.

"The letter didn't say what he wanted it for," Majewski said. "Development, presumably."

"He cannot be serious!" Alfredo cried. He doodled on the pad in front of him, drawing the word "No!" in three-dimensional block letters.

"He is," Majewski said. "He calls my office daily, waiting for an answer. But calm down, Alfredo. He annoys the hell out of me. I'm inclined to turn him down for that alone."

"That is good to hear," Alfredo said, drawing a dollar sign on the pad. "The island is quite small and very difficult to get to. Where the undergrowth is not completely impassable, it is very boggy and full of mosquitoes."

"So you've been there?" Majewski asked. "I was hoping to get you to do some investigating for us. Is it really haunted?"

Alfredo laughed and said, "No, not at all. There are many crows— an unusually large number, in fact. But nothing sinister, nothing magical. In fact, I am heading over there this morning, among other things to bury Maxmillian Wilder's remains. He was an old hermit that lived on the island for many years and built a remarkable little chapel."

"What else do you know about Maxmillian Wilder?" Majewski asked. "He was one of ours, you know. A Jesuit."

"Was he?" Alfredo said. He drew a skull on the desk pad. "I assumed he had taken holy orders, but he was one of us?"

He frowned, wondering if Charlie knew that. He seemed to know everything else about Brother Maxmillian Wilder. *Bruthamax.*

"Yes, he was a Jesuit, according to some letters and legal documents I accidentally found. But there's no mention of a Maxmillian Wilder in our records anywhere."

"None?" Alfredo was taken aback. "Why would the Jesuits expunge one of their own?"

"We don't," Majewski said. "We keep records on everyone, even the de-frocked."

Alfredo finished hearing confession and changed from priestly garb into jeans, a T-shirt, and hiking boots. He left his apartment at the rectory at St. Sophia's and headed for the Waterfront. From the top of the stone steps, he saw the Captain and his floating forest of a boat seemingly waiting for him.

"Here you are again, just when I need you," he said as he climbed aboard. "Do you have a sixth sense, Captain? Or is it always a coincidence that you are here whenever I need you?"

"I travel the river from sunup to sundown," the Captain said, "looking for those who are looking for a ride."

"Hahaha!" Sugarbabe screeched and flapped her wings on her perch next to the Captain. "No way, Jayzu! A little birdie told him! Me! Me! Me!" She danced around on her perch.

The Captain grinned and tried to cuff the crow with the back of his hand, but she leaped off her perch screeching with laughter.

"Can't get away with much with this old blabber-mouth around!" he said as he pushed his boat away from the dock.

"But no one knew I wanted to go to the island today," Alfredo said, thinking back on his morning. "Am I being spied upon?" he asked Sugarbabe.

"I know nothing," she said, burying her beak in her wingpit.

"Now that's a ding-dang lie, Sugarbabe!" the Captain said as he pushed the boat away from the dock. "You know everything that's to know all up and down this river. And on Cadeña-l'jadia!" He turned to Alfredo, winked, and then looked back at the bird. "Nothing gets by you!"

Sugarbabe pulled her head out and preened her breast feathers flat. "I know nothing about no spying," she insisted.

Alfredo laughed and said, "I suppose I do not mind being spied upon by crows, Sugarbabe. I had no idea I was that interesting."

"Oh," Sugarbabe said, "you're that interesting all right. You're Bruthamax's kin! That's why Charlie sent the magpies to follow you around, so they could tell him—" She suddenly stopped and glanced at the Captain. "Oops," she said. A moment later, she leaped into the sky and flew off.

The Captain threw his head back and laughed. "She never can keep a secret, that one!"

Alfredo smiled and then he frowned. "Why am I being spied upon by crows?"

The Captain shrugged. "They've got their reasons, I reckon."

He looked away suddenly, and Alfredo wondered if the Captain knew more about him than he let on. He felt somewhat disappointed that his new friend Charlie had watched him through the eyes of magpies. *Why did he not visit himself if I am that important?*

"But how did you know I would need a ride over to the island this morning?" Alfredo asked.

"Coincidence," the Captain shrugged, his eyes straight ahead. "I reckon."

The island's dark green forest loomed larger as they approached, and Alfredo felt his heart lighten. The Captain brought the boat to a halt on the shore at the inlet, and he leaped out. He offered to pay for the ride, but the Captain pushed his floating forest away from the dock tipping his hat saying, "G'day, Padre. Be back at sunset."

After waving good-bye to the Captain, Alfredo made his way to the old chapel. He opened the door and entered the patchwork of sunshine and shadows. Illuminated by several shafts of sunlight through the bird's-nest roof, Maxmillian's bones gleamed garishly white in the dim interior.

The skeleton was remarkably intact, considering it had been stripped clean of all soft tissue long ago by both vertebrate and invertebrate creatures on the island. He picked up the skull, and something dropped to the dirt. He dusted it off on his shirt and peered curiously at it: a large wooden bead of some sort. Or perhaps stone; it was rather heavy for its size. But the light in the chapel was too dim to examine it further. He put it in his backpack and continued with his task.

He carefully placed each of Brother Maxmillian's bones into a burlap sack and took it outside to a place just below the chapel, above the rocky point of the island's headlands. After he dug a hole, he placed the sack of bones into it and filled it with dirt. He took the small white cross he had fashioned from wood in the handyman's shop, upon which he had carved M. W., and pushed it into the dirt.

Charlie the blue-eyed crow flew in low and landed on a flat rock next to the grave.

"Hello, my friend," Alfredo greeted him, wondering again how much this crow knew about him. "I have buried Bruthamax's bones."

"I can see that," Charlie replied. "Why? They were not a health hazard, were they?"

"No," Alfredo said. "It is a human tradition to bury our dead. It honors them, we think."

"In that case," Charlie said, "may I join you in honoring Bruthamax? He was held in high esteem among us crows, you know, and we take any opportunity we can to revere his memory."

"Of course," Alfredo said.

Suddenly dozens of crows materialized from the trees surrounding the chapel, startling Alfredo. The crows dropped to the ground, surrounded Brother Wilder's grave, and bowed their heads. He was extremely touched by their reverence, and he bowed his head with them. In the language of the crows, he prayed, "Dear Lord Almighty, please receive our Brother Maxmillian Wilder, that is, Bruthamax, into your infinite peace. In his name, may you bless this island of crows and keep it safe from all harm."

"Amen," Charlie said, flapping his wings.

The other crows all flapped wings and shouted elegies to their hero: "The memory of Bruthamax lives in our hearts forever!" "Bruthamax! Where for art thou?"

"I had no idea," Alfredo said, "that after all these years Bruthamax is held in such high regard by so many birds. He has been dead for decades."

The birds wandered around murmuring more epitaphs to one another. A few picked flowers and laid them gently in front of the small cross.

"Bruthamax is legendary to just about every corvid family in North America," Charlie said. "Word flew out from Cadeña-l'jadia as soon as he died. Church bells everywhere rang out the news, even the bells at St. Sophia's."

"The bell-ringers were all Patua'?" Alfredo asked.

"Humans didn't ring the bells," Charlie said. "Crows did. They hung on the ropes by beak and claw until there were enough of them to pull it down. News of his passing spread by wing and beak after that. Thousands of ravens and crows, along with many jays and magpies from the entire river region, flew to the island for the Grand Funeral Roosting. Never in modern times has a human been so honored by us."

"One man meant so much to so many birds," Alfredo said. "Yet he was unknown among humans."

"Yep," Charlie said. "Sometimes that's just the way it is."

Gradually the crows dissolved back into the trees and sky, leaving Alfredo and Charlie standing next to the little wooden cross. "I brought lunch today, Charlie," Alfredo said. "I was hoping to bribe you into taking me down to Bruthamax's tree house."

"I can definitely be bribed," Charlie said.

The two walked side by side down to the flat gray rocks above the riverbank. Alfredo took a hero sandwich from his backpack, unwrapped it, cut it in half, and put one piece on a small flat rock for the crow. Charlie knocked the top bun off his sandwich and beaked a chunk of ham. He tossed it in the air, catching and swallowing it in one motion.

Within a few minutes, the sandwich was gone, both halves, though Charlie left most of the bun. "Someone'll eat it," he said, cleaning his beak in the sand.

"The Jesuits have discovered they own the island," Alfredo said as he stuffed the paper wrappings into his pack.

"No one owns Cadeña-l'jadia," Charlie said sharply. "You can't own anything you cannot carry in your two claws—or in your case, hands."

"Someone offered them a lot of money," Alfredo said with some discomfort. *No use mincing words.* "They want me to provide them with more information so they can assess the island's value."

"Val-yooo!" a mockingbird sang from the trees nearby. "Val-yoooo!" the call echoed through the trees.

"Value," Charlie said, his head tipped thoughtfully. "Now there's a word that means something completely different to humans than it does to me."

"Or me," Alfredo said. "But I worry that whoever made this offer wants to develop the island. They may want to cut the trees down and build houses. Or worse."

Alfredo imagined the lush forest all around him gone, replaced by some human nonsense—a shopping center or amusement park, perhaps?

"In that case," Charlie said, "it only matters if you Jesuits aren't planning the same thing."

"Probably not," Alfredo said. He picked up a small smooth stone and tossed it back and forth between his hands. "The island has a Jesuit-built chapel on it. It is more likely the Order will want to preserve it than have it torn down. I will do whatever I can to discourage them from selling."

"Cadeña-l'jadia owns itself," Charlie said. "Best you humans remember that." He unfurled his wings as he hopped off the rock and into the sky. "Shall we head down to the tree house?"

They traveled through the dense forest toward the tree house, the human on foot, the crow by wing. Hundreds of birds whizzed by—crows, magpies, jays, mockingbirds, and an assortment of other birds too small to identify. Many of them called out as the passed: "Greetings, Jayzu!" "Yahoo, Jayz-ZOOO!" "Grawky, Jayzu!"

He greeted them all back with a wave of his hand. "Grawky! Grawky!"

They came to the precipice Alfredo had encountered on his first visit to the island. "I have been here before, Charlie. I do not think I can get across this," Alfredo said as he looked over the edge at the sheer drop. "It is not too far down, but I am afraid I would either impale myself on the trees or smash up on the rocks."

"Follow me!" Charlie called out over his shoulder. "There's a bridge over this way."

Alfredo plowed his way through the thick undergrowth and found the crow perched atop a wooden post at the beginning of a swaying footbridge. "This bridge has been here over a hundred years," Charlie said. "Bruthamax built it."

The bridge seemed amazingly sturdy; though it had neither been used nor repaired in decades, it had not deteriorated. Charlie hopped down from his perch and started walking across the bridge. "Come on, Jayzu!" he said.

"Do you think it will hold me?" Alfredo asked as he yanked hard on the thick vine ropes.

Charlie leaped off the bridge and said, "I don't know, Jayzu, but it is the only way across the Boulders for the two-legged."

"Here I come," Alfredo said as he stepped onto the bridge. "Lord, please keep me in one piece." The old bridge swayed wildly from side to side as he crossed, but it held fast. He stepped onto a platform in the old tree on the other side of the boulder ravine and looked back at the bridge with admiration. "Bruthamax was quite the engineer."

"With a little help from his friends," Charlie said. "My ancestor Hozey the Younger and many other crows."

Alfredo imagined a scene of crows flying to and fro, carrying lengths of vine in their beaks across the Boulders to Bruthamax, who strung them through flat pieces of wood.

"That is even more amazing, Charlie," he said. "Humans and crows working together. Mighty impressive." He stepped off the platform onto short stubby branches that spiraled down the trunk all the way to the ground.

"This is marvelous!" Alfredo said on his way down. "A perfect natural spiral staircase—the steps grow right out of the trunk." He looked upward and shook his head. "While the branches above the platform provide a canopy of shade."

"Bruthamax had a way with the trees," Charlie said. "He had his own orchard near the tree house."

"Really?" Alfredo said, his dark eyebrows arching. "An orchard?"

"That's right," Charlie said. "And a pond, and a smokehouse."

He pointed a wing and said as he leapt into the air, "The tree house is this way! Follow me, Jayzu! And watch out. There are many wet places down there."

Alfredo looked back. The bridge had completely disappeared, and the dense forest closed in all around. "Good thing I have you to guide me, Charlie," he said. "I have no idea how to get back."

For a while, the ground was firm and dry, and he walked easily through the forest. His path became more difficult as the ground grew soft and wet with spongy bogs and dark pools. He stumbled on tree roots and an occasional rock hidden in the undergrowth. Overhead, the trees were hung with moss and vines, and hundreds of birds of many colors flew through the trees, all singing out at once.

Surprised and delighted at the plethora of flowers and vines that decorated the trees, Alfredo walked in wonder through tiny glens of miniature blue and yellow flowers that peeked up through the grasses. Star-shaped lilies of bright pink sprang from clumps of green spears amid an abundance of red and orange fan-shaped flowers he could not identify.

Charlie glided easily through the branches and trunks, helping Alfredo pick his way along the ground below. "Jayzu!" he called out, "Stop! You're heading into a bog. Go back!"

Alfredo tried to stop his forward momentum, but he tripped over a tree root and slid into a small pool of watery black mud. "Too late!" he said, pulling his mud-covered boot out of a shallow pool that he mistook for solid ground covered by tiny plants.

He tried to keep a better eye on Charlie after that, but the calls of many birds distracted his attention, and he found it difficult not to look up into the forest canopy. He was sure there was more than one birdcall he'd never heard before.

He waved at the swamp sparrows who trilled as he passed, and he called out a greeting to the chattering magpies. Underneath the birdcalls, crickets and other insects performed their own unique vignettes that somehow merged with all the other voices into an energetic song of life on a summer afternoon.

With so many birds flying among the trees, Alfredo lost track of which one was Charlie. He stopped and called out, "Where are you, Charlie? I cannot see you."

"Charlie?" a mockingbird mocked, "I cannot see you!"

"Charlie!" a raven rasped, "where are you?"

"Char-lee!" a red-winged blackbird trilled. "Char-lee, Charleee!"

"Up here, Jayzu!" Charlie called, "Right above you. The tree house is straight ahead."

"As the crow flies," grumbled Alfredo as he slogged through a shallow mud bog, trying to follow Charlie. He stopped next to an unexpected human-built structure, a hut constructed of small, rough-hewn wood planks. "What is this?" he asked.

Charlie landed on the roof. "Either Bruthamax's smoke house or his crapper," he said. "I could never tell which from which."

"Looks like the crapper," Alfredo said, noting the wood box with a hole cut through the top. "He had a smoke house, too?"

"Yep," Charlie said. "It got struck by lightning a few years back and burnt to the ground. But I didn't know it was the smokehouse, till now."

They continued on their way, and within a few minutes, Alfredo stood before a towering, black gum tree. "Bruthamax's tree house!" Charlie said.

Alfredo looked up, but saw nothing but a gnarly tangle of living and dead vines. "Where?" he asked, making his way around the massive, ivy-encased trunk. He craned his neck, squinting his eyes, hoping to discern a human-built structure.

"Up here," Charlie said, looking down at him. "The way up for the two-legged is around the other side."

He disappeared into the leaves, and Alfredo walked around the tree whose huge trunk was nearly encased in a variety of vines. Charlie dropped to the ground at the base of a graceful spiral of ivy and Virginia creeper that disappeared above into the great tree's interior. "Bruthamax climbed these stairs up to the treehouse," Charlie said, gesturing upward with his beak.

"What stairs?" Alfredo wondered. He unshouldered his pack and pulled out a machete he had borrowed from the gardener's shed at St. Sophia's. Hacking through a hundred years of vinage was no small task, but the effort revealed a series of wooden steps, stacked one upon the next, winding around a central axis and disappearing into the darkness above.

He tested the bottom step. It seemed sturdy enough and he wound his way up, hacking the thick growth of vines from the steps. He continued chopping away until his machete cut through a wooden deck made of smooth, straight tree branches lashed together by living and dead vines. He cut away the last of the vines and heaved himself onto the deck.

A crude railing of smooth, undulating lengths of whitewashed branches attached to posts enclosed the small deck, evidently a favorite perch for a multitude of birds. "Bruthamax slept outside on this bench in the summertime," Charlie said, pointing to a vine-encased bench.

"That looks more like a sofa!" Alfredo said and sat down. Over the years, vines had poured over the railing and formed a back.

Vines hung down from the tree branches in a curtain of green leaves, through which Alfredo finally saw it: Bruthamax's treehouse. He pushed through the hanging vines and stood before a small edifice, encrusted with tendrils of ropey gray.

Leaves rustled slightly in the branches overhead, and a voice called out, "That's too far, JoEd! Come back where I can see you!"

A crow dropped onto the deck, and Charlie said, "Jayzu, meet my wife, Rika."

"I am at my wit's end with that son of yours," Rika said irritably as she extended her wing in greeting. "Grawky, Jayzu! It is good to finally make your acquaintance. My husband speaks very highly of you."

"Grawky, Rika!" Alfredo said, blushing under her compliment as he brushed his hand across her outstretched wing.

Suddenly she whipped around and shouted, "JoEd! You come back here this instant!" But the little crow did not heed her. She turned around and said to Charlie, "Husband, please fetch back your son before he finds some breeze to blow away on!"

As Charlie took off, Rika said to Alfredo, "I swear by the Great Orb, Jayzu, it is harder with them out of the nest. They can do more, but at least when they were little, the nest kept them from wandering off or getting into trouble."

As she spoke, four young crows tumbled down onto the deck. "Oh!" Rika said. "And here's the rest of our family, Jayzu. Kreegans, say hello to Jayzu."

"Grawky, Jayzu," the four little crows said in unison, bowing low with their wings straight out over the deck. Alfredo got down on his knees to crow level, grinning at their squeaky young voices. He brushed their little wingtips with his hand, greeting each one in turn.

Charlie came back with JoEd in tow, nudging him into compliance. Even as the two crows landed on the deck, JoEd tried to break free of his parents' dominion, but Rika caught him by a tail feather and dragged him back. "JoEd, don't make me clip your wings," Rika scolded. Turning to Charlie, she said, "Husband, please try to talk some sense into your son!"

"Aw, Weebs!" JoEd complained. "You never let me have any fun. There's a whole world out there beyond this boring old tree."

"Listen to your mother, JoEd," Charlie said. "And say grawky to Jayzu."

"Grawky, Jayzu!" JoEd said obediently and brushed his wing against Alfredo's outstretched hand. "My zazu talks about you all the time."

"Well, JoEd," Alfredo laughed, "my new friend Charlie, your zazu, has told me all about you! I understand you have already learned to fly."

"Yes, Jayzu," JoEd said, puffing up with pride. "I'm an early bird, just like my zazu. And I am going to be a Keeper someday, too. I've already been chosen!"

Alfredo watched Rika jump up and dash off to keep JoEd's siblings from falling off the deck; they were playing King on the Mountain on the deck railing.

"Come, kreegans," she said to the fledglings. "Back up to the nest!" She scooped them up with her wings and pushed them up into the branches. With a great deal of fluttering and flapping, the little ones made it back to the nest. "JoEd!" Rika called down. "Please come and look after the others."

"Ah, Weebs!" JoEd said, but obediently he flew up to the nest.

Alfredo turned toward the tree house. "A work of art," he said. "Just like the chapel."

Years of ivy-growth had almost completely covered the tree house, in an ordered chaos of interlocking branches that held one another in place

"Where is the door?" he asked. "These vines have obliterated it. Do you mind if I cut away some of them?"

"Be my guest," Charlie said. "That stuff grows like weeds."

Alfredo cut until he uncovered the wooden handle of the door and hacked at the vines until the door appeared.

"That door has been shut for hundreds of corvid generations," Charlie said. "Ever since our beloved Bruthamax moved up to the chapel in his last days."

Alfredo yanked on the handle, and the door creaked opened on its wooden hinges. Darkness and scents of mold and dust greeted his senses. He fished a couple of candles from his pack, lit one, and stepped into the tree house and held it up. The trunk of the huge gum tree rose up through the floor and disappeared in the tangled branches of the Hozey-style roof. The walls comprised a solid mass of branches and vines so thick no daylight could penetrate.

Decades of leaves, twigs, and dirt littered the floor and the sparse furnishings: a small rustic table and a bench under a broken window, and a long narrow bed. A stovepipe chimney had collapsed into a crude fireplace.

Charlie and Rika walked across the threshold and into the tree house. "Oh, Husband!" Rika said. "Is it not a privilege to stand in the domicile of the great Bruthamax? To think he sat on that bench! Ate at that table!"

"Evidently Bruthamax constructed the walls in the Hozey way as well as the roof," Alfredo said as he held his candle aloft. "And over the years, the spaces completely filled in with these vines." He held his candle up as high as he could and gazed upward. Same as the roof."

"What's good for the roof is good for the walls, I reckon," Charlie said.

Alfredo melted the end of the other candle and stuck it to a table constructed of a single driftwood plank on three legs.

"How did Bruthamax build this by himself, I wonder," he said as he lit the candle from the one in his hand.

"He didn't," Charlie said from the doorway. "Hozey the Younger and his family helped him. Just like the chapel and the bridge."

"They say Bruthamax slept right here," Charlie said, walking over to a shallow box on legs constructed of split tree trunks.

Bruthamax's bed had been built up against the wall of the tree house, following its contours. "Nothing beats leaves for warmth and cushioning, you know," Rika said as she surveyed the bed full of tree debris and dirt. "Except perhaps feathers."

Alfredo laughed and said, "Yes, feathers are best!"

"As the family history goes," Charlie said, "Bruthamax made a winter cloak out of bird feathers. Crows, mostly, as we are the largest bird family on Cadeña-l'jadia. We, that is my ancestors, they all donated feathers, and Bruthamax sewed them together into a giant cloak that covered him from head to foot. Slept under it too, as the account goes."

"That must be where the stories come from," Alfredo said, imagining what the city folk saw. "They say a giant crow used to walk the shores of the island at night, fishing from the river."

"That would be Bruthamax," Rika said, nodding. "In his crow feather cloak."

"It could be made quite livable," Alfredo said, considering the possibility. "A bit of cleaning, really, is all the place needs."

"The glass is cracked," Rika said, pointing a wing toward the broken window above the table.

"And a little window repair," Alfredo said. "I wonder where Bruthamax got the piece of glass? And that piece of stovepipe? Surely they did not float here on the river!"

They stepped back out onto the deck. Charlie and Rika's kreegans perched on the railing, all eyes upon Jayzu. "JoEd!" Rika called up to the nest. "What are these kreegans doing down here?" She flew up into the branches. "Don't tell me that little judavoid has flown off again!"

Charlie flew out of the tree after his son, and Alfredo sat down on the bench. The young crows jumped from the railing into his lap, onto his shoulders and his head where they played King on the Mountain. One fell off his lap and onto the deck, where he discovered Jayzu's shoelaces. Another pecked at Jayzu's watch, saying, "Sparkly!"

Alfredo laughed and captured the young crows in his hands, one at a time, put them on their backs, and tickled them under their wings as they laughed and kicked their little feet. "All right, kreegans!" he said after everyone had been tickled at least once. He stood up, scattering the crows to the bench and deck. "It is time for Uncle Jayzu to go home."

"King on the Mountain!" shouted one of the *kreegans* as he leapt up to the railing. His siblings flew to the challenge, ready to unseat him and claim the top rail.

Alfredo said good-bye to Rika and spiraled himself down to the ground on the Bruthamax's stairway. As he walked below the tree house, he stumbled on a rock buried in dirt and leaves, and fell forward with a shout as he tumbled through rotten wooden planks into a shallow pit. Unharmed, he stood up and brushed the dirt from his hands.

He stood in a circular hole about five feet deep, lined with flat gray blocks of limestone. Near the top of the pit, a short length of a rusty steel pipe protruded through the stone. "A cistern!" Alfredo said in amazement.

Charlie looked down from the tree house railing. "What's a cistern?"

Alfredo leaped out of the pit and started uncovering the ring of gray rocks at the top. "It is a place to gather and store water," he said. "People collect rainwater in barrels and cisterns near their houses so they do not have to haul it. Water is quite heavy."

He looked up at the underside of the tree house. "But this one did not collect rain water. I bet this pipes water from a stream or a spring nearby." He kicked aside the dirt and leaves covering the pipe and followed it a short distance uphill, to a pond fed by a small, trickling stream.

"This must've been Bruthamax's water source," Alfredo said, pointing to the other end of the pipe. "It must have gotten clogged up over the years." He dropped to his knees and took a drink from the clear pool, sweet and cold.

He stood up, surveying the old hermit's water works. *It would not take much to get the cistern filled again.* But not today. "I must head back," he said to Charlie. "The Captain will be arriving at the inlet to pick me up shortly." Under Charlie's winged guidance, he walked back to the inlet, where the Captain and Sugarbabe awaited him. The Captain rowed in silence and Alfredo watched the green island recede, hoping one day he could come to this island and never leave. He imagined sleeping on the deck of the tree house, with everything he needed at hand's reach. Perhaps Charlie and Rika would not mind.

Alfredo could not stop thinking about the cistern underneath the tree house, wondering how Bruthamax could have built it by himself. He could imagine digging a hole that large, but with what? *And the cement to grout in the limestone bricks? Where did that come from? Where did he get the iron pipe? Surely not from Hozey!*

Clearly Bruthamax had a human helper, someone like the Captain perhaps? To bring him supplies and help with the heavy work ... but then why do the crows say he never spoke to a human after he came to the island?

He returned to the tree house a few days later, with Charlie again leading him through the bogs and dark forest. He brought a small, plastic tarp, a shovel, and a bucket and cleaned the dirt and leaves out of the cistern. Even the bottom had been lined with limestone bricks, and grouted with cement.

After he unclogged the pipe at the small pool, it sucked water in with a loud slurping noise. He ran back, hearing the sound of water falling as a stream poured into the cistern.

"This will take days to fill," he said as he and Charlie watched. He pulled a few branches across the top of the cistern and covered them with the tarp. He placed a few large rocks around the edge of the tarp to hold it down. "That should keep dirt and animals out, until I can build a more permanent cover."

He spent the night on the deck of the tree house, gazing at the stars up through the leaves. Corvus, the constellation of the raven, looked down upon him from high in the southern sky. He fell asleep long after midnight and slept soundly all through the night, until the *kreegans* dropped down on his chest just before dawn.

William Luther handed Father Superior Thomas Majewski a cup of coffee, saying, "The *Times* and the morning mail are on your desk, Father."

"Thank you, William," Majewski said, and he strode into his office. Moments after he sat down, Snowbell leaped into his lap. He stroked her back and scowled in distaste at the letter from an attorney on the top of his mail pile.

He reached for the *Times,* spreading the newspaper open over the dreaded mail. He read every page, including the Fashion and Real Estate sections. The Travel section sang like a siren. New Zealand! Amsterdam! London! Even a trip to New Jersey would beat having to deal with the matter on the top of his mail.

Majewski folded the newspaper carefully when he finished and added it to the stack next to the fireplace. "All right, my Snowbell," he said, "stop this procrastinating and get to work, you hear me?" He scratched the cat under her chin and then rifled through the mail.

The large envelope from Alfredo Manzi seized his attention. "That was quick—was it not, my queen?" he said as he tore it open. "I asked Manzi to send me a report on that island only a week ago." He settled back into his chair and pulled out the report. "Did he discover the talking crows?"

He read the note stuck on the first page:

Thomas–
My report on Wilder Island as you requested,
including photographs
—AM

He peeled it off and scanned the report. *Two miles long, one mile wide ... mostly wetlands ... dense swampy forest ... not enough trees for commercial logging ... no farming ... no mining ...*

He leaned back in his chair, took his glasses off and chewed the end of one of the ear rails. *No mention of talking crows. Of course not! They're not real. They never were.* He shamed himself for even thinking otherwise. They were always just a feature of Brother Maxmillian's insanity.

The same feature of Stella's insanity? Before her face materialized out of his memory, he leaned forward, put his glasses back on, and continued reading:

I have enclosed photos of the extraordinary little chapel that I told you about. There are no nails anywhere; everything was attached with living and dead vines that have since dried and hardened.

Majewski spread the photos on his desk and picked up the image of the chapel. "It looks like a bird's nest!" he said to Snowbell, who woke up suddenly to clean a paw. "That's at least interesting from an historical perspective, is it not? Perhaps the Order should restore that chapel. And the icons—our brother certainly had a gift—maybe I should take them to the Museum of Jesuit History.

He read the last paragraph of Manzi's report:

I have found Brother Wilder's residence on the opposite end of the island as the chapel. He lived in a tree house of the same general construction as the old chapel, except a bit more weatherproof. Like the chapel, it is extraordinary. I have enclosed a couple of photographs.

Majewski smiled at the photograph of the tree house. Manzi was right. It's absolutely enchanting, as if wood elves live inside. He rotated the photograph 180 degrees. Definitely a bird's nest.

He pushed the intercom button on his phone.

"Yes, Father."

"William, check my calendar and clear four days where I don't have appointments that can't be moved. Then book me a flight to Ledford. Yes, William. I'm going to Wilder Island."

"As you wish, Father."

—4—

Queen of the Night

"Oh my God!" Jade said. She stood at the sliding glass door in their living room, shaking her head and pointing to something in the backyard. Her hand covered her mouth in shock. "They know.""

"Who knows?" Russ asked. "And what do they know?" He looked over the newspaper at her from the couch.

"Oh my God," she said again, shaking her head. "They found me."

"Who found you?" Russ put the newspaper down, got up, and joined her at the window. "What is it, honey?"

Dozens of crows perched on their back wall, the little fence around the garden, and the backs of the chairs on the patio. Five dipped their beaks in the birdbath. Many more flew back and forth among the trees in the woods behind the house.

"Wow!" Russ said. "There must be a hundred of them! I wonder what's so interesting about our yard."

"They know," Jade said.

"Know what?"

"They know I have this." She patted the medallion through her shirt. "They know it's in here." Her voice rose slightly with each word. It's a token of some weird brotherhood of crows and humans! That's why they broke in and tried to steal it! They came back for it. They know where it is."

"Oh, please, Jade," Russ said, rolling his eyes. "How would these crows know what's under your shirt? I didn't tell them. That only leaves Willow B."

The cat looked up from his favorite chair. "Mrrr?" He blinked sleepily, licked his left paw twice, and put his head back down.

"And he says he didn't tell anyone anything," Russ said with a big grin. "They know nothing about you, Jade. They're crows. They're just looking for food, probably."

The crows stared directly at her. "Right," she said, backing away from the window. "Where's the food? We don't even keep a garbage can out there. They've never come into our yard before, not like this. And standing around the birdbath? Hmmm?"

"Hmmm, what?" Russ said irritably. He turned away from the window and looked at her with a frown. "They're birds, Jade. Birds go to birdbaths to drink and bathe. That's why we put it there."

"Don't you get it?" she said, her eyebrows crunched together. "I dreamed that a birdbath sailed through our window, and crows flew inside, and now they're standing on our birdbath."

"And you think they somehow picked it up and heaved it through our window?" Russ said. He looked heavenward with his arms out-stretched and shook his head. "It was a dream, Jade! Must you let it rule your life? And mine?"

"Okay, fine," she said with a long-suffering sigh. "You *don't* get it. Follow me."

She led him down the hall to her studio, stopping and turning toward a painting on the wall. "This was my first official painting. That is, the first one that ever got a frame. I called it *High Five*."

Five crows danced around the top of a birdbath, beaks open, laughing and brushing one another's wingtips above their heads. The blue-black feathers flashed iridescent red, green, and yellow, like tiny lights that appeared for a moment and quickly winked out, only to wink back on in another location.

"I've always loved this painting," Russ said. "You have so much talent. How old were you when you painted this? Before or after you dreamed they broke into your bedroom?"

"I was in fifth grade," Jade said. "Ten, I guess. These five crows came every day to the birdbath in Chloe and Smitty's yard. They had a very playful and silly side to them."

She remembered having fun with crows once. Before the night-mare started. Then it was crows on the road in front of Chloe and

Smitty's house, pecking at something. They looked up occasionally, pieces of white fur dropping from bloody beaks. Her cat, Blitzen.

She shivered. "But they eat dead things."

"We eat dead things," Russ said. He raised his eyebrows.

"Not off the road!" Jade said, wrinkling her nose.

"What difference does that make?" he asked. "Other than Miss Manners advises against it and we don't need small rocks in our stomachs to digest our food?" He put his arm around her. "It's only the food chain, dear. Crows eat road kill. They eat French fries and doughnuts and everything edible that we drop into the landscape. They ate a good many of the corpses during the bubonic plagues. The world would be a stinkier place indeed without our corvid friends."

"That's supposed to make me like them more?" Jade asked, frowning. "I wish they would go roost in someone else's yard."

Russ held up the painting of the five crows. "But you liked them once. And there they were, in your yard. Like they were your friends."

"I didn't have any friends," Jade insisted. "Just Abby. Chloe and Smitty lived out in the country. But there were always a bunch of crows everywhere." She shrugged. "I guess I played with them some. Once."

Russ placed the painting back down on the chair. He looked at his watch and said, "I gotta go, hon. Field trip this afternoon. I'm going to Wilder Island!"

"Lucky you!" Jade said. "I think."

She accompanied him down the hall and into the kitchen. Glancing out the sliding glass door to the backyard, she was surprised that the crows were gone. But a single black feather lay on the step. She opened the sliding door, reached down, and picked it up.

"Look at this," she said as she handed it to Russ.

"Looks like a tail feather," Russ said matter-of-factly and handed it back. He slung his pack over his shoulder and kissed her on the cheek. "I'll be home by six-thirty."

Jade took the feather to the studio and wondered how Russ knew so much. His family moved frequently, he had told her once. And he dealt with the constant uprooting and having to leave friends by burying himself in books. He read everything, he said. *He still does. That's why he's such a Mr. Know-It-All.*

Jade had the same best friend, Abby Mahoney, from first grade all the way through high school. She wondered how Russ survived his childhood without a best friend. How did he learn to be so warm and affectionate? He was very fun to be with and as gentle a soul as she'd ever met, other than her foster father, Smitty, maybe.

Russ was different from all the boys she knew in high school and college. He never came on to her. Not until that night in the Arizona desert when he completely swept her off her feet. She fell into a safety net of mutual affection he had built with his gentlemanly ways. *Such a sweet courtship!* Jade smiled at the memory. And their honeymoon the cave paintings in southern France could not have been more fabulous.

She sighed, remembering how it was Russ who'd convinced her to start painting again, and helped her turn their spare bedroom into a studio. Now she had a one-woman show coming up in Ledford's only avant-garde gallery. And she needed more paintings. She flopped down into a chair and examined the crow feather. "For something that seems so black, there are sure a lot of colors," she said as Willow B jumped into her lap. He sniffed the feather delicately before settling down for a nap.

The afternoon flowed by unnoticed as Jade meticulously painted the feather from the vantage point of a tiny creature walking up its central spine. A fabric of pigmented threads and gossamer film formed an oblique grid of tiny prisms that filtered and split light into transparent layers of color. Close up, thousands of tiny windows scattered the colors of the rainbow into a mosaic pattern of rectangles. From across the room, a black feather arced gracefully upward in a motion suggesting imminent flight.

RUSS SAT AT HIS DESK IN THE BIOLOGY department, re-examining the tiny blue flower from Wilder Island that Alfredo had given him. It was an orchid, he thought, but it was hard to tell in its dried, squished state. And part of it had crumbled away. He was eager to find one living and undamaged. As soon as Alfredo's Avian Anatomy class was over, they were heading to Wilder Island for an afternoon of scientific discovery. He had been looking forward to this day for weeks.

He put the dried flower back in a small plastic box and closed the lid. He walked over to his window and gazed out, his hands in his pockets. Bright and beckoning in the morning sun, Wilder Island called out to him, promising riches beyond his imagination.

I just know I'm going to discover a new orchid there. Jadum wilderii. He had always known that one day he would find a new and exotically beautiful flower and name it after his beloved yet eccentric wife. *Jadum wilderii.*

The white roof of the little chapel on Wilder Island glowed bright white and stark against the dark greens and shadows in which the chapel nestled. Russ fantasized it was a gigantic white flower—the *Se-lenicereus grandiflorus. More beautiful than any flower, my Queen of the Night. I fell in love with her the day I met her.*

Jade was a freshman, and he was a senior. From the first moment, he couldn't take his eyes off her. She was so beautiful, though a bit thin—she got carried away with painting sometimes and forgot to eat. He took advantage of her need and happily took her out for a bite whenever he could. She was kind of spacey sometimes but always full of fun and very, very sweet. She never gave him any sign that she would welcome a romantic advance from him, so he never made one. He spent his last year in college secretly in love with her.

When he told her he had gotten into grad school in Arizona, he thought she seemed happy for him, but there were no long, lingering looks when he left. They parted, and he wondered ever after what would've happened if he had taken her in his arms and kissed her passionately. "Spilled milk under the bridge," he had told himself. "Let it go. She's married to some lucky guy by now." But he could not forget her.

Out of the blue and in a weak moment of nostalgia, he sent Jade a postcard from Tucson. Joy of all joys, she called him a few days later. "As luck would have it," she said, "I'll be in Tucson in a couple weeks. Chloe and Smitty bought me a place in a workshop there. It's about making paint from the colored rocks in the landscape. Pretty cool, no? I'll be there for a few days. Want to get together?"

As luck would have it.

But was it luck? Was it just fate that brought him and Jade together finally? What is fate or simple obedience to the laws of the universe amid an infinite sea of variables? *Opportunity. That's all it is. There is no Almighty Oz that controls our lives. No horoscope, no tea leaves. It's all about luck and opportunity. You seize it or you don't.* Still, he felt that somehow in the grand order of the universe, he and Jade were meant to be.

He remembered the day like it was yesterday. He had driven to the airport and waited for her outside the gate. He recognized her instantly as she walked through the turnstile; she looked just the way he had remembered. *Blonde, beautiful, and green eyes, really green eyes.* He stepped forward, and she smiled. Oh, those eyes he had lost himself in years before just about devoured him again. They embraced quickly; she looked up at him, and he was history.

"What are you doing in southern Arizona, Russ?" she had asked him later, when they were seated in the dining room of her hotel. "Forgive me, but isn't this a desert? Seems like an odd place for a botanist. There's more dirt here than plants!"

"*Au contraire*, Mademoiselle," Russ said, waving his margarita at her. "Yonder desert teems with life. Granted, there's less of it here than in the Midwest, due to the scarcity of water, but the desert is surprisingly diverse in its flora."

Their food arrived, and Russ waited to continue while the waiter served them and bustled around filling water glasses. He hurried away only after he was satisfied their needs were filled.

"But really," he continued, "I'm here in Tucson because of its proximity to an area where the *Selenicereus grandiflorus* grows, the subject of my ridiculously intricate, yet fascinating, doctorate. Commonly known as the 'Queen of the Night,' the *Selenicereus grandiflorus* is a night-blooming cactus. Its flower is large and gorgeous, so someone started calling it an orchid a long time ago. But really, it's a cactus."

Russ stopped, blushed, and said, "Sorry for the diatribe. I can get pretty carried away sometimes." He attacked his steak.

"No. Really, Russ," Jade said, "I'm interested. Especially in a man who loves flowers! I like hearing about the scientific aspects of Mother Nature's jewels."

No wonder he was crazy about her. "Well, thanks," he said. "Most people find it boring. But the *Selenicereus grandiflorus* flower is incredible. It blooms only once a year—at night. And it only lasts for just that one night."

"Very romantic!" Jade said. "I'd love to see it, the *Selenicus grandiflorius*, in bloom."

He smiled at her attempt to pronounce the *Selenicereus grandiflorus. Cute and beautiful!*

After dinner, they sipped coffee outside on a wood deck cantilevered over a rock garden. The view was spectacular. The multi-story office buildings of downtown Tucson cast an impressive silhouette against the setting sun. The mountains to the east reflected the day's end in shades of watermelon and indigo in air so clear, you could almost see forever.

He took her for a ride in the desert, silently thanking the fates for arranging a full moon and a clear night. He stopped the car, cut the engine, and got out. He walked around to her side and opened the door. "At your request, my lady, right this way to the *Selenicereus grandiflorus* in bloom. It's not far."

They walked a short distance and stopped. He waited till she saw it—a large white flower, reflecting the silvery light of the moon and stars. Jade took a few steps and gasped.

And then he kissed her.

After that weekend, Russ spent a small fortune flying them both back and forth for visits, but he considered the money well spent and their time together precious. He loved her paintings and was wildly enthusiastic about her talent. "You should paint some more," he kept telling her.

"I know," she almost always said. "I want to, but somehow I can't." She looked so sad, and he didn't know what else to do, so he just took her in his arms and hugged her.

On his last visit, he took her out for dinner. Afterward, they went for a walk, and he asked her to marry him. "I love you, Jade. I've never loved anyone but you. And I want to stop this flying back and forth all the time. I hate it when you're not with me. Marry me?"

And she did! Life is strange.

Alfredo stuck his head into Russ's office and said, "You ready?"

Russ nodded and grabbed his backpack before heading out the door. They left the Biology Department together and walked to the parking lot behind the building. Russ drove them to the city boat landing, where a strange boat seemed to be waiting for them. He followed Alfredo aboard, admiring the artistry of the wrought-iron work.

"This is my friend Russ, Captain," Alfredo said.

"Pleased to meet you, Captain," Russ said, shaking the man's hand. He looked up at the branches and leaves that formed a canopy over the boat. "Nice work."

"Thank'ee," the Captain said with a nod.

He pushed off with a long oar, the tattoos on his arm coming to life as fish leaped over roiling waves, and birds flew in and out of the trees overhead. A large crow sat perched on the railing next to the Captain, gazing across the water as he rowed.

"You heard someone has offered to buy Wilder Island?" Alfredo said. "Henry Braun is his name."

"Yes," Russ said. "It's been in the papers. He wants to build some kind of casino resort. You Jesuits will turn him down, right?"

"I think so," Alfredo said. "In any case, I plan to do everything I can to convince my Order that the island is worth keeping."

"Be a cold day in hell," the Captain grunted as he steered, "before the crows'll let that happen."

The crow perched on the railing looked up at the Captain, squawking loudly as if it had an opinion to share. The Captain nodded and said, "No way, Jose!"

A barge blew its whistle as it took the right-of-way, and the shrill noise temporarily drowned out any conversation.

Russ gazed ahead at the mysterious island, inhaling deeply, filling his senses with the cool, moist river breeze. The island held his destiny, he was sure of it, beckoning and compelling him forward. *Jadum wilderii. I know you are there.*

"I'd give my left nu—" he said, turning to Alfredo, "ah, that is my left foot to discover a new flower, say an orchid. The papers I could write! Tenure for sure!"

"I suspect so!" Alfredo said, grinning. "That is why I want to show you the island, Russ. I am also hopeful we can turn it into a research station, where we can study the native birds and plants."

The Captain rowed into the inlet, and Russ looked up at several black birds circling above. "Crows or ravens?"

Alfredo looked up and said, "Ravens. You can tell by the wedge-shaped tail."

The Captain left the two men on the bank. "Back at sunset," he said and shoved his boat back into the river.

Alfredo pointed toward a vague path. "This way, Russ."

Immediately lost to its many wonders, Russ darted off the path and into the forest, calling out the names of plants and trees as if greeting old friends. "Ah, my lovely myrtle!" he said, plucking a leaf and holding it to his nose.

He stopped at a group of black ash trees. "Forgive me," he said sheepishly as Alfredo caught up with him. "But these ash trees—at least I think they're ash—are very unusual, to say the least. Look at the leaf! It's the right shape, but it's sure an odd color." He pulled a leaf off and examined it closely. "Almost blue-green." He put the leaf carefully in his notebook.

Alfredo conducted Russ through the forest, through stands of black spruce and white cedar, as well as balsam fir, dwarf alder, dogwood, and willow. Hundreds of birds flew among the trees, all calling out at once.

"It's hard to imagine a big city not a mile away," Russ said. "I can't hear it at all."

"Nor can you hear our feet crunching through the undergrowth," Alfredo said, "with all that racket up there!"

"I'm sorry." Russ cupped a hand behind his ear. "I didn't catch that."

"If you think this is loud," Alfredo raised his voice, above the din, "you must come and hear them in the spring. You cannot hear yourself think."

"Wouldn't you love to live here?" Russ said loudly. "I'd listen to this noise all day long, as opposed to the sounds of tires screeching, sirens, and planes landing and taking off."

I pray to the Almighty daily," Alfredo said, "that one day I will make this island my home."

Russ stopped to admire a cluster of willows growing along a tiny stream with a variety of different species of rushes lining the edges. "Wow!" he said, dropping to his knees. "Will ya look at that? I believe it's white Lady's Slipper, a rare find indeed."

"As I have been telling you," Alfredo said, "the island flora is extraordinary, Russ. There are many unusual plants, especially on the lower island, though I have not had the time to compare them to known species. Not exactly my expertise. But that is why I asked you here."

Russ took his camera out of his pack and took several pictures before making a quick sketch of the flower. After writing a few notes he snapped his notebook shut and stood up.

A noisy group of crows flew overhead, and the two men looked up. "One of the crow families that live on the island," Alfredo said. "Mother and father, three young ones, out for a fly."

"They do that?" Russ asked. "Take the kids out? They don't just toss them from the nest as soon as they have feathers and can fly?"

"Heavens, no!" Alfredo said. "Quite the opposite. The fledglings stay in the nest until they are several months old. The older brothers and sisters often hang around even longer and help care for the new generation of fledglings."

"Seriously?" Russ asked. "Extended crow families?"

"Yes," Alfredo replied. "The corvid even take care of their old ones, bringing them food when they cannot get it for themselves."

"Very kind," Russ said. "I had no idea. I guess I should read your papers."

"No worries!" Alfredo said with a grin. "I have not read any of yours either!" Both men laughed. "But perhaps we should, Russ. If we are going to be doing research on the same island."

They continued to walk, and Alfredo watched Russ's excitement grew. "There's years worth of research here! Things I've never seen before, not even in botany books. I'm completely awe-smacked, to use my wife's favorite term."

"To my knowledge, there is no where on Earth like this island," Alfredo said. "But wait until you see the orchids! The lower half of the island is very boggy with many springs that disappear underground and reappear elsewhere. Orchids evidently love that climate. Next time, we will go down there, though we will need to start earlier and pack lunch. And mosquito repellent!"

"I can't wait!" Russ said. "There are a few rare orchids in this state; it's a good bet one or two may be on this island. I'd love to find out what lives in these mosquito-infested bogs!"

"Perhaps even discover a new species, eh?" Alfredo said with a wink. "But yes, swampy and mosquito-infested, this island is all that. All yours, this mighty yet miniature kingdom."

"A research area in my own backyard," Russ said. "What a score! I was getting nervous about my tenure review next year, and about having the requisite number of publications. Imagine if I discover a new species!"

A group of crows swooped in low over the two men, cawing loudly. Much to Russ's surprise, Alfredo raised an arm and called out a greeting, and the crows returned the salutation.

"Nice!" Russ said. "I've never known anyone who learned crow calls. You're quite good! If I wasn't standing here watching, I wouldn't be able to tell the difference between you and them."

Alfredo smiled and said, "That was not really a call, *per se*. We tend to think of birdcalls as mating calls, but really most are not."

"So then," Russ said, stopping and turning his head toward Alfredo. "What was it?"

Alfredo shrugged and said, "Hello." He watched Russ's reaction carefully. No astonishment, just curiosity.

"Say it again, this hello," Russ said, looking at Alfredo intently.

"Grawky!" Alfredo said. "Grawky. The 'gr' sound begins in the throat. A guttural sort of growl almost as if you're clearing your throat and hacking up a feather. Grawky!"

Russ laughed and said "Grawky!" a few times until Alfredo nodded and said, "You got it! Grawky!"

"Thanks, man!" Russ said. "Grawky! I love it. It sounds so crow-ish! Grawky!"

"Grawky!" A call came down from the trees overhead. Russ laughed like a child and said, "Was that a crow or a raven? Or can you tell?"

"That was a crow," Alfredo said. "Ravens make much deeper, more guttural sounds." He looked up at the sky. "We should head back to the inlet. The Captain will be arriving soon."

"So," Russ said, as they backtracked through the forest, "how many other words do you know?"

Alfredo walked a few steps before answering. *How much should I tell him? He seems eager to know and not at all put off.* He took a deep breath and said, "The corvid language is composed of sentences, or phrases, rather than words. I used to think their language in terms of sounds is less varied than ours, due to anatomical differences, but that is not so. Corvid language is no less intricate than ours."

Russ stopped and took a bottle of water from the side pocket of his pack. Alfredo waited while he took a long drink and wiped his mouth on his sleeve. "Well, then I guess my question should have been: how many sentences do *you* know?"

"That is hard to answer as well," said Alfredo as he propped a boot up on a rock and retied the lace. "As I said, the corvid language is quite complex. I have only a rudimentary understanding of it."

He flinched a little at his lie. *I have as great an understanding of the corvid language as I do of English.* But he was not yet ready for

Russ to find out about the secret he had guarded so carefully since he was a child. Not yet.

"This is great stuff, Alfredo!" Russ said. "You are writing a paper, aren't you? I bet the department would find you a full-time faculty position."

"I have only just begun to scratch the surface," Alfredo said, shaking his head. "And I do not want a full-time faculty position. I am happy with my life the way it is."

"For God's sake, man!" Russ said, stopping and staring at Alfredo. "You need to publish! You'd have instant tenure at any university in the world. You'd be famous for-freaking-ever!"

"I do not want to be famous," Alfredo said, staring back. "My life is perfect. I am connected to a scholarly institution and the most marvelous field laboratory—this island. I have a cathedral when I desire human companionship. One day perhaps I will write about the corvid language. But not yet."

The birds were far less noisy than they had been earlier; the leaves and twigs crackled under their feet. Leaves fluttered on their branches, adding a soft percussive rhythm to the song of the wind. The Captain was waiting as they arrived at the inlet, and as they pulled away from the island, Russ said, "Thanks, Alfredo. This was fantastic! I can't wait to come back!"

"He does what?" Jade asked, her eyebrows arched in shocked suspicion. "Alfredo Manzi talks to crows?"

Russ shoveled a forkful of pasta into his mouth, dripping spaghetti sauce onto the table. "Um, hmm," he said. "I'm serious. He's translated some of their calls into English."

Jade speared a chunk of avocado and said, "You actually heard him talking to crows? You didn't perchance accidentally eat some loco weed on the island, did you?"

"No!" Russ laughed. "There are plenty of crazy-looking plants, though. But I did hear him speak to a small group of crows."

Jade giggled behind her napkin. "Did they answer?"

Russ popped a piece of garlic bread into his mouth. After chewing it, he said, "Yes. They did. I was pretty shocked at first, but there's no reason why we can't learn the language of other species. He taught me how to say hello." Russ put his fork down and drank a sip of water. "Grawky!" he said. "Grawky!"

Jade tried to repeat the crow's greeting, much to Russ's amusement. "The sound comes from down in the throat," he explained. "Alfredo says the crows have vocal chords of sorts way down deep in their throats. He says the crow's language is quite complex and may have as many words as any human language."

Jade shook her head and waved her fork at him. "That's just too hard to believe, Russ. How can crows talk to humans?" She rose from the table, took their plates to the sink, and returned with an apple pie.

He shrugged. "I can't explain the anatomy and physiology of it. I'm a plant man." He drank the last sip of his water and put the glass on the table, centered it precisely within one of the circle patterns on the tablecloth. He watched Jade cut the pie in half, quarters, eighths.

"But it's not all that crazy," he said. "Just because we can't understand the other animals doesn't mean they haven't developed a complex language."

Jade put a piece of pie in front of him. "Whip?" she asked, with the nozzle of the whipped cream can poised over his plate.

Russ nodded and said, "The unbelievable thing is that he won't publish."

The Great Corvid Council

D eep within the Ledford National Cemetery, Hookbeak, Aviar of the Great Corvid Council, emerged from sleep in an ancient white oak tree to contemplate the dawning of the day. The small hollow in the tree's massive trunk and the wide branch at its opening provided him shelter from storms as well as a wide platform upon which he could stand and even walk around a bit. He stood as high as he could and flapped his wings in his ritual morning stretch. Across the river, Cadeña-l'jadia floated on a river of glass, still shrouded in blankets of mist.

The military cemetery in which Hookbeak's tree grew formed the southwestern boundary of the city, on the outskirts of Downtown. Built in the early days of Ledford, its oldest gravestones bore dates from the early-1800s. The frequency of twenty-one-gun salutes had increased over the past decade, disturbing Hookbeak's peace. He supposed the humans had engaged themselves in another war somewhere.

"That is how they thin their populations," his friend Starfire had said. "That and the automobile."

Hookbeak endured the noise from the salutes without complaint. He had even stopped reacting, for the most part, to the sound of gunfire. Where humans gathered, noise ensued. But they always left food behind, which more than compensated him for a few seconds of annoyance.

He had hatched in the cemetery, and he had lived there his entire life. He built nest after nest in a new tree every year, and in nearly two entire decades, he and his lovely wife, Rosie, had hatched over one hundred chicks. Eighty-nine fledglings survived into adulthood—not a bad average. Not bad at all.

Hookbeak had quite lost count of how many grandchildren he had, or even how many generations he had spawned. Many of his children and their children flew in from time to time for a visit. He was always happy to see them, and grateful when they left.

He had lived alone in the old oak since his Rosie had fallen to the West Nile virus the year before. He missed her terribly, and he spoke to her frequently throughout his quiet solitude. *Rosie, my heart. My work here will soon be finished, and I will join you. Together we will fly into the Great Orb of Time. Wait for me!*

Today as Aviar, Hookbeak would preside over the Great Corvid Council, a thirteen-member body of crows and ravens whose objective was to keep the regional corvid population informed and healthy, as well as to keep historical and actuarial records. The Council would also discuss the sudden appearance of Jayzu, the newest Patua' in the territory. He just showed up out of thin air. Starfire was incensed at the very idea of an un-catalogued Patua' right under his beak.

A 'on Cadeña-l'jadia! The end times are indeed near, my Rosie! Hookbeak gazed across the cemetery toward the island. *I shall not see the new age.* He sighed. *But I do see it on the horizon. That will have to suffice.*

"Grawky, Starfire!" Hookbeak called out as his friend sailed into the tree and landed next to him.

"Grawky, my friend!" Starfire said after he dropped a barbequed chicken leg at Hookbeak's feet. "Breakfast for two!"

"What a pleasant surprise!" Hookbeak pecked a big chunk of chicken leg off the bone and rolled it toward Starfire with his beak.

"The Cub Scouts had a picnic at the park yesterday," Starfire said after he swallowed a chunk. "I managed to pluck this from the trash just before a mob of crows descended on it."

"One must be quick," Hookbeak said, "if crows are around."

The two ravens took turns grasping the chicken leg in one claw and pulling off chunks of meat. Starfire stood on the chicken bone and pulled off the last bits of flesh before letting it drop to the ground. He cleaned his beak on a branch.

"Very tasty," Hookbeak said. "Thank you most kindly, my friend. That should do me until after the council meeting. "Where is Jayzu?"

"Jayzu is waiting for us at the bench by the fish pond," Starfire said, opening his wings. "He's a short fly from the Council trees."

The two ravens left Hookbeak's tree and flew to a remote corner of the cemetery where the trees were tall and stood very close together. A man sat on a park bench near a pond, throwing bits of bread to a group of noisy ducks.

"Grawky, Jayzu!" Hookbeak said heartily as he landed on the back of the bench. "We meet at last! I am Hookbeak."

Starfire landed on the grass, folding his wings as he introduced himself. Jayzu brushed his hand across each of their outstretched wingtips. "I am pleased to make your acquaintances as well. I—"

The Aviar loomed over Jayzu and bore into him with his piercing black eyes. "The Council is quite curious about you," he said. "Many thought Bruthamax was the last of your kind. There are those among us, however, that know otherwise."

Starfire took a couple steps closer to Jayzu and said, "Indeed. And at least one among us who has predicted your coming."

Jayzu shifted his weight on the bench. "I am curious about the Council as well," he said. "But I have always thought that I am a freak of nature; I had no idea I had a 'kind.' I thought—"

"We are all freaks of nature," Hookbeak rumbled. "Are we not? What are any of us but miraculous answers to a unique set of utterly random circumstance?"

"Well, I guess—" Jayzu said.

Starfire flapped his wings impatiently and said, "Who is to say circumstances are random? But there is a larger picture than our mutual curiosity, Jayzu. Much larger." He hopped up onto the bench, eye-level with the human. "We believe your presence heralds a new age."

"Really?" Jayzu said. "A new age? Me? But I am just an ord—"

"Yes, you!" Starfire said vehemently. "That is what all the signs say. Ever since the Patua' mysteriously and suddenly disappeared some five hundred years ago, we have told our hatchlings stories of the return of a Great One, beloved by all. The Great One will bring the Patua' back from whence they disappeared."

Jayzu frowned and shook his head. "I am no messiah, Starfire. You have the wrong man. I am just an ordin—"

"We thought this Patua' was Bruthamax," Hookbeak interrupted. "But he did not bring the Patua' back."

"And you believe I will?" Jayzu asked. "You had the wrong man once. You still do."

"So our previous interpretation was wrong," Starfire said. He sharpened his beak on the edge of the park bench. "Not our stories. But here is an interesting fact: you and Bruthamax are of the same clan, the Jesuit Clan."

"The Jesuits are an order," Jayzu said, "not a clan."

"Order, family, genus, species, clan," Starfire said irritably. "Whatever you want to call it, you and Bruthamax are both Patua', you both came to Cadeña-l'jadia, and you are both of the Jesuit kin. We think this is not a coincidence."

Jayzu stood up and walked several steps away from the bench. He emptied his sack of bread crumbs into the pond, and the ducks scrambled, dashing to snatch up the morsels before they sank. He turned back to the two ravens on the park bench and said, "Then you probably will think it is no coincidence that I have spent my life among the Jesuits. I was placed in a boarding school at an early age, due to my crow-speech, as they called it. After that Jesuit high school, then Jesuit college, Jesuit seminary school—"

"Supporting my hypothesis," Starfire said, "of a Patua' Underground and the probable return of the Patua'. Right here, right now."

Hookbeak hopped down onto the seat of the park bench and said, "That remains a hypothesis, Starfire. Two data points is not a trend. Bring me proof." The Aviar turned his attention back to Jayzu. "Now we must go. Are you ready for the Council? These corvids can be rather formidable, and we are not all of like mind, and no one is the least bashful."

"Nor are humans all of like mind," Jayzu said, smiling. "I am ready, Aviar."

"Good," Hookbeak said as he flapped his wings and jumped to the ground. "Excellent. Let us go. The meeting place is just over yonder."

"I will see you at the Council Tree," said Starfire as he took to the air.

Jayzu and Hookbeak walked side by side toward a cove of oak trees a short distance from the pond. Most of the councilors had already arrived; Hookbeak could see many of them in the lower branches of the council trees at the edge of the cove. "Jayzu, please stay hidden back here," he said, "until I call you out."

Hookbeak walked into the clearing and flew up to the Aviar's perch, a branch higher than the rest on the tallest tree. The last councilor arrived, and the Aviar rose up tall on his branch, flapped his wings, and called out, "The Great Corvid Council convenes! Izzy?"

"Sound off, ravens!" Izzy, the Aviar's page called out in his crackly, adolescent voice.

Each bird called out his name and his territory, in accordance with the time-honored tradition of the Council.

"Hookbeak. Ledford National Cemetery," the Aviar rumbled.

"Starfire. Woodmen of the World Cemetery."

"Walldrug. The Boonies."

"Longshanks. The Timber Mill."

"Wingnut. Ledford Municipal Zoo."

"Fishgut. The Cannery."

"Restarea. Ledford Airport."

"All ravens present!" Iggy croaked. "Sound off, crows!"

"Athanasius. The Brewery."

"DeeJay. Downtown."

"Beamer. The Waterfront."

"O'Malley. Southlands."

"Ziggy. Cadeña-l'jadia."

"Joshwa. Ledford Landfill."

"All crows present!" Izzy yelled.

"Thank you, Izzy," the Aviar said graciously, before turning to address the Council. The page disappeared into the upper branches of Hookbeak's tree.

"What news of the territories, corvids?" Hookbeak's deep raven voice boomed through the branches.

"Runway 218's flooded again," said Restarea. "They are diverting air traffic."

"So that's why it's been so dang noisy around the Cannery," Fishgut said. "Like to shake the dang daylights out of a body."

"There's a new law in Cavron County," O'Malley called out. "All humans must carry an unconcealed gun in public at all times. Seriously. They're insane down there, afraid of everything. My brother-in-law, he even saw one poor slob shooting at his own shadow."

The councilors guffawed and flapped their wings in ridicule.

"Let us get the word out," Hookbeak said. "Cavron County is off-limits to all corvids. Any other news?" The Aviar looked around, and when no one spoke, he continued, "Very well. Most of you have heard the rumors that a Patua' again lives on Cadeña-l'jadia."

A hush fell at the mention of the lush green island of crows, uninhabited by humans for decades. The leaves quivered as the Council seemed to hold its breath.

"Bruthamax has returned!" Beamer shouted, and some of the crows erupted into a fanfare of feathers and beak. "Bruthamax lives!" The entire tree shook as the councilors danced upon their branches.

"Bruthamax is still dead, Beamer," Hookbeak said. "This one is called Jayzu."

The councilors settled back down, with a few last shout-outs, "Long live Bruthamax!"

"I seen him once, this new Patua', on the cathedral steps Downtown," DeeJay said. "All dressed in black. Looked kind of like one of us, only bigger. He threw leftovers from the monsignor's breakfast for us poor, hungry crows!"

The crows cackled and fanned their wings in approval. "I'll be joining you for church, come Sunday!" Beamer said.

"I heard Jayzu serves bacon," Joshwa said as he flew from his branch up to one near Beamer. "I haven't tasted bacon since the family moved out to the landfill."

"Councilors!" Hookbeak, the Aviar, spoke. "Please be serious. This is momentous. We have been waiting for this Patua' since Bruthamax.""

"I thought they all died out," Longshanks said.

"Bruthamax was the last of them," Walldrug said.

"We all thought that," Hookbeak said. "But evidently that is not so."

"Not at all," Starfire said, rising up on his perch. "There are a few in our area alone. But more importantly, we have expected the Patua' to reemerge for centuries, heralded by the arrival of one from the Jesuit Clan. We thought this Patua' was Bruthamax. We were wrong. It is this new Patua'. Jayzu."

The councilors muttered under their beaks to one another, some in wonder, "At last, the Patua' have returned!" some in doubt, "How do we know it is *this* Patua' we've been waiting for?" and a couple who believed the news irrelevant, "It is ludicrous to wait and hope this extinct species will save us." "What's a Jezyooit?"

Hookbeak rose up on his branch, flapping his huge wings. "Please let us now adjourn downward to the ground and greet the Patua'." He stepped off the Aviar's perch and sailed down to the clearing below. The rest of the councilors followed, gasping in dismay and delight. "A Patua'? Here? Now?" "Where is the Patua'?" "Why were we not told a Patua' would be here?"

"I am telling you now," the Aviar said. He paused a moment to allow the wave of wing shuffling and murmurings to cease. He turned toward the trees. "Jayzu! The Great Corvid Council awaits your arrival!"

Alfredo stepped out from behind the trees and walked into the very surprised group of corvids. "I am honored to be among you," he said quietly to the hushed councilors.

Many of them nodded to one another, mumbling their approval. A few waved a wing at him, and others called out their greetings and comments. "Yo! Jayzu!" "That's a Patua'?" "He looks just like a regular human!"

Hookbeak spoke. "And we are honored you came to us, Jayzu. Greetings!"

Alfredo held his hands out as a few of the councilors stepped forward to greet him.

"We were gladdened by the news of a Patua' on Cadeña-l'jadia," a raven said cordially. "I am Longshanks. Welcome." He brushed his wing across Alfredo's hand.

"Is it true, Jayzu," a crow spoke out above the muttering, "you are building a bird sanctuary on Cadeña-l'jadia?"

"Not yet," Alfredo replied, "but someday I—"

"Sanctuary? What kind of sanctuary?" one of the ravens interrupted in mild alarm. He wandered through the councilors on the grass as he spoke. "There are sanctuaries and then there are Sanctuaries, so we wonder exactly what you intend to do in this sanctuary. Some oddball sanctification ritual perhaps? Will you require feathers? Entrails?"

"No," Alfredo said, "I—"

"Sanctuary?" a few of the councilors said as they looked at one another in apparent confusion.

"What's a sanctuary?" asked a crow.

"It just means—" Alfredo started to say.

"Sanctuary—the word comes from the root, to sanctify," another crow replied sanctimoniously. "To mortify and cleanse the flesh."

Alfredo felt exasperated with some of the councilors, but there was little he could do other than wait politely and grab what chance he could to speak. He glanced at Hookbeak, standing silently next to him on the grass. *Will he not intervene and let me talk?*

"Ah," the raven who had asked the original question said. "It is a bathing place then. In this case, for birds. That does not sound so bad."

"Unless the cleansing of the flesh is done with blood, Restarea," a raven said. Hoots of denial circulated through the Council. "It has happened," he continued. "Human use of animals as sacrificial offerings for ritual ceremonies to appease their gods is well known."

"There will be no sacri—" Alfredo said and glanced at Hookbeak standing silently next to him on the grass. *Will he not intervene and let me talk?*

"Will this Patua', this Jayzu, be experimenting on birds in his sanctuary?" another raven asked. "Perhaps feather plucking for his rituals? Dissection?"

"A sanctuary is a refuge, Walldrug," Starfire said, impatiently waving a wing. "Safe haven. Rest stop. Now please, let us remember that Jayzu is Patua'. I daresay he reveres the corvid as much as Bruthamax did."

"Charlie of the great Hozey Clan," a crow said, "well, his wife told my wife that he told her that Jayzu knew nothing of Bruthamax."

Gasps of incredulous dismay pulsed through the councilors, and they looked at one another and Alfredo in disbelief. "Never heard of Bruthamax? How can that be?" someone hissed. "He knows not his own kin!" whispered another. "How can we trust him?"

Bedlam broke out as factions lined up against other factions. "Interventionist!" one side cried out, while the other shouted "Isolationist!"

"Are you all daft?" Starfire shouted, striding to the middle of the two groups. "Or just deaf? Did you not all just find it remarkable that there was a Patua' among us? Remember thinking the Patua' had completely vanished? Shocking as it is, Bruthamax is not known among humans outside of the city surrounding us."

The councilors quieted down as Starfire spoke. By the time he finished, dignity had been restored. A few seconds of silence reigned, and Alfredo seized the moment.

"That is true." He paused, momentarily shocked that no one interrupted. "Human knowledge of the Patua' is significantly less than yours. I am Patua' yet knew not there were others of my kind."

Thirteen pairs of eyes, some black, some blue, stared back in silence. "I did not know of Bruthamax until I came to Cadeña-l'jadia,"

Alfredo continued, grateful for the opportunity to continue speaking. Since then, I have learned much, thanks to the corvids for keeping his stories and sharing them with me. I am proud to be counted among Bruthamax's kin."

Most of the councilors softened and some even had a few sympathetic words of comfort: "Any kin of Bruthamax is a friend of ours!" "Long live the Patua'!" "Long live Jayzu!"

An explosive sound nearby scattered the councilors, and someone shouted, "Meeting adjourned!"

Alfredo was suddenly alone with Hookbeak and Starfire in the small clearing, but for several feathers that lay twitching in the breeze. He waited for a few minutes for the Aviar to speak, but the old raven kept silent and still as stone, listening. Not a creature stirred. Even the insects had been silenced.

"Thank the Great Orb for that explosion," Starfire said at last. "Nothing scatters the corvids like the sound of gunfire. Otherwise we would be beaking this to death till sunset."

"I thought it was just a car backfire," Alfredo said.

"It was," Hookbeak said. "But no matter, we accomplished what we wanted today."

"We did?" Alfredo said.

"Yes," the Aviar replied and leaped into the sky.

"Indeed, Jayzu," Starfire said. "Thank you." He flapped his wings and took off after Hookbeak.

"For what?" Alfredo called out after the ravens as they flew away. "What did we accomplish?"

He shrugged and walked back to the park bench where he had left his bicycle. Charlie flew out of the nearby trees.

"Where were you?" Alfredo asked. "I could have used a friendly face."

He got on the bike, and Charlie assumed his position on the handlebars. "You have many friends, Jayzu. Yes, I was there. In a tree on the edge of the clearing where you were. I heard everything."

Alfredo rode his bike out of the National Cemetery and through the huge wrought-iron gates onto Alhambra Boulevard. As they rode through the neighborhoods on the way down to the Waterfront, people smiled and waved at the man and the crow on the bike.

"Do you know how many Patua' there are?" Alfredo said as he waved back to an elderly couple out for a stroll.

"Where?" Charlie asked. "Here? Or in the world?"

"Here, and the rest of the world." Alfredo slowed down as he approached a four-way stop and sped up when he saw no cars coming.

"Well, we're working on that," Charlie said. "Starfire has been doing weekly Extraction Rituals for some time now on all the Keepers. It's a matter of coming up with the algorithms. And then there's constructing the chants. It's quite complex, and we're only working on the local database. I don't know if we could easily find out how many Patua' there are in the entire world."

"I see," Alfredo said. "Sounds like a computer program. Tell me more about this internal database."

"It's a lattice, actually," Charlie said. "The lattice has many branches, and each branch has many storage nodes where we implant data."

Alfredo turned down Water Street. The river lay in front of him, with Cadeña-l'jadia basking in the midday sun. As they passed St. Sophia's, the resident pigeons pecked at the sediments of earlier handouts left on the steps. "Am I in your database?" Alfredo asked. "Or do you know?"

"I have no awareness of anything in the database," Charlie said. "I don't know if you are stored in my lattice. The archives were set up to restrict any bleed over into the Keeper's memory, so as to not pollute the database."

"You never cease to amaze me, my friend," Alfredo said. "I never imagined the corvid had devised such sophisticated methods of archiving data. And your dedication is commendable."

"We love lists," Charlie said. He unfolded his wings to keep his balance as Alfredo rode over a rough patch of pavement. "We simply made them three-dimensional."

Alfredo knew that corvids have powerful memories, and though he understood well that these birds were as gifted by the Creator with intelligence and sentience equal to humans, he marveled at their invention. "Long ago, humans used to rely on oral traditions to store and maintain family histories and cultural lore. In the modern world, we rely more on external storage for our memories."

He stopped his bike at a red light, putting one foot on the curb and keeping the other on a pedal. A car pulled up next to him, a silver Bentley. The rear window went down, and a female voice said, "Good morning, Father Manzi!"

The woman in the backseat waved a hand out the window as Alfredo tried to see who had spoken. But the light changed, and the Bentley's chauffeur sped through the intersection before he had his other foot on the pedal.

"But our storage devices get full," Alfredo continued. "Or obsolete, or they break."

"That is a problem with tools," Charlie said. "But we too spend much time maintaining our database. Otherwise it too, would fall into decay."

Water Street turned steep as he rode the last few blocks to the Waterfront, where the Captain waited. "How does he always know when I am coming?" Alfredo asked.

"We tell him," Charlie said. "That is, we crows, magpies, jays, and the like. You can't go anywhere without being seen, and telling whoever cares about it."

Alfredo looked up; there were no birds flying overhead. None in the trees. "Why am I being spied upon, Charlie? I would tell you anything you ask."

As they arrived at the Waterfront, Alfredo slowed the bike to a halt and then hopped off.

"No one is spying on you, Jayzu," Charlie said as he leaped to a nearby bench and clutched the back with his feet. "At first, we did, till we knew what you are about. But now you're famous; some think you're the reincarnation of Bruthamax. You're a celebrity!"

"All aboard for Cadeña-l'jadia!" Sugarbabe yelled.

They rode in silence all the way to Cadena-l'jadia; even Sugarbabe was uncharacteristically quiet. When the boat stopped at the inlet, Alfredo jumped onto the sandy bank and waved to the Captain as he pushed his boat back into the current.

"Have you ever known another Patua', Charlie?" Alfredo asked. "Other than me and the Captain?"

The crow stood, and the priest perched on a driftwood log at the rocky point below the hermit's chapel. It had been a long day. Alfredo hardly remembered getting off the Captain's boat and walking the half mile to the rocky point. The Great Corvid Council was illuminating, yet he felt exhausted. He had not expected them to be so argumentative. He laughed at himself. *Like our congress, for instance?* Somehow he had envisioned them to be more civilized—to him, and to one another.

"One," Charlie said, "I have known one other Patua', for many years."

Jealousy surged through Alfredo, surprising him. *Am I envious that I might be sharing Charlie with another Patua'?* He bent his head back and looked up through the leaves at the sky. *Or am I jealous of Charlie?*

"Where is your friend now?" Alfredo asked. *Oh, to have a friend!*

"Rosencranz," Charlie said.

"The old insane asylum?" He had seen photographs in the library Downtown of the old hospital an hour outside of Ledford—an anachronism from the last century, part of the curious cultural lore of the city.

"Charlotte is not insane," Charlie said flatly, looking up at him. "Her family chucked her in Rosencranz when she was a teenager because she is Patua'. She's been there ever since. Twenty-five years."

"You have not seen her in twenty-five years?" Alfredo said to Charlie.

"I saw her last ten days ago," Charlie said. "But it's been quite a bit longer than that, though, since we have spoken."

Alfredo was aghast. "Just because she talked to crows? My mother was afraid people would think I was possessed by the devil. But no one ever thought I was insane. Our parish priest had me whisked me off to a Jesuit boarding school." *There but for the grace of God ...*

He had not thought of the family's parish priest in years. *"Try to keep this, uh, talent of yours hidden from everyone," Father Mario had said to him before he left for boarding school. "Use it only for the continued glory of God's creation. You must not let anyone else know. Make sure only God sees."*

Was Father Mario Patua'? Did he understand me better than I or my mother did?

"Tell me about your friend, Charlie," Alfredo said. "I would like to know another Patua'."

"Charlotte disappeared one day when she was seventeen," Charlie began his story. "I hadn't seen her in a few months. Rika and I had our first clutch that year, and I was in Keeper training, and just couldn't get away. But the magpies all said that men in white coats drove up in a big van and took her away. She was crying, they said, when the white coats put her in a tiny shirt with really long sleeves that they wound all around her.

"She kept screaming. All the way down the road, they could hear her screaming. The white coats took her to Rosencranz. That's what the magpies told me.

"I winged it over to Rosencranz, but couldn't get in, of course; what hospital would let a crow in, even during visiting hours? So I visited every windowsill, looking for her. I peeked and sometimes downright stared into every window, more than once. For two years, I came and pecked on her window nearly every day."

"I admire your devotion, Charlie," Jayzu said. "I cannot imagine.

"Then one day," the crow continued, "there she was! Just on the other side of the glass, sitting in a wheelchair with her hands folded neatly in her lap. But she did not see me.

"I pecked on the window, but she did not hear me. I called out her name. 'Charlotte! Yo! Charlotte! It's me! Charlie!' But she didn't look up. She just stared at her lap, and I wondered if she had gone deaf.

"I kept yelling and dancing and pecking, anything to get her attention. She didn't hear me, didn't see me.

"I didn't give up, though. Day after day, I showed up on the windowsill at the same time, trying to get her attention. But day after day, she didn't look up. Until she did! She finally noticed me through the glass! I nearly fell off the windowsill.

"'Charlie!' she said, with the big smile I remembered from long ago. Of course I couldn't hear her; the window was closed. Then she ran across the room and pasted both hands on the glass, as if to embrace me. I flapped my wings and cried out, 'Charlotte! Charlotte!' Great Orb, that was a wonderful day!

"Then a white coat came up to Charlotte and took her hands off the window, giving each one a little slap and then escorted her back to her wheelchair.

"'Charlotte!' I yelled as he wheeled her out of the room. I pecked on the glass. I shouted as loud as I could. Another white coat came to the window, opened it, and yelled 'Darn crows!' as she tried to smack me with a towel.

"She missed. 'Darn humans!' I yelled back at her.

"Though I waited at the window, Charlotte didn't come back that day. Or the next. I hung around, waiting and hoping for some sign of her. Days went by. I visited all the other windowsills again and again. Just as I was about to give up, there she was!

"I pecked at the glass, and when she looked up, I flapped my wings at her. But she didn't get up, didn't smile at me or say my name. I thought maybe she hadn't really seen me. But when no one was looking, she smiled at me. She wouldn't come to the window, though. Probably she was afraid they would slap her hands again. She never took her eyes off me until someone came and took her out of the room.

"That was eight years ago. I see her often, but through a closed window. I can't talk to her or hear her voice. But at least I can see her."

Charlie ended his story; crow and human sat without speaking for several minutes. The pulsating song of crickets emanated from hidden places in the grass. Several loons wandered along the bank below, pecking for tidbits between the rocks and grass. A few gulls orbited a fishing vessel on the river.

"I do not know what to say, Charlie, my friend," Jayzu said at last. "I am sad for your friend, being locked away like that. Surely her family visits?"

"Charlotte is alone, Jayzu," Charlie said. "No one visits. No one can understand her. But I am telling you, Jayzu, she is as sane as you or I."

The sky had turned the color of late afternoon. "It is time I headed home to Rika and my kreegans, Jayzu," Charlie said. "Before it gets too dark to fly."

Charlie left the priest and flew out over the river. The sun hovered above the western horizon, sending shimmering hues of yellow and orange across the river. All the way home, he thought about Charlotte and her years of silence.

He had never given up hope. Charlotte came back out of the graying. And now an idea tantalized him. *Jayzu could just walk in the front door of Rosencranz. And he could speak to Charlotte in the Patua'. What if ...* Charlie dared to hope ... *Jayzu could get her out of there? What if he could bring her here, to Cadeña-l'jadia?*

From the past, Starfire's voice boomed inside his head.

"I have lived a long time and have seen many things, but never have I seen a Patua' snatched back from the abyss, once he or she went into the graying. But none may know the future. Always keep hope in your heart."

Alfredo drew his mouth into a tight line as he watched Charlie take off and make a wide circle over the river. *Twenty-five years in an insane asylum! Why was Charlotte forsaken in such a place while I am allowed to live in this paradise? Why was I rewarded, and she was punished for being Patua'?*

His friend Charlie's anguish bore down on him heavily. "It is so unfair," Alfredo said aloud. "So unjust."

A voice from above replied, "I quote: 'There is no justice. There is only grace.'"

Alfredo looked up. A raven perched on the lower branch of a nearby basswood tree looked down at him. "And whom do you quote, NoExit?" he asked.

"The Grandmother's proverb," NoExit said. "There is no such thing as justice. Random mercies, perhaps, but no justice. That is a good thing for most of us. Our lives would be truly impoverished if ever all we got was what we deserve."

"Do you think so?" Alfredo said. "My species is forever expecting justice."

"Yet who among you has ever found it?" The raven flapped down to the ground, and Alfredo found himself nearly eye-to-eye with the elegant bird. NoExit wore his age with strength and dignity: his long, shaggy wreath of black feathers encircled his thick neck, draping over his breast and hanging nearly to his sturdy legs.

The sun touched the horizon, turning the river into liquid gold and bathing the island in stark, brilliant light. NoExit's feathers blazed with hints of refracted sunset, giving him a regal air of great wisdom and clarity. He hopped up onto the log next to Alfredo and gazed out over the river. Alfredo felt young and small next to him.

"Justice is a thing wholly imagined by humans," NoExit said. "You are not very good at it."

"Yet we try," Alfredo said, feeling a bit defensive. He sat up a little straighter. "Humans abide by the rule of law; that is what civilizes us."

"The law is an ass," NoExit said, "and an idiot."

Alfredo turned toward the raven, his eyebrows raised in surprise. "So said Mr. Bumble. Are you telling me you have read *Oliver Twist*?"

"Of course not," NoExit said, sharpening his beak on the log. "The saying has been in corvid lore for centuries, at least. Perhaps you should inquire as to where Mr. Dickens got it."

"Are you saying Dickens was Patua'?" Alfredo asked incredulously. "And that he stole the saying from the corvid?" The priest started to laugh.

"No idea," NoExit said. He flapped his wings a few times and refolded them into his sleek profile. "But the concept is intuitively obvious to the most casual observer. What is shocking is that it took your species until the nineteenth century for the very thought to even attain utterance."

The last of the sun seemed to disappear into the river somewhere upstream, taking all color with it. Downtown lights flickered on. A late barge chugged upriver, all lit up and blowing diesel smoke from its stack. All around, Alfredo could hear the sounds of many creatures browsing or hunting for their evening meal. The law of the food chain governed. He felt envious of such simplicity.

"We have a great many laws," Alfredo said. "Too many perhaps. But without laws, how could we even approach justice?"

"There is a vast difference between law and justice," NoExit said. "Perhaps therein lies the problem. The natural laws—the law of gravity, for instance—are absolute. Yet human laws, and therefore justice, bend with circumstance."

A multitude of young crows swirled above the trees, arguing over where they would roost for the night. Their noise seemed to irritate the raven, and he looked up at the ruckus.

"To change is to endure," NoExit said after the crows had passed. "That is what the Grandmothers say."

"You have mentioned the Grandmothers twice," Alfredo said. "Who are they?"

"Grandmothers are older female corvids with many generations of offspring," he said. "Similar to the Council, but they provide a female perspective. They do not concern themselves with the illusion of justice. Instead they seek the paths of grace and elegance."

"Grace and elegance?" Alfredo said, frowning.

"Have you ever found yourself on the horns of a dilemma?" NoExit said. "When adhering to the law produces more damage than breaking it?"

Alfredo nodded. "Many times."

"The Grandmothers will find a way through such times," NoExit said, "illuminating the way toward doing what is needed, as opposed to parsing the meaning of justice and the intent of law."

"The Grandmothers are wise," Alfredo said.

NoExit buried his beak in his wingpit and said in a muffled voice, "Mothers are inherently wise. Else they would fail as mothers, and their offspring would not thrive." He pulled his head out and continued. "Grandmothers are grandly wise, having raised many young, but they also have seen many of their kreegans die. What justice is there in the death of the young? Justice does not exist in nature, I tell you. Do not seek it there."

Twilight draped the island in shades of gray. City lights slowly twinkled on against the river's canvass that reflected the fading light of day. Crickets kicked off the nightly jam session of music makers in the insect world. A bell rang from the direction of the inlet.

Alfredo did not remember telling the Captain to return for him at sunset and was grateful that he had come anyway. *He always seems to know when I need him.* "That is my ride back to the city," he said. "I must say goodnight."

"Goodnight, my friend." NoExit flapped his great wings a few times and disappeared into the chapel.

—6—

The Eyes Have It

The trail of footprints leads to the edge of a roaring river. A woman with black feathers for hair sings an unintelligible song as she pulls fish after fish out of the raging current. She removes the hooks from their mouths and drops them into a wooden box and throws the hook and line back into the water. She pulls another fish out of the river and throws it into the box. She stands up and takes a shiny object from her pocket and hands it to me. She disappears with the box of fish and I open my hand. A flock of crows emerge and fly noisily away.

Jade lay still for a few moments, watching the dream recede, its colors and sounds coalescing into a stream of multicolored layers before disappearing into the folds of her memory. But she could still hear the singing, a haunting voice, thin and far away, a maddeningly familiar melody she could not name.

She wondered if she was insane. Why else would her dreams be leaking into her waking hours? *Go away! I know I'm awake. Go back into the night!* She shivered; that was how it started, the descent. *I couldn't tell my life from dreaming.*

Russ mumbled in his sleep, and the singing stopped. Jade got up quietly. After a trip to the bathroom, she went to her studio, closed the door, and flopped into the armchair.

Framed perfectly by the window, the full moon's face stared coldly down on her. *Like the face of the dead.* She took the black medallion on the leather cord out from under her nightgown. Moonlight flowed over the worn carvings on its dark surface. She turned it over in her hand a few times, tracing the silvery lines with her finger. *A hand intertwined with a crow wing.*

She leaned back against the chair. The window frame slashed the moon's face into two unequal pieces; one eye looked down upon her with a certain disdain, while the other hid behind the sash. Absent-mindedly, she rubbed the medallion back and forth gently across her front teeth. A shadow passed over the moon.

She leaped up and turned the light on. She attached a canvas to her easel, picked up a brush and a palette. Black paint flowed onto the canvas in broad, sweeping strokes that gave way to thin, curling tendrils. A face appeared out of the darkness.

Russ woke up to any empty bed. He got up, showered and shaved, and started down the hall. A sliver of light shone under the door to Jade's studio. He turned the doorknob and opened the door slowly, expecting to see her painting with enraptured attention.

Instead, he found her curled up asleep with Willow B in the over-stuffed armchair. He almost bent down to wake her gently, but the painting on the easel arrested his attention.

A portrait, more or less, of a woman. Long black hair swayed in turbulent currents full of stardust and tiny creatures of the deep. But it was the eyes that took him. The full moon reflected in pale gray eyes as it bathed the woman's face in silvery light. He felt as if she knew his every dream, every desire.

Jade materialized at his side and yawned, "Do you like it?"

"I love it," Russ said. "Those eyes! They just suck me in! They're like gateways into another dimension. I don't know how you do that! I swear to God, I can see forests and rivers and mountains—all in her eyes!"

"Really?" she said, frowning at the canvas. "You see all that?"

He gazed intently at the painting, shifting his weight to one foot as he tipped his head to the side. "Oh, I don't know if I actually *see* all that. But the way you painted it makes me imagine I did." He turned and faced her. "You're extremely talented, Jade. I don't know anyone else that can make me see a whole landscape in someone's eyes."

"I didn't mean to paint a landscape," she said. "I finally got an image of her. It's my mother."

"Oh," Russ said. "I see. You dreamed her, finally?"

"No," she said. "I wasn't dreaming."

"Really!" Russ said. *Oh God. Please don't go there again.* "Let's talk about it over breakfast, shall we? I'll go start the coffee." He planted a kiss on his wife's cheek as he went to the kitchen, relieved that he had escaped her morning madness.

HENRY BRAUN FROWNED AS HE LOOKED out his office window at his large estate. Over the years, he had spent a fortune on landscaping, a swimming pool, three gazebos, and his own private fishing hole. But it wasn't enough. Henry wanted more. More money and more fame. He loved being rich, and he wanted to be revered for the successful businessman he obviously was.

"Those damn Jesuits," he growled to his attorney, Jules Sackman. "It's just stall, stall, stall with them, and then without even the courtesy of a conversation, they turn me down. Worthless bunch of freeloaders never worked an honest day in their lives."

Henry the First's portrait stared disapprovingly down at him. *I'm sorry, Great-Grandfather! They just wouldn't listen to reason!*

He went to his desk, opened a rosewood humidor, and removed two cigars. After handing one to Jules, he peeled the wrapper of the other and licked it all over. He cut off the end with an ivory-handled cutter and lit it.

"Stop worrying about minutiae, Henry," Jules said, sitting up in the red leather chair and sucking on his cigar as Henry held the lighter to the other end. "We'll just bypass the Jesuits. Make them irrelevant. We'll go around them."

"How?" Henry said as he sat down in the armchair next to Jules. "They own the dang island, for God's sake. How do we get around that?"

"Eminent domain," Jules said, blowing a series of smoke rings toward the ceiling. "That's how." He crossed one leg over the other, revealing milk-white legs devoid of hair.

"Eminent what?" Henry said, turning away from the sight.

"Eminent domain," Jules said. "That's when the government—let's say the city of Ledford—condemns a property. That is, they take it, and in this case, sell it to someone who will develop it. Someone like you for instance. Someone who can promise what all politicians love to hear. Tax revenue and jobs."

"Are you serious?" Henry said, flabbergasted. "The city can do that? Just take over someone's private property like that? And sell it?" He didn't like the idea that the government could take a man's property, but if it would make Wilder Island his ... He licked his lips and glanced up at the portraits. Henry the First nodded.

"Yes," Jules said. He took a long drag from his cigar. "We just have to show the city government that developing the island with your casinos, hotels, restaurants, shopping mall, and amusement park will bring in some major cash and a significant number of jobs, without raising taxes on the citizenry. Whereas, the Jesuits pay no taxes on the island, provide no jobs, and are now shutting the island off to anyone but this Father Manzi and his birds. The politicians, who will be making the decision, will fall all over themselves to condemn Wilder Island."

Henry stared at Jules. "And these Jesus people are just going to roll over and let us do this? What about the chapel? Won't they claim it's a church and get out of this eminent domain thing?"

"The Jesuits will fight us perhaps, as other churches have fought condemnation suits," Jules said, flicking a cigar ash into a carved serpentine ashtray on Henry's desk. "But they will lose. They have no legal grounds; churches are not immune from eminent domain. Nothing is. We have a Supreme Court ruling on our side. But first you have to convince the city to condemn the property."

"Oh, I can do that," Henry said gleefully. He sucked on his cigar. "I have the city in my back pocket."

"Yes, Henry," Jules said, exhaling a long plume of blue smoke. "That's what you said about the Catholics, after you uselessly bribed the monsignor's know-nothing flunky at St. Sophia's. Do I need to inform you, as your attorney, that bribery is illegal?"

"Who said anything about bribery?" Henry asked innocently.

"I'm not going to bribe anyone." He glanced up at the portraits. Henry the First frowned down at Jules. *I'm not!*

"I am glad to hear that, Henry," Jules said, smiling as he puffed on his cigar. "Bribery is illegal, you know." He blew a smoke ring toward the ceiling.

Henry wanted to smack the sanctimonious face that sucked on one of his expensive cigars. *How many cops and judges have you bought off to keep your wife out of jail?* Henry knew all about Mrs. Sackman's gambling addiction—and how much Jules needed the money Henry paid him to keep her ass out of jail. *One of these days, you'll outlive your usefulness to me.*

"Once the city condemns the island," Jules said, the end of his cigar glowed as he paused to inhale, "they'll have it appraised for fair market value. Mind you, that'll probably mean a bit more than we offered the Jesuits, maybe twice. But you'll be happy to pony up ten million, won't you, Henry?" Jules exhaled a voluminous billow of smoke.

"Whatever it takes, Jules," Henry said. *You're mighty free with my money, lawyer.* But he was nervous. He hardly ever had to wait this long to get what he wanted.

The clock over the fireplace chimed the hour. Three o'clock. The big hand on the twelve, the little hand on the three. Like an L. For loser. He scowled at the clock and leaned toward Jules.

"Make no mistake, Jules. I'm going to have that island. Nothing is going to stop me. Not priests, not money, nothing." He ashed his cigar and leaned back in his leather chair. "And once it's mine, I'm going to blow that so-called chapel into the river. And then I'll scrape it clean of that overgrown, vermin-infested forest."

Henry Braun the First stared down from his gilded frame on the wall and whispered, *"You have the advantage. Go for it!"*

"What did you call this thing?" Henry asked Jules. "Imminent something?"

"Eminent domain," Jules said. "We didn't have a chance with the Jesuits, Henry, but with eminent domain, we do. Now, here's what you'll have to do while I file the appropriate papers. You will prepare a formal presentation to the city, with a fantastically beautiful, miniature Ravenwood Resort. Spare no expense, Henry. Never underestimate the power of eyewash, you know? Really glitz it up."

Henry had envisioned Ravenwood Resort many times, complete with two famous steam paddleboats from the last century. And a choo-choo! He had loved model trains when he was a kid and had spent many an hour building the little towns and landscapes for his trains to chug through. Who can resist a choo-choo!

"You'll also have to hammer home how much money Ravenwood Resort will bring to the city, Henry. And jobs. Don't forget the jobs. Emphasize how the chapel and the Jesuits have contributed neither money nor jobs, but don't bash the church. Do you catch my drift, Henry?"

"Yes," Henry said. "I know exactly what to say. And I'll build a model that'll knock their teeth out."

Jules stood up, straightened his sweater, and said, "Good, that is good, Henry. Now I'm afraid I need to head home. I'll call you tomorrow."

After Jules left, Henry finished his cigar alone in his office, enjoying a glass of Pinot Noir. *Silly priests. Shrewd businessmen they are not.*

He swiveled his chair around to face the portraits on the wall. Henry II and III gazed down at him with glassy stares. But Henry the First's eyes sparkled. "You get it, don't you?" He raised his glass to his ancestor. "To us, Great-Grandfather!" Henry the First winked and nodded as Henry swallowed the last of his wine.

A BLACK BIRD PICKS ME UP OUT *of bed. I hold on to his tail feathers as he flies into the horizon, his feathers and my hair streaming together like iridescent ribbons of light. Above a great rushing river, the bird's tail feathers come out in my hand, and I drop like a rock to the*

roaring waters below. Falling, falling, I finally splash down, down, down into a deep pool of water, cool and clear. Concentric ripples move outward from my point of entry, bubbling upward as I sink into a dark abyss.

Jade's eyes snapped open, and she gulped air as if she had been underwater too long. Feeling the solid bed underneath and hearing Russ's gentle snoring beside her, she tried to relax and breathe normally. But the images from the dream persisted, the feeling of falling made her dizzy, and she was unable to go back to sleep.

She rolled over and stared out the big bay window of their bedroom. She liked the curtains open at night, when all the house lights were off. The moon illuminated the woods beyond their yard with veiled light, and the shadows took shape, whispering seductively, beckoning her to enter. Wordless, insistent, breezy voices sought her out, hooked their tangled currents through the very fabric of her being, tantalizing her, tickling her with tales of wonder.

Russ snorted and flung an arm across her. The voices suddenly stopped, and the dark green and black shapes of the nighttime forest beyond the window. She patted Russ's hand, and soon he was snoring again.

She unwound herself carefully from his embrace and arose quietly. She made a cup of coffee in the kitchen, and Willow B followed her into the studio. She closed the door quietly behind him and sat at her easel for a few minutes, sipping coffee. Willow B jumped up to the armchair he liked to sleep in while she painted. Away off in the distance, she heard a siren.

The night sky was more gray than black, and she couldn't see any stars. Empty. *Like a canvas.* She turned on the lights. A blank canvas stared back at her from the easel to which it was attached, its flat white face momentarily blinding her with its brilliance. The dream that had awakened her cast an image upon the emptiness. She uncovered her paints and picked up a brush.

The underwater world of the dream flowed down her arm to

the paintbrush in her hand, and onto the canvas in front of her. She applied layer after layer of paint, color upon color as she worked to evoke a sense of being tugged down into the underworld realm of memory and dream, where sunshine, flowers, and birds recede into the upper-world of awakening.

Through a watery primeval forest stuffed with trees and leaves, sprinkled with occasional patches of flowery color, bubbles sprang merrily up and away to the interface of sky and pond, sparkling in the sun briefly before bursting. The painting's voice came from the vast darkness of underwater currents, filled with strange creatures that do not walk Earth's surface.

They dragged at her, those voices, pulling her deeper and deeper into the mysteries of her solitary universe. The canvas seemed but a thin, permeable membrane, pulling her into the underworld of her imagination. This painting told the story of the descent. It was breathtaking, exhilarating. And it scared her.

She put her brush down and turned her back on the painting. The sky beyond the window had turned pale gray; dawn was imminent. She picked Willow B up out of the armchair and sat down in the warm spot where he had been sleeping. He arranged himself on her lap, and she held fast to his solid warmth, trying to keep connected to the present.

Willow B had kept her from disappearing completely into her dreams once before. A vision of herself in her apartment during her last year in college leaped out of her memory, beckoning her into the past.

She saw herself painting, frantically painting. The madness in her younger self's eyes brought it all back—the entire descent, from the very first day she had given in to the irresistible harmonies of her imagination, to the very last, when they found her completely spent on the kitchen floor in her apartment.

She had shut everything out but the voices that told her to paint. The entire contents of her psyche begged for life, and she painted to its relentless pleas. For days, she had no memory of anything but painting, endlessly painting. One canvas would fall away, and another would appear, haunting her for its face. Irresistible, insistent, she was powerless against its demand.

It ate her alive.

Russ opened the door, poked his head into the studio and said, "You've been painting all night again?"

"Uh, no," Jade said, his voice shaking her out of the past. "Just part of it. Good morning, honey! I didn't hear you get up. What time is it?" She squinted at the clock on the wall.

"Time for coffee," he said as he bent down and kissed her good morning. "Want to keep painting? I can get my own breakfast."

"No," she said, getting up from the chair. "I was just daydreaming." She frowned at the painting on the easel.

"Looking good, babe," Russ said, putting his arm across her shoulders. "What will you call it? Will it be in the art show?"

"*Falling Backward*," Jade said. Icy tongues of anxiety licked away at her sense of worthiness. "But I'm not sure it will be ready for prime time by then. It's so rough still, so crude. In a bourgeois sort of way."

The opening reception for her upcoming art show at Jena Mc-Crae's gallery was less than a week away—her first show since she had started painting again. She wasn't worried about having enough paintings; her concern was how they would be received.

Russ made coffee while she scrambled eggs and made toast. "What if people hate my work?" she said after they sat down. "What if they think my paintings are bourgeois?"

Russ stared at her. "Are you serious?" he asked. "Bourgeois?" He shook his head. "Hardly, hon. Bourgeois means 'middle-class values.'" He made little quote marks in the air. "Really, hon, your paintings aren't about class values, so I wouldn't fret about it."

Jade blew across her coffee, watching the little bubbles roll along the surface and crash into the other side of the cup.

"But to regular people," she said, "bourgeois means 'tasteless' or 'boring.'" She made little quote marks in the air. "Like white bread—

you know, the icon of the consumer. Or refrigerator magnets. Sofa-sized paintings."

She wondered why people who bought paintings or sofas were called consumers. *It's not like they eat this stuff.*

"Jade," Russ said, putting his coffee down. "Listen to me. Your paintings are weird maybe, strange, enchanted, dark, disturbing, playful, mysterious. All that. Bourgeois, no. Where'd this bourgeois fetish come from, anyway?"

She remembered the moment, right down to the smallest detail. "Oh, a painting professor I had in college—Bill Williams—he used that word to describe my paintings at a final critique. I know it was a long time ago and in a different life. But it was such a stinging insult. It's clung to me like a tick ever since."

"Well, pull it out, hon," Russ said. "He was a jerk, probably jealous of your enormous talent and intricate imagination. Don't let it suck the life out of you. Let it go, okay? It wasn't about you or your paintings."

He got up from the table and put his plate and cup in the sink. "I've got to get to school," he said, kissing the top of her head. "I'll be in MacKenzie most of the day. The state science fair is down there this year, and I'm judging all the juniors and seniors. I won't be home till late tonight, so don't wait up."

Jade watched Russ back out of the driveway through her studio window and peel out, leaving behind a smoking layer of rubber on the road. She shook her head. "What is it with boys and hot rods?" she asked Willow B, who had taken up residence in the armchair.

The new painting on the easel called out to her, wanting completion. But it needed some time to dry before she could continue. "I don't know if I have enough time to finish you before my show," she said.

Not that she needed any more. She had completed ten new paintings, but Jena McCrae, the art gallery owner, wanted more. "I want you to bring some of your earlier work too," Jena had said. "Think of your show as a retrospective from today. Where you were then, where you are now."

Where I was then. Which then?

She stood before the closet where her older paintings were stored and said, "Well, then. Enough procrastinating. I am quite out of time."

She put her hand on the doorknob and hesitated. They were all there inside, the paintings that chronicled the details of her breakdown. Fear crawled up to her throat and squeezed. The memory of that time bore down on her with all its dread intact. *What if they suck me back down?*

Her hand closed around the doorknob, and she gasped for air. Anxiety threatened her resolve, and she almost let go. *Get a grip. They're just paintings. They can't kill you.* She jerked open the closet door. Before allowing her fear to stop her, she reached in and pulled out a painting and ripped the brown paper off.

Her face broke into a smile. "It's *Queen of the Night*, Willow B!" she cried. She set the painting on the arms of the chair above Willow B and stood back, savoring the memory of painting it in those early days of her romance with Russ. "I fell in love with him under this flower. God, who wouldn't have? A gorgeous flower that blooms but once, at night, under a full moon in the desert ..."

Pale and luminous, the white flower took the entire canvas. Spear-shaped petals of opalescent white enclosed dozens of delicate, pale yellow stamens swayed and undulated around the solitary pistil. Layer upon layer of sinuous shapes of translucent hues awakened memories of love lost and found.

"I love this painting," she murmured.

A sudden clap of thunder ended her reverie and she frowned out the window. "Where did that come from?" she said. In reply, big fat raindrops pelted the window and streaked down the slippery glass. Lightning flashed as she reached for another painting.

Frowning at her own handwriting, "12:01" scrawled across the paper wrapper, she tore it open and propped the painting across the arms of Willow B's chair.

Black birds clung to the brittle branches of bare winter trees against a cold, gray sky. A distant clock tower haunted the scene, its hands frozen at 12:01. "Remember that clock, Mr. B?" Jade said to the cat sleeping on the cushion underneath the painting. "It haunted me for weeks. Always stuck on the same time. One minute after twelve. Pretty well says it all."

Time runs through your life like water to the sea.

The memory of her apartment when she was in college enveloped her, with the clock centered in the window where she couldn't miss its reproachful face. Day after day, it had rebuked her, "You're late! You're late!" mocking her every moment. She had tried closing the blinds to shut it out, but it haunted her dreams every night, taunting her with the eternally missed deadline. Always running, forever late, never arriving.

Night after the night, the same dream had played over and over again: millions of clocks in many colors, all showing the same time—12:01. The clocks started out randomly and then each slowed or quickened their minute hands until they all ticked and tocked in unison. *Tick*, the clocks scolded her. *Tock*, they upbraided her. But the time never changed. 12:01. She buried her head in pillows, but the relentless *tick-tock* only grew louder.

"You did hear it, didn't you?" Jade whispered. "It drove me insane, the *tick-tock-tick-tock*." Willow B turned an ear sideways. "Remember how I opened the blinds, and the ticking and tocking stopped? And when I closed them, it began again?" She glanced nervously at the window as the tempo and rhythm of the rain changed. Tick-tock-tick-tock-tick-tock...

"Damn you!" she had screamed as the clock smirked coldly at her across the treetops, its face split in two by the hands stuck at 12:01.

She dragged her easel across the room and positioned it in front of the window. She attached a canvas to it, just large enough to block out that hateful face. "Ha!" she had said and stuck her tongue out at the clock she could no longer see.

But the white canvass tortured her with its blankness and commanded her to pick up a brush. She painted feverishly all day and all night. Exhausted, she flung herself on the couch and slept. When she awoke, the sun had gone down, and she flicked on a light. Winged shadows swirled around the room until one by one, they dove into the painting in front of the window, flying around the clock tower until at last they found places to roost in the gray branches of the winter trees. The clock condemned her with lidless eyes, its hands pointing to her doom. 12:01.

Thunder rumbled across the sky and the rain picked up its tempo as it beat upon the window. She dropped to the floor on her knees and stroked Willow B, asleep in the armchair. "That clock started it all. Like a big eye that never blinked and never stopped staring at me." She felt a distant purr deep within his sleeping bulk. "I'm sorry I neglected you."

In a frenzy, she had painted every waking moment and dreamed about painting when she slept. The imaginary boundary frayed between physical reality and the realm from which her paintings sprang. The completed canvasses morphed to life around her, and painted images became companions and critics that paced the room with her, argued with her, cried with her, laughed at her, comforted her.

The entire population of her psyche clamored for immediate voice and she gave in to the irresistible siren song. For days she had done nothing but paint, stopping only to stuff her mouth with crackers and wash them down with honeyed tea. When she slept, the beings that populated her paintings lived again in her dreams. There was no escaping them. Waking or sleeping, the voices owned her life.

"And then I crashed," Jade murmured. Willow B woke up and yawned. She scratched him under his chin. "You were there, Willow B. You saw it all. I lost track of everything—when to eat, when to sleep, when to go to class, my friends, time. I was alone in another world until the real one finally banged its way in."

God, it was loud.

When they found her in her apartment, she was thin, malnourished and speaking to no one but Willow B and the voices in her paintings. Her foster mother, Chloe, took her home and nursed her back to health. "It's as important to eat as it is to paint," Chloe had said as she poked another spoonful of food into Jade's mouth.

She wanted to paint sometimes but couldn't bring herself to actually pick up a brush. Fear stopped her; painting had opened the door to a terrifying descent. Just after Thanksgiving had passed that year, she took a brush in her hand and stared at a blank canvas. Nothing. Deader than a doornail, that place inside her that once demanded her to paint. Half dismayed, half relieved, she worried. *What if it never comes back ... what if it does?*

She shook the memory out of her head. "But it did come back, didn't it, Willow B?" She stood up and stuffed *12:01* into its quilted pocket.

The late afternoon sun broke through the clouds and illuminated the cat, sleeping in the chair.

HENRY BRAUN SAT BACK IN HIS LEATHER chair, his feet on his desk. "Eminent domain." He rolled the words around in his mouth again and again. He savored those majestic, beautiful words, caressing the sound with his lips. "Eminent domain."

They became his mantra, his obsession. They defined him, his life, his mission. He thought even the dictionary definition of "eminent" described him, Henry Braun, to a tee:

em·i·nent
1. High in station, rank, or repute; prominent; distinguished.
2. Conspicuous, signal, or noteworthy.
3. Lofty; high.
4. Prominent; projecting; protruding.

"That's me, eminent all the way down to the nose!" Henry chuckled, stroking the iconic family proboscis he had inherited from the ancestral Brauns.

He flipped the pages of the dictionary until he found the definition for domain: "a territory over which rule or control is exercised." He reread it several more times, memorizing it, before snapping the dictionary shut.

"Eminent domain!" he toasted the Henry portraits. "Wilder Island is our due and proper domain," he assured them.

He swiveled his chair around and faced the window. His own reflection stared back. *The Braun Legacy shall be legendary because of me, Henry Braun IV. My fame and fortune shall be greater than Henry I, II, and III combined.* He dared not say that out loud in front of their portraits. He didn't believe in ghosts, *per se,* but he always felt the ancestral Henrys were watching him, listening to every word he said.

Henry the First's trestle bridge disaster ruined him and darn near sank the family into the oblivion of poverty forever. It was an act of God, they said. *Act of God!* Henry smirked. *I'll show them all an act of God!* He turned back to the portraits.

"I will redeem you, Great-Grandfather," he whispered. "I will get Wilder Island back, make no mistake."

Never had the slightest shred of doubt cast a shadow on his vision of one day owning Wilder Island for himself and for his family honor. At last he had a found a way to get it.

"My Savior. Eminent Domain." Henry chuckled. The very act of saying the words pleasured him, tickling his tongue, his lips, his teeth. The words orchestrated his fate, trumpeted his desires. "Eminent Domain!" He sang it out like an opera singer, "E–e–e–e–e–e–min–ent Do–oh–oh–ohoh–main," in a crescendo from the upper registers of his rich and mellow baritone voice that cascaded all the way down to bass tones almost undetectable to the human ear.

Henry sang his tune over and over again. He postured with one foot up on a chair, a wine glass raised up high, as if he were lord of his domain. He watched himself in the mirror, singing, "E–e–e–e–e–e–min–ent Do–oh–oh–ohoh–main. E–e–e–e–e–e–min–ent Do–oh–oh–ohoh–main. "E–e–e–e–e–e–min–ent Do–oh–oh–ohoh–main."

When he tired of singing, he hummed the tune of his eminent domain soliloquy. With pencils and pens, he drummed out the rhythm. It became the background chatter in Henry's brain. He fell asleep in his chair, smiling like a child on Christmas night.

Homecoming

Charlie watched Jayzu string a rope between two trees and tie the ends to the trunks. He unfolded and shook out a large plastic sheet and draped it over the rope and hammered some sticks into the edges, pinning it to the ground.

Jayzu stood up and said, "That will keep the rain off me while I build myself a more permanent structure." He took a bedroll out of his pack and threw it under his tent. After he set up a small stove on one of the nearly flat rocks strewn about, he put a pot on it and filled it with water. Charlie swooped down from the trees above, landing deftly on a flat rock near Alfredo's chair.

"Tea time?" he asked.

Jayzu laughed. "No. I just like to get everything set up."

Charlie looked around the camp, at the tent, the bag of water hanging in the tree. "For what?"

"For later, I guess. This evening maybe. Or tomorrow."

"I see," Charlie said. "So you are moving in, or just staying the night?"

"At least the night," Jayzu said as he sat back in his chair. "I want to clean out the chapel and after that, maybe find a place to build myself a home."

Charlie had been delighted when Jayzu asked permission to establish his residence on the island. He and the priest had become fast friends, and he missed him when he was gone.

Jayzu reached into his backpack and pulled out a small bundle. "I found this under Bruthamax's bones when I moved them," he said. "It was too dark in the chapel to look at it, so I stuffed it in here. I forgot about it until today."

He unwrapped the bundle, and a small black orb tumbled out. He placed it in a sunny spot on a rock near Charlie's feet. "It seems to be some sort of trinket, carved from a very dense black wood, as far as I can tell. It was all caked with dirt when I found it, and I did not see the carving until I cleaned it. To me, it looks like a hand clasping a wing."

Charlie leaned down and took a closer look. "Charlotte had something very similar," he said.

"Really?" Jayzu said. "Charlotte had one of these?"

"She did," Charlie said. "She wore it all the time before they took her away. I've wondered where it went ever since."

Guilt stabbed Charlie from the depths of his memory ... he had tried to get it once, Charlotte's orb, in violation of the one corvid law against stealing. He broke into a house to get this orb, but he had not expected the little girl to be there. He had no idea who she was, but her terror still haunted his dreams from time to time.

Jayzu held the orb up. The sun reflected off the glossy black surface. "Does it have something to do with the Patua', I wonder."

"Yes," Charlie said. "The orbs are apparently ceremonial devices made by the Patua' long ago, but we do not know what they used them for."

A few young crows suddenly materialized in Jayzu's camp. They snooped around his tent and food box until Charlie shouted, "Hey! Gertrude! Ethel! JohnLeo! All of you! Be off!"

The crows reluctantly flew away, and Charlie said, "We have no laws against stealing food out in the countryside, Jayzu. A word to the wise."

Alfredo woke up under his tent and smiled at the racket from the forest outside. The din of hundreds of birds greeting each other had been building since the stars had winked out in the pale dawn sky. *Ah, Cadeña-l'jadia! May I never leave you.*

After a quick breakfast and a cup of instant coffee, he grabbed the tools he had brought with him and headed for the chapel. The Captain had raised an amused eyebrow as he approached the boat the day before, armed with a rake, a shovel, and his camping gear.

"It's a losing battle you'll be fightin' there, Padre," he had said, "trying to tame that forest."

"Just cleaning out the chapel," Alfredo had grunted a reply as he heaved his burdens onto the boat.

He left his tools outside and went into the chapel and said a brief prayer. *Bless my efforts in this humble chapel, oh Lord. And bless Minnie Braun, that is, Gabriella, for her generous contribution.* She did not want anyone to know she was Henry Braun's wife, she had told him. "Everyone and their dog will be after me for money."

She had floored him, handing him a thick stack of twenty-dollar bills. "For the chapel," she had said.

He cut away some of the green vines that had nearly enveloped the chapel and raked all the dead leaves, twigs, and branches from the interior to the outside. With a wet rag, he cleaned over a hundred years of dirt off the kneeler in the middle of the floor.

His fingers found a small hasp on the edge of the armrest. He pulled it, and the top of the armrest flipped open. "Well, what is this?" he said. A thin volume, a prayer book perhaps, lay inside the compartment. He removed it and opened the cracked leather cover, revealing a handwritten script scrawled upon a coarse paper.

He gingerly leafed through a few pages, but it was too dark to read the spidery handwriting. He wrapped the booklet in his shirt, left the chapel and went back to his camp. He sat in one of his chairs and unwrapped it carefully. The cover was not of leather as he had earlier thought, but bark that had been hammered flat and sanded smooth. The cracks were filled with some sort of resin. Was it sap? Fascinated by the age and author of the small journal, Alfredo's hands shook as he gently turned the page.

Maxmillian Wilder, Cadeña-l'jadia, 1863

The swim from Ledford to this island nearly ended my life. Though I had studied all the maps, and I knew where the deepest parts of the channel were located, I had gained not even a hint at the treachery below the surface. I am a strong swimmer, yet I was unprepared for the unpredictable and deadly undercurrents that lurked below this otherwise placid river.

As soon as I approached within a hundred yards of the island, the river sucked me below the surface and whipped me around like a rag. I was tossed and rolled every which way, and each time my head rose above the water, I gasped for air in the spray, coughing as the river dunked me again and again. Just as I was about to expire from lack of oxygen, the river released me. I sprang to the surface amid a rush of bubbles into a patch of miraculously calm water, where I floated on my back and rested while my lungs gratefully filled with air.

After catching my breath, I swam toward the island again. And again. Though maddeningly close, it remained inaccessible; the river made sure of that. Time after time, I tried to swim to the bank, but the river flung me back to the same pool of calm water. I exhausted myself trying to power my way through the obstreperous river until I finally gave up fighting. I rolled over on my back, put my machete on my chest and pointed my feet downstream. I turned myself over to the river's flow. Sooner or later, I would either land on the island's banks or drown.

I floated on my back with my eyes closed, and I lost all sense of time and direction. I was quite unaware when the river gently dumped me on the island's bank, face up. When I finally opened my eyes, a very large blue-eyed crow stood over me in the sand, beholding me with great concern.

"You live and breathe!" the crow said. "Grawky, Wayfarer! The name is Hozey–after my grandpappy, Hozey the Great. He was an Architect, you know–revolutionized the nest as we know it, he did. Great crow, Old Hozey. Proud to bear his name, I am."

The bird stretched a wing toward me, as if to shake my hand. I thought I was hallucinating, perhaps even dead. But I held my hand up in greeting, and the bird brushed his feather tips against my fingertips.

"That is certainly good news, Hozey," I said. "Though I reckon

I feel half dead." I sat up and felt as if I had been beaten in a boxing match. "The river was not gentle with me."

"The river is not gentle," Hozey said. "Still, you made it. That certainly speaks for itself. The river spat you upon the bank days ago. Looked like dead meat, you did. It was all we could do to keep the buzzards off you. Creepy, that circling thing they do." Hozey shivered, looking up as if he expected to see a vulture overhead.

"How long have I been here?" I asked. "It seemed only a few moments ago I was floating on the river." The memory of nearly drowning was strangely close, and though I was sure I had made landfall only minutes ago, my skin and hair were completely dry. I was also thirsty and very hungry.

"Nope. Three days," Hozey said, holding up a wing with three feathers protruding past the rest. "Three. You slept right here under the sun and stars. We kept you alive, we did. We dribbled water into your mouth from the river so you did not die of dehydration or get chapped lips. We shaded you from the sun so your skin would not get burnt to a crisp. One of us stayed right here with you, watching over you the whole time."

"Thank you very much," I said. "And thank heavens I was not eaten by a buzzard, though I imagine there are worse ways to decompose. I am Brother Maxmillian Wilder, by the way, but I do not know who I am named after. Perhaps no one. I am just a simple Jesuit monk looking for solitude."

"We know who you are, Bruthamax," Hozey said. "And, just so you know, you are not alone here, no sirreebob. No other humans, mind you, the river sees to that. But there are a few hundred crows, my family mostly. And a few ravens, they really like it here—no humans."

"That is why I came here," I said.

"Not that you will be lacking a body to talk to," Hozey said. "We crows will yack your ears off if you let us. But not the ravens, no sirreebob. Like pulling teeth to get them to talk."

Hozey led me into the forest to a spring where I drank until I thought my belly would burst. But it made my hunger pangs recede for a while.

Hozey took me all over the island, to places I would not have been able to go unguided. There is a great boulder chasm, beyond which is a landscape so pitted and pockmarked, it is nearly uninhabitable. One day Hozey and I will build a bridge across it.

I stayed on the solid ground on the upriver end of the island for my first year, living on nuts and berries and the abundant fish from the river. And I prayed—my whole life comprises one continuous prayer to the glory of God.

I have spent many hours talking with Hozey, and we have become close friends. He and his family helped me build a chapel above the rocky point at the island's upper end.

A few people have tried to reach the island, either by boat or by swimming, but none has been successful. Sometimes they ride by in boats, and I shout "Glory to God Almighty!" to them. A few wave back, but most just stare as if I am a madman. I must appear that way to them with my unshaven head, bark clothing, and crow-feather cloak.

But there were too many eyes trying to peer into my solitude, and Hozey told me the lower end of the island is much more secluded. He guided me there, far from the riverbanks through the most hostile lands full of dark pools, over which clouds of mosquitoes reign, and dense foliage that is near impossible to navigate through. Every other step, I sank knee-deep into sticky black mud.

Deep within the interior of this small island lies a paradise, where I have built a proper home in a giant black gum tree.

"Excellent, Bruthamax," Hozey said at my choice of tree. "Nice big branches. You can build yourself a platform right across those bottom ones—in the Hozey way of course. 'Only three bearing points,' that is what Hozey the Great would say. 'Four is unstable,' he always said. 'You will get unwanted rocking in the nest.' That crow really knew how to build. It was just in his bones, I reckon."

We spent about two months working from dawn till twilight, with Hozey's help, to build my one-room house up in this tree. It has all that I need, although I have wished somehow a stove would wash up on the shore! Every day after breakfast, I walk through the forest to the chapel. Every morning, I pray and give thanks to the Almighty for the incredible bounty of this island, and especially for my friend Hozey.

Alfredo turned the page, but the story did not continue. The next few pages were filled with doodles—outlandish plants with labels written in a fanciful text he could not decipher. He closed the journal and ran his hand across the cracked cover. *Brother Maxmillian's first year. I wonder if there is another journal somewhere.*

The chapel restoration involved cleaning and removing dead vines from the roof; Alfredo wanted to keep it as simple as it was when Bruthamax built it. "The chapel managed to survive over a hundred years of weathering," he had said to Charlie when finished. "There is nothing more I need to do."

With the chapel restoration complete, Alfredo turned his attention to building a small cottage for himself. He found a perfect site near the chapel, downhill from one of the island's many springs. "I want to build a cistern," he said to Charlie, "like the one Bruthamax built."

He hired a helper through an ad in the local free newspaper, *The Crow*. There was only one response, Sam Howard, who hailed himself as a sculptor as well as a carpenter, plumber, and electrician.

What a stroke of luck to find Sam! A jack-of-all-trades, and he's Patua'! Alfredo found out from Sugarbabe, who whispered, "He's one of y'all, y'know," when he had escorted Sam to the island for the first time. Sam blushed to his ear tips.

"No worries, Sam!" Alfredo assured him. "You are among friends here."

The Captain glared at his crow and said, "Sugarbabe, you are a blabbermouth for sure."

Alfredo and Sam hopped off the Captain's boat, and as they walked through the forest toward the site he had chosen to build his cottage, he greeted the corvids, returning their calls and encouraged Sam to do likewise.

"You are among friends here, Sam," he said. "Especially with me."

Sam nodded and waved as the crows and magpies yelled, but he did not utter a sound.

"The chapel is this way," Alfredo said, and he gestured with his head.

Sam nodded again and plodded along next to Alfredo. They walked in silence until they arrived at the chapel. Alfredo opened the door, and they stepped inside. "I want my cottage to look like this," he said. "More or less. Closed to the elements, except for light."

"Wow!" Sam said, as he grinned and looked around. "You really cleaned this place up!"

Alfredo's eyebrows rose up into his forehead and he said, "You have been here before?"

Sam's smile vanished. He wandered over to the kneeler and ran his hand along the smooth wood. "Once," he said. "Years ago."

"Really?" Alfredo said. "You and the Captain both." *So, that is three of us since Maxmillian. Why do the corvids insist I am the first?*

Sam scavenged as much of the construction materials as he could from landfills, roadside debris, and junkyards. Whatever couldn't be had from his various recycling sources, Alfredo purchased with the cash Minnie Braun, aka Gabriella, had given him to restore the chapel. She would not object, he was certain. But he never told her.

Alfredo purchased several RV batteries to provide what little power he needed. When one battery was spent, he would hook up a spare and take the dead one in to Ledford and have it charged.

Sam constructed a composting toilet out of materials he found or traded, and enclosed it within a small structure a short way downhill from the cottage, matching the upside-down bird's nest construction. He installed a narrow wooden door with a moon-shaped hole that opened to a scenic landscape of tall trees, medium-sized trees, bushes, flowers, and a few gray rocks poking through the tall green grass that grew wherever it could.

"Well, it ain't the toidy at the Waldorf," Sam had said, grinning. "But the view is better."

One of the ladies at St. Sophia's had recently remodeled her kitchen and gave Alfredo a used but still functional stainless-steel sink. "Boy, howdy," Sam said, pushing his hat back and scratching his head. "It's hard to not covet that sink, Padre. I'm doing a piece called 'Everything but the kitchen sink,' though in truth, it oughta be called 'Nothing but the kitchen sink.' This one's a beauty. I must have it!"

"Take it!" Alfredo said with a chuckle. "It is too large for my tiny kitchen."

"Thanks," Sam said. "I'll find you another one."

Alfredo made a sketch of the gravity-fed water system at the tree house, and said, "I have modeled it after the one Bruthamax, that is, Maxmillian Wilder built for his treehouse. One day perhaps I can take you to see it."

Sam understood the sketches well enough and built a similar arrangement that captured and moved spring water into a small cistern buried upslope from the cottage. A hand pump delivered water to the sink. "You can let your kitchen and bath water drain out into your, uh, yard," he said. "That is, out into the forest. It won't hurt the trees or plants."

Alfredo collected his sparse possessions from the rectory at St Sophia's and moved into his new cottage on Cadeña-l'jadia. He felt at home for the first time in his life. He loved waking up to the sound of the birds and stepping outside into a forest. Every morning, he walked to the old chapel for the Liturgy of the Hours, and on Saturday evenings, he said the Mass. Without a human congregation, he found it difficult to stay within the confines of the traditional celebrant/respondent verbiage set forth by the Second Vatican Council.

Whenever he needed to leave, one of the island's hundreds of friendly crows flew out over the river and summoned the Captain. Mondays and Wednesdays, the Captain took him to the boat landing on the east side of the river; from there, he pedaled his bike to the university. On Fridays and Sundays, the Captain ferried him to the other side of the river and let him off at the Waterfront; from there, Alfredo walked to St. Sophia's.

"Life is good," he said to the Captain as he ferried him back to the island, so beautiful in the late afternoon. The hermit's chapel glowed warmly amid the sun-drenched tops of the tallest trees and seemed to float above shades of green leaves and shadows.

He loved coming home most of all. He loved cooking in his tiny kitchen, at the small but completely adequate wood stove. He loved dining at the small table Sam had scavenged at a thrift store. And he loved looking out upon the sensuous lushness all around him.

Alfredo ate a quick supper at his cottage and strode up the path to the chapel. He clasped his hands at the kneeler, and said a prayer thanking the Almighty for his life, for his good friends, and for the abundance of Cadeña-l'jadia. Even after praying, he felt impoverished; his gratitude could not fill the growing hole in his heart. Ever since Charlie had told him about his Patua' friend Charlotte who lived in such unspeakable solitude, he felt a strange sense of shame at his good fortune.

He reassumed the praying position, bowed his head, and shut his eyes. *I am fine, Lord, thanks to the bounty you shower upon me. But I have much, while Charlotte suffers and is in need of your care. Please, Lord, may you rain your glory down upon her and ease her burden of loneliness.*

He left the chapel and spotted Charlie at the rocky point below, picking apart the carcass of some poor creature that had washed up on the rocks. He walked down to the customary place where he and the crow often sat and talked.

Charlie looked up and called out, "Jayzu!" and flapped up to the rock next to him.

"Everyone's talking about the new sanctuary," he said and cleaned his beak on the rock.

Alfredo's eyebrows went up. "Already? How? We haven't even started it yet."

"The news beaked out pretty fast after the Council meeting," Charlie said.

"I guess so!" Alfredo said, laughing. "So what is the general opinion?"

"Oh, generally positive, I reckon. But a few negative nellies claim it'll bring in a whole influx of foreigners wanting to immigrate here. But that's ridiculous."

Alfredo picked a blade of long grass growing out of the sand at the base of the log he sat on. "I just hope it is enough," He wove the blade through his fingers.

"Enough for what?" Charlie asked. "You can't please everyone, Jayzu."

He tore the grass into several pieces, letting them fall to the ground at his feet.

"Enough to keep Cadeña-l'jadia out of Henry Braun's hands."

"And if it isn't?" Charlie asked.

"I do not know," Alfredo sighed. "Then it is in God's hands, perhaps."

"As Charlotte has been in your deity's hands all these years?" Charlie asked.

Shocked at the crow's blunt statement, Alfredo started to protest. *But he is right. Are my prayers merely a statement of my passing the buck on to God?*

"Yes," he said with a sigh. "Just like that, I am afraid." He leaned forward, elbows on his knees, put his fingertips together and stared at the ground. An ant struggled with a pebble ten times its size. He felt suddenly tired.

"Though the Order turned his offer down, Henry still plots against Cadeña-l'jadia," he said, gazing out over the water. "I do not know how he will strike, but strike he will."

The gleaming white roof of the newly restored chapel, visible from both sides of the city, stirred up some new stories about the old ghost of the island's legendary hermit. "Brother Maxmillian has been reincarnated!" some people cried, until it became known that another Jesuit, Father Alfredo Manzi, had taken up residence on Wilder Island, and it was he who roamed its banks.

When Alfredo arrived at St. Sophia's with the week's supply of Communion wafers, people who used to just wave and smile at him, if anything, now wanted to touch his jacket or his shoe. His fall courses at the university had already filled up. "And it is only May!" he complained to Russ in his office before his Avian Biology class. "The last thing I want is to be a celebrity," he said.

"Oh well." Russ poured Alfredo a cup of coffee from his thermos and handed it across the desk to him. "That is the unintended consequence of your semi-hermitage on a island famous for hermits. People will make you into a legend before you know it, and you can go about your business again."

Alfredo took the coffee and wandered toward the window. "I don't want to be a legend. I just want to be a simple priest and scientist." He leaned against the wall and took a sip of coffee.

Russ looked skeptically at him. "That's the thing about legends, Alfredo. You don't really get that choice. You're either a legend in your own mind or in everyone else's."

Alfredo laughed. "But there is the third option. No legend."

"Real legends don't have that choice." Russ sat back in his swivel chair and put one foot up on his desk. "But look at it this way. It's job security, man! The university hired you as an adjunct, meaning they can jettison you anytime they want. But they won't if your classes are popular. As they obviously are, if the crowds are 'flocking' to you already." He grinned devilishly. "Instant tenure, maybe. And you wouldn't have to publish! I know you don't like writing papers."

Alfredo looked out the window. "I do like writing papers, Russ. I am just not ready to write up anything on the corvid language. And I love teaching. I enjoy the rare opportunity to interact on a meaningful level with people and maybe teach them a little science at the same time." He looked back at Russ. "I have no human companionship on the island. Nor at St. Sophia's, really. People do not look at me as a friend but as some kind of spiritual leader or therapist."

Russ's chair squeaked as he pulled his foot off his desk and crossed his legs. He poured himself another cup of coffee and offered the thermos to Alfredo.

"Why did you become a priest?"

Alfredo declined with a wave of one hand. "My mother sent me to a Jesuit boarding school when I was a young lad. And I guess I never left." He looked at his watch. "Speaking of my classes, it is time for me to go teach one."

Russ shook his head as Alfredo left his office, wondering what motivated the man. *He complains about his success and won't write up what will make him famous. What does he want?*

—8—

Sanctuary

"**P**erfect," Charlie said. "If you ask me."

"I did ask you," Alfredo said.

Crow and priest surveyed a possible site for the bird sanctuary Alfredo had dreamed about for months. Years, really, but until he came to Cadeña-l'jadia, he never imagined its reality. But here it was. The perfect place for a bird sanctuary.

On the west side of the island below the Boulders, the stream that flowed beneath them resurfaced and wound down a lazy path through a wide floodplain to the river. During dry seasons, the stream slowed to a tiny trickle; in wet years, the river inundated the entire area. Tall trees and brushy undergrowth lined the many small channels lined with rushes and grasses and flowers.

"I'm not a migrator," Charlie said. "Nor in need of rescue. My opinion may not be worth much."

Alfredo stood next to him, one foot on the ground and one foot on the log. He balanced a sketchbook across his knee and made a few broad strokes with a large, flat-edged carpenter's pencil Sam had left at the cottage. "But you are a bird; that is the perspective I do not have."

He looked up from his sketch to the scene before him and shook his head, frowning. "If only I had Jade's talent."

Charlie hopped up to Alfredo's shoulder and peered down at the sketchbook. "Oh, it'll do, I reckon. You've got the basic elements. Cliffs, rocks, water, a few trees."

A bell sounded from the direction of the river and Charlie jumped back down to the log. "Sounds like the Captain."

"Yes," Alfredo said. He put the pencil in his pocket and shut the sketchbook. "He is bringing Sam and Russ to help me move a few rocks and plants around."

"No business for a crow," Charlie said and took off toward the tree house. "I'll see you later, Jayzu."

A small forest seemed to float into the broad inlet, and after finding a suitable landing spot, the Captain leaped off and tied the boat to a tree. Sam and Russ disembarked with shovels and a pickax.

"Be back at sunset," the Captain said as he leapt back aboard.

"Don't work too hard!" Sugarbabe yelled from her perch.

"Thanks, Captain!" Alfredo said. He turned and gestured toward the future bird sanctuary. "This is it, gentlemen."

"Perfect!" Russ said as he surveyed the landscape. "The river will replenish the soil with nutrients and keep the plant populations healthy, which will provide a food supply for the birds."

"And the cliffs will shelter the cove from the cold winter winds," Alfredo said, pointing toward the limestone edifice. "Many of the island's ravens and raptors nest or roost in caves along that cliff face."

The three men spent the day moving and placing rocks across the main stream channel to create a wide, shallow pool. Russ moved some of the water plants that grew along the banks of the small stream to the edges of the new pool. "In time," he said, "this should all fill in with the other island flora—whatever the wind blows in and birds poop out. In a few years, this will be as lush and green as the rest of the island."

At the end of the day, they admired their work. "It doesn't look much different than when we started," Sam said, leaning on his shovel.

"That was the whole idea," Alfredo said, smiling. "It looks great. By the time the migrations start in the Fall, there will be plenty to eat."

The Captain pulled into the sanctuary under the late afternoon shadows. "Yo, Captain!" Russ called out. "Perfect timing! We just finished!"

The Captain grinned and waved, then picked up a large canvas bag and slung it over his shoulder. He jumped off his boat, walked over to the other men and put the canvas bag on the ground. Without speaking, he opened the flap.

"Beer!" Sam cried out as he leaned in to pull one from the ice.

"You are an angel of mercy, Captain," Russ said.

"Just the delivery boy," the Captain said. "You need to thank the Padre." He handed Alfredo a beer.

"Thanks, gentlemen!" Alfredo said, raising his bottle. "Thanks for your help, all of you."

After a brief celebration, they hopped aboard the Captain's boat. Alfredo got off at the inlet, waving as the Captain left with Russ and Sam for the city dock.

HENRY BRAUN TOOK A GULP OF HIS perfectly cooled coffee as he opened the Sunday *Ledford Sentinel.* An architectural rendering of the new Wilder Island Bird Sanctuary and Botanical Gardens was splashed across the front page. In shock, Henry spewed his coffee across the table, spraying his wife. Minnie said nothing as she wiped off her face and arms.

"Son-of-a—" Henry swore, over and over again as he read the accompanying article. He read it twice, a third time. "What the hell? A bird sanctuary?" He glowered at Minnie across the table. "Isn't the whole damn island a sanctuary?"

He stood up, shaking his head. "Those bastards." He picked up the newspaper and left the kitchen, scowling terribly all the way to his office.

Henry kicked his office door shut behind him and tossed the offending newspaper onto his desk. He picked up the phone and punched a few numbers, seething with impatience as he waited for his attorney to answer. "Dammit, Jules, what the hell do I pay you for?" he shouted into the phone. "Why didn't I know about this damn bird swamp before it hit the papers? I don't like being blindsided."

"Calm down, Henry," Jules said. "It changes nothing. They can build Notre Dame on the island, and it changes nothing. Churches are not exempt from eminent domain, as I told you; bird sanctuary is certainly not going to change anything. Just cool your jets. Is your presentation to the city ready? What about the model of Ravenwood Resort? These are the things you need to be worrying about, Henry."

Henry slammed down the phone. He strode to the window and jammed his hands in his pockets as he looked out over his estate. Two crows in the tree outside his office window mocked him, their sly smiles ridiculing his plans, his dreams. He shook his fist at them and spent the rest of the day moping, muttering vague threats, and punching the air with balled up fists. He phoned his attorney several times, relentlessly pestering him until finally Jules promised to come over for a nightcap.

Minnie Braun calmly ate her Eggs Benedict alone. She wondered for the millionth time why God had forsaken her so, and then she scolded herself. *Jesus never said, 'Take up your cushion.' Life is hard, and I have it so easy.* Easy, if all she considered was the comfort of the body. Her soul she had dedicated to Jesus, but who was there on Earth to hold her heart?

For years, she had listened to Henry talk about Wilder Island— owning it, subjugating it, and turning it into a money machine. His long-winded diatribes became a staple at the breakfast table, lunch table, and dinner table. Minnie never saw Henry in between meals, a scenario that was perfectly fine for both of them.

Priests, for God's sake! That's what Henry roared when he found out who owned the island. Minnie smiled to herself at the memory. *Oh, how he pouted and bellowed, threatening everyone clear up to God! The next day she wrote a big check to the orphanage run by the Sisters of St. Anne down in MacKenzie.*

She was a devout Catholic and hoped to think of herself as a good Christian as well. She had a comfortable life in Henry's big house where she lacked nothing. She was never hungry, never cold. But she felt enormous guilt at being financially supported by Henry; his most lucrative business deals often left someone else impoverished.

"It's business," he had said to her the first and only time she had mentioned that fact.

Minnie Braun's husband was a respected paragon of the business community. But she wished she could undo some of the damage he had done, though in most cases, she was incapable of remedying anything. Trying to warm the icebox in her heart, she bought coats and gloves for the poor children, and she arranged for groceries to be delivered to the soup kitchens. She constantly looked for widows whose rent needed paying, and poor children whose parents could not afford Christmas presents.

Over the years, Minnie had devised intricate ways to squirrel away money, a few dollars here, a few hundred there from her household budget. She shrewdly invested that money, Henry's money, and funneled the profits into her heart-warming projects. Frequently Minnie begged the Good Lord's forgiveness for what her husband would surely have called theft—just in case it was.

Minnie kept her charitable contributions secret from Henry. He would never approve of any of the places she gave his money to—that little Jesuit chapel on Wilder Island, for instance. She was charmed by the legend of Brother Maxmillian, and the restoration of his chapel had captured her imagination. While her husband fiddled with lawyers in his relentless pursuit of Wilder Island, Minnie funneled his money to Father Alfredo Manzi, whom she saw every Friday when he delivered Communion wafers to St. Sophia's.

Oh, the look of surprise on Father Manzi's face when I handed him twenty-five hundred dollars in cash! But she was grateful as well. *It is easier for a camel to pass through the eye of a needle than for a rich man to get into heaven.*

That's what she had said to Father Alfredo when he gasped at the size of her gift. Of course he knew she was the wife of perhaps the city's wealthiest man. But to everyone else at the church, as well as everyone except her husband and his attorney, she was known as Gabriella. No last name, just Gabriella. No one knew anything about her but her name and that she always dealt in cash.

Minnie needed a place to unload her guilt, lest it keep her from heaven. She unburdened herself in the confessional, but her real salvation came through her enormous gifts to the orphanage, and now to the hermit's chapel. She hoped to see it someday.

But her contributions did little to placate the gnawing guilt that chewed at the edges of her conscience. And when the cold reality of her loveless marriage bore down heavily on her, she found some comfort in escaping into fantasy, where she and Father Alfredo fed orphans on the steps of the hermit's chapel on Wilder Island. Of course she knew there were no orphans on the island, but the image comforted her.

ALFREDO BORROWED THE MONSIGNOR'S CAR after Mass and drove to Rosencranz Hospital for the Insane. The hundred-year-old building was nestled in the woods about an hour's drive from Ledford and about twenty minutes as the crow flies. Concertina wire atop the chain-link fence around the property discouraged trespassers as well as escape, should an inmate be capable of devising such a plan. The fence divided the tamed acreage of the asylum grounds from the thick, wild forest that forever threatened to encroach upon it.

He turned onto the long driveway that connected the rural highway to the Victorian-style building and its meticulously manicured grounds. A guard stopped him at the gate, pushing a clipboard at him, and he scribbled the name, Dr. Martin Robbins, onto the daily visitor's log.

"Follow this road around and you'll drive right into the parking lot," the guard said as he pointed toward the building.

Alfredo drove through the set of heavy-duty chain link gates crowned by the same concertina wire as the fence. Inside, a few neatly trimmed trees grew alongside the curvy asphalt drive. The old stone hospital building suddenly appeared in his view. A gazebo stood alone on the treeless lawn, encircled by a well-ordered flowerbed of mixed colors.

"Originally Rosencranz was some rich guy's mansion," Sam had told him. "He'd made a fortune in China in the opium wars, or so they say. And when he came back filthy rich, he built this huge house for himself and his twenty-three cats."

"Twenty-three cats?" Alfredo had said dubiously.

"That's what they say," Sam had said with a shrug. "Anyway, the mansion was supposedly the most expensive house in the US of A at the time. And Mr. Rosencranz, he threw legendary parties. Before he went nuts."

A guard motioned Alfredo straight ahead to the parking lot, blocking him from entering the service road that branched off the driveway. He parked the car and walked up the imposing granite steps, and through the heavy, metal-clad wood front doors. He stepped into the lobby, astonished at its opulence.

He stood upon a floor of huge slabs of polished white marble with streaks of black and gray. Polished wood and sparkling clean windows adorned the walls, evidently the original living room of the mansion. The pressed metal ceiling high above dwarfed the sparse furnishings—a receptionist desk, a few chairs and end tables huddled together near the front entry. The odor of institutional disinfectant permeated the air.

A sour-faced, middle-aged woman sat behind a plastic-laminate desk and credenza, which formed an unbreachable barrier between the outside world and the hinterlands of the institution. Behind her stood a row of offices, partitioned off from the lobby with wood-paneled walls with closed doors and curtained windows. She put down the book she was reading and greeted Alfredo with a frown. "Can I help you?" Her voice echoed coldly around the lobby.

Sound confident. That's what one of St. Sophia's young parishioners told him. The youngster was a master shoplifter who had rarely been caught because, as he said, "I just acted like I owned the place, so no one paid me any mind."

"Good morning, Miss," Alfredo said with what he hoped was a charismatic smile. "I am Dr. Robbins from Catholic Social Services, and I have an appointment with one of the patients."

"You got any ID?" she asked, her eyebrows arched suspiciously.

"Yes, ma'am," Alfredo said, withdrawing from his wallet the fake ID Sam Howard had made for him.

Truly, Sam is a jack-of-all-trades! Lucky for me, his skills go beyond cottage building!

The priest was uncomfortable with the deception, and he knew he was breaking at least one law. But there was no other way he could get access to Charlotte or her file other than to be a psychiatrist or medical doctor. *Charlotte has no family, Someone needs to look in on her. Forgive me, Father. I need to find out why she is here.*

NoExit's voice rang in his ears. "There is a vast difference between law and justice."

The sour-faced woman scrutinized his ID carefully, looking first at the photo, then up at him. Alfredo had taken great care to look the part of a shrink. He had donned a pair of plain-lens glasses and erased his iconic streak of white hair using small amounts of black dye. A gray sport coat over a blue button-down shirt, khaki trousers, and loafers finished out the ensemble of the handsome psychiatrist.

Evidently satisfied, she licked her lips and copied his name and address from his ID onto the guest register. She handed it back. "Who you want to see?" she asked indifferently, her hands poised over the computer keyboard.

"Charlotte Steele," Alfredo said. Charlie had told him that was the name on the smock she always wore when he saw her. He memorized the shapes of the letters and picked them from an alphabet Alfredo showed him: C. Steele.

She typed a few characters into her computer, and without looking up, she picked up the phone. "Yeah, Patrick," she said. "Bring Inmate 456191 to the patio. Yeah, Ms. Steele, that's the one. Yeah, there's someone here to see her." The sour-faced woman listened for a few moments and then laughed as she said, "I hear ya, pal. But whaddya gonna do? Right, okay, hon, thanks."

"Sign here," she said, pushing the register toward Alfredo. "They'll take her to the patio." She jerked her head toward the windows. "You can wait for her out there."

"Of course," Alfredo said pleasantly as he signed his fake name. "May I please have her file?"

She got up as if it might be her last act on Earth and walked the two or three steps to a file cabinet. She opened a drawer, rifled through its contents, and then another.

"I'm sorry, Doctor," she said, returning to her desk. "I can't find her file. All I can say is it must be in the archives. I'll send someone down for it and have it brought out to you."

Alfredo frowned, hoping to look like an irritated doctor. "That will be fine, Miss. Thank you," he said curtly. He turned toward the doors and stopped. "What is your name? I hate to keep calling you 'miss.'"

The sour-faced woman smiled. *She is actually rather pleasant looking.* "Dora Lyn, Doctor," she said. "One n, no e."

"Pleased to meet you, Dora Lyn," Alfredo said, smiling back.

He left the lobby through double glass doors and stepped out onto the patio. Several wheelchairs had been parked amid the few empty tables whose occupants were either asleep, with their mouths hanging open and their heads flung back, or they were staring blankly ahead. A tiny old lady babbled incoherently into her lap, shaking her head. An elderly stoop-shouldered man walked his wheelchair along the low stone wall encircling the patio, his slippers shuffling along the flagstone.

Alfredo was aghast. *This is where Charlotte lives? Among elderly dementia patients?*

"Charlotte Steele for Dr. Martin Robbins!" a loud voice shouted.

Alfredo waved, and said, "Over here, please." As the aide wheeled Charlotte over to meet him, she cried out and pointed to a flock of birds gliding by overhead. "Oh, look! The loons are flying to the river!"

She wore a blue denim jumpsuit that zipped up the front, the same as the patients in the wheelchair. A tag above her left breast read, "C.STEELE." A thick black braid fell down her back, almost to her waist. Her eyes arrested him for a moment, eyes the color of rain.

"She don't talk, Doctor," the aide said somewhat apologetically as he delivered Charlotte into "Doctor Robbins'" temporary custody.

Alfredo thanked him and wheeled Charlotte to a table in the far corner of the patio next to the stone wall that bordered the patio. A rose bush hedge so thick he could not see the ground through it grew up against the wall, closing in the two sides of the patio. *A most effective barrier.* Beyond the hedge stretched the impeccably manicured and treeless grounds of the asylum.

He came around to the front of her wheelchair so she could see him. "Would you like to sit in a regular chair, Charlotte?"

She squinted into the sun and held one hand up to her forehead like a visor. "Who is it?" she asked. "Who are you? You hear me? No one hears me."

"My name is Jayzu," Alfredo said. "And I hear you. Would you like to join me at this table?"

She nodded, ignored his outstretched hand, and stood up from the wheelchair. She sat down at the table, and Alfredo pushed the wheelchair up against the stone wall. He took a chair opposite her, with his back to the people on the patio—most importantly, the guards and orderlies. "Good morning, Charlotte."

Charlotte looked bewildered. "Who are you?" she asked suspiciously, her expression darkening again. "How do you know my name? Why are you here?"

"I am a friend of Charlie's," Alfredo said. "He asked me to come see you."

Charlotte's face lit up, and she cried out, "My Charlie? Where is he?" She looked out across the grounds toward the woods. "Is he here?"

"No," Alfredo said. "He is not here. But I am. Will you talk to me today? I will tell you all about Charlie."

He looked over his shoulder. The aide who had brought Charlotte to him was staring at them, but looked away as soon as Alfredo caught his eye. He turned back to Charlotte, who was placidly looking at him. "Charlie is well. He has a wife and a lot of children, and grandchildren, and great-grandchildren."

"Where is Charlie?" she asked. "Where does he live?" Her pale blue, almost gray eyes sparkled with lively interest.

"He lives on Cadeña-l'jadia, as do I, "Alfredo said. "It is a beautiful island in the river."

"Where is Cadeña-l'jadia?" Charlotte asked. "Is it that way?" She pointed toward the direction the loons had flown. "Or that way?"

"Oh, let me see," Alfredo said, and he looked around to gain his bearing. "North is that way, right?"

Charlotte nodded, "Yes, that is north, Jayzu. Is that the way to Cadeña-l'jadia?"

"No, it is toward the southwest," he said, pointing.

She nodded and looked, her hand shading her eyes from the sun. After several moments, she turned her eyes back upon him. "I want to go to Cadeña-l'jadia. I want to see Charlie. Will you take me there, Jayzu?"

Nonplussed, he held his breath for a few moments and then sighed. "Perhaps, Charlotte," he said. "Perhaps someday I can. You have been here a very long time, I know."

"Three thousand and eleven days. Counting today," she said. "But not counting the days in the graying."

He mentally calculated the number of days. *Eight years ago. That is about when Charlie said he got her to look up at him.* "The graying?" he asked. *Was she in a coma?*

Charlotte glanced beyond his shoulder toward the building and frowned. He turned around and saw an aide rotating each of the wheelchairs one-quarter turn until they all faced the building, away from the table where they sat. "So they won't burn on one side, Doctor," the aide explained to Alfredo. "We turn 'em every fifteen minutes."

Two of the tables were now occupied by elderly patients and their visitors. Alfredo wondered if they were doctors, or if these people had family that visited upon occasion. He turned back to Charlotte, who had gotten up from the table. He joined her at the stone wall as she leaned over and touched a red rose on the other side. "Oh!" she cried out suddenly. She withdrew her hand, revealing a spot of blood on the end of her finger.

He pulled a handkerchief out of his pocket and wiped the drop of blood from her finger. "What about the graying, Charlotte," he said as he guided her back into her chair. *Obviously not a coma. Severe depression, perhaps?* "How long were you in the graying?"

"I do not know." She shrugged. She sucked on her injured finger for a few seconds. "I did not count the days during the graying, because there was no night to separate the gray into days. But it was a long time, I think. Many years." She leaned back in her chair. "Do you know how many, Jayzu? How many days have I been here?"

"About twen—" Alfredo started to say before stopping himself to listen to the argument in his head. *Should I tell her? Yes, she asked. She deserves an answer. The truth shall set you free. But what if it devastates her?*

"You counted about eight years and three months' worth of days," he said after a few moments. "Charlie told me he found you eight years ago."

"Yes, Jayzu," she said. "But how many days was I in the graying?" Her eyes forced the truth from him.

"Eighteen years," he said, hoping his words would not crush her.

She stared at him for a few seconds. "Six thousand, five hundred and seventy days in the graying, plus three thousand and eleven days since the graying is—" She choked on the words. "Is nine thousand, five hundred, and eighty. She looked away from Alfredo as she brushed the back of her hand across her cheek.

Glory be to God! She is as lucid as I am, although I cannot do math that fast. But should I have told her? It seems to have made her very sad. Seeing her gray eyes full of tears made his heart ache.

Charlotte exhaled a long sigh and looked at Jayzu with great weariness. "I have been here longer than I thought."

Jayzu looked so distressed, she reached across the table and patted his hand. "Better to know than not know," she said. "In the graying, I did not know anything. I saw nothing, and I heard nothing, except once in a while, I heard screaming."

She shivered; the vastness of the graying billowed up at the edges of her consciousness. "Emptiness, Jayzu. Everywhere emptiness. No days, no nights. Only grayness." It called to her. Still. *Fall! Just fall in!* "It was very quiet in the graying, but sometimes I heard voices. *Fall! Just let go! Fall!*

"Do you remember when you came here?" Jayzu asked, his voice pulling her back. "Or why they brought you here?"

Charlotte put her hands over her ears, shut her eyes tightly, and shook her head back and forth. Needles and lightning bolts poked her, and she recoiled in a stiff paralysis that left her gasping in pain.

"Are you all right, Charlotte?" Jayzu's voice .

She looked at him, suddenly startled. *Where am I? Who are you?* The graying thinned, and a strange man was staring at her. The scent of the rose hedge brought her back to the patio. She pulled her braid to her front, unwound it and rebraided it. The grayness dissolved, and she sat in the sun at a table with a dark-haired man who said his name was Jayzu.

"They tricked me," she said. She frowned and her face darkened with an old memory. She was in the woods. *They came out of nowhere!*

"Who tricked you?" Jayzu asked. "Who were they? Where did they come from?"

"Jayzu," Charlotte said reproachfully. "I cannot answer a million questions all at once!"

"Forgive me, Charlotte," he said, smiling. "That was too many questions. Tell me who they were."

Her eyes darted back and forth as she searched for an answer deep within the wells of her memory. Finally her eyes focused again on Jayzu, and she said, "The foreign people."

"Don't kill me!" someone shouted from the patio.

Charlotte and Jayzu looked toward the direction of the noise. A patient was being escorted off the patio, yelling and waving his arms. "They're trying to kill me!" he shouted, hanging on to the doorframe as the aides tried to take him into the building. "Help me! Someone! I'm innocent!"

A couple left as soon as the patient disappeared into the hospital. The man put his arm around the sobbing woman and escorted her gently through the doors to the reception area.

"He is a foreign person," Charlotte said. "These people are all foreigners." She gestured around the patio to include everyone. "All foreigners, except you."

She felt the warm sun on her back and the solid chair beneath her. A few birds in the rosebushes fluttered and flapped. The man across the table was looking at her intently. He seemed concerned, but he did not make any move toward her.

"I do not know how I got here, Jayzu." She pushed a stray hair out of her eyes. "I was in my hidden place, where the little creek split in two and made an island. They found me, and I was very scared. They took everything from me. And then they took me." There was nothing more to tell or remember.

Charlotte looked up at the sky. Fluffy white clouds floated toward the west. After a few moments, it seemed to her that tiny multicolored drops of light fell from the blue onto her face. She shook her head back and forth quickly, her black hair catching its share of the light and twinkling with tiny flashes of shimmering color.

"Then the graying started." Her calm gray eyes focused on Jayzu. "I kept telling them it was coming, and they kept not understanding. Why could they not just speak English? They just kept yammering in their foreign language and sticking me and shooting lightning through me and—"

She gripped the arms of her chair and held her breath. A few moments passed, and she exhaled. "After a while, I could not hear them anymore at all, but they kept sticking me, and their mouths moved up and down like this." Charlotte stared myopically while opening and closing her mouth like a fish out of water.

Jayzu laughed, attracting the attention of the aide at the desk next to the doors. He frowned for a moment, and Charlotte was afraid he would make Jayzu leave. But the aide went back to the book he was reading.

"I do not remember anything after that," Charlotte continued.

"It was mostly gray, for a very long time. I lost track of the days." She sighed, leaning back in her chair and looking toward the woods. "Eighteen years."

"And when the graying ended?" Jayzu said.

Charlotte nodded. "When Charlie first came to the windowsill. But I am not in the graying anymore. I am seeing and hearing even if no one can hear me. Why can you hear me, Jayzu, and the others can not?" She gestured vaguely toward the patio.

An old woman in one of the wheelchairs suddenly erupted a string of nonsense in a singsong voice. No one paid her the slightest attention except for Charlotte. "What did she say, Jayzu?"

"I do not know," he said, shrugging his shoulders. "Charlotte, what language are we speaking right now, you and I?"

"Well, English!" She frowned in confusion at his question.

"Maybe I am silly," he said with a foolish grin that made Charlotte laugh. "But, you and I are not speaking English. They are," he gestured toward the others on the patio. "But we are not. And the old woman was not. I think she really might be mentally incapacitated, but you are not."

"But, Jayzu, how am I different from her?" She pointed at the old woman. "Why is she crazy," she drilled him with steel gray eyes, "and I am not?"

Jayzu stared at her strangely without speaking for a few moments. "I do not know the answers." He shrugged. "But I know you are not crazy."

"If I am not crazy, then why am I here?" Charlotte angrily waved at the bank of wheelchairs.

"Because to them," Jayzu said, "you sound like that old lady."

She considered Jayzu's words, her forehead wrinkled as she tried to fathom the idea that she was the foreigner. "There is no difference between her and me, then?" she said, her voice distraught.

Jayzu reached across the table and took her hand in his. "If any one knew the answer to that, Charlotte, neither you nor that old woman would be here. But you are not crazy, and she is—dementia is what they call it. People's brains wear out when they get old."

"I do not want dementia," Charlotte said, looking past Alfredo at the old woman and watching her head bob back and forth. "Am I old, Jayzu?"

"No," he laughed, "you are not old; you are what is known as middle-aged. Like me. You and I are probably around the same age. You have many years left. Probably forty, at least."

"How old are you, Jayzu?"

He looked at her with a strange expression of fear and sympathy, and he hesitated before he said, "You are forty-two, as I am."

Forty-two. Charlotte mouthed the words soundlessly. *Forty-two. Fifteen thousand, three hundred and thirty days.* She shook her head in disbelief.

"You do not look old," Charlotte said. "Then I am not so old either! I was afraid I had become an old lady and spent my whole life here in this stupid place!"

She looked down in her lap as her eyes stung with tears. *And Jayzu says I will live another forty years? Till I am eighty-two. Like the old lady in the wheelchair.* She forced her tears back and shut her mind to that thought.

"What do I look like, Jayzu?" she said. She tried to smile, but it felt gritty and tense.

He seemed surprised at her question and said, "Do you not have a mirror in your room?" Charlotte shook her head, and he continued, "Well, your eyes are sometimes very light blue and sometimes gray, like the dawn sky before the sun rises. Your eyebrows match your hair—black as Charlie's feathers. Your nose is straight and fits your face perfectly. You are a beautiful woman, Charlotte. You do not look old."

She blushed behind her hand. *I am beautiful?* "Oh, Jayzu! I wish I could see my face!"

A loud buzzer sounded, an ugly noise that made Charlotte cover her ears. A voice spoke over the loudspeaker.

"What did she say?" Charlotte asked. "They yell like that all the time, and I never know what they are saying."

"She said visiting hours are over," Jayzu answered. "But we do not have to pay any attention to that. I need to leave soon, but before I go, show me where your room is. I will tell Charlie, and he can visit your windowsill there every morning, before anyone gets up."

Charlotte's frown immediately vanished, and she lit up. "Oh, my Charlie! Charlie! Charlie! Charlie!" She clapped her hands and laughed. She rose from the table to dance around the patio, dodging the wheelchair people, singing in her strange babble that no one else understood.

The aide grabbed Charlotte and steered her back to Alfredo, who had gotten up from the table to follow her. "Thank you," he said as he took Charlotte's arm. After the young man was out of earshot, he said to Charlotte, "You will see Charlie soon, Charlotte. But come, let me escort you to your room."

She nodded, and the two walked arm-in-arm through the patients' lobby. At one end, a gigantic flat-screen television blared a popular soap opera to one very attentive woman amid a sea of snoring white-haired people in bathrobes.

Charlotte led him down a hall and into an elevator. "Third floor," she said, punching the button. "I am on the third floor."

When the doors opened, she nudged Alfredo to the right, keeping a strong hold on his arm. She opened the unlocked door to her room, a small cell that had space only for a single bed and a small dresser. He looked around the room, frowning. *It is so small!*

"Jayzu," Charlotte said. "Do not be sad for me. I love my little room. It is quiet and holds me comfortably. Much better than when I had a bed in the great room. It was so noisy all the time, all that yammering!" She put her hands over her ears and shook her head, her eyes large and glassy.

Alfredo laughed, and she took her hands from her ears. He felt humbled by her strength of spirit, her peace and humor with a life he would find unendurable.

"This is my sanctuary, Jayzu," she said, her gray eyes full of the moment, of him. "I do not need any more."

The elevator doors opened and Dr. Robbins stepped out into the lobby. Dora Lyn put her book down and looked at him curiously as he approached the desk to sign out. "I hope you had a pleasant visit, Doctor?" she asked as she pushed the visitor's log toward him. He had such a wonderful smile. It had been years since anyone had smiled at her with such ... what was it? —Attentiveness? That was it. As if he had actually noticed her as a person.

"I did, thank you," he said as he scribbled his name. "Did you ever find Miss Steele's file?"

"No, I am so sorry, Doctor," Dora Lyn said, blushing. "But I'm sure it is here somewhere."

"I shall return in a week or so for a follow up," he said with a warm smile. "Perhaps you will have located it by then."

"Sure, Doctor," she said.

He started to leave, and she said, "Uh, Doctor?"

"Yes?" he said, turning back around.

"Were you really talking to her?" Dora Lyn asked. "I mean, it's none of my business I know, but, well, I saw you two out on the patio, and it seemed like you were actually talking!"

He looked at her with a surprised expression on his face, and she continued, "I mean, she doesn't talk to anyone, that Charlotte. She hardly ever says anything. And when she does, it's just this squawking kind of noise. Do you understand her?"

Dr. Robbins did not reply, and she wondered if she was completely out of line for saying anything. "I'm sorry, Doctor, it's none of my business."

"No," he said, finally. "It is all right, Dora Lyn. We are trying a new therapy on patients such as Charlotte. By mimicking their quote-un-quote language, we hope to establish a connection with them, some of whom, like Charlotte, have not spoken an intelligible language in many years. It has shown great promise."

"I always thought she was in there, Doctor," Dora Lyn said, nodding her head knowingly. "You can tell by the eyes."

"The windows of the soul," he said and walked toward the door. As he reached for the handle, he turned and said, "God bless you, Dora Lyn."

"Thanks, Doctor," she murmured to his back. "God bless you, too."

—9—
What Is This Madness!

Father Provincial Thomas Majewski took a taxi from the Ledford airport and met Alfredo at the city boat landing. More than fifteen years had passed since he had last seen him. A few gray hairs made that white streak he had even as a young man a bit less noticeable, but he otherwise had not changed much. The same intense almost black eyes that seemed to see straight into your soul. And he had not lost the warm compassion that had made everyone want to turn him into a priest.

"Greetings, Father!" Alfredo said as he and the older priest embraced. "I trust you had a pleasant trip?"

"Alfredo, please," Majewski said. "Call me Thomas. We are old friends, and I want to take a break from being the father. I hope that is all right?"

"But of course, Thomas," Alfredo said.

They embraced again and after a few comments about their age and well-preserved appearances, the Captain ferried the two Jesuits across the river in what seemed to Majewski more like a floating chunk of forest than a boat. A crow swooped in under the canopy and found a perch on the railing next to the Captain, brushing his outstretched hand with a wing.

A secret handshake among crows and humans? Majewski frowned and immediately banished the thought. "I grew up not too far from here," he said as he looked downriver. "As the crow flies, probably fifty miles. A little town called MacKenzie."

"I have been there!" Alfredo said. "Are you planning to visit your family while you are here?"

"Oh, no," Majewski replied, shaking his head. "There's no one to see. My parents are both gone. They sold the house after I moved to

Washington, about twenty years ago. None of the rest of the family lives in MacKenzie anymore either."

"There is the old chapel," Alfredo said, pointing toward the island. "Or at least the roof, though it looks more like a tangle of dead branches from here."

"That's the miraculous chapel you told me about?" Majewski asked dubiously.

"Wait until you are standing inside," Alfredo said with a smile.

The Captain steered the boat into the inlet and ground to a halt on the sandy bank. The two priests jumped out, and after saying good-bye to the Captain, Majewski followed Alfredo up a sketchy path into the forest. He breathed deeply, inhaling the odors of a living landscape. Big city life had deprived him of the luxurious scent of soil and decaying plant matter and the natural cycles of birth, death, and regeneration.

He looked up at the forest canopy and was astonished at the sheer number of black birds perched on branches and flying through the trees. He felt as if they were looking down upon him, making snide comments to one another, ridiculing him with their raspy caws.

For God's sake, get a grip, Thomas! They're crows! They probably don't even notice I'm here. He stopped to catch his breath.

"My cottage is just ahead," Alfredo said. He waited while Majewski wiped his forehead with his handkerchief.

The cottage blended in well with its natural surroundings; they were nearly to the front door before Majewski realized it was there. Living trees comprised the walls, through which green vines had been interwoven, tying the structure together.

"My humble abode," Alfredo said. "You can put your bags inside, and then we will go on to the chapel."

"Incredible!" Majewski said. "Like it's part of the forest. I didn't even see it!"

"I wanted only the faintest human footprint here," Alfredo said with a smile.

Inside, Majewski looked up at the roof, constructed of interwoven driftwood branches. "It really does look like a bird's nest! Reminds me of the pictures of the chapel and Brother Wilder's tree house. You didn't build this all yourself, did you?"

"Heavens no!" Alfredo said. "I had a lot of help, from a local artisan as a matter of fact, Sam Howard. He helped me to restore the chapel as well."

He took Majewski's bags from him and set them in a corner next to a futon. "It doubles as my couch and your bed tonight."

"Very nice!" Majewski said, looking all around. "So cozy—I'm envious! A one-room cabin, perfect for one, but not two. Don't let me put you out, Alfredo. I can get a hotel in the city."

"Nonsense!" Alfredo said. "You will sleep here tonight. You are not putting me out." He raised a hand against Majewski's objections. "I will sleep where I normally do in the summer—in a hammock outside." He gestured toward the door. "Shall we go on to the chapel?"

Majewski felt the cares of his job in Washington DC recede as they walked through what seemed to him a primeval forest, unsullied by the artificial gods of commerce and greed, and the big business of religion. The utter joy of life abounded, in every leaf and stem, every feather and beak, every whisker and tail hidden in the bushes.

He stood in awed silence outside the little chapel for many moments. "It's like a living entity, as if it just grew here, right out of the forest floor."

"Much of it did!" Alfredo said. "Living trees hold up the roof, and several varieties of vine plants fill in the spaces between. Brother Maxmillian did a great job building it. All I had to do to restore it was clean it up and trim some of the vines. It was the inspiration for my cottage."

"I can see that," Majewski said as Alfredo pulled the door open.

They stepped inside. Sunlight infiltrated through the many open spaces in the roof, making a checkerboard pattern on the floor, giving the otherwise dark interior an almost cheery look.

"Reminds me of the basilica at our chapel in Rome," Majewski said, looking up into the upside-down-bird's-nest roof.

De la Torre's sister wrote about the Madonna della Strada! Coincidence, or—? He dismissed the thought. *Brother Maxmillian was a Jesuit. Why wouldn't he pattern his chapel after the Jesuit Mother chapel in Rome?*

"I thought so also," Alfredo said. "I like to think this chapel is the little sister to the Madonna della Strada. I am thinking of naming it the Madonna del Rio."

"Oh, that's lovely!" Majewski said. "The Lady of the River. Perfect!"

"It will never stick, I am afraid," Alfredo said. "The locals all call it the hermit's chapel."

"That works also," Majewski said, nodding.

The little chapel seemed to vibrate with the very essence of the Holy Spirit, and the old priest felt as if he suddenly weighed less. Even the act of breathing seemed easier. His burdens of guilt and anxiety floated away like balloons. For the first time in his life, Father Provincial Majewski felt the blessings of the Almighty raining down upon him. He felt a sense of peaceful acceptance enfold him, and he reveled in the luxury of the moment.

A ray of sunlight illuminated the kneeler in the middle of the chapel, attracting Majewski's attention. He went to it and ran his hand along the smooth armrest. "Brother Maxmillian prayed here," he said in awed reverence.

"I found a journal under here," Alfredo said and lifted the top of the armrest. "Brother Maxmillian's first year on the island."

"Really?" Majewski said, peering into the dark interior. "His own journal? Where is it now?"

"In my desk at the university. I found it before my cottage was finished, so I took it there to read and to keep it safe and dry. I looked at it under a microscope. Evidently Brother Max made his own paper and ink!"

"Fascinating!" Majewski said. "I'd love to read it sometime."

"I scanned it all into my computer at the university. I will e-mail it to you."

They made their way outside and down toward the rocky point. They stopped beside the hermit's grave and Majewski prayed, "Lord Almighty, look with mercy upon your good son, Maxmillian, and keep his soul in the peace and comfort of your most heavenly arms forever."

At that moment, a flock of crows burst from the trees and sailed overhead. Majewski was startled but not frightened by the intrusion—an unruly cacophony of raucous sounds from a noisy group of crows. "Strange coincidence," he said. "Those crows, I mean. Flying over just now. Like they were putting their two cents in." *I wonder if Alfredo knows what they said.*

"Many of them know me," Alfredo said with a casual smile. "Crows are extremely intelligent, Thomas, and very observant. It is rather well known that crows can pick a human face out of a crowd. Some of them watched me bury Brother Maxmillian's bones, and here we are standing on that very spot."

Majewski studied Alfredo's face for a sign. *Does he know about Maxmillian's sentient crows? Does he speak to crows himself?* Majewski was almost sure that he did, though he felt foolish for thinking so.

"Come!" Alfredo said, extending his hand. "Let us go back this way." He led Majewski back toward the chapel. He stopped and pointed to a pile of limestone blocks, bags of sand and a few tools. "Ultimately this will be a garden, but all I have complete is the pool."

Majewski heard water dripping, and he turned his head toward it.

A narrow rivulet poured over a stack of limestone blocks into a small pool surrounded by wildflowers and grass. "The water comes from a spring right out of these rocks. Sam and I moved a few to catch it. Such springs are everywhere on the island. My water supply depends on one of them."

Majewski cupped some water in his hands and drank. "Wonderful!" he said. "Nothing like water from a freshwater spring."

"Let us sit down," Alfredo said as he gestured toward a large gray slab of limestone. "This is a pleasant place to sit and contemplate the mysteries of the universe!"

"Indeed it is!" Majewski agreed, grateful for the opportunity to rest. "The pond is exquisite!"

Several crows materialized in the trees above the pond and looked down at the two men. Each time Majewski happened to catch the eye of one of them, it turned away. *Are they spying on me?*

"Alfredo," he started to speak. *I was just wondering, do you talk to crows?* He was dying to ask but immediately felt foolish for even thinking such a thought. *Imagine, the Father Provincial of the North American Chapter of the Society of Jesus asking if a human could talk to a crow!*

Brother Maxmillian's letter seemed to shout from the interior of Majewski's jacket pocket, *"De la Torre knew that some of us can!"*

Majewski took Brother Maxmillian's letter out of his pocket and handed it to Alfredo. "Coincidentally," he said, "I found this letter, quite by accident, the same day I received Henry Braun's offer to buy the island. It was written in 1852, by Brother Wilder to his uncle, the Father Provincial at the time, Antoni de la Torre."

"Really?" Alfredo said. "*The* Antoni de la Torre? Brother Wilder was his nephew?"

Majewski nodded and said, "You'll be more amazed when you read it."

Alfredo read the letter, feeling Majewski's eyes boring into him. *Does the Order know about the Patua'? Does Majewski? Is that why he's here?* He tried to keep his face expressionless as he flipped the page over and read it again. *God Almighty!*

"This is incredible," he said, handing the letter back.

"What do you make of it?" Majewski asked. "This claim of Brother Maxmillian's that he talked to the crows here? Is it not just the heretical babblings of a madman?"

Majewski has never heard of the Patua' then. Will he think I am a madman?

"Well," Alfredo said, "It could be that he was a madman and his uncle, the Father Provincial tried to hide his nephew's whereabouts during his life."

"But why?" Majewski asked. "Why would he do that? It's almost as if he wanted someone to eventually discover the island, and his nephew. What did de la Torre find so special about this island? Other than a place to stash his nutcase nephew."

Alfredo shrugged. "I do not know. There is really nothing here but trees and crows." *Did de la Torre know about the Patua'?* "Maxmillian would be a freak even in our time. A good question, though— why the great Father Provincial Antoni de la Torre would want him remembered." *I should ask Charlie of there were Patua' here before Bruthamax.*

Five crows dropped out of the sky and landed on the rocks on the edge of the pond. After dipping their beaks in the water, two of them jumped in and splashed water up over their back with their wings.

Alfredo recognized them all. Cousins–Charlie's nephew and nieces, Speedy, Blanche, and Zelda.

Speedy looked over at Majewski and said to his siblings, "That other one, he don't speak the Patua'."

"Nope. He's just regular," said Zelda. She and her sister Blanche flapped their wings over the water, splashing Speedy, perched on the edges of pond.

"Playful little fellows," Majewski said as the crows flew up to the trees above the garden. He followed them with his eyes, until they blended in with the shadows among the leaves. But he could almost feel them staring down at him.

"They make me laugh every day with their silliness," Alfredo said.

"Geronimo!" Speedy yelled as he tumbled out of the tree, beak-over-feathers into the pond. He disappeared for a couple of seconds before leaping out of the water and onto a rock above the pool. He shook himself soundly, flinging water drops all the way to the priests.

"So, do you think that Brother Maxmillian was insane?" Majewski asked. He turned his probing eyes on Alfredo

"I cannot know that," he said slowly, his face expressionless. *Well disciplined, like a corpse.* Even before his training as a Jesuit priest, he had developed the ability to hide his feelings and thoughts behind an impassive face. "But communicating with the beasts is not necessarily a mark of insanity. Look at St. Francis of Assisi. People no doubt thought he was insane in his time, yet now he is the revered patron saint of animals. Perhaps that was de la Torre's hope."

"That his nephew would be given sainthood someday?" Majewski asked incredulously. "*That* is insane. Do you actually believe that Brother Maxmillian talked to crows?"

Fear crawled up out of Alfredo's gut and into his mouth. His inner voices argued: *Does Majewski know about me? Is that why he is here? Tricking me into admitting I am a freak? Why not just tell him? The truth shall set you free! Or imprison me. He could have me defrocked, banished, and tossed to the dogs. But why would he do that? Tell him!*

The truth pushed against his teeth, and Alfredo locked his jaws, choking back words that could unleash an uncontrollable deluge in which he might drown. Betraying nothing of his inner turmoil, he stared back at Majewski and said, "The truth is, Thomas, I have never had the choice not to believe."

The whole truth is ...

"I have found," Alfredo continued, hoping his voice did not betray the fear he felt, "that corvids and certain humans—Brother Maxmillian, for one—are able to understand and speak a sort of dialect that harmonically overlaps the language of both species."

Why can I not just tell him! He already knows about Brother Maxmillian. What if he already knows about me?

"But that's preposterous!" Majewski said, wiping beads of sweat from his forehead. "Communication between the species! Impossible!"

The three crows stood at the edge of the pond facing the two priests. "Wonder what they're arguing about," Speedy said.

"He's got cookies in his pocket," Zelda said. "I can smell them from here."

"Oh?" Speedy looked sharply at Alfredo. "Suppose he'll give us some?"

"I'll die of boredom waiting till they stop yakking," said Blanche and took off for the sky.

"Is it?" Alfredo asked, raising his eyebrows as he watched Blanche fly away. "You did not think so at my PhD defense, Thomas, where you defended me against those very charges. And that was fifteen years ago!"

He stood up and walked over to the pond and reached absent-mindedly into his pocket. The two crows on the rocks looked first at his hand in his pocket, then up at him expectantly.

"Thomas," he said, as he tossed a chunk of chocolate chip cookie into the air. Speedy snagged the tidbit before it had achieved its zenith. "There is no reason, scientific or otherwise, why we humans cannot communicate better with other species—especially with the corvids, intelligent as they are."

Zelda waited patiently for her treat, but as soon as Alfredo lobbed it to her, Blanche flew in low and snapped it right out of her beak.

"I'm sorry, Alfredo," Majewski said, shaking his head. "I remember your PhD, your fascinating experiments testing for corvid sentience with mirrors and complex pathways to food that required planning and tool making. And, you reported on some rudimentary sounds and correlated them to some pretty simple phrases. But it's utterly preposterous to claim that is a language." He shook his head in dismay. "How can you believe that and still call yourself a scientist?"

He will find out sooner or later. The longer I hold back the truth, the more it makes me look like a liar. Tell him!

Alfredo tossed a chunk of cookie to Zelda, who caught it deftly. "Thank you, Jayzu," she said and flew after her brother and sister.

"My dilemma is whether or not I can still call myself a priest," Alfredo said, quietly surrendering. "Thomas, I have this ability too. Preposterous or not, I, like Brother Wilder, understand and can speak the language of the corvid, fluently. I have had this ability as long as I can remember."

"What is this madness?" Majewski cried out, shaking his head in bewilderment. "I came here prepared for Dr. Alfredo Manzi to debunk Maxmillian Wilder's claim, to remind me that the Almighty made but one sentient creature, mankind." He shut his eyes and his mind to the image of Stella, her hands reaching out to him, pleading. "Forgive me for being flabbergasted, but this is just too incredible."

"I am sorry, Thomas," Alfredo said. "I wish I could relieve your distress. But you are a man of science yourself. Can the highly respected linguist Dr. Thomas Majewski see not madness and heresy, but the miracle of a complex language and culture of another sentient species that has been here on Earth longer than we have? Can you not behold this wonder of creation and rejoice?"

Silenced by his internal confusion, Majewski did not reply for several minutes. All around him, the visible and invisible natural world contradicted any need for such turmoil. The trickle of water into the pond seemed to repeat its cadence over and over again, "Why can't you just *be*?"

At last he took a deep breath and said, "I've seen a lot in my time, Alfredo. I've been sore amazed more times than I can count at the wonders wrought by the Almighty. But discovering this letter and the hidden talent of our Brother Maxmillian several weeks ago—quite frankly, it's kept me awake at night ever since. It's not so much that I think speaking the language of the animals is so preposterous. It's that, well, you see, my sister, Stella—"

Majewski squeezed his eyes shut with his thumb and forefinger, suddenly overcome with emotion. For a wild moment, he thought Alfredo might have known Stella, and he wished he could unburden himself of her tragedy. And his guilt. But the words would not come to his lips. From the well of his memory, the last image of Stella's face emerged. The shock and betrayal on her face broke his heart. *Her big brother sold her out. That's what she thought. I never got to tell her the truth.*

"Your sister?" Alfredo said. "Was she like me?"

"Yes," Majewski said, trying to compose himself. The water dripping into the pond grew suddenly louder, crying out with watery voices, "Just like me, just let it be!" He focused on the sound of the tiny stream spiraling down to the pool in a continuous song that had no beginning, no end. No choice, no questions asked. Or answered.

Stella's face in his memory was unbearable, but he could not banish her. "They thought she was handicapped when she was younger, because she didn't speak to any of us until she was almost five. Before that, she'd babble away all day long. But only with crows."

He paused, remembering Stella and her pet crow. *What was his name?* "And when she grew up, she walked and talked more among the crows than she did with humans, until finally she only talked to crows. That's when they said she was insane. I helped them capture her and haul her off to the asylum."

A tiny bird flew down to the pond and sipped a few beakfuls of water before taking off again. The stream continued to fall over the edges of the rocks and into the pool, oblivious of the bird, of Majewski's sister or his guilt. It wore on him, this guilt, eroding his sense of worthiness, relentlessly pursuing him like a bloodhound. Ever since he had read that letter.

"I understand why people think we are insane," Alfredo said. "The Patua' does not resemble any human language, and it frightens people. I have managed to lead a relatively normal life—if you call the priesthood a normal life—in a safe place where I could speak in this tongue without persecution. I know others have ended up in insane asylums, just like your sister. Some take their own lives."

"Suicide? Oh dear Lord!" Majewski said, horrified. His hand went to his breast.

"Forgive me, Thomas," Alfredo said. "I intended to offer you some comfort; instead, I burdened you. I am very sorry."

Majewski nodded wearily and said, "I know that, Alfredo. It's not like I haven't had that thought myself. But until recently, I have kept her safely stuffed in some dark corner of my past. And then I found the letter. Since then I have had almost no peace. Stella's face invades my thoughts during the day and haunts my dreams at night."

"But why, Thomas?" Alfredo said. He reached out and put his hand on the older man's knee. "What happened? Where is Stella now?"

Majewski watched the ripples that emanated from the water falling into the pond, large bubble floated outward, endlessly created, and endlessly destroyed against the rocks around the edges. Such was his torment. *Where is she? They never told me. I never asked.*

"I don't know," Majewski said, his shoulders sagging. "I wish I had tried harder to persuade my parents not to incarcerate her, but she was out living in the woods like a heathen. That's what my mother said. Turned out she wasn't. She was with her old nanny. Mimi, she called her." He hung his head, raking his hands through his hair. "I can't get it out of my mind."

"Thomas," Alfredo said, reaching over and putting his hand on top of Majewski's. "Forgive yourself. You did not know."

Majewski nodded. The two men sat in silence for a several minutes. A lone cricket in the garden chirped out the late afternoon temperature. Water fell relentlessly into the dark pond, at the mercy of gravity and other forces far beyond its ability to avoid or control, in a continuous downward journey to merge at last with the sea. *As we run down our own pathways to death ...*

Guilt and shame kept Majewski from telling Alfredo that after his parents' deaths, he had hired an attorney to write the checks to the mental institution where Stella was. He didn't want anything to do with Stella, didn't even want to know where she was. There was plenty of money; she'd be taken care of for the rest of her life. He had relegated it all to a dim corner of his memory. Until that accursed letter.

A barge on the river blasted its horn, disturbing the peace in the garden and jolting Majewski out of his dark thoughts.

"I see the shadows are now long, Thomas," Alfredo said. He stood up and offered a hand to Majewski. "The sun will set in a half hour or so. Let us go to my cottage, and I will fix us some tea."

Majewski tore his eyes from the little waterfall and said, "Wonderful!" He took Alfredo's hand and stood up. As they walked the short distance to the cottage, it seemed to Majewski that the entire forest had suddenly come alive with motion and sound. A few small animals scurried through the undergrowth, and hundreds of birds all called out at once. Crickets chirped in the grass, and buzzing insects flew past his face.

Majewski forgot Stella and his burdens of guilt in the wonder all around him, his senses sharpened. The forest seemed more colorful than living things ought to be. He felt lightheaded from the many fragrances of life and death co-mingling in his nose.

Once again, they were almost at the doorstep to the cottage before Majewski realized it. "Sit down, make yourself comfortable," Alfredo said after he opened the door.

Majewski sat down at the table in the corner, and Alfredo filled the kettle and put it on a small cast-iron stove. He tossed a few lengths of small branches into the stove and within a few moments, he had a small fire going.

"That was fast," Majewski said. "I'd still be down there, blowing and praying."

Alfredo laughed, pushing a small piece of wood into the stove. He closed the door and stood up. "I have gotten very good at building fires, living here. I otherwise would have starved by now. Or learned to love raw food."

Majewski pulled the cord on the lamp over the table, and the light came on. "What's this?" he said, looking down at the black fob in his palm. "Did you carve it?"

"No," Alfredo said. He walked over to the table, wiping soot from the stove off his hands. "I found it beneath Brother Maxmillian's bones in the chapel. I also found pieces of cord and a crucifix, which I buried with the rest of him."

"I see a hand maybe," Majewski said, looking through the bottom of his glasses. He squinted, leaning closer to the light. "Or is it a wing?"

"I thought I could see both," Alfredo said. "A wing and a hand."

"Interesting." Majewski let go of the fob and watched it swing back and forth on its cord. He felt lightheaded and wanted to tear his eyes away, but could not. Back and forth, back and forth. Alfredo was talking, but he couldn't hear him as the room dissolved into a shadowy twilight. Nothing remained but the aura of light from the lamp and the black orb swinging back and forth in front of his face.

His head swam in confusion. *Where was Alfredo?* He saw a withered old man kneeling at the prayer bench in the hermit's chapel, his long white hair illuminated by a single shaft of sunlight. His lips were moving, but Majewski couldn't understand what the man was saying. Was he praying? Suddenly the old man turned, and Stella's face stared at him.

"Thomas?"

Disoriented, Majewski called out, "Alfredo! Where are you?" He squinted into the light. "Stella?"

"I am right here, Thomas," a familiar voice said. His right arm was shaking involuntarily.

"Thomas!"

Majewski blinked. The vision evaporated, and Alfredo stood next to him shaking his arm. "Thomas! What is the matter? Are you all right? Thomas?"

CHARLIE FLEW OVER THE RIVER TOWARD Ledford searching for his nephews, Floyd and Willy. After chatting with a few local crows, he found the two young brothers playing games in the park next to Ledford City Hospital. He landed on a bench and called out to them, "Over here, fellas. I've got a job for you two. Espionage."

Floyd and Willy loved intrigue; they had watched many spy movies as fledges, from their nest at the drive-in movie theater.

"Oh, yeah," Willy said and landed on the bench next to Charlie.

"Who, what, when, where, why?" Floyd asked, a second behind his brother.

"Follow me," Charlie said as he took to the air. "This way."

The three crows flew across the park and into the neighborhood beyond. The landscape below gradually changed from neat little rows of houses with adjoining yards to larger and larger estates behind huge stone walls and wrought-iron gates.

At 10 Woodland Drive, Charlie, Floyd, and Willy swooped down to the wall surrounding a sprawling mansion with many gables and chimneys and a satellite dish. The three crows looked down at the gray stone walls nearly covered with ivy and Virginia creeper. Huge windows in white frames stared out toward the horizon.

Charlie gestured with his beak toward the mansion and said, "The man of the house, Henry Braun, is among the richest in Ledford."

"Pretty fancy digs," Willy said approvingly. "We'll be puttin' on the ritz after this one."

"I just love big old houses," Floyd said. "One day I want to live in a house with white curtains flapping in the breeze, and pies cooling on the windowsills.

"It's a spy caper, boys," Charlie said sternly. "Your primary job is to spy on Henry Braun. No looking for sparklys, and no stealing. You got that, Floyd? Willy?"

"Gotcha, Boss," Willy said.

"You can count on us," Floyd said.

"Do not let Henry Braun leave your sight," Charlie said. "Perch on his windowsill and observe his every move. You're going to need to pay a lot of attention, boys. I'm counting on you two."

Charlie drilled them with his intense blue eyes. "Don't let him notice you. He hates crows. He may even hate all birds, for all I know. But he particularly hates crows. A word to the wise, fellas."

"Hates crows," Floyd said. "Perhaps we should be incognito, eh?"

Willy smacked his brother with a wing.

"Now get to it," Charlie said. "Let me know if you hear anything about Cadeña-l'jadia. I have a session with the Archivists the rest of today and tomorrow, but I'll check on you the day after."

Willy and Floyd nodded solemnly. "We'll keep our ears and eyes open," Willy said. "No worries, Boss."

Floyd and Willy knew Ledford like the backs of each other's wings. They'd flown virtually everywhere in the city since the day they fell off the roof of the projection booth at the Raven Wind drive-in theater, one of the last of its kind in the state.

They had spent little time in the rich folks' neighborhoods, however. What was the point? These humans never even left a covered trash can outside. They built special houses for their rubbish that were locked and emptied by authorized personnel once a week. Even their landscapes were kept impeccably free of everything edible. Not even a blade of grass was out of place, let alone a misplaced or lost sparkly.

Before they fledged, the two brothers, kreegans of Charlie's sister, Eliza, watched a different movie every night from the nest at the drive-in theater. They loved to act out different scenes from their favorite movies. Floyd was fascinated with manners and food and loved movies that featured exotic, faraway places. Willy loved Westerns and science fiction. And they both loved movies about clandestine operations and spying.

Floyd and Willy liked to hang out in the blocks surrounding the university campus, on the windowsills and in the trees surrounding the student apartments. Much to their delight, every apartment had its own television—miniature movie theaters as Floyd called them. Every night they found a windowsill to perch on while they watched their favorite shows.

The two crows never went to roost hungry, thanks to the many dining establishments and fast-food joints located near the campus. Every night for weeks, they selected a new restaurant, raiding the trash containers in the alley after hours. Both crows cultivated a taste for international food.

Willy loved it all, spicy, not spicy, raw or cooked. Except for calamari. "Like trying to eat rubber bands," he said.

Floyd embraced any flavor or dish, as long as it was presented with tasteful elegance. He was especially partial, however, to the English Tea Gardens, where ladies sat in elegant finery, sipping brown liquid from delicate white cups painted with exquisite artistry.

The two young crows stayed hidden way up in the big tree in Henry's backyard, watching. Waiting to watch mostly, until Henry was in his office. They watched him smoke cigars, shout on the phone, and yell that he needed more coffee, or lunch, or his suit, or tie.

They were fascinated by the Henry's little choo-choo train that went around and around a miniature island with a big boat moored at a little dock. It was very beautiful; hundreds of little lights sparkled like diamonds, rubies, and emeralds. At least once a day, Henry turned them all on, ran the choo-choo around its tracks, and sailed the boat out into the miniature river.

The first time they saw the little train blow its whistle, a small puff of steam issued from its smokestack, and the crows were amazed. "Is that cool or what?" Floyd said to his brother.   Willy   nodded and replied, "Man, I'd love to have one of those. I'd ride that little train around all day long!"

"And I would preside over the lovely paddleboat," Floyd said. One of his favorite movies featured a romance on a big riverboat, and he was dying to fall in love with a young lady crow on one. "I would serve exotic coffee and tea and delectable pastries on the deck every morning, and champagne with wild mushroom perogi in the evening!"

"Perogi?" Willy looked at Floyd in shock. "Are you nuts? No one serves champagne with perogi! Cognac, perhaps. But champagne? Ish!"

"Don't knock it till you've tried it," Floyd said with an air of superiority. "It's quite scrumptious, actually. I wouldn't serve *cabbage* perogi with champagne, however. Now, that would be disgusting."

They watched from the windowsill: Henry sitting down in his armchair; Henry turning on the television; Henry flitting through the channels. He settled upon a conversation between several people sitting around a table. Within minutes, his head dropped to his chest.

"Gad!" Willy said after a few minutes. "How dreadfully dull! I'm falling asleep too. What say you, brother, that we flee to yonder tree whilst the object of our spying naps in front of the tellie?"

"Capital idea!" Floyd said. "It is half past time for tea, anyhoo."

The two crows flapped to a different tree and perched on a branch where they could still see Henry, or at least his bald spot sticking up over the back of the armchair. "I say, old chap," Willy said after Floyd passed him an imaginary cup of English Breakfast tea and a blueberry pastry, "I cannot fathom how you can sip a cup of tea, hold a crumpet, *and* keep purchase on this branch at the same time."

Floyd looked at his brother with an air of superiority and said, "That is because I have the lithe soul of a dancer, my dear brother. While you, I fear, inherited the corpulent spirit of the bovine."

A sliding door opened below the two crows, and a thin, petite woman with dark hair tied up in a bun stepped outside. She set a covered tray down softly and called out, "Grawky! Did I hear someone say it is tea time already?"

"I say, old chap," Floyd leaned over to Willy, forgetting about the imaginary crumpet, which fell to the ground below. "What the bloody hell was that?"

"Why, I daresay someone is speaking in the Patua'," Willy remarked. "Perhaps it is Henry Braun's maid, or his spouse. Perhaps she wishes to attract our attention."

Willy raised a claw up to his eye and peered down at the woman on the patio through an imaginary monocle. "Really! Another Patua'! What a lovely coincidence! Perhaps we should see if she knows anything important about Henry Braun," Floyd said as he took one last sip of tea from an imaginary fine English bone china cup—white, upon which delicate pink flowers were painted.

"I say! 'Tis a capital plan, old boy!" Willy replied. "Let us fly down and greet her good morning."

"Bloody grand idea, old chap!" Floyd put his teacup down carefully on the branch. Wiping his beak delicately with an imaginary polished cotton napkin, embroidered with pink flowers to match the teacup, he turned to his companion and said, "Shall we?"

The two crows flew down to the patio, landing at the woman's feet. Willy bowed low and said, "Grawky, Madame! It is an honor and a pleasure to make morning salutations!" He could be very eloquent.

"Indeed, fair lady," said Floyd, not to be outdone. He bowed so low his beak scraped the concrete. "My colleague and I beg for the occasion, nay, privilege, to make the acquaintance of such a lovely and gracious lady."

"Well, for heaven's sakes!" The woman blushed. "My darling kitty has maligned you! He told me there were, how did he say it, 'crows masquerading as dandies drinking tea in the trees.' Dandies indeed! Finely mannered gentlemen is more like it!"

She motioned for the crows to seat themselves and they nodded approvingly to each other. "Miss Fair Lady, ma'am," Floyd said, as he surveyed the contents of the tray on the table. "I daresay you've exhausted yourself on our behalf this morning! And we have yet to be formally introduced. I am Floyd of the Drive-In, at your service, fair lady!"

Minnie bent over and giggled as she brushed her hand across Floyd's outstretched wing. "My pleasure, I am sure!"

"Likewise," Willy said, bowing and stretching out a wing. "I am Willy of the Drive-In."

"My name is Minerva," she said, brushing her hand through Willy's feathers.

"Minerva," Willy said, nodding approvingly. "A lovely nom de plume, wouldn't you say, my brother?"

"Who could think otherwise?" Floyd said with a low bow. "Pleased to meet you, Miss Minerva."

"Oh, please!" Minnie said, blushing. "No one calls me that except my husband. Call me Minnie."

"But of course," Willy said, "Miss Minnie."

"Thank you," she said. "Now, let's have some tea and crumpets, shall we?"

She sat down on a chair, uncovered the tray and put three cups and three plates on the table. Two apple fritters peeked out from beneath a cloth napkin in a small basket. She took one, cut it in half, and put the pieces on the crows' plates.

With unimpeachable manners, Floyd and Willy dipped their beaks into their tea and nibbled delectable pastry with Minnie Braun. After he finished his last crumb, Floyd wiped his beak on his napkin and said, "To what do such humble fellows as my brother and I owe this marvelous repast?"

"Oh, pshaw!" Minnie said, waving her hand at Floyd. "It's just tea and some baked goods from the grocery store."

"Nay," Willy said, shaking his head. "No two crows were ever so less deserving of sweeter confections than the exquisite products of your culinary art, as well as and not less than, the delight of the company of a maid so fair."

Minnie looked confused for a moment, then smiled and said, "As easily I could say, to what do I owe the occasion of such a delightful visit from two handsome, well-mannered, and dare I say, well-spoken crows?"

The crows looked at each other for a moment, and Floyd said nonchalantly, "Why, nothing other than our hope to share tea with a beautiful lady!"

"Oh, fiddle-dee-dee!" Minnie laughed, waving the hand at the two crows. "Enough of the honey-beaked speech! What are you fellows up to, really? Are you spying?"

The two crows looked at each other again, abashed. "She knows," Floyd hissed through his beak.

"Well, Miss Minnie," Willy said, "we did hope to acquire news or developments thereof that interest the master of the house, that is, about possible future plans he may or may not have concerning Cadeña-l'jadia, that is, Wilder Island to you folks."

"I see," Minnie said. She glanced over her shoulder and leaned toward the crows. Floyd and Willy leaned in toward her.

"He's just crazy to get that island," she whispered. "He keeps saying the same thing over and over again. 'Condemnation for the priest, eminent domain for Henry Braun.' I have no idea what that means.

He's not the least religious, so I don't think he's talking about heaven or hell. He just keeps repeating it, over and over again. 'Condemnation for the priest, eminent domain for Henry Braun.' And then he laughs." She sat back and wrapped herself in her arms. "It is a not a happy sound."

"Eminent domain," Floyd said. "Izzat so?"

A door slammed in the house, and Minnie looked anxiously over her shoulder again. "Minerva!" a male voice boomed out the windows.

"Ta-ta for now, fellas!" Minnie said. She quickly put the cups and plates back on the tray and darted into the house, leaving the fritters on the table.

"What is eminent domain?" Willy asked, beaking a chunk of fritter and flying up to the tree.

"Beats me, old chap," Floyd said, grabbing the other fritter and following his brother. "But isn't Miss Minnie just the bomb?"

—10—

The Keeper's Trance

The fermented mildornia berries tasted bitter in his beak, and Charlie felt his stomach rebel, but he had long since learned to control the impulse to puke it all back up. All around him and the other Keepers, the Shanshus chanted the Starting Verse, the Calling of the Trance.

Shim shu vig zhi gimki cot
Za zho glik fa vesh ni bu
Och o mishka sen say vox
Min goy mob y fin ga sook
Shim shu vig zhi gimki

The words meant nothing in any language to anyone save the Archivists of the corvid databases. Carefully constructed of sounds in sequence, each tone and space conveyed a command, involuntarily understood by the specially trained Keepers.

Za zho glik fa vesh ni bu
Och o mishka sen say vox
Min goy mob y fin ga sook

Charlie felt his legs stiffen as the mildornia berries took effect. His vision blurred and his beak locked. Though he could blink his eyes, paralysis settled in his wings and feet. His awareness diffused, and he couldn't distinguish himself from his surroundings. He was one with the rest of the Keepers, one with the Shanshus, one with the Archivists, and one with the great tree in which the Encoding Ritual took place.

As Charlie sank deeper into the trance, an image arose from his own memory lattice. He saw his younger self stumbling over his own feet, meeting Starfire for the first time. Regal and elegant, the old raven called out, "Grawky!" and flapped his wings in greeting. "Blue eyes?" he had said. "You are not yet old enough to be a Keeper."

"Yes, sir. Blue eyes, sir," Charlie had stammered as he grazed wingtips with Starfire. "I'm three years old, sir. My family lives on Cadeña-l'jadia. We've all got the Hozey-blue eyes."

He had been proud the day Starfire probed and measured his memory capacity and chanted his archival lattice into place, even though he had a headache that lasted for several days afterward. It was worth it; he could hold an exceptionally large lattice, and that made him an especially valuable Keeper.

Charlie remembered well those early days of his training as a Keeper, where he learned all the verses to all the chants. He had spent months with the Shanshus, learning how to sing the verses that put the Keepers into a semiconscious paralysis. *Soon my JoEd will report for his training.*

The Shanshus' chanting grew louder, more insistent, and irresistible:

Zhan gink voor man ink fan zhee
Klee zhor mel toc vix kin go klan
Vak jist rax vor gonz chi vang
Slix yor wa dot szi zho bak

The intonations shrank Charlie's awareness of himself, collapsing his personal memories into a temporarily repressed state, so as not to bleed into the Keeper data he was about to receive. He lost all sensation in his body. He could not move, other than to blink his eyes.

The Shanshus' verses cajoled Charlie into the Keeper's Trance where he lost all awareness of past, present, and future. Time ceased; all that existed was the Shanshus' chanting. Devoid of senses and memory, his awareness knew no bounds and began an expansion that if left unchecked would become indistinguishable from the universe. The crow who knew himself as Charlie would dissolve into the vast emptiness. The Shanshus chanted a boundary that surrounded his awareness and kept his own self—his memories and attachments—intact beneath the trance.

He could hear nothing but the Shanshus, see nothing but a vast darkness as they chanted the Opening Verse of the Emplacement Ritual.

Blik blak glok mok shoo
Zik zak clok bok voo sim coo

Charlie sensed a broadening of space, as if the universe had become instantaneously larger. The chanting slowed and faded into a low hum. The Archivist stepped forward and leaned over him, uttering the Unfolding Verse, a somewhat melodious conglomerate of syncopated sounds that awakened the archival lattice embedded in Charlie's memory.

All other Keepers and Archivists had receded beyond Charlie's consciousness; he was aware only of his own lattice unfolding and Starfire's voice floating somewhere above it. The old raven chanted the Unfolding Verse until the lattice completely expanded into the void space.

Quo fol hozhu gak flo ming
Zinj vox von mi aoh zam
Plak egh zhi gum nond qua yi

The lattice filled Charlie's awareness with a tree-like structure, comprising a trunk, several main limbs, hundreds of secondary branches with thousands of auxiliary branches that ended in fan-shaped arrays of twigs. Thousands of nodes, located on every branch and twig, were programmed to receive specific data packets.

Starfire intoned a cadenced phrase that opened a node on one of the branches, which glowed with a pale blue light. After a few moments, he chanted another sequence of alliterative verse that encoded genealogical data upon a ribbon that glowed with colored light.

Charlie watched the rainbow-colored ribbon vibrate as Starfire harmonically encoded it with data. The ribbon drifted through the branches of the lattice, seeking the unique node that would open as soon as it felt the specific vibrations intoned by Starfire's chanting. A node opened, capturing the ribbon, then it closed, and its color changed to yellow. Charlie blinked twice, paused, and blinked two more times, signaling Starfire the data ribbon had been emplaced.

Starfire began another refrain, encoded another data ribbon, and again Charlie watched it laze through his lattice until the unique blue node opened, received, and turned yellow. Over and over again, Starfire repeated the sequence. All day and far into the night, he emplaced data into Charlie's archival lattice. Finally, as the night sky gave way to a pale gray dawn, Starfire chanted the Resting Verse:

Coo shul ay maas vay wu oh
Bu ee ray shon boy on wee

MAJEWSKI AWAKENED TO THE SONGS OF birds. Nothing else—no train whistles, no car horns, no screeching tires, no sirens. Just birds, a great many of them all chattering at once. *This island is a paradise. So far from Washington. Heaven should be this wonderful.*

The gray sky spoke of the coming dawn. He sat up and stretched. He could hear Alfredo outside talking to the birds. A strange, guttural squawking sound. *The language of the crows.* He pushed Stella back into a corner of his memory and rose from his bed and dressed.

"Good morning, Thomas," Alfredo said, as he came through the door. "How did you sleep?"

"Like a baby," Majewski said. "I have not slept that well in weeks, if not years." He sat down at the table and eyed the strange carved fob hanging from the lamp.

"I am glad to hear that," Alfredo said with a smile. "I was worried about you last night. I thought you had gone into some sort of trance."

"Just some jet lag," Majewski said, waving his hand. "I felt a little dizzy, that's all. Don't give it another thought."

He watched a hummingbird through the open window as it hovered above a honeysuckle vine and plunged its long beak into a flower. Such a simple life. Majewski was envious.

He took the cup of coffee Alfredo handed him and said, "You know, Alfredo, after teaching for three decades, I took a desk job at Jesuit headquarters in Washington. I thought I could make a difference."

He watched the hummingbird outside the window poke its beak into another flower.

"Got all the way to the inner sanctum, to the office of the North American operation. But what a hellhole it is, headquarters. You have no idea, Alfredo. The place where you'd think brotherhood and Christ-love reigned, you have to watch your back more than perhaps anywhere else on Earth."

"Unlike the shark-infested pools of academia," Alfredo said. He put a plate of bacon, eggs, and toast in front of Majewski.

"But academia does not pretend to be about brotherly love," Majewski said. He picked up a piece of bacon and bit the end off.

"I have been to Washington DC a few times," Alfredo said. He sat down at the table with his plate. "I found the city itself to be loud and ugly. I have never had any use for such a place, and the political intrigues of the Jesuits, or academia for that matter, never interested me. I just want to be away from all that noise, free to discover the sacred secrets of creation."

Majewski took a drink of coffee and leaned back, looking out the window. *I never want to leave this place.* "It's noisy," he said, nodding. "Constantly. It's all a distraction. But I'd like to leave this earth knowing I accomplished something, Alfredo. My oath as a Jesuit is the furthering of the human spirit in the glory of God. I don't feel like I've done anything of the sort."

He thought of the stack of letters on his desk, from attorneys suing the Order. And his job was to somehow turn them back, deny or at least delay.

"I'm not furthering anyone's spirit," he said. "Or glorifying God at all. I don't even say Mass anymore. I fear I'm nothing but a therapist with a lot of power, a large budget, and the thankless job of managing hundreds of insecure, arrogant, ambitious, ego-driven, so-called holy men with graduate degrees."

Alfredo laughed and said, "That about nails us, does it not?"

Majewski waved his toast at Alfredo. "Present company excepted, of course. You are most humble and don't seem to be arrogant or ego-driven. You are the icon of all I ever wanted to be, Alfredo. No, seriously." He held a hand up and turned his head away as if not listening to any protests. "Your scholarship is excellent. Do not discount your contribution. Your postgraduate work on corvid behavior is still the authority on the subject. And I am envious of your freedom, your life here."

Majewski watched a robin swoop down to the ground and hop around for a few seconds before pulling a fat worm out of the ground. *The Law of the Food Chain. So simple. So easy to understand.*

"Have you thought about retiring, Thomas?" Alfredo said. He sipped his coffee. "You have served the Order for your whole life. Perhaps it is time to step off the merry-go-around and do something that replenishes your spirit."

"I'd love to retire," Majewski said. "But what would I do? Come to Wilder Island and build myself a cabin? Watch birds all day?"

"Research!" Alfredo said. "May I interest you, as a linguist, in the first study of the corvid-human dialect?"

A magpie flew to the windowsill and walked back and forth scolding, it seemed to Majewski.

"Cre–ak cre–ak, sca–reee!" The long, blue-black tail whipped up and down, punctuating whatever it was saying.

"Do you understand the speech of magpies also?" Majewski asked. "I know they are corvids, but that didn't sound much like crow-speech."

"Very astute observation, Thomas," Alfredo said, smiling. "The magpies and jays have thick accents—for lack of a better word. Just as we have many different speech patterns within our country—the Southern vernacular is different from the New England accent, yet both are American English and readily understood by English-speaking folks. But to answer your question, I can speak with all corvids, though crows and ravens are generally more interested in talking to me."

The magpie pecked on the windowsill, screeching. "Ka-rawk! Ka-chek! Ska-wee!"

"What did this magpie say?" Majewski asked.

"She said, 'More bacon next time, if you please!'"

"All that?" Majewski said. "I only heard about three or four different sounds, less than ten syllables." He mopped up the last of his eggs with a piece of toast, wondering if he should save it for the magpie.

"Yes, Alfredo said. "I did hear all that. I hear more nuances within the corvid speech than you and most other humans do." The magpie pecked impatiently on the windowsill, and he tossed her a bit of toast. "I think the same must be true for composers. They hear more in the music than we average folks do. They understand and can speak its language more fluently than the rest of us. I cannot help but wonder if this ability, whether in hearing music or the language of the corvid, may be inherited."

The magpie turned her attention back to Majewski, croaking at him earnestly, her tail whipping up and down as she paced back and forth on the windowsill. "As in a Patua' gene?" Majewski said, somewhat aghast. He put a corner of his toast on the windowsill, and she snapped it up. "While I want to say that's preposterous, it's certainly a scientific approach."

The magpie pecked on the windowsill. "Cree-ak-ak-ak!"

"What a little piggy you are!" Majewski said with a smile. He put a larger piece of toast on the windowsill.

The bird looked down at the bread, then at Majewski. "Cree-ak-ak-ak!" she said, and pecked the windowsill.

"We've cracked the human genome," he said, wondering what the magpie wanted, "this is true. But identifying a particular gene that causes a certain trait is not very straightforward, Alfredo. Frequently there is a pair or set of traits that occur together. Or a protein that switches a gene on or off. It's quite complicated."

"I know that," Alfredo replied. He put a bit of bacon on the windowsill; the magpie beaked it and flew away. "But there is some evidence that the trait runs in families, a bit more rare than twins, but we do see some continuity that does not appear random."

Majewski frowned. "We? You've been talking about this corvid-human language with others?" Only yesterday he felt almost indignant disbelief at the very idea. And now he was intrigued, in spite of his doubts. And jealous.

Alfredo left the table and came back with a coffee carafe. He filled their cups and said, "We means me and the Great Corvid Council. Over the eons, they have constructed a huge database of genealogical information, such as all Patua' births, deaths, marriages, etc., of all crows and ravens, since the beginning."

Majewski's mouth dropped open, and he shook his head in astonishment. He reached for the sugar bowl. "The Great Corvid Council? A governing body keeping track of the Patua'? And I thought merely talking to these creatures was incredible!" He stirred a teaspoon of sugar into his tea, watching the mini-maelstrom he created.

"Indeed," Alfredo said. "I am embarrassed at times at my own ego-centrism. The corvids have quite humbled me, yet I still sometimes catch myself being amazed. At what? That another species has evolved a highly sophisticated oral tradition that is excruciatingly detailed yet completely organized, accessible, and is thousands of years old? How dare I?"

Alfredo stood up and cleared the table. He filled the small sink, adding the leftover warm water from the teakettle. "The Captain will be here in an hour or so to take you to the mainland. What would you like to do in the meantime?"

"Let me help you, Alfredo," Majewski said. He grabbed a towel and dried as Alfredo washed their breakfast dishes. "I'd like to visit the chapel again before I leave," Majewski said.

Charlie remained incapacitated even after the data ribbons of Patua' births, deaths, and marriages had responded to Starfire's Sorting Chant and had disappeared into the storage nodes. Though he had no ability to respond or even feel surprise, he heard Starfire chant a strange verse he had never heard before:

Aka-kaka-gak-a-zhak
Eeka-keeka-geeka-zheek
Uku-kuku-guku-zhuk

Charlie watched a single node suddenly glow purple and eject a small white fireball that flashed and glittered in the dim interior of the lattice. It was not a data packet; it did not unroll into the typical ribbon, but bounced through the lattice like a shiny rubber ball.

Charlie felt vaguely puzzled by the fireball ricocheting through his lattice. It seemed to be severing connections between the nodes, which gave up a puff of white light just before they went dark. He had no capacity to react, but he understood that something was terribly wrong, and he blinked rapidly until he heard Starfire reciting the Rescue Verse.

Zhoomoo weemwoo oomee moo
Oomoo weemoo shoomee woo

Moments before he lost consciousness, a cool breeze flowed through Charlie's lattice, as it suddenly shut down.

Starfire chanted the new verse, designed to access the Keeper's own lattice. "We are missing Patua'," he had told Hookbeak. "I think I can locate them in the Keeper's memories."

Though Hookbeak had vehemently forbidden him to even think about it, Starfire nonetheless pursued his hypothesis. He had wandered through the lattices of several Keepers and had found nothing. "I know they are there," he had insisted to Hookbeak. Charlie had volunteered for this search, having understood the importance of finding the missing Patua'.

When the strange fireball ejected from Charlie's lattice, he made a quick copy of it and transferred it to his personal lattice for later analysis. Of course it would be like studying a snapshot of a multidimensional object, but it was the best he could do. *If only I could dive down the node that ejected it; I could at least find where it came from.*

Foamy spittle appeared on Charlie's beak, and he began to shake. Starfire recited the Rescue Verse and watched Charlie's eyes continue to blink rapidly. His breathing was labored. *Great Orb! I cannot lose another one!*

He chanted until he was hoarse, then exhaled in great relief when Charlie's blinking finally slowed, then stopped. The crow's chest rose and fell with the rhythm of a deep healing sleep. Starfire posted a novice to watch over him while he slept and wrapped himself in his own thoughts, contemplating the fireball in Charlie's lattice.

Never had he seen such a phenomenon. Clearly it had come through the Archival Lattice into Charlie's personal memory. That was not supposed to happen, and he wondered if the sphere was a sign that the lattice had suffered some structural damage during the ritual. *Perhaps I need to run a diagnostic on the Archival Lattice.*

Starfire glanced at Charlie, who remained deep in a near-comatose state. He was grateful the crow had volunteered for a personal lattice search. Jayzu's sudden appearance had invigorated Starfire's cherished hypothesis of a secret underground into which the Patua' had disappeared centuries ago. The idea had enchanted the raven for years; he was an historian after all. He had spent much time searching the archival lattice for clues to their whereabouts, and then Jayzu suddenly appeared out of nowhere.

"We didn't know about him," Starfire had told Hookbeak. "Jayzu is not in our database."

When Starfire heard the rumor that Floyd and Willy had found a genuine Patua', he summoned them both for questioning, releasing them several hours later, wrung dry of every piece of information they knew about the new Patua'.

He recalled the day the two brothers told him how they liked to perch in the tree at the edge of the duck pond on the campus of the university in Ledford. It was a popular place for students, occasional faculty, ducks, geese, and crows to eat lunch.

"A man strolled by," Floyd said, "a man with a white streak in his hair."

"And when he threw chunks of bread into the water for the ducks, I said to Floyd, 'I like a man who feeds the animals. It shows true character and compassion.'"

"And then he sat down on the bench below us," Floyd said, "and took out his lunch."

"A ham sandwich from the look of it," Willy said. The two brothers nodded at each other, remembering.

"And potato chips," Floyd said. "He had potato chips."

"So I said I loved potato chips," Willy said. "And he looked up and saw us."

"And then," Floyd said, "he put two potato chips on the bench next to him, and he said in a loud voice, 'I like a crow who joins me in conversation befitting an educated mind.'"

Floyd and Willy cracked up and high-fived each other. Starfire rebuked them and said, "And then what happened?

"We, uh," Willy said, "dropped down and introduced ourselves." He turned to Floyd and reenacted the scene for Starfire. "Grawky, Mr., uh—"

"Grawky, fellas," Floyd said, taking the man's part. "I am Father Alfredomanzi."

"Father? I asked him," Willy said, his head cocked to one side. "Father of whom?"

"And he said, 'Father of no one,' Floyd said. "And then he told us he is a Jayzooit priest." He turned to his brother. "Isn't that right, Willy?"

"Yah!" Willy said, nodding. "A Jayzooit priest and a perfessor."

Starfire had presumed that all Patua', living or dead, resided in the vast, interconnected corvid database. Ever since Bruthamax, who had provided a huge repertoire of names, dates, and locations of the descendants of the lost tribes of the Patua' living in America, they had kept track. The question continued to haunt him. "Why was Jayzu not in our database?"

Charlie awoke at dawn; the effects of the mildornia berries had not completely worn off. Generally the Keepers needed three full days to recover, and he had had but one night, after undergoing a particularly rigorous ritual. He perched dizzily on his branch and watched ghost images of memory nodes opening, while colorful ribbons of memories leaped forth for a few moments before diving back into the closing node.

"Forgive me, Charlie," Starfire rumbled, as he struggled to pay attention, "for putting you through such a lengthy ritual. We had an enormous volume of data to emplace. I hope you are not too fatigued."

"No problem," Charlie said, trying to discern the raven amid the memory streams. "I could use a bite to eat, though. And some water."

"A strange thing happened during our, uh, experiment," Starfire said. "Something ejected from your lattice, something I have never seen before. At that moment in your trance, you began blinking quite rapidly, signaling that something was amiss. That is why I brought you out." He looked intently at Charlie.

Charlie swayed a bit on his branch, and Starfire put out a wing to steady him. "Forgive me. I should not burden you so soon after your ritual."

The other Keepers were already awake and devouring a carp that the novices had brought to the tree. The raven motioned them to bring some food to Charlie. Famished yet stiff from the effects of the mildornia berries, Charlie gulped down all he could eat within minutes. "I feel almost corvid again," he said, picking a bit of fish gut from his breast feathers.

"There is more," Starfire said, "on yonder branch where the rest of the Keepers are feeding."

Charlie managed to half walk, half fly the short distance to the group of Keepers. There was still plenty of fish.

"Nice that we get fed so well," a fellow Keeper said to Charlie, "doncha think? Right after we wake up and all? That is true civilization at its finest, if you ask me. I'd go through the Keeper's Trance every day if I could eat like this the next."

Several Keepers flapped their wings and croaked their agreement. "It really rocks not to have to find your own food in the morning," one of them said.

"Unfortunately," another said, "the mildornia berries can only be eaten once every full moon. Eat the berries too often, and they're poison. You'd keel over dead by morning."

"They say if you stay in trance too long," someone else said, "you'll never come out of it. And then you spend your whole life being a zombie Keeper. You're just a data repository. No flying, no mating, no anything but mildornia berries and carp. 'Course they have to force feed you 'cause you can't do anything for yourself, being in permanent trance and all."

Charlie wondered if that was how the world seemed to Charlotte, those years she spent in the graying. How different was that from the trance? Where the surrounding world fades and all that remains are one's oldest memories in the darkness?

ALFREDO AND MAJEWSKI WALKED TOWARD the chapel with the morning in full swing. Majewski saw more birds of all kinds than he ever imagined—crows, blue jays, mockingbirds, sparrows, finches, orioles—in the trees, on the ground, flying, on the chapel roof. And they seemed to be all talking at once.

"Thomas," Alfredo said as they walked, "are we safe from Henry Braun? I had assumed that was the purpose of your visit, to talk about how to fight him off."

"The purpose of my visit," Majewski said as they arrived, "was to see for myself this wondrous place. And to hear from you that our Brother Maxmillian was insane because he talked to crows, and they didn't talk back."

Alfredo laughed. "Sorry I could not deliver, Thomas!"

"Oh, you delivered all right. Have no fear!"

They entered the chapel. Majewski went to the kneeler and said a silent morning prayer. When he finished, they left the chapel, and Alfredo indicated they should turn down the path toward the rocky point. "I like to sit down here watching the river flow. It is quite a lovely view," he said as they walked.

"To answer your question, Alfredo," Majewski said as he followed Alfredo, "I do not intend to allow Henry Braun to get his greedy little hands on this island, if for no other reason than he's an unctuous, self-serving slime-ball. Forgive me, Father." He blessed himself as he looked upward.

"What if someone in the Order hears about it?" Alfredo asked. "I mean, can you just turn down five million dollars like that? The chapel is not exactly the Notre Dame Cathedral, however sacred and charming you and I find it to be."

He stopped and pointed to a log. "The view is pretty fabulous from here."

"The riverfront down in MacKenzie isn't this nice," Majewski said. "There's a lot of activity out there! Barges, boats, water skiers."

A barge blew its horn, warning a couple of speedboats that had crossed right in front of it. Majewski turned toward Alfredo and said, "The matter of whether we sell the island is completely up to me. But, we are going to be proactive and turn this island into a conservation easement, which is a legal instrument that is frequently used to preserve and protect a wetland or a wildlife area from development, both of which we have here." He gestured all around them.

"I see," Alfredo said. "What would that look like? Who would own the island? What about the chapel? Would it be torn down?"

"I wouldn't think so," Majewski said. "I envision that the trust will own the island, thanks to a generous donation from the Jesuits. The chapel will remain Jesuit property, and you will continue on as its pastor. The Order can take a tax write-off, you remain on the payroll. No one will bat an eye."

"Excellent, Thomas!" Alfredo said, laughing. "That is excellent. Very poetic."

"I thought so," Majewski said with a twinkle in his eye. "I got the idea when you told me you wanted to build the bird sanctuary. I've got an attorney working on conservation easement documents as we speak. I'll have her call you. Kate Herron is her name. She probated Brother Maxmillian's estate for us. And she lives in Ledford, so she has some knowledge of the island. Get together with Kate and figure out how to set it up. I'll pay her fees and will back whatever you come up with."

Several crows flew over their heads and landed at the river's edge where they plucked a meal from the rocks. "Tell me, Alfredo," Majewski said as he watched, "did you know there was something special about the island before you came?"

"I had heard of the island," Alfredo answered, "when I was a graduate student. I came across some strange stories of talking crows on Wilder Island, and the name sat in my memory all these years. Then one day, I had gotten tired of promising little old ladies that Jesus will receive them in heaven if they would only hand me a check, and I made my way here."

"People need spiritual guidance, and we need to eat," Majewski said. "I don't care for the money-grubbing we have to do either. But it is necessary."

"A necessary evil it seems," Alfredo said with a sigh.

"Evil?" Majewski said, almost angrily. "Evil is the sex-abuse the church has been kicking under the rug for centuries." He sighed wearily. "I'm sorry, Alfredo. I'm just so tired of it all."

He picked a small yellow flower growing out from under the rock he was sitting on and sniffed it. He twirled the stem between his thumb and forefinger and watched the petals blur into one.

"The Jesuits do much that is good, Alfredo," he said. "Our universities and schools all over the world have helped lift the veil of ignorance from the human race for more than five hundred years."

A bell sounded from the direction of the dock. "That is the Captain telling us he is here to take you to the mainland," Alfredo said as he stood up. "We will go by my cottage on the way, and you can grab your suitcase."

"I envy you this life you have made for yourself," Majewski said as they walked. "You could have a department chair somewhere, but you choose instead to live here among the crows. You are a brave soul, my friend. I envy you. May God bless you."

"Tell me, Alfredo," Majewski asked after they left the cottage for the inlet, "do you think that at one time all humans could speak to the corvids?" He could hardly hear himself with the racket in the forest. *There must be hundreds of birds up there, all chattering at once.* "That would certainly have been a helpful trait."

"True," Alfredo said loudly. "I suppose the entire race could at one time, but one must wonder then, why would such a useful trait die out? It seems more likely the Patua' were a race of humans, with genes similar enough to interbreed with the other races. In any case, according to the corvid histories, there were many more Patua' in times past than now, before the Protestant Reformation and counter-reformation."

"Those were volatile times in Christendom," Majewski said, wrinkling his brow. "Our Order had just been born. Surely if the Patua' were of sufficient numbers to be persecuted, the Jesuits must have known of them, wouldn't you think?"

He followed Alfredo across the small stream that gurgled softly through its rocky course. "Fare thee well!" it seemed to whisper. Majewski stopped and picked a yellow flower growing along the water's edge. He pulled a small bible out of his briefcase and carefully put the flower between its pages.

"I would think the Patua' must have been known to the Order," Alfredo said as they started to walk again. "The botanical lore of the Patua' is said to have been vast. That alone would have been highly appreciated."

They arrived at the inlet where the Captain was waiting. A crow perched on the rail, seemingly chatting away, Majewski noticed. But there were no other crows around. *Is it talking to the Captain? Is he Patua' too?*

The two priests embraced. "You have given me much to think about," Majewski said, "and I am deeply grateful. My life in Washington DC has isolated me from the grand mysteries of the universe, both scientific and spiritual. I have missed both."

"You are welcome here any time, Thomas," Alfredo said. "And I hope you will consider a Patua' research project."

"Oh, I am interested," Majewski said, a broad grin streaking across his face. "You can count on that. I just don't know how long it will take me to divest myself of my duties."

He sailed away on the Captain's boat, looking back at Alfredo waving to him from the banks. He imagined Stella living on Wilder Island, happily gabbing with the crows. He shook his head at his own fantasy.

If she even lives.

He took one last look at the island.

Dear Lord, grant me this kind of peace someday.

11

Eminent Domain

"The River Queen will remain in permanent dry-dock here on the west side of the river," Henry told the small group of Ledford city officials as he pointed to the lovely miniature riverboat. "You'll be able to see it from Downtown and the Waterfront. There'll be a ferry coming in from both sides of the city, docking on the rocky point below the old chapel ruins. We'll have a marker there, commemorating Maxmillian Wilder's life and legacy."

Henry Braun stood while eight others sat in chairs around the architectural model of Ravenwood Resort. The mayor, his secretary, and six heads of city departments were there: Planning and Zoning, Environment, Tourism, Economic Development, Water, and Neighborhood Relations.

Of the group, Henry was sure he had four of them in his pocket: Tourism, Economic Development, Water, and the mayor himself. They all saw the light, even if they might've needed a little shove in the right direction. *That's a majority!* He chuckled to himself. *I've got this in the bag!*

The model around which they all were seated was huge. Complete with lights and running water, the miniature *River Queen* bobbed up and down in the current generated by her own paddlewheel. Gone were the overgrown forests of Wilder Island and the newly restored hermit's chapel. Trees obediently lined the sidewalks and cobbled streets instead, and tidy green lawns of manicured grass bordered with flowers surrounded concrete-lined fountains sporting sculptures of leaping fish.

Henry turned a switch on a transformer, and a small scale-model train emerged from a tunnel. Eight pairs of eyes followed the tiny steam engine around the little island as it blew its whistle and flashed its lights. "What resort would be complete without a train?" Henry asked the smiling faces around the table. "Completely electric, so no smokestacks or smog—just a little steam puff every now and then."

The tiny train rolled past groups of miniature people walking along the boardwalk next to the river and chugged past hotels, restaurants, and the amusement park, where the Ferris wheel spun like a hypnotic pinwheel of lights. "The train will shuttle people anywhere they want to go," Henry said, pointing to the tiny track. "To the casinos, the shopping mall, restaurants, Kid Land. Anywhere they want to go. Free of charge. They just hop on and off as they wish!"

The officials watched the little train begin another loop; a tiny puff of steam erupted from its engine. The whole scene was rather enchanting. Henry saw the smiles, the relaxed shoulders. The officials were charmed, he thought with a smug smile. *Who can resist a choo-choo?* Just about time to move in for the kill.

"Over here," Henry said, "is Kid Land." Colored lights adorned the miniature Ferris wheel, roller coaster, and water park slides that presided over the amusement park. "Complete with day-care workers and lifeguards to look after the youngsters while Mommy and Daddy are at the gaming tables!"

Henry pushed another button on the control panel, and the *River Queen* sputtered to life. He steered the boat around the island, and said, "Ladies and gentlemen, this is a replica of the old *River Queen* paddleboat that traveled up and down the river in the last century. She's been in dry dock, getting renovated into the first riverboat casino in the state. In Phase II, I'll bring in her newly restored sister, the Delta Dawn."

"Yes, Henry," the director of the Water Department said, "I'm sure she's very pretty. But what's the bottom line here? You ask us to condemn this property? What's in it for Ledford?"

"I am glad you asked that," Henry said magnanimously. "Bottom line: Ravenwood Resort is Ledford's cash cow. In perpetuity. Right now, Wilder Island is nothing but a mosquito-infested swamp, to say nothing of the unsustainable crow population, which has for decades been too large for the island to handle. I am talking about progress before crows."

Henry was proud of the slogan he made up, "progress before crows." He paused for a drink of water, looking around the room as he unscrewed the top of the bottle. Predictable scowls and smiles all around.

"Ravenwood Resort is a recreational facility that the entire city can enjoy," he continued. "But the greatest gift Ravenwood Resort will give the city of Ledford is to fill its coffers with tax revenue, as well as provide up to eleven hundred new jobs."

No one stirred for a few moments, until finally the mayor remembered his cue.

"Very provocative, Henry," he said. "Now let's see some numbers."

"Of course," Henry said. "That would be my pleasure. If I may direct your attention to the screen?"

A colorful pie chart sprang to life as Henry turned the data projector on. Circling the pie chart on the screen with a laser pointer, he began his speech. "We expect a gross revenue of fifty million dollars in the first year after Phase I completion. Triple that when Phase II is complete. We estimate city revenue from our operations to be in the neighborhood of eight million per year, once we get going. Maybe more."

Henry heard a low whistle at the other end of the table. He nodded and said, "Exactly. Please note, ladies and gentlemen, that I have broken down our expected revenue from each of the operations. Casino income, that's the biggest slice at 78 percent." Henry zeroed in on each segment of the pie chart in their turn with the laser pointer. "Hotels and Restaurants, 13 percent; Amusement Park, 7 percent, Ferry, 2 percent." He rattled off the numbers, his words falling like coins from his mouth.

"The current level of gross receipts tax on all Ledford business transactions," he said, advancing the slide on the screen to another pie chart, "is 7.38 percent. The state takes 5.2 percent, leaving 2.18 percent for the city of Ledford. Now, 2.18 percent of 50,000,000 is ..." Henry stopped again to advance the slide, pausing an extra second or two for effect.

In the largest font possible, "$1,090,000.00" glittered and sparkled like a jackpot against a soft background photo of the future Ravenwood Resort.

Jade opened her eyes. Willow B's face was not two inches from hers; his golden eyes seemed to have bored through her sleep. After scratching him behind the ear for a few minutes and listening to his raspy purr, she stretched and sat up. She could hear Russ in the shower.

"We're going to Wilder Island today, Willow B," she said as she put her robe on. "Crow Island is more like it, though. We're going to be in a land trust. I don't know what that means exactly, but I guess we'll find out."

Crow Dreams. Crow Island. Crow Backyard. The little messengers from the beyond, trying to tell me something. Maybe someone is dead. Russ had rolled his eyes at that one. But he had not offered a plausible and scientific explanation for the frequency of crows in her life.

"You live in a city that has a plethora of them," Russ had said. "They're freaking everywhere, hon. And besides, you've been painting them since your childhood, so this is evidently not a sudden phenomenon."

"I rest my case!" Jade cried. "Crows have haunted me my entire life!"

Curiosity overwhelmed her anxiety and fantasies in the end, and she was excited at the opportunity to see the famed island. Besides, Russ would be there. And the Jesuit—he would be there too. Probably the crows liked him, and she would be safe by association, so really there was nothing to worry about. Really.

Clear and blue, the river sparkled in the morning sun. Russ was driving, so Jade could unhook, admire, and even lose herself in the scenery. The newly restored chapel was especially beautiful in the morning shadows. Elegant and silent, its roof a bleached, gray-white tangle of dead branches cradled within the saturated greens of the dense forest under a clear blue sky. *Like a painting.* Jade smiled, thinking of the hundreds if not thousands of Wilder Island paintings flooding the Ledford art market.

"Do you think the Jesuit says Mass for the crows?" she said. "Do they listen to his sermons, or ignore him and think about breakfast, like we do?" She visualized a flock of crows in the chapel. "Do they eat the bread and drink the wine?"

"The Jesuit's name is Alfredo Manzi," Russ said, looking at her sternly. "He is my colleague and my friend. Can you please show a little respect? Please?"

"I promise," Jade said, "I will be the perfect picture of the college professor's elegant wife."

"In your dreams!" Russ said with a grin. "And what a bore! I'll settle for the eccentric yet not totally bonkers wife of the college professor. Think you can manage that?"

"I'll do my best," Jade said with a satyr-like grin.

"I love you, babe," Russ said, shaking his head. "God help me."

He parked the car, and they walked down to the dock where a floating iron forest on pontoons glided soundlessly into one of the slots. "Yo, Russ!" the Captain called out as he tied off the boat. His hat in one hand, he extended the other and invited them to climb aboard and join the red-haired woman seated on one of the benches.

"Hi, I'm Kate Herron," she said, extending a hand. "I'm the attorney for the land trust."

"Nice to meet you," Jade said. "I'm Jade Matthews, and this is my husband, Russ."

"And here comes Sam," Kate said with a grin.

An old, beat up, flesh-colored pickup truck roared into the parking lot, spraying gravel as its driver slammed it to a halt. A window went down, and an arm appeared and opened the door from the outside. A sandy-haired man in tight blue jeans and a red plaid shirt jumped out and hollered, "Morning, Captain! Don't be taking off without me, now!"

He leaped onto the boat, and Jade said, "Sam! I thought I recognized that old truck! You coming to Wilder Island too? For the land trust meeting?"

"I am!" Sam said. "I guess you are too! That really rocks. Hey, Russ! Nice to have you aboard!"

"Thanks," Russ said, shaking Sam's outstretched hand.

Sam put an arm around Kate and gave her a hug as the Captain pushed the boat away from the dock with his wooden oar. Jade admired the beautiful, honey brown wood, finely carved with waterfowl and fish leaping through foamy waves. With a start, she noticed that a crow perched on the railing next to the Captain as he rowed. *I guess that's not too unusual in these waters, next to an island full of crows. But who has one as a pet?*

Russ nudged her arm and pointed upward. Her amazement increased at the full grandeur of the Captain's boat. Tree trunks of wrought iron and chased metal held up a canopy of branches and leaves over their heads, through which flew a few small birds, both real and crafted of metal.

The Captain steered the boat around the northernmost tip of the island and into the quiet waters of an inlet. Alfredo stood on the bank, waiting for the Captain to throw him the rope.

"Thanks, Captain!" he called out after his guests stepped off the boat.

"G'day, Padre." He tipped his hat and shoved off.

"Great day, is it not?" Alfredo reached to shake Russ's hand.

"Alfredo, this is my wife, Jade," Russ said, his other hand on Jade's back.

"Russ has told me about you!" Alfredo said, his hands encasing hers. "You are an artist, a painter, he tells me."

"Yes," Jade said, taken aback at his warmth and sincerity.

"I presume you all met each other on the way over?" They all nodded, and he continued, "Good, good. Jade, I hope you find inspiration here."

"I'm already inspired," Jade said, blushing, "just from the boat ride. The island is so beautiful!"

"She'll have a painting done by Sunday night," Russ said with a grin. "It'll be extraordinary. Tell them about your show, honey."

Jade blushed again and said, "It's a one-person show at Jena McRae's gallery Downtown. I'll send you an invitation to the opening reception. It's next Friday."

"I will be there," Alfredo said. "I know Jena's gallery well."

"Send me one also," Kate said. "I love art shows!"

"Me too, Jade," Sam said. "You know I'm a fan of your work." He winked at her.

"You two know each other then?" Alfredo said, pointing to Jade and Sam.

"We do," Jade said. "We worked on the Urban Art Project the city put on last year. Were you here then? People brought all their discarded metal and stuff, and a group of sculptors, Sam for one, made it into a big art piece for the park next to the Waterfront."

"Yeah," Sam said. "Jade brought the most amazing stuff to the project. It was great fun!"

"Then you are aware of Sam's artistic talents," Alfredo said. "You will be pleased to discover his latest work in the chapel garden!"

As they left the dock, Jade looked back over her shoulder several times, half expecting to see a swarm of crows following her. She heard birdcalls everywhere but saw no crows.

They walked up the embankment and onto a path. "My cottage is just over there," Alfredo said, pointing, "but I will take you the long way around, through the chapel and the gardens."

Where are all the crows? Jade looked all around her and into the tree branches overhead. She stumbled on a rock, and Russ grabbed her hand and directed her attention to the plethora of wildflowers all around them.

"Aren't they gorgeous?" he said. "You'll have to come back with me sometime and paint while I find a whole new flower unknown to mankind."

The chapel roof appeared through the trees, and a few minutes later they stepped into the garden. An assortment of pink-and-white water lilies and irises decorated the pond.

"You must have a green thumb, Alfredo," Russ said. "This is beautiful."

"Thank you," Alfredo said. "I am but a humble gardener."

"Oh my God!" Jade said. "That's incredible!" She turned to Alfredo. "This is what you were talking about! I'd recognize Sam's work anywhere."

A metal sculpture arose from the pond, an unexpected assemblage of the rusted remains of derelict automobiles juxtaposed against shapes cut from discarded stainless steel milk tankers. From any angle, the view was breathtaking, each component an integral part of the whole, in a mosaic of shadows and spaces that reflected in the polished surfaces of the stainless steel. Elegant upward motion suggested the reach for the divine, brought gently back to earth by the mundane decomposition of the rusting junk that once littered the urban landscape.

"Yes," Alfredo answered for Sam, smiling proudly. "This is a very recent addition to the garden. A Sam Howard original. Signed right there." He pointed to the signature carved into the metal base. "I was lucky to find Sam. I hired him to help with the restoration of the chapel. The sculpture in the pond was his idea. It just appeared one day. As if it grew overnight."

Alfredo looked admiringly at the sculpture. "Sam also built my cottage. But as you observe, his true calling is to art."

"I see a giant bird about to take off," Kate said. "Or land—I can't tell which. But I love how you pick up the rubbish of the industrial age and make us forget that it was once all just litter."

"One man's junk," Sam said with a grin, "is another man's art. Modern American artifacts—that's what I call this stuff. It's all over the place. Good thing it's mostly free."

"Sam," Jade said as she walked around the pond, "this is your finest work ever!"

Sam squinted up at the sculpture. "I think so too. I had one of those rare moments we all pray for, when the thing you haven't quite envisioned just rises up and seizes you."

"And you just let it come through," Jade said, nodding. "It has a life of its own almost, and it pulls you along."

"Yep," Sam said. "Like that."

Two crows flew into the garden and perched in a tree near the pond and disappeared into its shadows. Four luminous blue eyes stared down at Jade. She returned to Russ's side and grasped his hand and stole a glance back at the tree. The eyes were still there. Eyes without bodies, hanging like blue globes in the darkness.

"What amazes me, Sam," Russ said as his hand closed around hers, "is how you managed to evoke a green forest using rusty junk metal. It's like portraying the miracle of life using what's essentially road kill."

Sam threw his head back and laughed. "That's a good one, Russ! Urban Roadkill. I'll have to create that one. But yes, that's where I get a lot of my raw material—all along the highways. Car parts, pieces of buildings, farm equipment. Anything metal—gutters, pipes, corrugated siding, old furnaces, air-conditioners. Mufflers and license plates—those are everywhere—but occasionally I pick up something cool like a radiator or an engine fan."

"Very green," Russ said. "I'm impressed, Sam!"

Jade tried desperately to not look at the two crows in the trees. *Why am I so nervous? It's not like they're going to come down and attack me.*

"I'm the queen of recycling," Kate said. "Anyone who picks up rubbish in the landscape is my hero. Especially if they make art with it." She smiled coyly at Sam, who looked down at his feet.

"The chapel is so lovely from the river," Jade said suddenly, hoping Alfredo would get them out of there and away from those eyes. "I can't wait to see it up close, Alfredo! Can we go in?"

"But of course!" he said. "Sam? Would you mind heading over to my cottage and making the coffee? We will be there in fifteen minutes or so."

"Sure thing," Sam said.

"I'll go with him," Kate said. "I've gotten the tour already."

Jade noticed the goofy look on Kate's face when she looked at Sam, who blushed deep red and grinned stupidly at the ground. *Hmmm. Love blossoms on Wilder Island.* She turned back toward the tree where the two crows had been. *They're gone.* Relieved, she turned to follow the others.

"Shall we?" Alfredo said, indicating the direction they should take.

"Greetings, fair lady!" a voice above them said.

At least that's what Jade thought she heard. She slowed down and looked up into the tree under which they walked. A blue-eyed crow stared back. "I beg your pardon?" she said, glancing quickly toward Russ and the others. None of them noticed her or the crow. When she turned back, the crow still gazed down at her.

"Alfredo," Jade said, walking quickly to join him, "Russ told me you have deciphered some crow words, but do they also speak English? I think that crow just spoke to me! Or am I crazy?"

"Careful how you answer that, Alfredo!" Russ said with a grin. "At least the crazy part!"

Alfredo smiled and said, "You are not crazy, Jade! It is possible that the crow spoke to you. They are very intelligent birds and have marvelous vocabularies. I have been able to teach them a few English words here and there as well. What did he say?"

"'Greetings, fair lady,'" Jade said. "At least I think that's what he said."

Alfredo frowned and said, "Interesting. That is not one of the phrases I taught them." He shrugged. "But crows are very magnanimous, and this one could have picked it up anywhere. Many of these crows fly across the water to the city."

"I didn't know crows spoke English," Russ said, one eyebrow

raised. He turned to Jade and said, "Or perhaps I should say, I didn't know you understood crow."

Jade felt her cheeks burn as everyone looked at her, expecting an answer. "I—I don't," she stammered. "I just thought the crow said something. It sounded like English."

"They can be taught to speak a few words of most any language," Alfredo replied. "Just like parrots, though I do believe both birds understand what they are saying."

Jade looked back for the crow as they started along the path to the chapel. It was gone.

HENRY SMILED AT THE HEADS OF THE five city departments that formed the condemnation committee. "Just over one million dollars, folks. And we expect that to double in the first five years." He circled the sparkly numbers with a red laser pointer. "Think about it. Over a million dollars for the city, and all you have to do is condemn Wilder Island and watch the money flow in."

The mayor started to clap, cutting off Henry's conclusion. He was nodding and smiling as he looked around the table. No one else joined his applause.

"Now just a damn minute," the Planning and Zoning Department director said as he smacked the table suddenly with his palm. "Mr. Braun, you've yet to swing this casino park of yours through the permitting process." He gestured toward the extravagant model of Ravenwood Resort. "This is adorable, but how do we know you're not just blowing smoke? Let's see some details. I for one am not going to vote until we see exactly what you plan to do."

Henry watched the mayor sink back into his chair. *The coward!*

"The island won't support a large human population," Environment piped up. "It's full of bogs and swamps and places where the water's found its way down cracks and fractures. You'd have to bring in a mountain of dirt to fill all that in."

"Well," Henry said amiably, "that'll be my problem, now won't it? It's a matter of money and machine. I got both."

"Well, you don't got a building permit," Planning and Zoning said in a vaguely mocking tone.

Henry clamped back the anger that surged up from his gut. *Stay calm!* That's what Jules had said. *Think before you speak. Look out the window, get a drink of water, do something, anything, to keep your cool.*

He reached for his water bottle, and as he took a sip, he noticed the two crows on the windowsill. He thought they looked familiar and then reminded himself that all crows look alike. But he didn't like how they stared at him and wondered if they were bugged.

"And until I see your plans for a sewage treatment facility, and a plan for maintaining safe drinking water and controlling run-off," Environment was saying, "you won't get one. And I suggest, Mr. Mayor, that Mr. Braun be so required to submit some details before we vote. Do you really want an environmental disaster on your hands?"

Henry pulled an exceedingly white handkerchief out of his pockets and wiped the beads of sweat from his forehead. The crows on the windowsill had not broken their gaze. He wished he could throw his shoe at them. *Calm, stay calm.*

"Now, now," the mayor said soothingly, looking toward Henry. "There's no need to come all unraveled here. Mr. Braun has already promised us complete compliance with everything. Isn't that right, Henry?"

"Absolutely!" Henry said, grateful the mayor had come to his aid, finally. "Ravenwood Resort will be eco-friendly. We'll be helping save the environment by using as much timber as we can from the island's own forests."

Henry savored the appalled expression on Environment's face. "And we'll be using the island's natural filtration system—its vast network of underground caves—to filter and process our wastewater. Through these natural wetlands, we'll actually return cleaner water to the river than when we found it!" He smiled broadly all around the model.

"Are you insane, Henry?" Environment said angrily. "You think you're going to pump sewage underground and have it come out as spring water? You'll never fly that by my department without precise and complete code-compliant engineering drawings and—"

A car alarm went off outside the building, its shrill, urgent tone screaming through the open window. Henry licked his lips, trying to stay composed. "Enough!" he wanted to shout. *Careful! Stay calm.* He took a deep breath. It was hard to remain calm, too hard almost, with these simpletons going on and on about such trivia. He clenched his mouth shut tightly.

The alarm suddenly stopped. Henry exhaled and took out his handkerchief again. He wiped the sweat from his forehead and smiled broadly.

"I'm going to hold your feet to the fire on this one, Henry," Planning and Zoning said. This is sewage you're talking about here. You can't just pump it underground or into the river. We need to see how you plan to—"

Henry inhaled slowly and deeply as he counted to ten. Just like Jules had taught him. *Exhale two, three, four, five, six, seven, eight.* He wished he couldn't hear his heart pounding in his ears.

"Gentlemen, gentlemen," he said, smiling with an overly robust pretense of camaraderie. He ignored the sour look on Neighborhood Relations's face. "I intend to fully comply with all your rules, codes, and regs. Have no worries! Trust me! This is just an overview of Ravenwood Resort. I am merely submitting a proposal today."

He turned to the mayor and smiled. *You were supposed to back me up on this one!* "Surely I am not expected to pay the enormous expense of hiring engineers before I have your condemnation?"

"Mr. Braun is correct," the mayor said, nervously shaking his head. "The entire set of engineering drawings isn't required for us to condemn the island under eminent domain. Let's cross that bridge when we come to it! Meanwhile, Mr. Braun has shown us a reasonable proposal of what he intends to do with Wilder Island. Let's continue with the condemnation proceedings, and if the committee so decides, we shall require Mr. Braun to submit the required documentation to build the resort."

"Mr. Mayor," Environment said, "of what use is it to condemn and kick the Jesuits and the birds off the island if he can't come up with a viable plan? Then what? How will you explain that to the people? Some of them, most of them I'll warrant, love the island. You'd best tread carefully here, Mr. Mayor. Mr. Braun must show us he has a viable plan before we vote to condemn."

Henry watched the mayor start to cave, and he resisted the strong temptation to pick up his chair and heave it at the unctuous little weasel. *Calm! Stay calm!* He heard Jules's voice. He looked out the window. *Damn those crows! They're like little spies, watching my every move.*

"Mr. Braun," the mayor said, licking his lips nervously. "You know I'm a supporter of Ravenwood Resort. But these gentlemen speak truthfully. The public is quite sensitive to environmental concerns—issues of water quality and the like. May I remind you, I'm an elected official, and the mayor appoints all the department heads around this table. That is, me. We must tread very delicately here, or the public will flay us alive."

I'll flay you alive, you miserable pantywaist. The two crows on the windowsill smirked at him behind their beaks. He looked away. *Inhale two, three, four ...*

His hand found the switch to the choo-choo, and he flipped it on. The tiny train steamed to life and began its winding way around the island. It calmed him, and he watched it for a few moments, feeling his anxiety diminish. "Folks," he said after a few moments of watching. "Ravenwood Resort has something for everyone—jobs, fun, money. I promise to comply with all building codes and laws. I can say no more to convince you. I'm in your hands."

Silence permeated the room for a few moments, except for the tiny sound of the little choo-choo, cheerfully chugging around the island. Tourism and Economic Development scowled at Planning and Zoning, who glared at Henry. Environment tapped irritably on the table with his pencil. Neighborhood Relations scribbled furiously while Water causally doodled upon their respective covers of their Ravenwood Resort proposals.

Finally the mayor spoke. "Yes, well, thank you, Mr. Braun. Wonderful presentation, just wonderful. The ball is now in our court, my friends, and we'll take this all under advisement. We'll have a decision for you in a week or so, Mr. Braun."

ALFREDO OPENED THE DOOR TO THE chapel, and the roof seized his guests' attention. They gazed upward through the white branches Bruthamax and Hozey wove together, to the blue sky beyond.

NoExit and his family peered down from their nest, and Alfredo nodded to them. He directed Russ and Jade's attention to the singular bench and kneeler in front of the altar. "Marvelous, is it not? The old hermit hacked it from driftwood," he said. "It is held together by railroad spikes. Brother Wilder must have salvaged them from that trestle bridge catastrophe."

"How'd he get the wood so smooth?" Russ said as he stroked the top of the kneeler. "It's like polished stone."

"The river and the sandy beaches did most of it," Alfredo said. "The sun and time did the rest. Evidently Brother Maxmillian picked up whatever lumber he needed from the riverbanks. The timber mill upstream loses a log now and then, and many end up here."

Jade wandered to the place where Alfredo had found Brother Maxmillian's remains. "Whatever happened to the old hermit?" she asked. "Did he die here on the island?"

"Yes," Alfredo answered. "His bones were in here the first time I visited, just about where you're standing, Jade."

She looked at him with a stricken expression and then down at the floor, as if she expected to see the old hermit's bones.

"They were picked clean and pure white," Alfredo said as he walked over to where she stood. "I collected them all and gave him a proper funeral. His grave is outside."

Jade shut her eyes tightly, shaking her head murmuring, "No, no, no."

"I am so sorry!" Alfredo said, taking her arm and moving her away from the spot. He handed her off to Russ. "I did not mean to upset you." *What a strange woman she is. And Russ is so straight-laced and down-to-earth.*

"You didn't upset me," Jade said weakly, sagging against Russ. "I just thought for a moment I saw his dead body, and several crows and ravens were eating him." She shivered. "They all had these really cold blue eyes. I had a dream about one, and it—"

"My wife has an extremely vivid imagination," Russ said, interrupting her. "Sometimes it gets the better of her."

Blue-eyed crows and ravens eating Brother Max's flesh! That was not her imagination. How did she know? Is she clairvoyant? Though abashed that he, a scientist, would entertain such a thought, he couldn't think how else she would know. He recalled her claim in the garden that a crow had said, "Greetings, fair lady!" He looked at her closely. *I wonder, is she Patua'?*

"That is an interesting anomaly about the crows on the island, Jade," he said. "Crows are born with blue eyes, like human babies. But in the vast majority of cases, their eyes turn black or brown as soon as they're ready to leave the nest. Except for this island. For some reason, a lot of crows' eyes stay blue all their lives."

"Really?" Russ said. "That's interesting. But I suppose not entirely surprising that a genetic enclave exists here, considering the island is cut off from the mainland."

"Indeed," Alfredo said. "While it is a short fly for these birds, and many leave for new territories elsewhere, evidently enough have stayed on the island to keep those blue eyes in the gene pool. I am quite charmed by them."

"Well I'm not," Jade said. "I keep dreaming of crows. And they're not very nice."

Alfredo looked at Russ with raised eyebrows. Russ merely shrugged, shook his head, and rolled his eyes.

"Alfredo," Russ said, looking up at the roof, "it must get pretty wet in here when it rains."

"It does," Alfredo said. "Sam and I wove a few more branches in, to keep it slightly drier in here than it was. I do not have to be here during increment weather, however. The Good Lord will accept our prayers anywhere."

"Do you say Mass here?" Jade said suddenly. "Does anyone come?"

"Every Sunday," the priest said, "at dawn. No humans, of course, but a few birds usually attend—crows mostly. Saying Mass in this chapel is more like a meditation. I do miss a congregation, I suppose. But you are welcome anytime if ever you wish to attend."

"Perhaps," Russ said. "This place reminds me of my altar-boy days somehow. Don't ask me why."

As they left the chapel, Jade gasped. Dozens of black birds perched on the chapel roof, and many more were on the ground, walking or pecking. "Oh my God," she said, "what are they doing here?"

Alfredo laughed and said, "They live here! They noticed I had visitors and are curious. They will not harm you."

Jade skirted around the other side of her husband, avoiding even a glance at the crows hanging around the chapel.

Sam and Kate had coffee made and the table set with cups, plates, and a large platter of cookies when Alfredo arrived at the cottage with Russ and Jade. "Sit down, everyone," Alfredo said, gesturing toward the small table. "It will be a bit tight, but we are all friends."

After they were seated nearly elbow-to-elbow, Jade pointed to the fob on the end of the lamp chain and said to Russ in a whisper, "Look at that!"

"Look at what?" Alfredo said, as he brought a carafe of coffee to the table. "Oh, yes, is it not marvelous? I found it in the chapel. I think it must have belonged to Brother Maxmillian."

"Jade has one almost exactly like it," Russ said. Jade nudged him to be quiet. "Show it to him, honey!"

"You have a similar piece?" Alfredo asked. "May I see it?"

He put his hand out, and his sudden interest made Jade recoil. Russ nudged and her said, "C'mon, honey, show it to him. No one's going to take it from you."

"What is it?" Kate asked.

Reluctantly, Jade drew out her medallion on its leather cord and held it up to Alfredo without taking it off. "It was my mother's," she said, her hands shaking. "At least that's what I've always believed. I never knew her, so I don't really know."

Alfredo held Jade's medallion carefully. "They're astonishingly similar," he said, dropping both. "What a delightful mystery that we each have one!"

Jade dropped the medallion back under her shirt and blurted out, "I have dreams about crows all the time, mostly scary ones, but sometimes my mother is in them too. One time I thought the crows were trying to steal this, and I've been hiding it from them ever since."

"Interesting," Alfredo said. He felt a certain kinship with her, but he wondered why she was so reluctant to show him her orb.

"What is it?" Kate asked again, taking the fob at the end of the lamp chain into her hand. "It feels like stone, yet it's so delicately carved."

Sam took a turn examining the fob. He tapped it against his teeth and said, "It's definitely wood. A very hard wood. Can't tell what kind, though."

"You said you found it in the chapel?" Russ asked.

"Yes," Alfredo said. "Under the old hermit's bones. Evidently he wore it around his neck."

Jade made a distasteful face and looked out the window. Alfredo poured coffee into everyone's cups. *Was Jade's mother Patua'? Why else would she have had an orb? If her mother was Patua'...*

Jade reached for the cookie platter and took two. After a few bites, she said, "Alfredo! These are wonderful! Where did you get them?"

"I baked them," Alfredo said with a smile as he sat down, "in my easy-bake solar oven!"

The others laughed uproariously. "Seriously?" Jade asked. "You baked them? I had no idea you were so talented." She bit into her second cookie.

"I love to bake," Alfredo said. "My grandmother taught me when I was a boy. I used to help her bake pies at Christmas, and dinner rolls every Sunday. I bake the Communion wafers for St. Sophia's to supplement my generous stipend from the Jesuits."

"Truly a man of many talents," Kate said. "Priest, scholar, baker. Who knew?"

She pulled her briefcase up to the table and opened it, saying, "All right then. Welcome, board of directors of the Friends of Wilder Island Land Trust! As you all know, the Padre and I hammered out the land trust in the last couple weeks. Here are the bylaws and the articles of incorporation." She tossed several spiral-bound booklets onto the table.

"First, a little history," she said. "Henry Braun approached the Jesuits to buy the island, and we turned him down. But that hasn't stopped him."

"What does he want to do with the island?" Jade asked.

"He wants to turn it into a casino resort park," Alfredo said. "Evidently he is not happy with his current wealth."

"Wow," Sam said. "He lives in a freaking mansion, has a chauffeur drive him around in his Bentley, and he wants more. What a pig!"

"Even as we speak," Kate was saying, "he's presenting a proposal to the mayor and certain city department heads, asking them to condemn the island as a nuisance—what did he call it, Padre?"

"Fallow," Alfredo said. "And derelict."

The fob on the lamp chain swayed slightly as if in protest. Jade finished her second cookie and grabbed another off the plate. She looked around the table. Everyone else was still working on cookie number one. She put the third cookie on her plate and put her hands in her lap, hoping the others had not noticed what a pig she was.

Russ shook his head, frowning. He reached across the table for a cookie. "But how can he do that? The Jesuits said they wouldn't sell."

"He's using the eminent domain laws," Kate said, "to force us to sell the island to him. But, he won't succeed, at least not this time. The land trust is a done deal, as of yesterday morning at 8:13 a.m., thanks to all of you for doing the electronic signature thing on the Internet."

Jade took two quick bites from her cookie and put it back on her plate. She chewed slowly, trying to savor every bite. Trying to not think too much about the remaining cookies on the platter.

"Thanks to you, Kate," Alfred said. "I am impressed and amazed at how quickly you got the land trust drawn up and filed. I just hope this land trust will be enough to stop Henry Braun."

"What's eminent domain?" Sam asked, dunking his cookie into his coffee.

Two more cookies on the plate. *Russ has had two now, Kate two, Sam two. Me three.* She glanced at Alfredo's plate. He had not finished his first.

"It's a right guaranteed to the government," Kate said, waving her cookie as she spoke, "to condemn and sell private property to another individual for the purpose of development. Up until recently, it was only used to acquire property for roads and public buildings. But now, eminent domain is a tool to condemn private property for private commercial development, though this is flabbergasting to the vast majority of us."

"But what about the Jesuits?" Russ asked. "Will they let us make a land trust out of their island?"

Jade studied her cookie, resisting the urge to cram it into her mouth. One of the chocolate chips had melted in the oven and hardened into a shape that resembled a crow in flight. *Oh God, stop it!* She bit the crow off and ate it.

"The Jesuits donated the island to the land trust," Alfredo said. "It was the Father Provincial's idea to do this. In fact, the whole land trust was his idea. Things might have turned out a lot differently had Henry Braun not been so annoying. It just really irked Majewski—the idea of anyone tearing down a consecrated Jesuit chapel to build a casino."

Jade finished off her third cookie and drained her coffee cup. Sam took the second-to-last-cookie from the plate.

"And even when I told him," Kate said, laughing, "that the island would probably be assessed at upward of Henry's original offer of five million dollars, his reply was something like: 'Henry Braun could offer me the golden gates of hell, and I'd still rather see our chapel and nothing but several thousand crows on Wilder Island.'"

I thought heaven had the golden gates. Oh, wait. Pearly gates. Hell's gates are more valuable than heaven's?

"Speaking of the chapel," Jade said, "what will become of it?" She poured herself another cup of coffee from the carafe, wondering if someone was going to take that last cookie.

"The Jesuits will keep ownership of the chapel and the small plot of land it sits on," Alfredo said. "And I will say Mass every morning to my congregation of crows, same as I do now."

"But, Kate," Russ said, looking up from the proposal, "wouldn't it be easier to fight eminent domain if the Church still owns the whole island? Aren't churches immune?"

Jade tried to ignore the last cookie. She looked out the window. A crow flew by, shrieking, "Give me a cookie!" Startled, she glanced at Alfredo. Did he hear it?

"Legally," Kate said, "nothing can stop it—not even the Catholic Church. A land trust can't stop eminent domain either. We can only prescribe what will be done with our island if we're forced to sell it." She picked the last cookie off the platter, broke it in two, and returned one half to the plate.

So that's how you do it! Just take half! Jade resisted pouncing on the other half.

"But, how can this be?" Russ asked, aghast. "How can the city condemn private property, for God's sake? For a gambling resort? That's just wrong. And there's nothing we can do?"

"We're not complete victims," Kate said. "We can fight back."

Russ reached past her, took the last cookie off the platter, broke it, popped one piece in his mouth, and left the other on the plate.

Dang! I should've made my move. She wondered how many times the cookie could be broken in two.

"We have some protections built into the land trust," Kate said, "that'll make it hard for him to build his casino. But if he wins the eminent domain battle, he'll still fight us tooth and nail to thwart the intent of the land trust. And he's got a lot more money than the five of us combined will ever see."

Jade's resistance broke down, and she snatched the last quarter of the last cookie and popped it into her mouth, all in one piece.

Alfredo went to the kitchen area and brought back a plastic container. He opened it and refilled the cookie platter. Jade reached over and took one, followed by Russ, Sam, and Kate.

"Does anyone want more coffee?" he asked with an amused smile. Everyone shook their heads, and he sat back down.

"What about endangered species?" Sam asked through a mouthful of cookie. "Or a wilderness designation? Can't we go that route too?"

Alfredo shook his head, but before he could speak, Kate said, "First we would need to get a Wilder Island animal on the endangered species list."

"Aren't the blue-eyed crows unusual?" Russ asked, turning to Alfredo. "Have you ever heard of a population of crows with blue eyes anywhere else?"

"No," Alfredo said. "But even so, it is difficult to imagine convincing anyone that crows of any eye color are an endangered species."

"Too bad crows can't talk, eh?" Kate said. She winked at Alfredo. "That'd get us on the list pronto!"

Alfredo stared at the attorney. *Does she know?* He had met with Kate a few times since Majewski left and wondered if he had told her. *Surely she would have let on by now.*

"They do talk, actually," Russ said, waving a cookie at Kate. "Alfredo has discovered they have a rich and varied vocabulary."

"Do tell!" Kate said, a wicked smile on her face. "I have long thought that all the animals have some form of language. If only we could understand it."

Jade nodded in agreement, and Sam stared at Alfredo with a fearful look.

"The corvid have an extensive vocabulary," Alfredo said with what he hoped was a relaxed smile. "As richly varied as any human language, I think. They have a significantly more intricate language than we humans give them credit for. As do many other animal species."

Sam visibly relaxed as Kate nodded. "That's true," she said. "We assume we're alone at the top of the evolutionary heap, when in fact we have merely clawed our way to the top of the food chain. And we're not alone there either."

"We're our own predators," Russ said. "What other species can make that claim?"

"Black widow spiders can," Sam said.

"But they eat their prey, Sam!" Kate said with a grin. "Humans just kill each other."

"Speaking of predators," Sam said, "this whole eminent domain thing seems like human preying on human to me. I mean, this is America, isn't it? And we're supposed to just roll over, let the government take away our private property, and hand it over to the highest bidder? I just can't stomach it."

Alfredo remembered his conversation with Charlie about property and ownership. *"You cannot own anything you cannot carry ..." Perhaps the corvids are right. All this fuss about ownership. In the end, the Earth owns itself. We borrow pieces of it and entertain greedy illusions that it is ours.*

"Hardly anyone can," Kate said. "That's the main advantage we have; public opinion on our side, whether or not people approve of the casino park."

"We need to rally the folks of Ledford to our cause," Kate continued after taking a bite of cookie and washing it down with a gulp of coffee. "So, we need a brand, a logo." She turned to Jade. "You think you can come up with one for us?"

"I can!" Jade said.

"A brand?" Alfredo asked, blinking and frowning. "Why do we need a brand? We're not selling anything."

"Indeed we are, Padre," Kate said. "We're selling an idea. We want to get the folks of Ledford stirred up and rally around a place they will never see, if we have our way."

"Never underestimate the power of the brand," Sam said.

"Right," Kate said, throwing a quick grin at him, "Wilder Island is part of the history of this city, a legacy that's owned by everyone. That's the only way people, religious or otherwise, have beaten eminent domain condemnation."

"It's true," Jade said. "Ledford loves Wilder Island. People have developed a whole relationship to it, almost like a religion, or at least a mythology. I doubt many will want to see it paved over with slot machines and hotels."

Alfredo looked out the window at his private Garden of Eden. He hoped that the people of Ledford would support the island remaining intact and not need to come see for themselves what they were protecting. *I do not want to share it with anyone.* He scolded himself for his selfishness. But it was the truth.

"That's our point," Kate said, nodding. "That the island is neither fallow nor derelict. But beyond all that, Wilder Island represents the heart and history of Ledford. That's how we fight Henry Braun's eminent domain project."

The Friends of Wilder Island Land Trust spent the rest of the afternoon discussing ways in which to engage the people of Ledford to rally to their cause. Just before sunset, they heard a bell ring from the direction of the inlet.

"That is the Captain," Alfredo said, "coming to take you home."

12

Catching the Wind

"**H**usband!" Rika shrieked as she dropped to the tree house deck. "JoEd's flown off again! I just don't know what to do with him! He won't mind, he won't listen." She paced back and forth, flapping her wings. "Every single time I turn my back, he's gone. I cannot keep my eyes upon him every second! He's not the only fledgling I have to look after!"

"He's a chip off the old block, my love," Charlie said, following her around the deck. "My mother pulled her feathers out over me, too. The nest has gotten too small for him, I reckon. But let me take him off your wings for the rest of the day. I'll show him a bit of the outside world."

Charlie flew off looking for his errant son and found him on the riverbank. Though a plethora of dead fish and other delectables littered the river's edge, JoEd was not interested. His eyes were upon the city across the river. Charlie knew that look; he'd had it himself. *Our JoEd will be leaving us soon. I must prepare Rika.*

"Zazu!" JoEd cried when he saw Charlie. "I wanted to see what was beyond the nest, and I flapped my wings one or two times, and here I am! Look at that!" He pointed a wing toward Downtown. "Someday I want to go there, Zazu!"

Charlie grinned at little JoEd and said, "And someday you will. But today, let's fly all the way around Cadeña-l'jadia."

As father and son flew off together, Charlie remembered how his curiosity had nibbled away at his common sense when he was JoEd's age. Thank the Orb his mother sent him to Starfire when she did. *JoEd should begin his training soon; no use letting all that energy go to waste.*

"This is Cadeña-l'jadia," Charlie told JoEd as they rose above the treetops of the island. "Your homeland and your heritage."

They flew around the southern tip of the island and headed up-river toward the bird sanctuary, a very popular place for not only migratory birds, but island and city birds as well. Charlie and JoEd landed in a tree and watched the panorama in front of them.

Shorebirds of all sizes littered the shallow quiet water; waders, fishers, skimmers, and a dozen or so white pelicans fished from the bank. Rowdy groups of crows and magpies flew in and out of the trees that lined the banks, swooping down from time to time to catch a mouthful of fish the pelicans inadvertently let fall out of their beaks. A group of loons played a noisy game of splash-tag, beating the placid water into a tempest as they belted out insults to each other in melancholy voices. Waves fanned out in all directions and struck the shorelines with a slurping sound.

"Nice job Jayzu did, eh, JoEd?" Charlie said to his son.

"What did he do, Zazu?" JoEd asked.

"Well, he and his friends moved some boulders around a bit so that this large pool would form and all these birds would have a place to feed and hang out."

"Why did they do that, Zazu?"

"Jayzu loves birds," Charlie said. "He is Patua', like Bruthamax was. He knows this island belongs to birds."

Father and son flapped their way to the edge of the pool, where they both found more than enough morsels of fish to fill their stomachs. "Shall we?" Charlie said, gesturing toward the sky with his head.

"Let's!" JoEd jumped into flight, following Charlie as he flapped up to the limestone cliffs. Vertical and horizontal fractures split the cliff face, creating rectangular patterns of rock and shadows. They came to a landing on a ledge near a great fissure in the cliff wall. "I can feel air coming out!" he said, his beak turned toward the dark cleft in the rock.

"There are many caves in these cliffs, JoEd," Charlie said. "They go way back underneath the island—and some are joined together by tunnels. Bruthamax lived in these caves during the cold time of year. But he used them year-round to travel back and forth between his tree house and his other house on the other end of the island."

They watched a raven glide into an upside-down V-shaped crack in the cliff. "Is there a nest in there?" JoEd asked.

"Probably not this time of year," Charlie said. "Though the ravens roost in these cliffs year-round. But don't go looking for them! They like their privacy and won't take kindly to a young crow sticking his beak where it doesn't belong."

Charlie leaped off the cliff flapping his wings, and JoEd followed. As they flew out over the river, the sight of Downtown in the morning sunlight captured JoEd's attention, and he could not take his eyes off it.

"That is where your mother hatched, fledged, and lived until I brought her to Cadeña-l'jadia," Charlie said, dipping a wing toward Downtown. "See those green trees over there, next to that really tall building? That's where your weebs and I met."

He remembered how Rika had knocked him beak-over-feathers the first time he had ever laid eyes on her. She was a beauty. Fredrika Eliza Katarzyna Antonina Stump was her given name, but she was known to everyone simply as Rika. It was love at first sight. When Rika called his tune, he came dancing.

JoEd could hardly take his eyes off the sparkling jewel across the water as they continued their journey upriver. On and on, flying close to the sheer limestone cliffs that rose right up out of water. Father and son played in the gentle, capricious winds that blew constantly downriver from the north.

"Watch me, Zazu!" JoEd said as he caught an updraft.

Charlie shouted, "No! JoEd! No!" But it was too late.

"Whooooaaaaa!" JoEd cried out as he shot upward like a rock from a slingshot.

"JoEd!" Charlie shouted, looking all around for his wayward son. "JoEd!"

But there was no sign of the young crow.

JoEd struggled for consciousness. A large black figure hovered over him, but he just couldn't focus on it. *That's one big raven.* Struggling to his feet, still woozy from having the wind knocked out of him, JoEd realized this was no raven, but a human all dressed in black, except for the streak of white hair on his head. *He must have some corvid in him. He looks like Starfire.*

He cast a blue eye upward at the beakless black bird above him. JoEd's head cleared, and he leaped to his feet as he cried out, "Jayzu! It's me, JoEd!" He put out a wing in greeting.

"JoEd!" Jayzu said as he brushed his hand across JoEd's feathers. "Grawky! You are a long way from the tree house."

"I am!' JoEd said, puffing up his chest. "My zazu and I flew all the way here!" He stopped for a moment and shook his head. "Wait a minute! Where's my zazu? We were just looking at the raven cliffs! Where did he go? How did I get here?"

"Well, I do not know, JoEd," Jayzu said. "You just fell out of the sky."

JoEd looked confused for a few moments. "Ohhh," he said, nodding his head. "I remember now. I was riding a jaloosie. Which way are the cliffs, Jayzu? I need to find my zazu!"

"That way," Jayzu pointed. "It is not far."

JoEd flew up over the trees. The river shimmered blue and white in the afternoon sun and in the distance, he saw a single black speck flying back and forth. "Zazu!" he shouted and flapped his wings as hard as he could.

"Zazu!" he called out as he flew until Charlie was close enough to hear him.

"JoEd " Charlie said angrily as they met in the sky. He smacked his son with a wing, nearly knocking him out of the sky. "You scared the beezle out of me! Where in the Orb have you been?"

"I'm sorry, Zazu," JoEd said. "The jaloosie flung me all the way to Jayzu's house!"

"Jaloosies can turn you into jelly," Charlie said sternly. "Especially the ones along the raven cliffs—they're killers, and you should stay away from them. Let me show you a couple of tricks, but let's get away from the cliffs."

JoEd and Charlie continued flying upriver, following the riverbank. They cut across the little inlet and rounded it. "The jaloosies here are not as wild," Charlie said as he caught one and whooshed upward. He flipped himself out of the thermal and returned to JoEd's side.

"Now you try it," Charlie said. "Jump in like normal, but don't let the jaloosie grab you! Get right back out. Like this!" He jumped into another jaloosie and somersaulted out of it in a mass of feather and beak that somehow righted itself into JoEd's otherwise unruffleable Zazu.

"Try it!" Charlie said.

JoEd leaped into the jaloosie and felt it tumble him backward, but he did not let it take hold of him. He darted sideways, shrieking as he tumbled tail over beak.

"After you practice awhile," Charlie said, "you can do more than one flip-out. Watch this!" He rolled into the jaloosie, which spun him around like a top before releasing him.

"I want to do that!" JoEd cried out. He jumped in the way Charlie had and laughed all the way through four revolutions. "Wow! Zazu!"

"Hey there, Flyboy," Charlie called out after a few more spins in the jaloosies. "Let's go home! Your mother is probably imagining us both dead somewhere."

"Okay, Zazu," JoEd said. The young crow looked down at the island as they winged homeward. "Look! There's the tree house, Zazu! It is so small!"

Catching the Wind opened with eighteen of Jade's paintings at Jena McCray's eclectic gallery in Downtown Ledford. Jena's place attracted a broad range of buying clientele. The reception she put together was incredible—simple and elegant, with enough wine to get people talking and loosen their checkbooks, but not so much as to promote accidental drunkenness.

Russ was enormously handsome in his tux, and Jade was touched that he was so willing to put on the dog for her night. Nibbling nervously on one of the exquisite canapés Jena had provided, she could hardly catch her breath. So many people wanted to talk to her, tell her how much they loved her work, how it spoke to them in ways that art never had before. *And here I thought this would be my final, solitary journey into the bourgeois.*

"Jade, dahling, it's so mah-velous to see you. Mwa. Mwa." A woman with penciled-in eyebrows and flaming red hair had appeared, kissing the air in front of each of Jade's ears.

"Hello, Twyla," Jade said, smiling as cordially as she could. Twyla Spitzwater was the art critic for the *Sentinel*, well known for her scathingly sarcastic articles.

"She likes being known as eccentric," Jena had told her before the reception, "without actually being so. In her youth, she was very attractive, but alas, Twyla is a woman who cannot bear to age gracefully. She's going kicking and screaming."

"Speaking of bourgeois," Russ said into his wine glass. Jade jabbed him in the ribs with her elbow.

"I'm so glad you could make it to my opening," Jade said.

She tried not to stare at Twyla's outlandish appearance. Her overly dyed hair had taken on the texture of a bird's nest, and a layer of powdery makeup caked heavily on her cheeks only called more attention to her undulating wrinkles. Impossibly thick false eyelashes looked like caterpillars above her eyelids. Her lips were painted a brick-red color, outlined in black.

"Tell me about *Catching the Wind*," Twyla said as she sipped her wine and looked at Jane over tinted glasses shaped like cat's eyes. "Why that title?"

"I took a hiatus from painting for several years," Jade said. "Most of the paintings in this show are the first gust, so to speak, since I've returned to painting. The wind that used to drive me still blows. I'm trying to catch it."

"Interesting," Twyla said. She pinched a morsel off her plate between long, spiky fingernails painted to match her lips and plopped it quickly into her mouth. "Would you hold this a moment, dear?" She handed Jade her canapé plate and wine glass as she scribbled a few notes in a small pad. She looked back up at Jade over her glasses. "And why had you stopped painting?"

Jade felt like she was being probed for a soft spot, a sign of weakness. She didn't want to tell Twyla that she had been in a state most of the world would call temporary insanity. Or that she had quit eating and sleeping and wandered nomadically through foggy memories and dreams.

"I stopped hearing the wind." Jade hoped that would be enough. Twyla nodded and scribbled some more in her pad.

"And why did you stop hearing the wind?"

"Isn't Jade the most exciting artist we've seen in a long time?" Jena said as she put her face in between Jade and Twyla. "It is so unusual," she continued, "to sell half the show at the artist's reception. Especially a new artist on the scene. Don't you agree, Twyla?"

"Indeed," Twyla said as if she thought the opposite. "I always love to introduce new talent to the community."

"That was the purpose of having her show at my gallery," Jena said sweetly. "I hope you'll give Jade a nice write-up in your column on Sunday. Meanwhile, forgive me for interrupting, but several of my customers want to meet Jade. I am afraid, Twyla, that I must steal her from you."

Jade handed the wine glass and canapé plate back to Twyla, and Jena whisked her away. "You are a smash hit, my dear!" Jena said as they left Twyla scowling. "She likes your work, I can tell that. And you too. It'll be interesting to see what she writes in her column on Sunday. But promise me you will not take anything negative she might have to say personally, okay? She'll throw some darts at me, but I don't care what she thinks. It's my gallery. And I'm ecstatic."

Jade nodded, wondering why anyone would not like Jena. Her gallery was fabulous, and she was very successful.

A wealthy client of Jena's, a woman in her fifties, stood before *Catching the Wind*, the title painting of the show. "Gabriella, let me introduce Jade Matthews, the artist," Jena said.

The woman turned and gushed enthusiastically as she took Jade's hand. "I'm so pleased to meet you! I just love your paintings, Ms. Matthews. The colors and the richness! I can just feel the crisp air in this one.' She gestured toward *Catching the Wind*. "I can almost hear the wind blowing those leaves along the pavement! I don't know how you do it!"

"Thank you," Jade said. "I heard it too—the wind. I'm glad to know it comes through."

"Oh," Gabriella said, "it does. I've never experienced anything like it from a painting. You are uniquely talented, Ms. Matthews."

"Perhaps you should hang it next to this one," Jena said, directing the woman's attention to *Leave Me*. "The two together would be lovely, don't you think?"

Leave Me, a playful celebration of leaves falling from trees, leaves blowing around, and leaves collecting on doorsteps, captured the vivid reds and yellows of the summer sun. Leaves fell from their trees, playfully riding the winds of fall, oblivious to the coming winter's death.

"But that means I must buy two!" the woman said.

"Exactly!" Jena said, and both women laughed.

Jade laughed too, though nervously.

"Well," Gabriella said, "they do look lovely together. All right! You talked me into it, Jena! I was going to buy another one anyway—that sweet little one of the crows dancing around the birdbath—but my husband absolutely loathes crows, and I'm afraid I would never get it into the house. How much do I owe you?"

Alfredo walked from the docks at the Waterfront where the Captain had left him to Jena's gallery on Pomegranate Street. When he arrived, several dozen people chatted while helping themselves to the food and drink. He walked in and stopped dead in his tracks, chilled to the bone by the face in the painting across the room.

It is Charlotte ...

The eyes dragged him forward, eventually. Painted with the palest hues of pink, blue, and green, those eyes pulled him into the patterns and promises of another world on the other side. He stood before her, enthralled and astonished. He wanted to get closer and closer, dive into them, bask in days of warm sunshine and nights of star-sprinkled heaven.

He looked at the title of the painting. *Ave, Madre.*

Hail, Mother. Jade's mother, Charlotte. Of course. Though she doesn't look anything like her. He turned and scanned the crowd, trying to find Jade.

"Father Manzi!" Jena cried out, waving as she approached with Jade. "What a pleasure to see you!" She gave the priest a quick hug and said, "Please let me introduce the artist, Jade Matthews."

"Alfredo!" Jade said and took his hand. "I'm so happy that you came! Russ is here somewhere, as are Sam and Kate."

"Here I am!" Sam said. "And here's Kate!" Jade greeted Kate with a hug and Sam with a playful punch to the shoulder.

Alfredo said, "My pleasure, Jade."

"I see you all know each other," Jena said.

"Yes, I know Sam from way back," Jade said. "But Alfredo and I have only recently met. He's a colleague of my husband's in the biology department at the university. But I had no idea he's an art collector!"

And I had no idea Charlotte is your mother. Alfredo felt suddenly lightheaded and inhaled slowly, trying to keep his thoughts from running away. *And you are Patua', of course! The crow spoke to you in the chapel garden, not in English, but Patua'!*

"One of my gallery's best clients!" Jena said.

"When St. Sophia's was remodeled," Alfredo said, "they needed new paintings of the Stations of the Cross. Jena helped me find interested artists. I simply recommended them to the monsignor."

"Oh, you're too modest!" Jena said, giving Alfredo a gentle shove. "That was quite the largesse for a number of our local artists. But aren't Jade's paintings just fabulous?" She turned and gazed at *Ave, Madre*. "I feel like I'm gazing into my own mother's eyes."

Alfredo looked again at *Ave, Madre* and then back at Jade. Her blonde, curly hair and green eyes did not remind him in the least of Charlotte's pale gray eyes and long, straight black hair. But there was something about her face that did.

"This one's my favorite," Sam said, gesturing toward the painting next to *Ave, Madre*. "*Winter Wonderland*. You got amazing depth in just two dimensions, Jade. Incredible."

A sunbeam coming through a window illuminated the particulate matter floating in the air. The rich, exquisite surface of many brush strokes pulled the viewer into the warm light, where images of flowers and dragonflies floated on warm, lazy breezes.

"That's what the world outside my studio looked like one day last winter," Jade said. "There was this amazing sunbeam. The contrast was exquisite—the sparkling clear landscape covered with snow outside, and a mosaic of color in the dust particles of the sunbeam inside. I couldn't resist."

"Truly superb, Jade," Alfredo said. "I feel like I am gently falling through stardust. You manage to evoke many senses beyond the visual."

"*Willow B*," Kate said, pointing across the gallery to the painting of a gray cat. "That's my fave. It's like you can almost walk into it; the mounds of fur seem like trees. Oh! And the little critters running around everywhere. I just love them!"

Jena excused herself to attend to a refreshment issue. Sam and Kate wandered off toward *Willow B*, leaving Alfredo and Jade alone.

"You truly have a gift," Alfredo said to Jade. "Your paintings are simply magnificent." He turned toward *Ave, Madre*. "She is your mother?"

"I don't know who my mother was," Jade said with a shrug, facing her painting. "This woman is from my imagination. Or perhaps one of my dreams. I was an orphan, and you know what they say about us—always looking for our quote-unquote real parents."

"I am sorry, Jade. Losing your mother must have been difficult," Alfredo said. "We all long for the Holy Mother who nurtures us all. Perhaps orphans feel her presence more acutely than the mothered."

Jade shrugged again. "I never knew her. I was a foundling, as they say. She's my fantasy mother." She pointed at her painting. "My real mother left me in the woods in a basket with nothing but a blanket. And that strange medallion like the one you have." She smiled without joy. "To haunt me."

Alfredo touched her arm sympathetically. *Yes, Jade, your mother had one of the orbs. And she is Patua'. As you are.*

"Fortunately, there was a happy ending," Jade said with a smile as she patted his hand on her arm. "I was raised by foster parents whose love and nurturing are one reason I'm here today in this gallery full of my paintings. And Russ is the other."

"Other what?" Russ said, suddenly appearing by Jade's side.

"My other husband," Jade said with a wicked smile. "I was just confessing my bigamy to Father Alfredo."

Alfredo laughed and said, "Jade was telling me how grateful she was to have such a supportive and nurturing husband."

Jena McCrae strode toward them and pulled Jade away. Without apology, she said over her shoulder, "Sorry, gents. Another sale on the horizon!"

Russ wandered off toward the refreshment tables, leaving Alfredo alone. He strolled through the gallery, admiring Jade's paintings and mentally arranging his finances in consideration of purchasing *Ave, Madre*. He spotted Kate by herself in front of a large painting and walked over to her.

"Jade's so talented," Kate said as they stood together in front of *Falling Backward*. "She said this came from a dream she had about falling from the sky into a pool of water."

"Yes, she is," Alfredo agreed. "She is gifted with a sight most of us do not have."

"Thank God for artists, eh?" Kate said.

"Indeed." He looked over his shoulder, making sure no one approached. "Kate, I need some lawyerly advice. How would one go about getting someone released from Rosencranz?"

"The mental hospital?" Kate asked, raising her eyebrows.

"Yes."

"Okay," she said slowly. "And who may I ask wants whom released?"

"I do," Alfredo said. "She is a friend of mine."

"And why do you want her released?"

"Because she is not crazy."

"Then why is she there?" Kate asked.

"As far as I can tell," Alfredo said, hesitating before replying, "it is just a language issue. She cannot speak English."

Kate looked at him intently. "Can we go outside and chat, Padre? I'm in sudden need of fresh air."

Alfredo followed her out the door and onto the sidewalk. "Truth time, Padre," she said. "What exactly is this language issue?" When he didn't answer, she bit her lower lip and nodded slowly. "I see. It's the language of the crows, isn't it?"

He stared at her in shock. *Did Majewski show her Bruthamax's letter? Did Sam tell her?*

"For God's sake," Kate said, "I'm not an idiot. Do you think I can't put two and two together? 'The corvid have an extensive vocabulary'—your own words, no?"

Several people came out the door of the gallery. Kate started walking down the street, pulling on Alfredo's sleeve. "Padre," she said. "I know. I know about you. I know about Sam. And I know about the Captain. So, drop this charade, okay?"

"B-but, how?"

"I suspected as much," she said. "But Sam told me."

"Sam told you?" Alfredo felt deflated, his façade breached.

"Yes," she said. "I forced it out of him. First I tricked him into telling me about you." She laughed at Alfredo's shocked expression. "Oh, stop! I'm a lawyer; that's what we do!"

Kate took his arm, and they walked slowly back to the gallery. "And then he let it slip that he'd been to the island once before you hired him."

Alfredo nodded. "He mentioned that to me too, but he did not seem to want to talk about it."

They stopped at a traffic light and waited for the pedestrian light. A paper cup flew out of a passing car, striking a vehicle parked next to the curb. "Got one!" a voice yelled as the brown liquid dripped off the hood.

"People!" Kate said shaking her head. "No freaking manners."

The light turned, and they stepped into the street.

"Sam brought his twin sister's boyfriend Andy, whom we know as the Captain, to the island a few years ago," she said after they had crossed. "Sam's father had beat him dearly to death before throwing him in the river to drown."

Alfredo stopped and stared at Kate. "Oh, dear Lord!" he gasped. "the Captain? But why?"

Kate nodded. "Sam's sister was pregnant with his child. She hung herself, thinking Andy was dead."

Alfredo gritted his teeth against the surge of anger in his chest, and his eyes burned with hot, stinging tears he would not let fall. He cried out in anguish, "God Almighty, can there be no end to the suffering of your innocent children?"

"I know," Kate said as she looked up at him. She took his hand and led him to a bench on the sidewalk. They sat side by side in silence while Alfredo struggled to compose himself. His heart ached for Sam, for the Captain, for Sam's sister, the unborn dead child.

He saw Charlotte wandering alone within the silent stone walls of Rosencranz. *Dear Lord, please look after her until I can.*

"I want to help you, Alfredo," Kate said. Her voice brought him back to the Downtown sidewalk. "And I want to help your friend. But you have to trust me. Does she speak the language of the crows? And is that really why she's in a mental institution?"

"Yes," Alfredo said, without hesitation. There was nothing to hide. Kate knew it all, everything, apparently. He stood up and offered Kate his hand, and they resumed walking back to the gallery.

"Apparently about twenty years ago," he said as they walked, "she lost the ability to understand human language. She is otherwise a very intelligent, lucid woman who has endured twenty-five years of confinement and the abandonment by her family with amazing grace."

They stopped outside the gallery. "I have to get her out of there, Kate. It is unbearable for her." *And me.*

They sat down on a planter next to the door. Kate looked at him intently and said, "As your attorney, I must ask you this: are you in love with her?"

Alfredo frowned. "I do not know what that means, exactly. I feel great affection and attachment for her. I admire her and worry about her. I want her life to be better. I enjoy her company. Is that what 'in' love means?"

"If we're lucky," Kate said, smiling. "But what about romance? Have you two kissed or anything?"

Alfredo laughed. "No. The thought has never occurred to me. Nor to her, that I can tell."

"Like you would know," Kate said with a grin.

Alfredo frowned again. "I do not think I have romantic thoughts."

He had thought he was in love once, before seminary school. She was another graduate student in the department. Beth. But when she discovered his so-called gift, she freaked out and broke up with him. He had been crushed, though grateful she never told anyone about his crow-speech. But he had vowed never to let anyone know again. He buried himself in his dissertation, and after he was awarded a PhD, he immediately entered the priesthood.

"Friendship can be very romantic," Kate said. "But I had to check, you know, if anything else was going on. People do crazy things for sex."

A car drove by slowly. Music boomed out its open windows; a

female voice screamed out the lyrics, something about love and pain.

"I have never participated in the sex act," Alfredo said, stiffly, feeling his face redden.

Kate cracked up laughing and hugged him. "Oh, Padre! That is what we hoped to hear from all our priests! But seriously, sex is wonderful! It's like a glue that holds two unrelated people together."

The door to the gallery opened, and several people walked out, discussing where to go for a drink. "How about the Saddle?" a man said. "No!" the woman on his arm said. "No sports bars!"

"So, where will you take her," Kate asked, after the group had passed, "assuming you can get her out of there?"

"I have not yet decided," Alfredo said. "But before I imagine myself and her at a bridge we may never cross, I want to find out if I can get her out of there at all. If so, I will find her a safe place where she will be happy. But not at my cottage, if that is what you are thinking."

"I was," said Kate. "What is her name, by the way?"

"Charlotte," Alfredo said. "Charlotte Steele."

After the last guest left the gallery, Jade and Russ stayed to help Jena tidy up while Sam, Kate, and Alfredo drove to the Double Elbow, a popular Downtown pub known for good beer, buffalo wings, and whose relatively quiet atmosphere made conversation possible. A few tables against the windows surrounded an interior dominated by two L-shaped bars with stools.

By the time Russ and Jade arrived, the others were already seated in a booth in the far corner. Sam poured them a beer from the pitcher on the table.

"I need man food," Russ said after he slid into place. "I must've eaten a hundred of those delicate little tea cakes or whatever the hell they served at the reception. Like eating air. A man needs meat."

Sam laughed and clapped his hands. Alfredo regarded Sam with a new sense of tenderness. *He has endured much suffering. Grant him happiness now, Lord, with this loving woman, Kate.*

"I hear ya," Kate said, giggling, "but we've ordered wings. Do real men eat chicken?"

"Whenever possible," Russ said with absolutely no expression on his face.

That seemed hilariously funny to everyone, except Alfredo. He smiled anyway, though he could not fathom what the joke was. His conversation with Kate had illuminated his alienation from his fellow humans, and he was envious of his friends' banter and easy enjoyment of each other.

The wings arrived, and for a few moments, everyone had their mouths full and their fingers covered in reddish-orange spicy sauce. "Ya know," Jade said between bites, waving a wing bone at her companions. "I only realized last year why they call these buffalo wings. I wondered for a long time how buffalos and wings could wind up being the same food. I just thought it was one of those things frat boys come up with, you know, for their keg parties—because it's more manly to eat buffalo than chicken."

Everyone chuckled, shaking their heads. Alfredo furrowed his brow and said, "I always thought they were wings of chickens from upstate New York. And I wondered what was so special about that. And how would we ever know if they did not come from Buffalo?"

"Thanks, Padre," Jade said as the rest of the group erupted in laughter. "I'm glad to know I'm not such a black sheep, that others think like I do."

"Not very damn many," Russ said with an affectionate nudge.

"Your husband speaks the truth, Jade," Alfredo said. "But in the end, we are all just strangers in a strange land, are we not?" *We are Patua' in a strange land, you and I.*

"Hear! Hear!" Kate said with mock sternness. "Let's not have such lonesome talk when there are friends all around. How about a tribute to Jade for a fantastic art show!"

They toasted Jade and each painting that sold. Alfredo had arranged with Jena to purchase Ave, Madre, but he did not tell Jade. *She will see it hanging in my cottage. Or the chapel.*

The waitperson brought a new pitcher of beer, and Alfredo filled everyone's glass. "Speaking of art and artists," he said when he finished, "I have been seeing flyers up around Downtown. Seems the Friends of Wilder Island are having an arts and crafts fair and art auction next weekend at the Waterfront."

"That's right!" Jade said. "Sam and I put a proposal in to Parks and Rec, and we got the permit that same day! The city loves people to come Downtown on the weekends—that's what they told us. They're trying to promote the Waterfront too. Sam and I are both contributing work to the art auction, and we have at least half of the artists saying they'll put stuff in too!"

Alfredo observed Jade intently as she spoke. Her eyes sparkled with excitement, and every once in a while he thought he caught a glimpse of her mother. He squinted his eyes and listened to the lilting quality in Jade's voice, so like Charlotte's.

"Perfect timing!" Kate said. "The city's going to announce their decision to condemn Wilder Island on Thursday."

"How do you know that?" Jade asked, tilting her head to one side and wrinkling her brow.

Alfredo almost laughed out loud. *I have seen that exact expression on Charlotte!*

"My vast network of spies," Kate said with a wink. "Seriously, there are no secrets among lawyers and politicians." She turned to Russ. "But we gotta be ready. You have things set up with KMUS, Russ?"

"Yes," he said. "The students at the university radio station are ready to roll on Friday night. They'll broadcast us live from the Waterfront. After we explain the issues—condemnation, eminent domain, and why we might want to keep the island the way it is—there'll be time for people to call in and comment or ask questions."

Their server came by the table and dropped off another pitcher of beer. He picked up the empty plates and napkins and left the check and several individually wrapped hand wipes.

"Hey," Sam said as he cleaned the red hot sauce from his fingers. "As long as we're on KMUS, how about we put on a beg-a-thon? Like they do on public radio, you know? I mean, we need to raise some bucks, don't we? We've made some money selling booths for the fair, and we'll make a little more from the silent auction. But we could rake in some serious money if we put on a beg-a-thon."

"What the devil is a beg-a-thon?" Alfredo asked.

HENRY BRAUN APPLIED FOR A PARADE permit, not coincidentally, for the same weekend as the Friends of Wilder Island Art Fair. Just as Kate Herron had her network of informants, so did Henry. He too knew exactly when the mayor's announcement to condemn Wilder Island would occur. He planned to fire up the *River Queen* and start parading her past the city boat docks on both sides of the river for the entire weekend. There would be free food and drink for the crowds he hoped would gather on the docks to ogle his beautiful *River Queen*.

"You can't have the docks at the Waterfront," the city clerk said. "On account of the art fair. You can have the city boat landing on the other side, though."

"What art fair?" Henry growled.

"I just stamped their permit," the clerk said, rifling through the previous day's paperwork. "An outfit called the Friends of Wilder Island."

Who the bloody hell are the Friends of Wilder Island? They'd better not get in my way!

"Oh? Whose name is on the permit?" Henry said magnanimously as he pushed a five-dollar bill across the counter at the clerk.

"Let's see," he said, looking through the bottom half of his bifocals at the permit. He carefully ignored the bill on the counter. "Here it is. There were two applicants, Jade Matthews and Sam Howard." He scribbled the names on a scrap of paper and pushed it and the money toward Henry. "There is no charge for this information, Mr. Braun." The clerk looked over his shoulder and smiled at the video cameras behind him.

"Thank you," Henry said cordially as he pocketed the bill.

He walked out of City Hall and stepped through the open door of his Bentley and into the backseat. Jules Sackman sat waiting for Henry, sipping a latte and reading the newspaper.

"Who the hell are these people?" Henry Braun growled to Jules as the car pulled away from the curb. "Friends of Wilder Island?"

"Everything is named after the island in this city, Henry," Jules said, sipping his latte. "Don't let that make you paranoid. Probably just a band of dilettantes and their gigolos."

"I don't want probably, Jules. I want facts. I want answers," Henry growled. "Who the hell are Jade Matthews and Sam Howard? And who's behind them? A bunch of bleeding-heart, liberal tree-huggers, I bet."

ALFREDO SPENT THE NIGHT AT ST. Sophia's, as it was too dark to return to the island after he left his friends at the Double Elbow. He tossed and turned, unable to find sleep. He missed the sounds of the night on the island, and the evening's revelation kept his mind running. *Charlotte is Jade's mother!* The knowledge filled him with a strange mixture of dread and excitement.

How old is Jade? Early twenties, I would guess. Was Charlotte pregnant when she was taken away? Did she give birth at Rosencranz? Dora Lyn had not been able to find Charlotte's file at his last visit, which he thought would tell him everything he needed to know about Charlotte's arrival, treatment, and residence at Rosencranz.

The headlights from a passing car infiltrated the gap between the curtains, sending a geometrical pattern of light and shadow darting across the ceiling.

Charlotte never mentioned a daughter. He frowned in the darkness. *Maybe she's not Jade's mother after all.* He turned over in bed again, his back to the window.

He slept fitfully, disturbed by vague dreams of a blindfolded Charlotte with arms tied behind her back, and a baby in a basket crying faintly. He woke up feeling as if he had not slept at all.

He left the rectory at St. Sophia's as soon as the sun came up and found the Captain and Sugarbabe docked at the Waterfront. Funny how they always knew when to pick him up.

"It ain't rocket science," Sugarbabe squawked. "We left you here yest'aday. You didn't g'home last night. Where else would y'be at this hour, than here wantin' for a ride?"

The Captain chuckled and gave his crow a treat from his shirt pocket. He pushed the boat out into the river. Alfredo wondered again how old the Captain was; his craggy and sun-wrinkled face somehow defied age. *How many years ago was he left for dead in the river?* Sam was in his mid-thirties, he knew. But the Captain seemed far older. "How long have you been running the river, Captain?"

The Captain looked up at the sky for a moment and then at Alfredo. "Many years. I forget." His face seemed to cloud over, and he turned his eyes back to the river.

Alfredo left the Captain in peace and inhaled the cool, clear morning, reviving his sleep-deprived body. The river's flat and calm surface reflected the forest and sacred chapel of Cadeña-l'jadia like a mirror.

"Ah, Bruthamax's Roost," Sugarbabe said. "'Tis always a beautiful sight."

Alfredo nodded. "That it is."

He bid farewell to the Captain and Sugarbabe and entered the thick forest He smiled up at the birds flying through the branches of the trees and walked the path to his cottage. It was good to be home. He opened the doors and windows to the fresh air and then left to find Charlie.

He walked past the chapel and down to the point where Charlie pecked at his lunch from the cracks and crannies of rocks and driftwood.

"Grawky, Jayzu!" Charlie said. He cleaned his beak in the sand and hopped up onto the driftwood log where Alfredo had seated himself.

"Charlie, I have reason to believe Charlotte has a daughter!"

The crow shook his head. "How do you know this?"

Alfredo told him about Jade's painting of her unknown mother that bore an uncanny resemblance to Charlotte. "And she has that orb."

Charlie paced back and forth across the log. "Well, I guess it's possible. In the half a year before they took her away, I was in Keeper training then and couldn't visit her." He stopped and looked at Alfredo. "But Charlotte has never mentioned a child?"

"No, but she seems to have forgotten a great deal of her life." Alfredo gazed across the river for a few moments. "I wonder ... could the stress of a difficult childbirth have caused her to forget her native human language?"

"I don't know," Charlie said. "I have an archive session with Starfire tomorrow. Perhaps he will know the answer to that. He has seen a few Patua' fade into the graying. At the very least, he will be very interested in adding a new Patua' to the database. And that she has one of the orbs."

Charlie flew off, leaving Alfredo alone on the log. He watched a few crows flipping themselves through the jaloosies out over the river. *Sometimes I wish I were one of them. So free of the madnesses we humans have created.*

—13—

Mirrors and Other Illusions

Starfire completed the last Keeper session and fell into a dreamless sleep, exhausted. He awoke suddenly, several hours before sunrise, his mind filled with a single thought. The fireball that streaked through Charlie's lattice. What is it?

He had been busy with the Keepers for days, performing the monthly data emplacements, and whatever spare time he had was devoted to discovering the mysterious holes in the lattice. There had been no time to examine the mysterious fiery object he had copied from Charlie's lattice. Until now.

He summoned the fireball from his memory, and it appeared behind his eyes, flashing as it spun, just as he had seen it in Charlie's lattice. He had not expected it to come over in multiple dimensions—highly polished, black as raven feathers. And he could wander all around it.

What is it? Where did it come from? What is it trying to tell me? Starfire was sure the fireball was a message of some sort, whether from the archive itself, warning of a possible data corruption, or a breach in the lattice, or—?

He recalled suddenly that Charlie had started blinking rapidly at the same moment the orb had been ejected. Did he see it? Even if he did, he would not have brought into consciousness any memory of the Emplacement Ritual, or even the experimental extraction ritual he was under when the fireball appeared.

Starfire opened the main archival lattice through a meditative state. The mildornia berry-induced trance was necessary only to introduce or extract large volumes of data into the Keeper lattices. Starfire only wanted the answer to one question: *what is it?*

He chanted up the vast body of historical data regarding the use and care of the Archival Lattice, a sort of trouble-shooting compendium of tricks, observations, and advice from countless chief Archivists over many millennia. But there was no mention of the lattice suddenly spitting up fireballs. Or anything else for that matter.

The lattice is but an archive of events already occurred, Starfire reasoned. *It knows nothing of the present moment or the future. Is this sphere some sort of messenger, programmed to eject at a specific time?*

What if—? What if the fireball is a secret archive that was placed into the lattice before the Patua' went underground? A signal, perhaps? A signal to us, the future corvid, that the Patua' have returned?

He called up the Patua' lattice within the archive. He felt sure the fireball was related to the Patua', if only because it was the Patua' lattice in which it appeared. Determined to pry the secret from the lattice, he searched for the right question to ask. *Dump fireball subset Patua',* he commanded the lattice. Nothing. He changed the chant: *Dump fire orb subset Patua'.* Several seconds went by before a node opened and spit out a data packet. Starfire watched it gracefully unfold into a ribbon of sound.

RB OF UA'1405 CE ATUA' mae hun eds t re uryseed e rbs th 1586 E Pat 'man cr pt hi d n Gregor U y

The incomplete data stream annoyed Starfire, and he replayed the data ribbon. Such errors were not uncommon and usually were due to a glitch in the chant. The new data ribbon unfolded, and to Starfire's chagrin, it was again incomplete.

The old raven was troubled, though he told himself it could be any number of things. He tried not to fear the worst—holes in the lattice. Trying to quell fear with reason, he reminded himself over and over again that the diagnostics he ran would have revealed such structural damage to the lattice.

The twenty-one-gun salute at a military funeral in the cemetery in which the tupelo tree grew catapulted Starfire out of his meditative state and into the bright, sunny morning. He stretched his wings and muttered an expletive. He never was able to shut out the sound of gunfire.

He perched within the murky shadows of the huge tree, pondering the fireball. *What is it?* Though he had worked for much of the night to find the answer, he had not even been able to discover what it was not; that maddening broken data stream had suggested a far greater problem.

Starfire wondered how extensive the holes were and if Patua' data was lost. And why were there holes in the lattice at all? A stray chant gone awry within the lattice?

The incomplete entries were over six hundred years old, he reasoned. Perhaps the holes were due to lack of maintenance, in which case a little housekeeping would take care of the problem. But the data was stored at the boundary of the lattice, whose edges were ragged and frayed, as if part of the sector had been torn away. *What could do that*? he wondered. *How much data have we lost?*

Beyond the worrisome aspects of a possible systemic problem with the lattice, Starfire felt sure the missing data would answer many questions, and he was certain this was not a solitary, random event without connection to anything. The fireball had ejected during an Emplacement Ritual; he had just finished inserting Jayzu into the Patua' area of the archival lattice. Ever since, Starfire had harbored the feeling that Jayzu's name in the lattice had triggered the fireball.

He stood up on his branch, flapped his wings several times, and took to the air. It was time for breakfast. He flew toward the river and spied Hookbeak on the ground near some poor creature a car had hit and flung well off the road.

"May I join you, my friend?" Starfire asked as he landed next to the carcass.

"Help yourself," Hookbeak said through a beakful. "There is plenty here."

Starfire snagged a chunk of flesh and swallowed it. "I love possum!" He pecked off another bite.

"Grummrummrumm," Hookbeak agreed. He swallowed the chunk of flesh in one gulp.

"I have found some disturbing holes in the lattice," Starfire said. "I do not know as yet how large or how extensive."

"Holes?"

"Yes," Starfire said. "During a routine Keeper session, a strange fireball popped out of the Keeper's personal memory lattice and into the archival lattice. I felt free to copy it to my own lattice and examined it later."

"What?" Hookbeak said sharply. "Why was there a bleedover between the Keeper's memory and the archives at all? Was the Keeper not under trance deeply enough?"

"No." Starfire shook his head emphatically. "Nothing was amiss in the trance, or anywhere else. As yet, I do not know what it is or why it was ejected from the Keeper's lattice. I queried the database, and I discovered the holes."

Hookbeak stepped on the carcass and pulled off a chunk of meat. He gulped it down and helped himself to another. "So you think the fireball has something to do with the holes?"

"Seems so," Starfire said. "But I do not as yet know what the connection is."

"Has data been lost?" Hookbeak cleaned his beak on the grass.

"Yes," Starfire answered. "But I don't know how much yet. The holes occur randomly in the lattice, and we have lost some corvid historical data. But the greatest damage is to the Patua' trees."

He beaked another piece of the road kill and swallowed it. "I had hoped that this problem could be fixed by a defragmentation procedure, but no such luck. I must look to other causes."

"Such as?" Hookbeak asked. He thrust his thick beak into the possum carcass.

"Bugs," Starfire said. "That is my greatest fear."

"Bugs?" Hookbeak withdrew his head and stared at Starfire.

"Bugs eat things," Starfire said. "They eat everything, from flesh to petroleum to data; they eat it all."

✦✦✦

ALFREDO RENTED A CAR IN LEDFORD and drove to Rosencranz. The day had dawned with cloudy skies and a cold drizzle, but by the time he was on the road, the rain had stopped and the clouds started to break up. He had looked forward to another visit with Charlotte. Other than Charlie, there was no one in the world he wanted to talk to more than Charlotte.

He wondered how many Patua' languished in mental institutions. Like Charlotte. And Majewski's sister, Stella. Not insane, just unable to communicate. *I should tell Majewski about Charlotte.*

He pulled onto the county road toward Rosencranz and left the urban realm of Ledford for the pastures and cornfields of the country. *Charlotte may have a daughter!* She had never mentioned she had a child. *Did she forget? Or am I only imagining Jade is her daughter?* There was no way he could ask Charlotte without upsetting her, he knew. *I hope Dora Lyn has been able to find her file. That should tell us everything.*

He signed in at the gate and entered the obedient landscape of Rosencranz Hospital for the Insane. He drove past the gazebo, but it was too dark inside for him to tell whether Charlie had arrived yet. He parked the car, donned his fake glasses, grabbed his briefcase, and entered the lobby through the heavy front doors. Dora Lyn wore her usual grimaced expression as he approached the reception desk, which changed the moment she saw him to one of giddy delight.

"Dr. Robbins!" she gushed, looking him over from head to toe. "You look great! Have you been working out or something?"

"Ah," Alfredo said self-consciously, "no." But he had been working on the tree house, and before that, his cottage.

"Yard work," he said. "I put in a pond in my backyard. I did a lot of digging."

"Really?" Dora Lyn said, putting her chin in her hand and leaning on her elbow. "It sure looks good on you, Doctor."

He set his briefcase on the tall counter between them and opened it, hoping she did not see him blush. He withdrew a bouquet of flowers and handed it across the counter to her with a big smile.

Dora Lyn had warmed up to him on his first visit, but he still wanted to look at Charlotte's file. "Bring her flowers," Sam had told him. "Nothing special, just a little nosegay from the grocery store. Might help her remember where that file is."

Alfredo had laughed. "I always thought men gave flowers to women to make them forget something!" But he had taken Sam's advice and bought a small yet cheerful bouquet on his way to the asylum.

"For me?" Dora Lyn giggled as she took the flowers. "You shouldn't have, Dr. Robbins! They're lovely." She put the flowers in a small vase on her desk. "I'll get these little beauties in water once I get you squared away with Miss Charlotte."

Miss Charlotte! Much better than Scarecrow! Alfredo smiled, amazed at what a few flowers could do. "Did you ever locate Charlotte's file?" he said. "Remember you could not find it last time I was here?"

"I do remember, Doctor," Dora Lyn said, wrinkling her brow. "And yes, I did locate it, but there's nothing in it. I'd say someone forgot to put its stuffings back, but no one has asked for it in the entire time she's been here. I'm sorry, Doctor. I don't know what to tell you. But I'll keep looking."

"Thank you, Dora Lyn," Alfredo said. "I am quite grateful for all of your help. What would I do without you?"

Dora Lyn blushed and smiled. "Just doing my job, Doctor."

"No, you do above and beyond," Alfredo said, smiling warmly. "At least for me. I would hate to be here on your days off!"

"I would hate that too, Dr. Robbins," Dora Lyn said, smiling back. "I'm off on the weekends, same as you, probably."

Alfredo laughed and said, "I try to leave my work at the office on the weekends, but there are times when I work all the way through."

Dora Lyn nodded sympathetically. "Not me!" She giggled. "Really, Doctor, it's just crazy here on the weekends. The girl who sits here on Saturday and Sunday? Dumb as a post. An inmate walked right past this desk and out the door last weekend, and she never even no-ticed." Dora Lyn rolled her eyes.

"What happened?" Alfredo asked. "Did he escape?"

"Nope, but he would've gone clear to the highway if a visitor hadn't reported an old guy in his pajamas wandering around in the parking lot."

The phone on her desk rang, and she held up a forefinger as she answered it. Alfredo wandered to the windows opposite the patio and gazed across the lush carpet of grass to the gazebo. A black bird perched on the apex of the roof. *There is Charlie!*

He heard Dora Lyn hanging up the phone and returned to the desk. "It is a beautiful day," he said. "Perhaps Charlotte would like to step out for a stroll, out to the gazebo and back. Is that permissible?"

Dora Lyn glanced toward the gazebo and then rolled her eyes as she said, "Yes, but surprise-surprise! First you have to sign a form."

She fished a sheet of paper out of a compartment on her desk. "I trust you, Doctor, but you know, protocol and all. We have to keep track of the patients. And since that patient nearly escaped last week, well, you know."

"Of course," Alfredo said.

"Sign there," she said as she put an X next to the signature line. "They didn't have the money to hire enough security guards to watch the whole building, so they put video cameras everywhere." She low-ered her voice to a whisper. "Even in the restrooms!"

"No kidding!" Alfredo shook his head as he scribbled his faux name illegibly on the form. "I will have her back within the hour."

"Take your time, Doctor," Dora Lyn said, waving him on with a smile. "Miss Charlotte's on her way down. They're taking her to the patio. It'll just be a minute."

"Thank you, Dora Lyn," Alfredo said.

"I don't know why they don't let her come down by herself," she said, smiling up at him. "She wanders the place on her own all day long." She shrugged. "'Course they lock all the patients in their rooms at night. I guess someone still adheres to protocol in this Mickey Mouse outfit."

"Now, Dora Lyn," Alfredo laughed.

"I'm serious, Doctor," she said. "This is not a mental institution! It's a halfway house for the senile, a place for rich folks to stash and forget about their pesky old demented parents." She giggled self-consciously into her hand. "I'm sorry. I shouldn't go on like that. But I'm sure glad we're moving to a real hospital."

"Oh, no problem," Alfredo said. He was grateful for the information, but was taken aback by her frankness. The building and its grounds had virtually no security. And that Miss Charlotte pretty well had the freedom to wander anywhere patients were allowed to be during the day. But at night she was locked in her room. *That* disturbed him. Charlotte's tiny room was on the third floor. *What if there is a fire?*

He started toward the doors to the patio and was stopped short by a sign that he had not noticed when he walked in: We're Moving! Without reading the rest of the sign, he turned back to Dora Lyn and asked, "Really? The hospital is moving? When? Where are you going?"

"That's right, Doctor!" Dora Lyn said, giggling. "We're moving, lock, stock, and barrel in about two weeks! A brand-new building over in the state capitol! It will be so nice to get out of this stinky old place. It was built more than 150 years ago, you know. And it wasn't even a hospital! You can tell, can't you?"

"Oh, it is a bit old-fashioned perhaps," Alfredo said. *Moving! You cannot move now! Not yet!*

"Well," Dora Lyn said, "it used to be a mansion that old man Rosencranz lived in till he died." She looked over her shoulder as if checking to see if someone was listening. She lowered her voice. "He went out of his mind, and his spinster sister took care of him. But she ran out of money way before that, on account of Mr. Rosencranz lost his fanny in the crash of '29. Some say that's what made him lose his marbles too."

She giggled behind her hand and looked over her shoulder again. "Anyhoo, so Rosencranz's sister, she took in a few invalids, to help pay the bills. And after he died, she stayed on, and kept on, and by and by it became Rosencranz Hospital."

"I see," Alfredo said.

"But we don't have really crazy people here," Dora Lyn said, shaking her head as she looked out the windows at the patio. "Just folks who forgot themselves. Alzheimer's, you know, that's what most of them are here for."

Alfredo looked through the windows at the people on the patio. *Charlotte does not belong here.*

"The new building will have state-of-the-art security," Dora Lyn said. "No more inmates just waltzing out of here in broad daylight. And I'm getting a brand-new computer!"

"Sounds wonderful," Alfredo said. He looked at his watch.

"Oh!" Dora Lyn gushed. "I'm so sorry, Doctor! Prattling on like that when you have work to do!"

"No problem." Alfredo smiled. "But I do need to go."

He left the lobby though the double doors to the patio, anxiety gnawing at his stomach. *Moving in two weeks!* The state capitol was more than a hundred miles farther away from Ledford.

CHARLOTTE CHARGED THROUGH THE DOOR ON her own two feet, shouting over her shoulder at the aide, "I am not crippled! I do not need your damn wheelchair!"

Jayzu said something to the aide, and he let her go. "Jayzu!" Charlotte cried and flung her arms around Alfredo's neck.

"Hello, Charlotte," he said, laughing as he peeled her arms away. She loved his laugh, so full of joy. She had missed him tremendously in the days since she had last seen him. But here he was! Smiling at her and holding her hands! He led her to a table on the patio, and they sat down.

"So, how are you?" he asked, putting his briefcase on the empty chair beside him. "You are looking well."

He looked at her so intently, she wondered if there was something the matter with her face. She brushed a few stray hairs from her eyes. "I am very happy to see you, Jayzu," she said. "I have been counting the days. Six."

"Only six?" he said with a twinkle in his eyes. He reached into his briefcase, pulled out an object wrapped in purple tissue paper, and handed it to her. "I brought this for you, Charlotte."

"A present!" she said. "I never get presents, Jayzu! Is it my birthday?"

"No," he laughed. "It is just something I thought you needed to have."

She peeled the paper away carefully. "A mirror!" She stared at her image in it for many moments. "That is me," she murmured. She turned her head to each side, trying to see as much of herself as she could. She touched her face, her nose, her lips.

She gazed into her own eyes, gray like the clouds that roll through the sky. Scene after scene played in their depths—of wheeled chariots pulled along by great horses, of torches on cave walls painted with wooly mammoths, of dark passages filled with the dead. The sensation of falling flooded her with fear. She screamed and threw the mirror to the patio, shattering it.

Jayzu stared at her in shock. All of the patients on the patio, their doctors and visitors, stared at her. A custodian appeared with a broom and dustpan and swept the glass into a dustpan and took it away.

"I am so sorry, Charlotte," Jayzu said, ignoring the cleanup and the stares. He took her hands into his. "Forgive me, please?"

The warmth of his hands calmed her, and she stopped shaking. "I saw myself in the mirror," she said, shuddering anew as she recalled the frightening image. Jayzu moved his chair closer to her. "I was in my room, and I was old and wrinkly all over." She choked her fear back. "I was thirty-one thousand, six hundred and thirty-seven days old."

Tears burned her eyes, but she didn't want Jayzu to think she was a crybaby. She pulled her hands away and put them in her lap.

She hung her head, squeezing her eyes closed and digging her finger-nails into her palms. "I do not want to live that long, Jayzu," she said, her voice flat and final.

Alfredo had no idea the mirror would upset Charlotte so. *She saw herself still at Rosencranz as an old woman. She could live another forty years; that is what I told her.* But he had been trying to make her feel that her life was not over, not despair at four more decades in this place. But could he even suggest a different life?

He could not bear to see her in such anguish, and he wanted to take her in his arms and rock her gently, soothing away her fear. He checked his watch. *Charlie is waiting at the gazebo.* He stood up and put his folded arm out. "May I take you for a walk around the garden, fair lady?"

Charlotte opened her eyes. She stood up and giggled as she took his arm. "Oh, please! That would be so lovely!"

He led her through the lobby, past Dora Lyn, who smiled and waved. Out the front door and down the steps to the sidewalk. Alfredo did not see Charlie on the gazebo rooftop and hoped he was inside. They crossed the service road and stepped onto the lawn, and Charlotte immediately kicked off her shoes. She ran across the grass, laughing in sheer delight. She wiggled her toes in the soft, cool green grass, squealing with delight at the sun, the blue sky, and her unexpected freedom.

Charlotte's face was paralyzed into a permanent smile as they walked across the grass. There was even a little color to her otherwise pale cheeks, and her gray eyes were alight with the simple joy of being alive. She seemed to inhale the entire landscape with each breath; Alfredo knew it had been many years since she had felt the bare earth on her feet.

They climbed up the concrete steps to the gazebo. "I have always wondered what is in here!" she said, her eyes sparkling with the excitement. "I imagined I lived here, except it was far, far away from Rosencranz! On an island just like Charlie's."

They sat down in wrought-iron chairs around a small table, their backs to Rosencranz and facing the wild woods beyond the grounds. A black bird flew out of the forest and into the gazebo. After orbiting the table where Charlotte and Jayzu sat, it perched on the back of one of the empty chairs.

"Grawky, Charlotte!" the blue-eyed crow said.

"Charlie!" Charlotte cried out and opened her arms. Charlie hopped over to the arm of the chair, and the two nuzzled each other with wings and hands.

Charlotte's laughter melted Alfredo's heart, though he felt a little envious of their physical affection. He imagined her arms around him, and he nearly cried out as a strange energetic exhilaration rushed from his tailbone upward and outward, spreading tingling warmth all the way to his fingertips.

He wished he had Jade's talent; he would paint Charlotte. Her smile as she gazed upon Charlie with such tender love, her hand gently touching his beak, her black hair and Charlie's black feathers, flashing hues of red and blue. And her gray eyes, sparkling like crystals. *God Almighty, she is beautiful.*

The gazebo's ivy-covered lattice walls faithfully blocked Charlotte and Charlie's playful interactions from anyone who might happen to look out a window of the asylum. Alfredo glanced up the road toward the guardhouse at the driveway entrance, but he could not see it.

The gazebo would also conceal an escape over the fence. He turned and looked toward the forest beyond the gazebo. Barely visible, it was intergrown with trees and vines and topped with a coiling layer of concertina wire. *Through it or under it, that is.*

"Cadeña-l'jadia is like the forests we used to play in," Charlie was saying when Alfredo tuned back in to their conversation. "Many trees, large and small. And all the aromatic herbs you could ever want!"

"Jayzu," Charlotte said, turning suddenly toward him. "I want to go to Cadeña-l'jadia right now. Take me to Charlie's tree house, please?"

He stared into her pale gray eyes, wondering if she had read his thoughts. "I would love to do that, Charlotte," he said. *You have no idea how much.* "But it is very complicated, and I cannot just walk out the front door with you."

"Jayzu is right, Charlotte," Charlie said. "We might have to trick them."

"Trick them?" Charlotte said, her eyes growing big with excitement.

Alfredo frowned at Charlie, wishing he had not made such an implicit promise to her. "We do not know how to get you out of here, Charlotte," he said, "yet. But we, that is Charlie and I, are working on a plan."

She clapped her hands and then pulled her arms in and covered her mouth as she drew in a great breath. Her eyes danced with delight, and Alfredo could not resist the smile that she brought to his lips.

Alfredo looked at his watch and said, "I must take you back now, Charlotte. It is just past an hour since we left the building."

"I do not want to go back," she said, frowning. "I want to stay here with you and Charlie."

Charlotte looked over her shoulder at the building. Her shoulders sagged as she turned back to face him. "When will you come back, Jayzu?"

"Very soon, Charlotte," he said. "In less than fourteen days."

"I will be patient," Charlotte said, squaring her shoulders and folding her hands on the table. "Fourteen days is not very many."

Charlie said good-bye, and Alfredo escorted her back to the building. She walked as slowly as she could without stopping, delaying the moment when they would have to part. She held her tears back when the elevator door closed, and he rode down to the lobby without her.

"How'd Miss Charlotte like her walk?" Dora Lyn asked as Dr. Robbins signed out. *What a hunk!* He didn't wear a wedding ring, which she hoped meant he wasn't married. *Or he's gay. That'd be my luck. The handsomest sweetest men are always gay.*

"She did!" he said with an irresistible smile. "I think it was good for her to leave this building, even if it was just out on the lawn." He reached for the log, and she handed him a pen.

"Yeah," Dora Lyn said. "I don't know how she hasn't just flipped out, ya know?" She looked out the window at the gray people in wheelchairs, all facing the other direction. "She's not like the others."

"Oh?" Dr. Robbins said. "How so?"

His black eyes seemed to penetrate her very soul. "Well," Dora Lyn said, "she babbles in this strange language no one can understand, like Miss Rosie out there." She jerked her head toward the wheelchair brigade. "But ever since she sort of woke up from her sleepwalking, after she'd been here, oh jeez, twenty years maybe, and that's when she started babbling, well, she didn't seem crazy, just sort of, I don't know, in the wrong place."

"That is interesting, Dora Lyn," the handsome doctor said. "I have had that sense as well."

She leaned forward toward him and whispered, "Do you think it was aliens?"

"Aliens?"

"Yeah, you know, like space aliens." She glanced back out the window toward the gazebo. "They say she had disappeared for weeks before they brought her here. She was fine until then, but whatever happened to her, she couldn't talk no more. Not a word."

"Really?" Dr. Robbins said. "Were you working here then?"

Dora Lyn was pleased that he was so interested in what she had to say. And that she knew things about Charlotte that he didn't.

"I was!" she said, beaming a smile at him. "They brought her in all tied up in a straitjacket. They sedated her, because she screamed so much, they said. And then after she got here, God knows what they did to her, but she was all docile like, until maybe seven or eight years ago, or so."

Dora Lyn remembered her out there on the patio; among all the gray, faded people, Charlotte's black hair had stuck out.

"They shaved her hair all off," Dora Lyn said, wondering why that made the doctor wince. "And they kept cutting until she started 'talking' again. Quote unquote."

"Does anyone know why she suddenly started talking?" the doctor said. "Quote unquote."

Dora Lyn brushed a stray hair out of her face. "Nope. But she just up and got out of her wheelchair and started talking that alien language. She smiled a little, but she always looked so sad."

Dora Lyn looked out at the patio as the aide rotated the wheelchair people. "She's just not like the others."

Alfredo left Rosencranz and drove back to Ledford, thinking about what Dora Lyn had told him. *They shaved her hair off?* He had almost lost his temper when he heard that. Her long beautiful hair she kept in a thick braid down her back.

They let her have long hair, Dora Lyn had said, after she started taking care of herself. "You know, like brushing it and taking care of her own teeth and stuff."

She does not belong there anymore. Even Dora Lyn sees that. I need to bring her home to Cadeña-l'jadia.

And the argument began.

Are you nuts? his voice of reason demanded. *You want to take an inmate in the insane asylum where she has been her entire adult life to a deserted island?*

But Charlotte is not insane, his compassion argued. *How can I just leave her there?*

The choice was clear: get this innocent woman out of this prison or do nothing but conform to the madness that put her there in the first place. *What would be gained by that? I would have bragging rights that I obeyed the law? The law that is an ass?*

Just because the law is an ass does not mean you have to be one, his rational voice argued. *Did you want to go to jail for kidnapping under "the law is an ass" defense?*

The "We're Moving" sign appeared in his thoughts, and he felt a surge of panic. He wanted to turn the car around and return to Rosencranz, go in and get her, take her to the car, and drive away.

The law is an ass, and I am insane.

Charlotte stayed in her room, refusing to go down to the dining hall for the evening meal. She sat at her window looking out over the forest on the other side of the fence. A tear rolled down her cheek. *He is gone. Jayzu is gone.* Fear billowed up in her chest. *What if he never comes back?*

A parade of nameless faces strolled through her head, faces she could not name, and they stabbed her with grief and loneliness. The gray-haired woman with the red cheeks and the warm smile. A young boy with black hair like hers. A young man playing a guitar, a cigarette stuck to his lip, dangling on the edge of a song.

A dark shadow flew to her window and landed on the sill. "Charlie!" she cried and put her hand on the glass, tears raining down her face.

Alfredo returned the rental car and walked to the Waterfront where the Captain was waiting to take him home. The late afternoon sun felt hot and sticky, and he could not wait to be back on the cool island, away from all the noise and heat of the city.

He jumped aboard, and the Captain pushed away from the dock. Sugarbabe clutched the railing and flapped her wings a few times before folding them neatly at her sides and settling down on her perch.

"And how's Miss Charlotte?" she asked Alfredo.

He was surprised Sugarbabe knew anything about Charlotte. "She is just fine, Sugarbabe. We went out for a walk today, which she enjoyed very much."

"Right kind of you to visit her," the Captain said.

"Do you know her also?" Alfredo asked in surprise.

The Captain gazed ahead for a minute or two, his brow knitting and unknitting as if he were in some mental anguish. "Once, long ago, I knew someone like her," he said finally. "We were like peas in a pod, she and I. But her mother hated me, on account of me and her being too much like me, if you catch my drift."

"I do," Alfredo said.

The Captain nodded. "Her daddy forbade us to see each other. We did anyway, on the sly, like. But he found out."

The Captain's jaw worked up and down, and his face bore such anguish, Alfredo wanted to comfort him, to lay his hands on the man.

"Her daddy had a couple of thugs beat me near to death and toss me in the river. I never saw her again. I don't know what happened to her. She just disappeared. I like to think someone like you maybe is visiting her somewhere."

Sugarbabe leaped from her perch to the Captain's shoulder and rubbed her head against his cheek. She remained there as he pushed his oar into the water again and again.

Sam never told him? Alfredo had no idea what to say. He had been consumed with self-pity lately over his loneliness, yet both Charlotte and the Captain had endured much greater suffering than he ever had. *No one ever beat me.* Though he could not leave the Jesuit boarding school his mother and her priest had sent him to, he did not really want to. And once he graduated high school, he was free to do anything he wanted.

University, seminary school. Now this. He watched the island come closer and closer, the gnarled white roof of the chapel nestled luminously in its aura of millions of shades of green.

Alfredo watched, almost hypnotized as the Captain, his oar, and the river became a single entity. The oar pushed its way through the water and then sailed overhead in a fluid circular motion that propelled the little boat toward the island. He wondered who else the Captain boated around the river, without charge.

"Captain, you have taken me back and forth between Cadeña-l'jadia and the city several times, yet you do not allow me to pay you. Surely you must need income?"

The Captain continued to row. After a few moments, he looked over at Alfredo and said, "I receive such payment as I need from them that I carry. Some pay in currency, others trade for the goods I need." He looked out over the water. "Most folks are full of chatter. Their minds are running like rats on a wheel, and their mouths are running to escape their fear. They wear me out."

The oar sliced through the water, parting the fishes and birds from air and foam. "You, Padre, are quiet inside. When I stand beside you, I am quiet inside."

CHARLIE FLEW INTO STARFIRE'S TUPELO tree in the old Woodmen's Cemetery as the Chief Archivist was instructing a novice. "As every fledgling knows," Starfire said, "First Crow and First Raven brought many great gifts to the skinny, pathetic humans shivering in their darkness, the greatest of which was agriculture. The Patua' Clan, as this family would one day be called, took the instructions of First Crow and raised the arts of farming and animal husbandry to heights never achieved by humans since."

The novice, a great-great-great-great-grandchild of Starfire's, fidgeted on her branch, and the old raven stopped speaking, glaring at her until she settled down. Charlie was amused, recalling his own early days as a novice. The long stories of corvid interactions with the humans were only marginally interesting to him then, and he understood this one's impatience to get on with her training.

"For many thousands of years," Starfire continued, "the Patua' were renowned among humans for their expertise in botany and medicine. Their fields produced the most abundant grain, their trees the largest fruits. Some said they whispered to the plants to grow. They were the envy of the land for their farming methods. But, as the lust for power among the other humans grew, the Patua' became targets of envy, fear, and hate. As we know, the Patua', for all practical purposes, disappeared in the sixteenth century."

"Were they killed?" the novice asked.

Starfire stared coldly at her for a few moments, and Charlie feared for the youngster. A novice simply does not interrupt the Chief Archivist. He was relieved that Starfire did not strike her. "We have long thought they were," the old raven said, "being that they essentially vanished during a time of great religious fanaticism among the rest of the human species. We now believe that they were not killed but disappeared among their own kind. Hiding in plain sight as it were."

"How did they do that?" the novice asked.

"They stopped being Patua'," Starfire said. "They stopped talking to the corvids and stopped farming. They went into other trades like carpentry and weaving and blacksmithing."

The old raven paused to sip some water that had collected in a small aluminum tin he had long ago brought back to the tree—with remnants of chicken pot pie stuck to its sides and bottom. Whichever generation of his offspring happened to be in the nest enjoyed the largesse, picking it clean of even the burned-on grease spots. Over the years, the tin had become one with the tree, wedged into its very hide, and it collected enough water for Starfire to drink at will without leaving his tree.

"The problem was and is," Starfire resumed speaking, "that the Patua' were so very good at hiding. Too good. They hid so well, they forgot who they were. And so began the self-persecution of the Patua'."

"The Patua' killed each other?" the young novice asked in shock.

"By no means!" Starfire's deep raven voice nearly knocked her off the branch. "The Patua' are quite gentle souls. No, the Patua' disappeared from the corvid. They hid their ability to speak with us. They simply merged with the general population of humans, and as our current working hypothesis goes, the Patua' trait became diluted in the human gene pool, so there are naturally fewer of them."

"What is a gene pool?" the novice asked.

"Never mind that!" Starfire boomed. "The point is, the Patua' were ultimately dissolved into the larger non-Patua' human population. It is in this way that they disappeared. And because regular humans cannot speak to any of the animals, let alone us, they fear and revile those who can—the Patua'. Families hid their Patua' offspring; often they never left their houses."

Starfire moved to the hollow in the trunk of the tree saying, "But enough of this chatter. It is time to begin." He reached in, pulled out a clawful of dark blue paste and dropped it at Charlie's feet.

He motioned Charlie to ingest the fermented mildornia berries and continued speaking to the novice. "These are dire times. We must rouse the Patua'. But first we must discover where they are. The archival lattice contains scant few, yet I am certain there are many Patua' hiding among the humans."

"Have the bugs been exterminated?" Charlie asked.

"I think so," Starfire said. "I have introduced several pest-control chants into the lattice and that should take care of it. If there are a few remaining, we have algorithms now to detect them and stop them in their tracks. But we have a formidable task ahead of us to repair the damage. Now eat!"

Charlie choked down the bitter mildornia paste. Within seconds, the effects began—the locking of his feet around the branch, the numbing sensation that traveled up his legs and all through his outer layers of flesh and feathers, leaving his vital organs intact and functioning. He began the syncopated breathing that helped facilitate the opening of his lattice.

As a Keeper, Charlie had participated in the emplacement and retrieval rituals many times, and even a few repair jobs to correct spoiled data. But this was the first time his own memories would be used to patch holes in the lattice.

Starfire and the novice chanted the elementary verses of the Shanshu that put Charlie into the first level of the Keeper's Trance. He fell, enjoying the familiar weightlessness of the mildornia paralysis, as it dampened all sensations of the body. He watched his memory lattice snap open and expand outward in all directions. Many nodes glittered like multicolored stars that twinkled and blinked in the secret twilight.

Starfire chanted the verses he had devised for this ritual:

Vibzu bashki gax
Noxim ghazh blut a rek

Charlie had never heard that chant before and watched all but the purple nodes blink shut. After another series of unfamiliar chants, the purple nodes seemed to turn inside out, revealing layered filaments of the palest hues undulating in the lattice energy field.

Starfire raised his voice as he chanted another verse, and one of the filament pods enlarged, engulfing Charlie into its glowing interior. He blinked his eyes once, paused, and blinked twice more, signaling that he was on the threshold of the mildornia trance.

Starfire chanted several more verses, encoded with commands and questions directed at the Charlotte entity in Charlie's memory. "Where did you get the orb, Charlotte? Who gave it to you?"

Charlotte's voice came through Charlie's beak with a strange warbling sound. "'Look at my birthday present, Charlie! My Mimi, she gave it to me! It is very old she said. She used to wear it all the time, and I always loved it, and now it is mine!'"

"Who is Mimi?" Starfire's chanting came again through the darkness, urgent and demanding. "Who is Mimi?"

"Charlotte dances around; the orb hangs around her neck." Charlie stopped talking for a few moments and then resumed. "She is babbling." His head moved back and forth quickly. "The words come too quickly, faster and faster. I cannot understand; it is too fast."

Charlie's breathing became irregular and frantic. Starfire chanted softly, a verse that slowed the memory flow. Charlie's head stopped moving back and forth, and his breathing resumed its half-trance rhythm.

"Who is Mimi?" Starfire repeated the chant.

"'Mimi!'" Charlie's Charlotte voice cried out happily. Charlie swayed slightly on the branch.

"Who is Mimi?" Starfire's voice boomed through the lattice.

"An old woman," Charlie said. "Charlotte gives her a basket. She is crying, and the old woman grows smaller and smaller. She is gone."

A cracking white fireball suddenly tore through the image, and Charlie watched Charlotte dissolve back into the data ribbon. But before the ribbon could return to its node, the fireball destroyed it. The ribbon wound through the lattice aimlessly, with nowhere to go.

"The orb!" Starfire's chant reverberated around the lattice.

"Where is the orb?"

The fireball bounced into the lattice, severing an entire section from the main trunk, and hundreds of nodes went dark. An automatic alarm went off, sending a preprogrammed command. He blinked rapidly, involuntarily responding, but struggling to speak. The lattice collapsed, and the fireball disappeared.

Charlie felt Starfire's wing steady him as he heard the Shutting Verse. Before the memory of the ritual had completely disappeared, he opened his eyes. He forced his beak open and croaked, "Ug," and he fell into unconsciousness.

—14—

The River Queen

Henry Braun awaited the mayor's press conference with Jules. The sun came in through a tall window, casting a swath of light across the Persian rug. Two crows stared in the window at him; he got up from his chair, walked over to the window and drew the curtains closed.

"Why can't I keep those foul birds off my windowsill," he growled. The darkened room oppressed him, but that was preferable to having those damn crows watching his every move.

Jules laughed at Henry's unintended pun. "They're probably spies," he joked. "Sent over by the good Father Manzi."

But Henry was in no mood for jokes. He switched a lamp on and sat down in his chair. Henry the First smiled down on him from the paneled wall above. "No worries, Henry!" he said. "The island is as good as yours!"

Of course it is! Thank you Great-Grandfather! Somewhat relieved of his anxiety, Henry pushed a button on a remote control device, which opened a cabinet on an adjacent wall, revealing a large flat-screen television. He pushed another button, and the screen came to life.

"Here's the moment you've been waiting for, Henry," Jules said. "Think about it, Henry! You've won!"

Henry glanced nervously at the soundless screen, wishing Jules would shut up. "Yeah, but what if someone steps up and outbids me?"

"Step up from where, Henry?" Jules offered him one of his own cigars from the humidor on his desk. "Relax. Seven more days and the island is yours."

"Don't jinx it!" Henry snapped, nervous that Jules had used the number seven. *My unluckiest number.* He bit off the end of his cigar and bathed it thoroughly with his saliva before letting Jules light the end.

"That would require someone with a greater passion than you to own the island, Henry." Jules leaned back in his chair. "Don't you think we would know by now if there was another interested party?"

Henry shrugged. Logic was no comfort at a time like this. The mayor's face appeared on the screen, and he turned up the volume.

"Good citizens of Ledford," the mayor's flabby mouth said. He licked his lips and smiled into the camera. "It is my great pleasure to announce that, after a two-week period in which you the public has a right to comment, the city of Ledford hopes to condemn Wilder Island as a nuisance under the country's eminent domain laws. I am certain that the good people of this city will agree that we should move forward and develop the island into a resort park, as Mr. Henry Braun has proposed. Or perhaps a shopping mall, or a business park, all of which would bring money and jobs to our city."

In great relief, Henry wiped the sweat from his forehead with his handkerchief. He relaxed into his chair and inhaled deeply on his cigar. Henry the First smiled warmly down upon him. He exhaled gratefully.

"Once the island has been properly developed," the mayor's said, his head bobbing like a large bird, "the revenue from the island will be such that we can do away with property taxes altogether. Wouldn't that be nice? Perhaps the city could end the gross receipts tax on all goods. How about them apples? More money to spend, more jobs. Folks, we are on the threshold of a new future for our fair city. A whole new day of prosperity."

A gaggle of reporters crowded around the mayor's podium, and all shouted their questions at once. "Will the people have a say who buys the island?" a reporter managed to shout above the rest.

"Wilder Island will be sold to the highest bidder," the mayor said. "Seven days after the commentary period is over."

Seven again. Henry's sense of well-being breached, and a shroud of catastrophe loomed suddenly over him. *What if the investors dou-*

ble-cross me? He had invited his wealthiest friends in the business community to a picnic on the island, where he would plant his own flag, claiming the island as his. *What if* ... his shoulders slumped, and he raised his suffering eyes up to the portraits of his ancestors.

"Be a man!" Henry the First said, his stern face whipping Henry into an upright position. "Only women whine about what will be. Seize today, and tomorrow is yours!"

+ + +

DR. RUSS MATTHEWS, BOARD MEMBER of the recently established Friends of Wilder Island Land Trust, happened to be in his office when the TV station called for comment on the city's eminent domain ruling.

"I'm disappointed," he told the reporter. "We will rally the people to say no to developing the island. Wilder Island is a landmark in this city. The very identity of Ledford is tied up in this island. Commercial development will destroy it, whether it's Henry Braun building a casino resort, or Joe Schmoe building a mall or a motor speedway. It's a matter of who we want to be, who we want to project to the outside world."

"How do you intend to stop it?" the reporter asked.

"With a grassroots uprising," Russ answered. "We need to stand up, all of us, and just say no to destroying this jewel in our midst. Some things money can buy. Our Wilder Island heritage isn't one of them."

The phone rang again as soon as Russ hung up with the reporter. "Pull the trigger!" Kate said on the other end of the line. "Launch the beg-a-thon!"

+ + +

HENRY AND JULES CONVENED BACK IN his office after another superbly cooked dinner. Whatever Minnie's faults were, Henry always appreciated his wife's culinary talents, though he hardly ever told her so.

Why should he? Did she ever thank him for providing her with such a luxurious and opulent mansion?

The six o'clock news replayed the mayor's afternoon announcement and showcased the spectacular model of Ravenwood Resort as an example of what could be done with the island. The camera zoomed in on the adorable little *River Queen* and its tiny lights.

"Everyone in Ledford is invited!" Henry's smiling and somewhat giddy face said as the camera panned slowly over the paddleboat. "Come on down to the city dock on Saturday or Sunday for a free ride around Wilder Island on my beautiful *River Queen!*"

Several local radio stations broadcast a Public Service Announcement on behalf of the Friends of Wilder Island Land Trust. The student-run station at the university broadcast a panel discussion with Dr. Russ Matthews and Dr. Alfredo Manzi on the condemnation ruling.

"Help us save Wilder Island from the bulldozers!" a woman's voice came over the airwaves. "Come on out to the arts and crafts fair this weekend at the Waterfront. We've got over two hundred artists featuring all things Wilder, and a silent auction to help keep our island wild. Stop by the Friends of Wilder Island booth and buy a share in the island, get a free flag with the Wilder Island logo, and become part of the land trust. We need your help!"

Henry reached over to the radio and shut it off with an angry twist of his wrist. "Who the hell do they think they are anyway?" he growled. "The freaking Public Broadcasting Service? For crying out loud, are they trying to dupe the public into buying into their land trust scheme?"

"As a matter of fact," Jules said blandly, "some of these stations subscribe to much of the programming from PBS. Your tax dollars at work, Henry."

Henry scowled at Jules, wondering why his attorney seemed to enjoy toying with him. "I'm not talking about the university's commie student radio station," he ranted. "I've had just about enough of this sham outfit, this so-called land trust. I want you to do something about it, Jules."

"Like what, Henry?" Jules swirled the wine in his glass.

"Discredit them," Henry said. "Find something wrong with these troublemakers—the Matthews, for instance. Dr. Smarty-Pants college professor and his so-called artist wife. Find out why Manzi showed up here all of a sudden. Who can trust a Catholic priest these days? Find out who else is involved in this scam to cheat me out of my rightful inheritance."

His hands shook as he poured himself a glass of wine, slopping a few drops onto the floor. He moved his shoe back and forth across the wet spot, disbursing it over a wider area.

"And then what, Henry?" Jules said. "Beatings with a rubber hose? Cement overshoes? You won, for God's sake! The city condemned the island."

The wine Henry spilled had disobediently beaded up on the waxed hardwood floor. He scowled at the red raindrops and patted his pocket for a handkerchief.

"Look, Henry," Jules said, "you're taking the whole town for a ride on the *River Queen*. You think they've got something better? An arts and crafts fair? Selling worthless shares in a land trust? Don't make me laugh!"

Jules laughed, and Henry tried to calm his anxiety. The drops of spilled wine on the floor reminded him of blood. His blood. *My blood, sweat, and tears have all gone into this island!*

"While you're at it," Jules continued, "give 'em all five bucks and let 'em waste it in the casino. You'll hook 'em all, and they'll stop thinking about their beloved island. Let this commie rabble, as you call them, rattle their chains till the crows come home, for all the good it'll do them."

Henry dropped the hanky to the floor and moved it around with his foot, staining its pure white perfection.

+ + +

THE ART FAIR CELEBRATING THE WILDNESS of Wilder Island opened on Friday evening, the day after the mayor's press conference. The people came out for the fair, and both sides of the river swarmed with humans. Jade and Russ met Alfredo at the Waterfront boat landing and walked up the stone steps to Riverside Drive, which had been closed to vehicle traffic for the fair.

The wind picked up and carried lighthearted music that bubbled forth from a calliope on board the *River Queen* across the river. "I feel like thumbing my nose at it," Jade said. "Except it's quite lovely. Too bad Henry Braun owns her."

"Jeez," Russ said as he looked across the river, "look at the size of that crowd!"

"Hopefully most of them are coming over here," Jade said, grasping his hand and leaning into him. "The boat landing is right there too, next to the *River Queen*."

"So ironic," Alfredo said, shaking his head. "Henry on one side, us on the other. Wilder Island in the middle."

A small crowd had assembled around the KMUS student radio station booth where Alfredo, Russ, and Kate would participate in a live discussion regarding the future of Wilder Island. A television news station's cameraman panned around the fair-going crowd as the reporter blathered something about the mayor declining his invitation to attend.

"Good evening, ladies and gentleman," the disc jockey began. "This is KMUS, streaming live from the Friends of Wilder Island arts and crafts fair at the Waterfront here in Downtown Ledford. We are here tonight to discuss the fate of our island in light of the mayor's announcement today that the city has condemned the island under eminent domain laws."

A few people stopped to listen. Jade and one of Russ's students handed them flags bearing the Friends of Wilder Island logo—the skyline of Wilder Island in front of a huge full moon. Jade had taken particular delight in modeling a subtle image of a crow into the moon.

"Our guests this evening are MU biology professors Dr. Russ Matthews and Dr. Alfredo Manzi, both board members of the Friends of Wilder Island Land Trust. Manzi, we should note, is also the pastor of the old hermit's chapel on the island. And lastly we have Ms. Kate Herron, attorney for the land trust."

The DJ's voice boomed out over the loudspeakers, attracting more people to the live broadcast. Flags waved, and a few people called out, "Save Wilder Island!" The music from the calliope swelled for a moment before disappearing on a downriver breeze.

"Before we get into the ramifications of condemnation," The DJ said, "let's start with the basics. Ms. Herron, can you tell us exactly what does condemnation under eminent domain laws mean?"

"It means the government can steal your property!" a man shouted.

The small crowd waved flags amid catcalls and shouts of disapproval: "They can do that?" "Down with Braun!" "Preserve the wilderness!" "Wilder Island!"

"It means 'compulsory purchase,'" Kate replied, after the noise had abated somewhat. "The Fifth Amendment to the US Constitution grants the right to local, state, and federal governments to condemn and confiscate private property, so long as it's subsequently used for the public good, and the owner is paid a fair price. But the property owner has no choice. He must sell."

A man in the back yelled out, "Get the government's hands off my property!"

Flags waved wildly, and the crowd shouted, "No! No! No!"

"The government can just sell your property to a private developer?" the DJ asked, turning the mic up. "I thought they could only do that, take your land, for roads, bridges, schools maybe—things like that."

"That's been the traditional use of the eminent domain clause," Kate said, nodding. She looked over her mic at the crowd. "But a couple years ago, the Supreme Court expanded the definition of public good to include creating jobs and increasing revenues to the government. That automatically expanded the permissible land uses under which government bodies may exercise eminent domain. Prior to that, it was used, as you said, for schools, hospitals, roads, et cetera."

"But, why?" the DJ asked. "It seems so un-American."

The people in the crowd nodded, and the man in the back hollered, "It is un-American!" He led another chant of "No! No! No!"

The television station's cameraman panned around the rowdy crowd again, and Jade wished momentarily that the guy in the back would be quiet. But she quickly changed her mind, realizing that was what the land trust was trying to do—stir the people up. *I hope this makes it to the evening news.*

"What about the chapel?" the DJ asked. "Aren't churches protected from eminent domain?"

"No," Kate said. "Nothing is protected. Not even churches."

"They're going to tear down the hermit's chapel?" a woman shouted out from the crowd. The crowd blew up again, waving flags and yelling, "No! No! No!"

"Is Wilder Island doomed then?" the DJ asked, turning his mic up again. "Is this a done deal? Is there nothing we can do?"

"We've got two weeks," Kate said. "And we plan to be heard."

As the Friends of Wilder Island prepared the arts and crafts fair for opening night at the Waterfront, the *River Queen* was released from her moorings at the timber mill, and by late Friday afternoon, she had docked at the city boat landing. Like a siren song, the calliope aboard the beautiful paddleboat beckoned Ledford residents to come aboard for a free tour. Complete with two restaurants, a pub, and a daycare center, the *River Queen* also offered slot machines, bingo, and blackjack.

Henry had never had children of his own, but somehow he knew what kids liked. He spared no expense on the childcare center, with video games, jungle gyms, playhouses with miniature functioning appliances, and a plethora of building blocks, erector sets, and Lincoln logs. Big floppy pillows and blow-up furniture gave the childcare center a cartoonish aura.

While the folks of Ledford crowded the decks of the *River Queen* and stood in line to play the slots, Henry sat glued to the television in his penthouse apartment on the roof. The live KMUS broadcast, televised from the arts and crafts fair at the Waterfront really irritated him, but he couldn't bring himself to shut it off.

"So, if the city condemns the island," the DJ said, "the trust will be forced to sell it to the highest bidder?"

The camera panned to the flag-waving crowd shouting, "No! No! No!"

Dammit! I should have had flags made. Henry's stomach hurt. The relentless calliope down on the deck had given him a headache. He wished he could turn it all off, the TV, the calliope, everything, and just have some peace and quiet.

"Yes," the attorney Kate Herron said, tossing her red hair back over her shoulder. "But the land trust has two protective overlays, which ensure that while we can't stop eminent domain, we can force whoever buys the island to conform to our restrictions on what may and what must be done with it. We've restricted the land use to a bird sanctuary and botanical research station. And we've got a ninety-nine year lease with the Jesuits on the chapel, which they still own."

The crowd cheered, and Henry picked up the remote and muted the sound with an angry flick of his wrist. "What the hell, Jules? Is she blowing smoke, or does that commie land trust think they can tell me what to do with my island?" He peeled his eyes away from the television and looked at Jules. "Can they?"

"Relax, Henry," Jules said, waving his hand at the image of Kate Herron on the TV. "I've never heard of such a thing as telling someone what they can and can't do with their private property. It's quite un-American, don't you think?"

"Damn right." Henry said. *Don't play with me, you overpaid land shark. One of these days ...*

"But if it'll make you feel better," Jules said, "I'll file an injunction against this land trust having any legal status to demand anything."

The television had taken Henry's attention, and he made no reply.

"While we can't protect ourselves from eminent domain in the court of law." Kate Herron said into the camera, "the Friends of Wilder Island Land Trust has the legal standing to represent the interests of the island in court. And, we can catalyze public sentiment to save it from development. Which we fully intend to do."

Henry glared at Jules. "She's full of crap, Henry," Jules said. "There is no stopping eminent domain."

"I understand we can all become members of the land trust," the DJ said. "Is that correct?"

"Yes," Alfredo Manzi replied, "anyone may purchase shares in the land trust. We invite the entire city out to the arts and crafts fair, where we have a booth staffed with volunteers to sell shares in the island."

Henry snorted. "My arse! Soaking the public for worthless shares in a bird swamp, you swindling hypocrite!" He threw a pillow at Alfredo Manzi's image on the TV.

"Oh, they're not entirely worthless, Henry," Jules said. "People can line their birdcages with them."

Both men laughed. Henry opened the humidor on the end table next to him, took out two cigars, and handed one to Jules.

"We do not advocate saving Wilder Island for nostalgic reasons only," Russ Matthews was saying as the two men lit their cigars, "though people do have a right to their lore, their stories, the connection to their past. But look at the revenue this island generates by its very solitary existence in our midst."

Henry burst out laughing. Shaking his head, he looked in amazement at the TV. "Oh, that's a good one! Revenue from the bird swamp!" He slapped his knees, laughing. "They can't be serious!"

"The city logo features the Wilder Island skyline," Russ Matthews said, as if listing the glorious money-making opportunities the island was engaged in. "The tourist industry relies heavily on the island, as do many businesses for their brands—the Cold Raven Brewery, the Crow's Nest, for example."

"Correct," Kate Herron said. "Wilder Island is by no means derelict, so the assertion that the island produces nothing is just flat wrong."

I'll flat wrong you, you miserable tree-hugger. Henry shook his fist at the TV. He hated attorneys, all of them. Up to and including his own. *Slimy bastards!* But he retained Jules. As he had told his wife, Minnie, "I need a lawyer to keep me out of the trouble that I wouldn't get into if there weren't any lawyers."

"We must all rise up and say no to condemnation," Kate Herron said. "The only weapon we have is public sentiment; that's the only thing that will save Wilder Island."

Public sentiment? We'll see, my pretty, where public sentiment lies after they ride on my River Queen!

"We are not opposed to development or entertainment," Russ Matthews said. "But we ask: can this Ravenwood Resort not be built somewhere else?"

"Good question, Dr. Matthews," the DJ said. "Perhaps Mr. Braun could answer that, but he elected to not be with us tonight."

"Bastards never invited me," Henry growled as he muted the sound. He leaned back into the couch, puffing out seven smoke rings as he exhaled.

"Oh, but they did, Henry," Jules said. "You turned them down, remember? We decided you wouldn't engage with them at all because it doesn't serve our interests to debate them. Remember?"

Henry grumbled into his chest. It was true; he didn't want to be their straw man. He had dignity.

"Forget about them!" Jules said, waving his cigar in the air. "Fight fire with water! Convince the people of Ledford that your resort has something wonderful for everyone in the family, while this land trust has a dark, spooky island that no one other than the priest is allowed to step foot on."

Henry nodded dully and stared at the soundless TV. He wished Jules would shut up. He got up and left his penthouse and scowled when Jules joined him at the railing.

"You did a great job refurbishing this old bitch, Henry," Jules said as they looked down on the deck below. He took a long drag from his cigar. "When I first saw her, I didn't think you'd be able to clean her up. But she's a classy lady now."

"She's a beauty, Mr. Braun!" someone yelled from the deck.

Henry waved and yelled down to the man, "Come back tomorrow, you hear? Catch a ride on the *Queen!*"

CHARLIE AND HIS YOUNG SON JOED perched in the branches of a basswood tree, listening to strains of music that wafted across the river from the calliope on the promenade deck of the *River Queen*. JoEd gazed in fascination at the beautiful paddleboat. Elegant yet perky, the *River Queen* charmed him with her bright red paint, white trim, and golden railings. Oh! And the big red paddlewheel! He had never seen anything so amazing.

JoEd had spent his entire fledgehood deep in the swamps and forests of Cadeña-l'jadia and in the branches above the tree house. Ever since that day his zazu had taken him around the periphery of the island and he'd beheld his weebs's homeland across the river, buildings mesmerized him. When his zazu told him the *River Queen* was a building that floated on water, he could hardly believe it.

But believe it he did as he watched her float slowly down the river and dock at the city landing. Speechless with awe, JoEd couldn't take his eyes off the magnificent *River Queen*.

"Zazu," he said as he turned toward his father.

"Go!" Charlie said, without waiting for his son to ask. "Fly on over and check it out. But be home by sunset; you know how your weebs worries."

Without a word, JoEd took to the air and flew across the river toward the *River Queen*. The music got louder as he approached, and he realized the bugs crawling all over the boat were actually humans. He looked back toward Cadeña-l'jadia. It seemed so far away in its brooding green solitude. But the colorful riverboat and the teeming life it hosted were irresistible to JoEd. Though his heart was beating very fast, and he was a little scared, he bravely flew right to the roof of the *River Queen* and grasped the golden railing that wound all the way around the topmost layer of the boat.

JoEd had only ever seen one human up close—Jayzu. He looked down upon the humans milling around and said out loud, "How do they tell each other apart? They all look the same!"

"Not really," a voice said. JoEd turned to see another crow standing on the roof.

"The differences are subtle," an older crow said, "but after a while, you can see them. Some you can even pick out of crowds, but those are special humans."

"Like Jayzu?" JoEd asked. "He lives on Cadeña-l'jadia."

"Everyone knows Jayzu," the crow said. "He is Patua', like Bruthamax. But you can tell even the regular humans apart if you live around them long enough. You get to know who is naughty and who is nice."

"Oh," JoEd said. "What do the naughty ones look like?"

"It's not what they look like," the crow said. "They're all butt-ugly if you ask me. But there among the masses are those who distinguish themselves by their actions, be they good or evil. Those humans we know. The others, well, they're a bit like cattle, don't you think?" He peered over the edge at the people milling around the docks.

Before JoEd could ask what cattle meant, another crow joined them on the roof.

"Hey there, Antoine," the new arrival said. "How're things?"

"Oh, not bad, Tobias," Antoine said, "not bad at all. Thanks for asking. Say, young fella," he turned to JoEd, "you got a name?"

"JoEd," he croaked, wishing he sounded more grown-up.

"Well, grawky there, JoEd," Tobias said.

"First time he's seen so many humans, that's what he said," Antoine told Tobias. The two crows nodded knowingly.

"Must not be from the city then," Tobias said. "Place is crawling with 'em."

"He just flew in from Cadeña-l'jadia for the festivities," said Antoine. "There's but one human there."

"Ah," said Tobias, cocking his head to one side. "He's a friend of Jayzu then.'

The sights and sounds of the paddleboat astonished him. There was so much to see! So many humans! More crows landed on the railing, and JoEd scooted over to make room. Three more crows came in for a landing on the roof and cackled their greetings to Antoine, Tobias.

"I'm JoEd," he said, putting a wing out to the young female crow next to him. "Are you from around here?"

She brushed her wing across his and said, "I'm Shannon. I was hatched and fledged Downtown. That's the best place for festivities!"

"My weebs came from Downtown too!" JoEd said. "I've never been there though." He looked across the river toward his mother's homeland. So beautiful, how it sparkled like water almost.

"Are you here for the festivities?" Shannon asked.

He didn't know what festivities meant, but so far it seemed to be a good thing. Lots of noise and excitement, and there were delicious odors in the air, all new and enticing.

"I didn't know about the festivities," JoEd said. "I came to see the paddleboat. That's what my zazu said this is."

"Oh, I didn't know that!" Shannon said. "I watched it float in like a great big duck, kind of, except it looks more like a house."

A couple of humans came out onto the deck below them and leaned against the railing. They waved their arms and shouted some things JoEd couldn't understand.

"Do they have festivities often?" JoEd asked Shannon. "I'm from Cadeña-l'jadia, and this is the first time I have been to any festivities."

"All the time," she said. "But this one looks like it's going to be a doozy!"

Many dozens of crows arrived on the rooftop over the next half hour, and it seemed to JoEd that they all knew each other. There were a great many crows on Cadeña-l'jadia, and he knew them all, but here were so many new beaks! He walked through the growing crowd of crows, introducing himself. He tucked every one of their names into the lattice of his memory.

And the names of the new food.

"Man," Antoine said, "I love hot dogs. One of the human's greatest inventions, if you ask me."

"Nah," Tobias said, "it's the French fry. Oh! Glorious fries! I could live off them, I tell you what."

JoEd had never seen a hot dog or a French fry and had no idea what they were, but they sounded exotic and tasty. "Is that what I smell?" he asked. "Hot dogs and French fries?"

"And hamburgers," said Antoine, "which also means pickles and onions."

"Thank the Orb humans are so clumsy," Tobias said, "else we wouldn't eat so well."

"Yes," Antoine agreed, "they are quite wasteful too, bless their hearts. And come morning, we, the mighty volunteers, shall clean the docks of burgers, fries, and whatnot for our human brethren."

Tobias chuckled and said, "Indeed. Though it is a thankless job, we are dedicated."

"Dedicated to gluttony," a new arrival said.

"May we never have less!" Antoine shouted.

"Gluttony! Gluttony!" the crows all cried out to the humans below and to the skies above. "Gluttony!"

"Good thing we came early," Antoine said to JoEd. "You just stay put right here. We got good roosting and front-row seats to the banquet. There won't be any roosting spots, good or bad, come sundown. You just wait; there'll be food everywhere, come morning. All over the decks, all over the riverbank, the docks. Everywhere."

The world beyond the island captivated JoEd. *Paddleboats! Festivities! Food everywhere! And a doozy!*

The beg-a-thon ended, and Alfredo, Russ, and Kate found Sam and Jade were mobbed by people at the land trust booth. Everyone, it seemed, wanted a share in the future of Wilder Island. They jumped in, and the five of them sold shares until the crowd dwindled enough that they could leave the booth in the hands of the volunteers.

The fair occupied two city blocks along the Waterfront, two double rows of booths, one on each side of Riverside Drive. The mysterious Wilder Island forest had long attracted many artists, who generated a multitude of art from all its seasons. The variety of ways in which people used the black birds and tree line silhouette of Wilder Island as art motifs was astonishing, from the sublime to the ridiculous.

"This is how the people of Ledford show their love for their island," Alfredo said as the friends strolled past the booths at the arts and crafts fair.

Paintings of all genres depicted the island's many moods: *The Cliffs of Wilder Island; Wilder Island in the Mist*; *Storm on Wilder Island*; *Wilder Island at Dawn*; *Sunset*; *On a Lazy Afternoon*; *In the Snow*; *In a Thunderstorm*; *Wilder Island under the Full Moon*; *New Moon*; *Quarter Moon*; and *Dark Nights* of no moon.

Many artists painted the seasons of Wilder Island Forest: in the fall as the deciduous trees said good-bye to summer in a spectacular rain of colors; the bare winter grays and browns against gray skies; and the blessed relief of spring, expressed by the subtle colors of the flowering trees.

There were literally hundreds of photographs of trees and crows and of the wild river thrashing the shores of the island. The hermit's chapel appeared in many, sometimes as a holy shrine, sometimes as a dark, enigmatic witness to the island's solitude. Whether singular or in flocks, on the wing or perch, crows and ravens rose to the unusual occasion of stardom at the fair, as icons of the wild mystery of the island.

The love for Wilder Island appeared in the more mundane objects as well. Crows, ravens, and island silhouettes appeared in T-shirts, key chains, hats, candles, coffee mugs, handbags, and backpacks.

"Limited only by the boundaries of the human imagination," Alfredo said, "gifted to certain individuals more than others. Like Jade and Sam."

Jade blushed and waved him away, saying, "In some circles, it's considered madness."

"In others," Sam said with a grin, "it's considered a vow of poverty."

"Let's count how many famous artists died in the poor house!" Kate said cheerfully. "There's Vincent van Gogh, Beethoven—can we include musicians too?"

"Oh, shut up!" Sam said, giving Kate an affectionate shove.

They wandered past a booth of wrought-iron work featuring a coat rack, constructed such that when coats were hung upon it, the crows appeared to be flying off with them. "That would be perfect for your cottage," Jade said. "Don't you think, Alfredo?"

"I'm hungry," Kate said. "Can we stop and eat some of this fine food that has been tantalizing my nose and stomach since we got here?"

"I too am hungry," Alfredo said. "I had breakfast once, long ago. On a distant island." He smiled wanly at the laughter from his friends. "What? Priests cannot be hungry?"

"Oh, no," Jade said through her chuckles. "The thing is, we're just not used to the idea that priests can have a sense of humor."

Am I not still human? He laughed to himself. Priest, Patua'—what did it matter? *I am still an outcast.*

"Some of us don't think of you as a priest," Kate said with an impish smile. "You're incognito tonight, though, aren't you? Without your little white collar?"

Alfredo laughed and said, "Oh, I never wear those! I have a hard enough time with laundry issues on the island without having to care for priestly fashion accessories. Besides, I do not think that God requires my throat to be chafed with stiff, scratchy collars to serve him." *Not that I am much of a priest.*

"Can't you just be 'off duty'?" Russ asked, making little quote marks in the air with his fingers.

"Well, yes," Alfredo replied. "Except I'm never really on duty. I have no congregation that needs my ministrations. Other than baking pre-consecrated Communion wafers for St. Sophia's, I'm just an ordinary Joe. Part-time priest, part-time professor, full-time human."

"Right," Kate said, looking at Alfredo through squinted eyes. "You're an ordinary Joe, Padre. And I'm the tooth fairy! Now, where shall we eat?"

The delightful flavors of many cuisines wafted all around the fair, tantalizing even the most resolute. "There's tons of food," Sam said. "We'll eat well, real cheap, whatever we do. I've spent just about every waking hour in the last month planning and arranging this shindig."

"And," Kate said as she linked her arm into his, "he subjected the food and beverage purveyors to more scrutiny than the artists and craftspeople."

Jade laughed and said, "That's true! He was like a rabid dog with the Burger Shack guy."

"No franchises," Sam said, laughing. "That was the number-one rule. We want local people and local establishments only; that's what I told 'em. Same as the artists."

"Sam!" Jade said, sniffing the air. "Do I smell Thai?"

"Yes, ma'am," Sam said, tipping his baseball cap. "I tried to represent all the flavors the people of this city like. We've got India, China, Japan, Vietnam, Thailand. And of course all the usual American, Mexican, and European suspects—corn dogs, burgers, tacos, corn-on-the-cob, croissants, perogi, brats. You name it, we got it."

The numerous microbreweries of Ledford were well represented also, thanks to Sam's rule against franchises. Colorful labels sported such names as Two Crow Brew, Red Raven Ale, Bog Birch Beer, and Crow's Eye Wild Lager. Wilder Island Brewery, the city's oldest and finest, committed all profits from their number-one selling beer, Crow Wing Ale, over the weekend of the arts and crafts fair to the Friends of Wilder Island Land Trust.

The friends found a table and sat down with their food and beer, laying out a smorgasbord of international cuisine. They ate till they could hold no more.

The sun set gorgeously, reflecting brilliant red, yellow, pink, and orange hues off the fluffy clouds that floated on the horizon. A large flock of crows appeared above the treetops on Wilder Island. Coalescing into a swirling spectacle of black wings, the crows flew a great circular flight pattern against the last colors of the sunset.

Reminiscent of the famed photograph in the city library, *Murder of Crows*, the crowds at the fair and milling around the *River Queen* gasped in delight. A roar of approval and applause erupted from both sides of the island, and for a few moments, a pervasive sense of community overtook human and crow, and the spirits of both species soared.

JoEd Blows His Mind

Henry slept on his riverboat, but he did not sleep well. All night long, he was plagued by dreams of an angry river inciting the wind to blow, battering his beautiful River Queen to smithereens. While clouds poured down rain, the River Queen capsized. Alone, he bailed bucket after bucket of water, but the more he bailed, the more it rained. Just before she rolled over and sank, Henry woke up, drenched in sweat.

At dawn, he got up, showered, and shaved, and slammed down a shot of bourbon to stop his hands from shaking. He strode purposefully down to his usual breakfast—bacon and eggs over easy, a slice of burnt toast, no butter, and a cup of black coffee. He read the *Wall Street Journal* as he ate, ignoring the bustle of the workers around him as they prepared for the city folk of Ledford to come aboard for their free ride.

Saturday morning dawned bright and beautiful; the decks and docks had been picked clean of food by the crows. The crew cleaned up the rest of the trash, and the *River Queen* was ready to roll. Henry abandoned the idea of circling Wilder Island—his dreams the night before of an angry river destroying his beautiful lady quite convinced him. "We'll go up the river to the mills," Henry told the Captain and crew, "and down to the old stone bridge."

The people of Ledford flocked to the docks to wait their turn for a ride on the lovely *River Queen*. An endless stream of ice-cream sodas and hot dogs flowed while Henry handed out baseball caps and T-shirts displaying the Ravenwood Resort logo, and free tokens for the casino. Television and newspaper reporters circulated among the crowd, filming the revelry and occasionally interviewing a citizen.

"Tell us how it feels to be waiting for a ride on the historic *River Queen*," the television reporter asked as he stuck his mic into the face of a carefully coifed, middle-aged woman.

"I'm ecstatic," she gushed. "Is this gorgeous or what? Can you imagine? A ride on the glorious *River Queen*? Oh, be still my beating heart!" Putting her hand to her bosom, the woman closed her eyes as if taking a moment to regain her composure.

"So," the reporter said, winking at the camera, "I take it you'd like to see the *River Queen* permanently parked at Braun Enterprise's proposed resort on Wilder Island?"

"Oh my God!" The woman went into another round of passionate yet ambiguous exclamations. "Can you imagine? Oh! Right across the river! In our own backyard! Can you imagine?"

As the *River Queen* paddled upriver, the reporter sidled up to a small group of people leaning on the handrails. "Tell the folks out there in TV land how it feels to sail on one of America's historic paddleboats!"

"Oh, we love it!" a woman said. "I've always wanted to ride on a paddleboat, you know. I'm so happy I got to experience this!"

"Truly," a man said. "This is a wondrous experience! My great-granddaddy was the Captain of the *Delta Queen*, back in the day. That was a sad day, when the paddleboats stopped running the Big Muddy, I'll tell you what. I'm just downright grateful to Henry Braun for bringing this piece of American history back to us."

The ride on the *River Queen* was a big hit. Though the paddleboat stayed well in the middle of the deepest part of the channel, most people had never been that close to the mysterious island, and the opportunity to observe its secrets was tantalizing. Nor had they ever been on a riverboat.

"Take some pictures of people having a good time," Henry said to the television reporter he had invited. "I want their smiles all over the evening news, you understand?"

The *River Queen* made quite a spectacle indeed, cruising up and down the east side of the river. A contingent of crows clutching the golden railing atop Henry Braun's apartment added to the people's amusement, but not to Henry's.

"Damn crows," he growled at them, waving his arms, trying to scare them off. The crows cackled back in laughter—at least that's what Henry heard. "I'll have the little bastards shot if they don't get off my boat."

"Don't do it," Jules had told him the evening before when the crows began to arrive. "It's illegal to discharge a firearm in the city limits. And don't shoot the crows, it's a violation of the Migratory Bird Act. Remember you're on a mission here. You want people on your side. You want to appear reasonable, not like a hot head with a gun. Put it away, Henry."

AT FIRST LIGHT, JOED OPENED ONE eye. After a few seconds of bewilderment, he remembered where he was and opened the other eye. A momentary wave of guilt washed over him for breaking his promise to his zazu that he would be home by sunset that day before. He would go home today, explain to his weebs how fabulous and wonderful the *River Queen* was, that he was simply unable to tear himself away. JoEd hoped she would understand.

Many crows still snoozed on their roosts all around him, including Antoine. JoEd waited quietly, surveying the scene below. Antoine was not kidding; there was food everywhere. *Maybe I will find a hot dog.* He leaped off the railing and down to the deck. Before him lay a veritable feast, and he picked at a morsel. "Is it a hot dog, I wonder?" he said out loud. "Or is it a doozy?"

"That," Antoine said as he came in for a landing next to JoEd, "is a French fry."

"It's incredible," JoEd said through a beakful of the most delectable food he had ever tasted.

"This is a hot dog," Antoine said, pushing a piece of reddish something or other at JoEd.

"Wow!" JoEd said after a few pecks at it. "Better than the French fry! These humans know how to eat!"

He and Antoine wandered through the rubbish, picking at a burger here, a piece of caramel apple there. The sun rose to hundreds of crows feasting on the largesse left by the crowds the night before.

"Had enough, kid?" asked Antoine.

JoEd nodded. He was stuffed. The two crows flew back up to the railing above Henry's apartment and watched a dozen or so humans issue forth and fruitlessly attempt to chase the crows off the decks.

"The only thing's going to get rid of them boys," Antoine said, shaking his head, "is the hot dogs and burgers and fries getting all eaten up or tossed into the river. You'd think they could figure that out."

"Good for us they can't," JoEd said. "That was some pretty easy pickings. I usually have to work harder than this to get food on Cadeña-l'jacia."

"That's why we like to live among humans," said Antoine. "Great food and lots of it. Leaves more time for riding the jaloosies."

JoEd gazed across the river at the dark green shadows of Cadeña-l'jadia. He really should be getting home, he knew. But there was just too much excitement. Too much food!

"And there's even more food across the river," Antoine said. "Big crowds at the Waterfront yesterday. They dropped tidbits everywhere, and not just hot dogs. Everything! You ever had Thai, JoEd?"

The young crow shook his head. "Come on, son," Antoine said as he leaped into the sky. "This is going to blow your mind!"

The two crows flew together across the sparkling river toward the Waterfront. When they arrived on the scene of the arts and crafts fair, JoEd saw that many crows and other scavengers had already arrived. But no humans. He followed Antoine as he swooped up and down, and in between the colorful art fair booths. They passed up many delectable tidbits on the street, and he wondered if they would ever find any Thai. Not that he knew what Thai meant, but the last two days with Antoine had considerably broadened JoEd's world view, and he supposed that eating Thai would too.

Finally Antoine dropped to the street and pecked at a chunk of food. "Nope," he said, shaking his head. "I don't know what it is, but it ain't Thai." He pecked at it a few more times. "It's good, though!"

"Better even than a hot dog!" JoEd said with his beak crammed with whatever it was. "Is it a doozy?"

"Nah," Antoine said. "Wait'll you taste Thai; that'll be your doozy, I reckon." He lifted his beak into the air. "I know it's here somewhere. I can smell it."

The two crows took off again, and JoEd followed Antoine back through the streets. "Ah!" Antoine said. "There it is!" He swooped down to a trashcan next to a tent, picked out a small container, and dropped it to the ground. "Yep, Pad Thai. Long, flat noodles, a few peanuts and some stir-fried veggies." Antoine said triumphantly. He hopped down to the pavement and pecked at the Pad Thai. "Oh, yeah!" he said after he swallowed a bite. "Pad Thai! You gotta try this, JoEd! It's just out of this world!"

JoEd picked a piece off the street and dropped it immediately. "Whoa! That has got some kick to it!"

"That's how we like it," Antoine said, chuckling. "You get used to the heat after a while."

JoEd ate very well on Cadeña-l'jadia—plenty of fish guts, small rodents, even an occasional egg. But he'd never even heard of spice, let alone imagined what it did to food; he pecked at the Thai food, though it burned his eyes even to get near it.

"After a while," Antoine said, "you crave it hot."

JoEd could not imagine craving the burning sensation in his beak and all the way down his throat. He slurped some water from an abandoned cup.

"Here," Antoine said, tossing JoEd a piece of a honeybun he dug out of the trash. "Eat this. It'll take some of the sting away."

The honeybun soothed JoEd's burning beak, and he returned to the feast before him. Perusing the food choices strewn about the streets and sidewalks, he sampled a croissant with cream cheese and orange marmalade from the French Riviera Bakery and declared that it was his favorite food of all time. When he tasted the souvlaki from the Greek Cafe, he changed his mind—until he discovered the amazing flavors of Japan.

"Teriyaki!" JoEd said to Antoine. "That's my favorite!"

"Have you tried the calzone?" Antoine pointed a wing toward the Little Italy trashcans. "Tobias found a mushroom-broccoli-mozzarella over there. Sweet!"

"Oh, yeah!" JoEd said, amazed again at the world of flavors that had visited his beak. "The absolute best!"

Stuffed beyond belief, JoEd couldn't take another bite. Antoine motioned him up to the lower branches of a tree. He wondered if he could even fly. "Hey!" JoEd called out after he had hauled himself up to the branch next to Antoine. "Isn't that Jayzu down there?"

THANKS TO THE EFFORTS OF A MULTITUDE of crows and a few humans who ate and cleaned up all the rubbish that had been dropped by the crowds the evening before, the Friends of Wilder Island arts and crafts fair opened on Sunday morning with clean sidewalks and streets. The doors of the local Downtown churches flew open and disgorged the early worshippers, who came in long lines down the sidewalks to the fair on the Waterfront.

The evening news the night before had showcased some of the art donated to the silent auction, to be held at noon. People rushed to the Friends of Wilder Island booth to put in last-minute bids, and while they waited, volunteers sold them shares in the land trust and gave them free colorful brochures cleverly disguised as calendars. They explained the mission of the land trust and how support from Ledford residents would be the only way to save it from development.

Everyone who entered the booth received a free lapel pin that said "Friend of Wilder Island" and a raffle ticket for a free T-shirt or baseball cap with the land trust logo, a blue-eyed crow against the silhouette of the island at sunset.

"Just send this postcard to the mayor," Kate said as she handed one to a passerby on the street in front of the booth. "Tell him how you feel about our island. They're pre-addressed and pre-stamped for your convenience! Just sign it and send it!" she said, pointing to a nearby US mailbox.

The postcard featured the painting Jade had donated to the art auction, *The Wilder Side*, on the front, with the text "Save Wilder Island!"

The Wilder Side was a raucous carnival of trees and flowers, birds, butterflies, and bees that beckoned the viewer to step forth into its unknowable secrets. Buried in the familiar, the untamable still maintained a fragile presence woven into the varied assemblage of plant, bird, and insect. Hinting at deeper mysteries more ancient than ours, layer upon layer of paint created a sense of another dimension. The painting enchanted, whether one chose to contemplate its greater secrets or to just luxuriate in the rich surface textures and color.

The Wilder Side was among the larger donations at the silent auction, as was Sam's sculpture, *Roadkill*. Comprised of rusted metal objects cast off by motor vehicles along the interstate, the sculpture featured a large raven picking at the wreckage of a shiny red convertible, the victim of an inelastic collision with a sparkling blue sedan. From a short distance, the raven appeared to be perched amid a sea of brightly colored red, blue, and silvery flowers.

Russ chuckled as he stood before *road kill*, remembering the first day he'd met Sam at the quiet pool in the garden of the hermit's chapel. Sam materialized at Russ's elbow and stood for a moment looking at his own piece.

"Thanks, man," Sam said, clapping Russ on the back. "Thanks for the idea. I'm going to give you and Jade the model—it's a miniature replica of the big one, about yay big by yay." Sam mimed the approximate size with his arms. "It'll go right into your garden in the backyard, next to the fountain."

"What fountain?" Jade asked, laughing. "I mean, thanks, Sam!" she turned to Russ and said, "Honey, can we build a fountain in the backyard?"

"Absolutely," Russ said, also laughing as he hugged his wife's shoulders. "But seriously, Sam. Thanks. I mean that. I love it, really. And I'm honored that you were inspired by my offhand remark."

Alfredo looked at his watch and then up at the bandstand and said, "We need to go, Russ. The open-mic discussion starts in about five minutes."

"Later, hon," Russ said and gave Jade a quick peck on the cheek.

During breaks from the live music—a local band called Hermit Crow—Russ and Alfredo facilitated live televised discussions about issues surrounding the Wilder Island controversy, if Ravenwood Resort became a reality. People strolled through the bandstand area, stopping to listen for a few minutes or longer, and anyone who so desired could step up to the mic and make a comment or ask a question.

Russ and Alfredo took their seats at a folding table on the bandstand. "Greetings, folks!" Russ said, his voice strong and clear. "Welcome to the Friends of Wilder Island lunch-hour discussion. First on the agenda is lunch."

A few people chuckled as Russ turned to the priest and said, "I've got brats and kraut from the German-American kitchen. What's on your plate, Dr. Manzi?"

"Oh, I've got a sampling of everything from the Taste of Thai booth, including dessert," Alfredo said.

"Smells great," Russ said. He turned toward the crowd. "So, folks, while Dr. Manzi has a few bites of his lunch, let's get things rolling."

He stood up, mic in hand, and strolled to the edge of the bandstand. "It's a lovely day for a fair." He smiled at the people below. "And doesn't Wilder Island look gorgeous in the morning sun?"

"Like a jewel!" a woman near the bandstand said.

"An emerald isle in the river!" her companion said.

"Our island is indeed a precious jewel," Russ said. "But some think it has greater value as an urban playground of greed and waste.

That is the choice before us, folks, whether to turn Wilder Island into an urban playground, or to preserve it as a lone sliver of wilderness within urban Ledford."

"Wilderness!" a man shouted.

More people wandered into the bandstand area, most of them bearing hats, flags, and lapel pins bearing the land trust logo.

"But if it's declared a wilderness, will we ever get to see it up close?" another man asked in a loud voice. "Or will we just continue to see this jewel, as you call it, from across the river?"

"Yah!" his female companion yelled out. "We want to visit our island."

"Virtually no one has set foot on the island," Russ said to the crowd, "ourselves excepted, and the fact is, if we are successful in our fight, very few will ever step onto its banks."

A few people booed and hissed. "Everyone is invited to Raven-wood Resort!" a voice from the back shouted.

"On the other hand," Russ continued, trying to see who had spoken. One of Henry's shills, no doubt. "If Ravenwood Resort replaces the island as we know it, a great many people will visit, but everything we love about it, the wilderness, the crows, will be gone."

"What's the diff?" the same voice shouted. "Either way, we don't have to see no crows!" A handful of people around the man laughed and clapped and patted him on the back.

"But you bring up a valid point," Russ said. "So, why do we need wilderness if no one can see it? Would we rather have an urban play-ground open to everyone?"

Alfredo stood up, leaving his partially eaten lunch on the table. "I can take it from here, Russ." The crows moved in on his lunch as he spoke to the crowd. "Why do we need wilderness at all? I would like to answer that with a quote from Edward Abbey, noted author and outspoken defender of wilderness."

He pulled a small notebook out of his shirt pocket and opened it. "'The love of wilderness,'" he read, "'is more than a hunger for what is always beyond reach; it is also an expression of loyalty to the Earth, the Earth which bore us and sustains us, the only paradise we shall ever know, the only paradise we ever need, if only we had the eyes to see.'"

A few people laughed and clapped. Alfredo smiled as he closed the notebook and put it back in his pocket.

"Too bad most of us will never see it!" the man in the back shouted.

"Somewhere along the way," Alfredo said, ignoring the heckler, "we gave ourselves the illusion of dominion over the Earth, which has all but severed our connection to the web of life. We built great cities, where we concentrated power and wealth, while we impoverished our spirits and our wild lands in the search for more money."

The crowd had grown, but was still smaller and quieter than Friday evening A few people waved flags; most just nodded and seemed to be listening intently. *Perhaps it is because they have just come from a blistering sermon.* A few crows had collected in the trees surrounding the bandstand, staring down at him. Or was it his lunch?

"Often we lose ourselves in these artificial landscapes," he continued. "Cities weigh heavily on the hearts of men and women, and we must be able to escape them, even if it is just in our imaginations. In wilderness, we find ourselves. As we cherish one of our last wild places, let us become aware of our connection to it and impose surrender upon ourselves."

"Surrender?" the man at the back of the crowd shouted. "Never!"

The calliope on the *River Queen* suddenly started up, and Alfredo glanced across the river. A line of cars had formed at the road leading to the parking lot at the boat ramp, and a crowd had gathered at the paddleboat.

"Yes," Alfredo said. "Surrender, as the old hermit, Brother Wilder, surrendered to this wilderness we are now trying to preserve. He chose this wild island as a refuge from the world of cities and men, where he spent his life in solitary contemplation of the glory of creation."

"Who has time for that?" the man in the back shouted. "Some of us have to actually work for a living!"

Alfredo's face did not betray the anger he felt surging in his chest, and he continued without reaction to the heckler. "While most people do not desire such lengthy solitude, it is through these pristine and unaltered wild lands that our spirits connect us to the Earth. As we gaze upon our island from across the river, its wilderness lives within us all; let us not now throw it away for a few pieces of silver."

The crowd cheered and many clapped. Before Alfredo could continue, a small crow dropped from the sky onto the table, and beaked a noodle from Alfredo's plate. The crowd laughed, and Russ said, "It must be about time for open mic. Does he want to make a comment?"

Alfredo turned off his mic and said to the crow, "Well, hello little fella!"

"Don't you know me, Jayzu?" the crow said, looking up.

"Of course I know you!" Alfredo said in a very low voice. "Grawky, JoEd!" He smiled as he put out his hand, and JoEd brushed it with his wingtip.

"Grawky, Jayzu!"

"Grawky!" Russ said as he offered his hand and giggled like a schoolboy when he felt JoEd's feathers grazing his skin.

Nine more crows dropped down to the table, all talking at once. Russ's mic amplified their caws and squawks over the loudspeakers. The crowd laughed and cheered at the show on the bandstand. The crows seemed to have the upper hand, helping themselves to the lunch plates of the two professors.

"Is he talking to those crows?" a woman standing close to the bandstand said.

"Nah! He's just pretending he's talking to them!" a man next to her shouted. "Fake!"

"Looks like they're shaking hands," her companion said, "—that is, wings. Hand and wing."

"Is that real, Mommy?" a young boy on his father's shoulders asked. "Is that man really talking to those crows?"

"Sounds just like a bunch a crows to me," the woman next to him said.

"If he's talking, them crows sure aren't listening," the little boy's daddy said.

"If that's talking," the man next to him said, "I can talk crow too!" He put his fists in his armpits and did a funny dance while shouting, "Caw-caw! Caw caw caw-caw!"

The little boy laughed and called out, "Caw! Caw!" as he flapped his arms up and down.

"Antoine," JoEd called out to his new friend, "come say hey to Jayzu."

"Hey," Antoine said, bowing low to the table, with wings extended outward. "The pleasure is mine." He straightened up and brushed a wingtip against Alfredo's outstretched hand. "I am honored, finally, to meet the great Jayzu."

"I am honored as well, Antoine," Alfredo said, glancing sidelong at the crowd. A few people were frowning and shaking their heads, but others seemed entertained more than shocked. "A friend of JoEd's is a friend of mine!" He held out his hand.

"I smell Thai!" Antoine said, raising his head.

"Right here," JoEd said, pointing with his beak toward Alfredo's plate.

Antoine beaked a fat noodle and swallowed it. "Ah!" he said raising his head. "Extra spicy! That's how we like it!"

Alfredo watched in stunned silence as the crows wandered back and forth across the table, noisily pecking at the luncheon entrees. Within a few minutes, the table was a complete mess, with food strewn all over. Anxiety and fear gnawed at him, but the people below the bandstand seemed to enjoy the fiasco on the table. They laughed and clapped and cheered for the birds. A few called out: "You go, crows!" "They're really eating his lunch!" "Do you think they planned this?"

"Now that's some class-A brat," Tobias said, finishing off the last bit of Russ's sandwich. "Still don't care for the kraut, though!"

Russ grinned at the crow eating his sandwich, as if he was enjoying himself. Everyone seemed to be at least amused, Alfredo noticed. *Except me.*

A man took the mic, turned his back on the bandstand, and said to the people, "This is not real, folks. Just a publicity stunt with a bunch of trained birds." He turned to Russ and Alfredo and said, "You expect us to believe you're actually talking to crows?"

The crowd fell silent. The crows looked up momentarily and returned to their luncheon on the table. Russ glanced at Alfredo. "We are definitely for real," he said.

He stood up, mic in hand. "This is not a stunt, folks. We're as surprised as any of you that these crows showed up at our discussion today. And happy to share our lunch, as if we had any choice!"

He looked at the crows with an expression of feigned exasperation. The crowd roared as one of the crows flipped Russ's abandoned plate over, scattering sauerkraut and crumbs.

Alfredo admired the way Russ's humor had gotten the crowd laughing again. His knees were shaking, and he wished he could sit down, but a crow stood in his chair, pecking at the last remnants of Pad Thai on his plate.

"My colleague," Russ said, his arm extended toward Alfredo, "Dr. Alfredo Manzi, well-known and respected scientist, has studied crows for his entire life, including their language."

Alfredo had been uneasy since the crows first landed on the table. He felt like Russ was dragging him over a precipice he had feared his entire life.

"We humans are not the only creatures on Earth that speak a bona fide language," Russ was saying. "So do whales and dolphins. Almost everyone has even heard recordings of their sounds, right?"

The majority of the heads in the crowd nodded amid a swell of murmuring.

"Well," Russ continued, "so do the corvids, as Dr. Manzi has learned in his research."

Alfredo felt the tingling needles of adrenaline preparing him for...what–? He saw no fear on the faces in the crowd. *It is not as if Russ is lying to them*, his rational voice said. *There is nothing uncanny here, really.*

Russ stopped and turned to Alfredo. "Tell them about your re-search, Dr. Manzi."

Alfredo frowned and said through clenched teeth, "What the hell are you doing, Russ?"

"I'm telling you to stop being such a weenie," Russ said, through his smiling teeth with his mic behind his back. "You're a scientist, man! Now stand up. Talk science to them. Don't let them go away thinking any of this is fake. Or supernatural."

The people waited for Alfredo to speak. A breeze came through the bandstand, carrying the calliope's ridiculously merry tune. He glared at Russ. His legs felt like rubber, and his stomach jumped into his throat. But he turned his mic on and faced the crowd. "It is true," he said.

"Smile!" Russ hissed through smiling teeth.

Alfredo looked out over the small crowd for a few moments. *They are my students, and I am in a classroom.* He moved out from behind the mess and the crows on the table, brushing the bits of food off his clothing. Russ smiled approvingly, and the crows continued to scavenge for every last morsel on the bandstand.

"Crows and their raven cousins are extremely intelligent birds," Alfredo said, his voice sounding stronger than he felt, "with an extensive intercultural language that I have studied for many years."

You are a scientist, man! Russ had reminded him of that one critical weapon he had against fear: reason.

"In that time, I have managed to learn a few of their words, phrases actually, such as how to say 'hello,' which is what you were seeing here today." That was an under-exaggeration, he knew. *Sometimes it is best to deliver the truth in small bundles.*

"Riiight!" the heckler from the back shouted. "You expect us to believe that "

"Does he think we are fools?" the man next to him shouted. "Crows don't talk!"

"Teach us how to say hello to the crows!" the little boy on his father's shoulders yelled, and the crowd cheered.

Alfredo explained in great detail the guttural sounds and within minutes, the people were yelling, "Grawky! Grawky! Grawky!" Their noise attracted other fair goers, and soon the crowd had grown to several hundred, all shouting, "Grawky!" and waving their arms and flags.

"Grawky!" JoEd called out, though the crowd did not hear him over their own noise. "Grawky!"

Several more crows flew down to the table, chowing down while the others flapped their wings and called out, "Grawky! Grawky!"

"We love our crows!" a woman shouted from the crowd. "Long live Wilder Island!"

The people cheered, waving their flags, hats, and arms.

"Wilder Island!" they shouted. "Wilder! Wilder! Wilder!"

"What're they saying?" Antoine asked Alfredo.

"They love you," he said. "And they are all friends of Cadeña-l'jadia."

"Well, by golly, so are we!" Antoine shouted. "Right, JoEd?"

"That's right!" yelled little JoEd. "Cadeña-l'jadia forever!"

Antoine led the others upward into an ever-expanding spiral as they all shouted out, "Cadeña-l'jadia forever!" He turned them all back, and they flew a last low circle over the crowd and headed toward the river.

"Grawky! Grawky! Grawky!" the people shouted and waved until the crows had vanished from sight.

THE AIRWAVES AND THE NEWSPAPER came alive with opinions, viewpoints, sales pitches, and pleas, as the media captured the weekend's events on both sides of the river in the struggle for the body, soul, and future of Wilder Island. From the Waterfront and the Friends of Wilder Island arts and crafts fair, to Henry Braun and his *River Queen* parading back and forth in front of the city dock, the citizens of Ledford indulged themselves in food, drink, and merriment as they considered the choice before them.

The Sunday evening news featured the crowd at the bandstand shouting "Grawky! Grawky! Grawky!" while Russ and Alfredo looked on haplessly behind a table full of crows eating their lunch. All of Ledford watched continuous reruns of a video of Alfredo and Antoine greeting each other, wing to hand. By the time the ten-o'clock news had ended, the majority of Ledford residents had learned how to say hello in crow.

"Dr. Manzi brought a trained troupe of talking crows to the table this afternoon," a reporter said with vague tones of dread in her voice. "He claimed he has decoded their language, and taught the small gathering what he says is the crow word for hello." She rolled her eyes as the camera showed the crows eating right off the table.

Jade laughed and said, "Oh, look at you two with all those crows! They look like lawyers pacing back and forth as they argue. That's hilarious!"

"And completely eclipsing an historic event of our two species greeting one another!" Russ said, shaking his head. "Leave it to the media to spew innuendo, half-truths, and outright lies, and call it news. I wonder how much Henry Braun paid them to say that."

"Total propaganda!" Henry Braun's television face said. "This is just a flimsy cover for the utter nonsense this land trust outfit is trying to perpetrate on us. This is nothing but a joke, folks! These phonies want to prioritize crows over people! Why can't they share the island with the city of Ledford?" he asked innocently as a scene of crows feeding at a dumpster filled the screen.

"My Ravenwood Resort will be completely environmentally friendly," he crooned as the black birds picked at the garbage, "and open to the many, while this, this bird park is open only to crows. We leave it to the good people of Ledford to decide."

The station broadcast its reporter's footage of Henry giving balloons and candy to children, roses to their mothers, and prospectuses to their fathers. Henry's voice played continuously in the background, basted in heartfelt concern for his fellow man, appealing to the very freedoms guaranteed by the US Constitution.

"And what do you think of the planned Ravenwood Resort?" the reporter asked, sticking his microphone into the face of a woman with frothy blue hair.

"Oh, I just love to play slot machines!" a woman said. "So much fun! And on the historic *River Queen!*"

"I hope he builds it," a man said. "The sooner the better! Ledford could use some entertainment. For the love of mike, how many stock and feed shows can a person go to?"

"Even if it means destruction of the crow population on the island?" the reporter asked.

"When did flying rats become a protected species?" demanded a man with an ugly sneer. "They're vermin, that's all. Braun Enterprises is going to drain that swamp and bring us a new, beautiful, and clean resort for our families."

"They say after Henry Braun does that, we won't have any more mosquitoes," another man said. "I'd be in favor of that."

"Don't know why it's taken so long to drain that swamp," his wife said. "It's a health hazard, I tell you."

The camera cut to a smiling, magnanimous Henry Braun striking a pose in front of the beautiful *River Queen*. "Other than for nostalgic reasons," Henry asked, "why should we save Wilder Island? Why not turn this otherwise derelict land into a resort we can all enjoy?"

Dora Lyn put her knitting down and stared at the man on the TV. The announcer had said the man's name was—what was it? Dr. Alfred Manzer? She was sure she'd never seen him before, a man with a thick streak of white through his black hair. But it was his voice that had attracted her attention and made her look up from her knitting.

He was awfully handsome and she listened for a few minutes to him read from a small notebook and then plead to keep Wilder Island wild. "Who is he?" she said to her mother, who was deaf as stone. "I know that voice from somewhere."

—16—

Unmentionables

Russ awoke suddenly to the sound of the doorbell ringing. Jade gently snored beside him in the dark room. He raised his head and looked at the clock on the bedside table. It's freaking four in the morning. Who the hell is it? He got out of bed, grabbing his cell phone as he shoved his arms into his robe. He tripped over his slippers and stumbled into the wall.

Jade woke up and said, "What is it, honey?"

"Someone rang the doorbell. It's probably some neighborhood prankster, but I'm going to check it out." He left the bedroom and walked down the hallway to the front door.

"Oh, Jesus!" he said, as he opened the door to flames on the porch. He quickly grabbed the fire extinguisher from the kitchen and sprayed the small fire till it went out. He shoved the cinders with his foot—a few pieces of painted canvas and burned fragments of the frame. "Sonofabitch!" he said angrily. "Who would do this?" He took his cell phone from his pocket. "Nine-one-one, what's your emergency?" the voice on the phone said.

"Someone started a fire on my front porch."

Jade appeared in the doorway. She gasped and pointed to the blackened mess on the porch, crying out in wordless anguish at the smoldering ruins of *The Wilder Side*, the painting she had donated to the silent auction.

"The cops are on their way," Russ said, taking her into his arms.

She shook her head and leaned against him. He walked her to her studio and put her gently in the armchair. Willow B jumped into her lap. "I'll take care of everything, honey. You just hang out in here, okay?"

The police officers left just as the treetops glowed with the first light of morning. Russ opened the door to the studio and said, "Well, that's that, for whatever it's worth. They pretty much said there's no chance they'll ever find out who did this." He squatted next to her chair and took her hand. "You going to be all right, hon?"

She nodded and smiled weakly as he kissed her hand. "We have a breakfast date with Sam, Kate, and Alfredo this morning," he said. "Remember? Are you all right to go? We can postpone it if you aren't up to it. I know they'll understand."

Jade shook her head. "No," she said through a sigh. "Let's go. I don't really want to be here right now."

They met the other Friends of Wilder Island at a popular twenty-four-hour eating establishment near the university, the Komodo Dragon. "You know the students call this place The Commode," Russ said to Alfredo as they slid into a huge booth upholstered in red lizard skin.

"How very appetizing!" Alfredo said, chuckling.

A stuffed Komodo dragon hanging from the ceiling stared down at Jade. Grotesquely comical, the gigantic lizard swayed gently on its ropes, a giant claw raised in a friendly greeting, and his long tongue frozen in a permanent licking gesture. One eyeball glared down at Jade, and she squirmed under its unblinking scrutiny.

After ordering breakfast, Alfredo, Kate, and Sam listened in shock as Russ told them about the fire on their porch.

"Oh, no!" Kate said, shaking her head. "Not *Wilder Side!*"

"What kind of low-life bastard would do something like that?" Sam said. "I'd like to beat the crap out of him." He balled up a fist and punched his other palm. He shook his head a few times and blew hard through his teeth. "I just can't stomach it."

"I am distraught, Jade, that someone could destroy such a beautiful piece of art," Alfredo said. "There is much evil in the world."

"The same evil that wants to destroy Wilder Island," Jade said.

Alfredo nodded. "It is indeed, Jade. Our only hope is to stand together against it."

They held each other's glance for a few moments. *Why is he looking at me like that?* Ever since the night of her reception, whenever their eyes met, he wore the strangest expression. *Like he's seeing me for the first time. I wonder if I have mascara all over my nose.*

"I am amazed at you, Jade." Alfredo smiled, and his expression changed to kind concern. "You are so composed after such a horrific attack."

"You didn't see me when Russ opened the door," Jade said with a smile as she rubbed her nose. "I try not to think about how hateful it was." Russ put his arm around her as she choked up. She drew in a deep breath and sat up straight. "But I'll paint another. I'll paint a hundred more. I will not be beaten."

Her friends burst into applause. Jade blushed deeply, but she kept her head up and smiled.

"Well, whoever did it," Sam said, "paid a lot of money to destroy it. Out of the $18,750.00 we made from the silent auction, Jade's painting brought us $5,500.00."

Jade gasped. Her hand flew up to her face to cover her open mouth.

Russ asked, "Who bought it?"

"Someone named Gabriella," Sam answered.

Jade noticed Alfredo's head turn suddenly toward Sam. *Does he know her?*

"Gabriella who?" asked Kate.

"Just Gabriella," Sam said. "She didn't leave a last name."

"Gabriella," Jade said. "I've met her. Short, thin black hair wound up in a bun. Fifty, maybe sixty?"

"That's her," Sam said with a nod. "Real nice lady. I asked her if she wanted to be on our mailing list, and she said no, she'd keep up with us in the news."

"She bought two paintings at my art show," Jade said.

"Well, she's obviously your biggest fan, then," Russ said. "You should send her a Christmas card."

"If I knew where she lived, I would," Jade said.

Alfredo's eyes dropped to the table in front of him, and Jade watched him frown. *He knows who Gabriella is. A church person, maybe?*

"Did you look at her check?" Kate asked.

"She paid in cash," said Sam.

"Cash?" Russ said, raising his eyebrows. "Who goes around with almost six grand in their pocket?"

Jade looked across the table at Alfredo's inward stare. *He knows Gabriella. And he can't tell us who she is. Why?*

The waiter set a large tray loaded with their breakfast on an adjacent table. In rapid succession, he pulled each plate off and put it down in front of the appropriate recipient.

Jade looked up at the Komodo dragon, which stared balefully down at all the food on the table. *The poor thing looks hungry.* She was tempted to offer it a bite, until she thought she saw a small drop of saliva fall from its leathery lip.

Gabriella! Alfredo felt his stomach turn over when he heard her name. He saw the whole scenario at once. *Gabriella, aka Mrs. Henry Braun, bought Jade's painting at the auction. Henry had it destroyed. Or more likely, one of his hired thugs did.*

"Surely," Kate said, mopping up the egg yolk on her plate with her toast, "Gabriella didn't take the painting away herself? Was she alone? Who picked it up? Where'd the painting get delivered to?"

I should have returned her calls. The secretary at St. Sophia's had forwarded several phone messages to him from Gabriella yesterday. But he had not answered. He tried to tell himself that he had not had time to call her, but the truth was, he felt that she had developed a fondness for him that made him uncomfortable.

Could I have prevented this destruction of Jade's paintings had I called her back? Fear jabbed through his guilt. *Has Henry harmed her too?*

"No," Sam said. "She said a workman would come after it and take it to the library. She wanted it hung next to the *Murder of Crows* photo."

"That would have been the perfect place," Alfredo said ruefully. "How very generous of her." *In contrast to her husband's destructive greed.*

"Who came and got it?" Jade asked.

Sam shrugged. "I don't know. Some guy picked it up Sunday night when we were taking everything down. He had the receipt, so we let him take it."

The waiter cleared the table and refilled everyone's coffee cups. He put the check on the table, and Kate pushed it toward Jade. "I believe you're the treasurer for the trust?"

"Does that mean I have to pay for breakfast?" Jade asked in cautious fear. "When does my term end? Can I resign right now?"

Kate laughed, as did the others. "No, you may not resign! No— seriously, Jade, the treasurer pays the bills. Your first act is to order up some checks. I'll put this on my credit card, and you can reimburse me from the funds in the land trust."

"We have funds?" Jade asked with a grimace.

"Uh, yeah," Russ said. "We sold a few more things at the art auction—your painting and about fifteen grand more for a few other odds and ends. Remember?"

Jade slapped her forehead and giggled. "Sorry! I'm a dope."

She's certainly not a dope. Again, she reminded him so much of Charlotte, a vast innocence perhaps. *Her mind freely wanders like her mother's. Russ seems to keep her feet on the ground, though.*

"Sam," Kate said, "tell everyone how much the beg-a-thon brought us! '

"We pulled in almost a million and a half bucks," Sam said. "Mostly twenty-dollar shares." He pulled a small piece of paper out of his shirt pocket and read: "We also sold eleven shares at the hundred-dollar price, six at the thousand-dollar level, and one at the ten thousand." He looked up with a grin.

Russ whistled, and Alfredo said, "Bravo!" clapping his hands.

"Really?" Jade asked. "We got that much from the people of Ledford?"

"Well, I haven't gone through the names and addresses yet," Sam said. "But I think they're all from the Ledford area."

Kate pulled a calculator from her purse and said, "The population of metropolitan Ledford is one point two million. At twenty bucks a pop—"

"That's seventy-five thousand people," Russ said, frowning. "Not exactly a large segment of the voting public."

"Five percent," Kate said, snapping her calculator shut.

"That's it?" Jade asked. "Just 5 percent gave that much?"

"Yep," Kate said. "And we've only just begun!"

Alfredo was impressed too. *That means there is more to be had from the people of the city.* And then his own words haunted him: *"I had gotten tired of promising little old ladies that Jesus will receive them in heaven if they would only hand me a check."*

What are we offering the people of Ledford? A wilderness they will never see up close? He shrugged.

A necessary evil, it seems.

The five friends said good-bye to one another on the sidewalk outside The Commode. Sam jumped into his flesh-colored pickup and screeched his tires as he peeled out.

"Boys!" Kate shook her head at his taillights. "Need a ride to the docks, Padre?"

They walked a few blocks to her car, and she unlocked his door. "I found out that your friend in Rosencranz is a ward of the state." She pulled out of the parking lot. "As you imagined. But not for the usual reason."

Kate turned onto University Boulevard. "And I found out her real name."

Alfredo stared at her, and adrenaline shot him up with a strange jittery fear. "It is not Charlotte Steele?"

"Charlotte is her real first name," Kate said. "Her full name is Charlotte Estelle Majewski."

Stella? Alfredo sat in stunned silence. *Stella?* He shook his head. *No, it cannot be. It is a coincidence.*

"Majewski's a pretty common name," Kate said. She stopped at a red light and turned to Alfredo. "Tell me, is she related to Majewski?"

Alfredo shook his head dumbly. "I honestly do not know." *What are you, a lawyer?* He mocked himself. *Charlotte Steele. Charlotte*

Estelle. You know who she is—Majewski's sister. He looked out the window at Wilder Island, green and beautiful, wishing he could vanish forever into its mists and shadows.

"Well," Kate continued, "it would certainly be easier if Majewski was her brother. If he is, he can get her out."

Alfredo did not answer. *Majewski is Charlotte's older brother! And Jade's uncle!* His mind reeled with the consequences of these facts. *Majewski cares a great deal about his sister. Will you hide this information from him, knowing his anguish over her?*

"But this family never visits," he said angrily, dismissing his own thoughts, as well as the compassion he had felt for his friend Thomas. *He could have tried to find her.* "No one does but me."

"Well, anyway," Kate said, "Mr. and Mrs. Majewski died in 1990 and the family lawyer set up a permanent trust fund with Rosencranz as the beneficiary, for Charlotte's upkeep until she dies."

Alfredo felt as if he had been stabbed in the heart. *Until she dies?* He heard Charlotte's voice in his memory. *"I do not want to live that long, Jayzu."*

"Evidently they wanted to hide the family surname," Kate said. "As long as Charlotte is confined to Rosencranz, they collect their rent, which these days is around ten grand a month."

"They do not care about her!" Alfredo said tersely. "Why can I not become her legal guardian?"

Kate turned into the parking lot at the boat landing. After she parked and cut the engine off, she turned to Alfredo and said firmly, "Rosencranz is her legal guardian, Alfredo. There is no way around that. Why not just ask Majewski if Charlotte is his sister? He could get her out.'

"No!" Alfredo said harshly, and then he quickly apologized. "Forgive me, Kate. I do not know what came over me." He looked across the river at the island. *Why not tell Majewski? Kate is right ... if Charlotte is his sister, he might even get her released from Rosencranz.*

"Why not?" Kate asked again. "Seems to me that would be the easiest way."

Without looking at her, Alfredo shook his head.

"What is it?" Kate asked. "What are you afraid of?"

"What would he do with her?" Alfredo asked. "He does not speak the crow language."

"I see," Kate said, nodding. "You want to bring her to the island." She tapped her fingers on the steering wheel for a few moments before turning to Alfredo and looking at him with a calm and reserved expression on her face.

Suddenly she shouted, "Are you nuts?"

ALFREDO SAT AT THE ROCKY POINT BELOW the hermit's chapel, recalling how Kate had nearly flayed him alive with words. "You can't bring an inmate from a mental hospital to the island!" she had said. "It's a freaking primitive wilderness, remember? That's what we've been fighting for! For God's sake, Alfredo! Where would she live? Don't tell me in your cottage!"

After he denied such intent, or at least claiming he had not gotten that far with his plans, she had backed down somewhat. "Good. Don't even think about it," she had said. "Find somewhere else for her. But don't tell me, okay?"

But where could he take her that would be any different than Rosencranz?

Charlie flapped to a landing on the driftwood log next to him, interrupting his thoughts. He smiled at his friend and lifted a hand in greeting.

"Grawky, Jayzu!" Charlie said, brushing a wing across Alfredo's hand. He folded his wings and scraped his beak back and forth across the log several times. "What's up, man? You look a little down in the dumps, as they say."

"Charlie," Alfredo said, "in less than two weeks, Rosencranz is moving all their patients upstate. We must get Charlotte out of there before they move her. I must break a few laws to do that, and I risk jail if I am caught. But if I do not get Charlotte out of there, I am afraid she'll be a prisoner at Rosencranz forever. My heart tells me one thing, my rational mind another."

He picked up a stick from the ground and peeled away fronds of rotten bark. "I am an alleged man of God, I beg him for guidance. But for the splendor of nature, he does not speak to me. I do not know where to turn for answers." He bent over and traced the outline of a crescent moon in the sand and erased it with his foot.

"Deities can be spectacularly subtle," Charlie said. "That's been the corvid observation of human gods in general over the years."

"As well as spectacularly unhelpful," Alfredo said as he drew the outline of the grounds of Rosencranz in the sand. "Sometimes God wants us to find our own way, I guess."

"Well, it might help if you ask a yes or no question," Charlie said. "Then the deity could catch a bush on fire, which would be a yes answer I would think. However, silence could also be construed as consent, albeit far less dramatic."

"The Almighty has indeed forsaken me," Alfredo said with a rueful laugh. "And in my own silent darkness, I must consider committing a crime that could imprison me and leave Charlotte in Rosencranz without anyone to visit her." He drew a curved line in the sand. The driveway.

"But is it not a crime to leave her there?" Charlie asked.

"It is indeed," Alfredo said. "I am on the horns of a dilemma."

"The Grandmothers have a proverb," Charlie said. "The horns of all dilemmas grow from the head of the same beast."

Alfredo laughed bitterly, remembering NoExit's words: *"Have you ever found yourself on the horns of a dilemma? When adhering to the law produces more damage than breaking it?"*

"The dilemma is indeed a beast," he said with a sigh. "Obey the law and commit a crime. Disobey the law and commit a crime. Either way I am gored."

He traced a circle in the sand. The gazebo.

"We corvids have but one crime," Charlie said. "That makes things a bit simpler."

Alfredo traced two large rectangles near the gazebo. The building, the parking lot. He marked Charlotte's tiny room with a rock. "One law? Just one?"

"No stealing," Charlie said. "That's it, our one law. Though it constantly undergoes reinterpretation to fit the circumstance—that's one of the Grandmother's duties. It is very cumbersome, the Grandmother's task, requiring both reason and compassion."

"It would be considered a form of stealing if I take her from there." Alfredo sighed, sitting up straight. "But what would I do with her if I could? Where will I take her?"

There were some very kind folks at St. Sophia's, he had reasoned many times. *But they would not be any better at communicating with Charlotte. Chances are she would end up right back in Rosencranz.*

"I cannot house her in my cottage," he said. "It is too small for two humans. And, it would be unseemly for a priest and a woman to co-habitate." He heard Kate's voice almost snarling at him, "Don't even think about it!"

"What about the tree house?" Charlie said. "You are nearby, more or less. And I would be there to look after her, and so would Rika. Charlotte would never be lonely again, nor suffer any lack of companions to talk to."

Alfredo almost laughed out loud, imagining how Kate would take to that idea. "Perhaps I should live in the tree house. Charlotte would undoubtedly be more comfortable in my cottage, which has running water. It is more suited for a woman, I think."

"It is too exposed here, Jayzu," Charlie said. "People would see her. And then they would talk. That could never be good for Charlotte, and perhaps people would try harder to come to Cadeña-l'jadia."

Alfredo nodded slowly as he pondered the crow's words. He bent back down to the sand and drew a large rectangle around the building, the parking lot, and the gazebo. He added a small square, for the guardhouse. "It is true," he said thoughtfully. The last thing he wanted was to attract attention to his crime. He placed small x's all along the fence line. The concertina wire.

"Word will get out very quickly that an inmate has escaped Rosencranz. We would not want people to see someone matching her description here on the island." *Oh, the rumors that would create!*

"Let's bring her to the tree house," Charlie said. "You could sleep on the deck, or underneath it, while the three of us—you, me, and Rika—teach her how to live there. Then you go home to your cottage, and Charlotte is safe from being seen. She would love living in the tree house. I know she would."

Alfredo s own happiest memories resided in a crude tree house that he had built himself. He had spent most of the daylight hours in the summer there, with his only friends, a few crows. "All right, Charlie," he said. "Let me gather a few things. I reckon it will need a good cleaning, at least."

Life in Bruthamax's tree house with her old friend Charlie could not be worse than her life in Rosencranz. I can look after Charlotte until she can manage on her own.

Armed with candles, matches, and cleaning supplies, Alfredo followed Charlie to the tree house. He slogged through the bogs and fens below the Boulders, trying to recognize where a different texture of leaf and shade of green heralded solid ground. Though he had been to the tree house many times, he still could not find his way on his own. He had only discovered the last time that Charlie had never taken him the same way twice.

"Duck weed," Charlie called down from above after he stepped into a hip-deep hole full of tea-colored water.

"Oh, crap!" he swore, pulling himself out. He kept a closer eye on Charlie after that. Though he had a few close calls, he arrived at the tree house without further mishap.

"Grawky, Jayzu!" Rika said, as he stepped onto the deck of the tree house. 'Nice to see you again, dearie."

"Grawky, Rika!" Alfredo said, brushing his fingertips against her outstretched wing. "It has been a while—since just after I got to Cadeña-l'jadia. I thought I should tidy things up a bit, in case we bring Charlotte here. And I need to check out what is here in the way of kitchenware—you know, pots and pans, dishes and such?

"Well, dearie," Rika said, "you'll be bringing some comforts for the lady, I reckon. A tea kettle, for sure. And a nice cup. And maybe a bowl. I reckon Bruthamax ate right out of the pot he cooked in. That will never do for the lady." Although crow beaks cannot be wrinkled up in distaste the way in which the human nose can, her tone clearly expressed that image.

"Yes," Alfredo said, laughing. "I am sure you are right. Human males, when left on their own, can be quite, how shall I say—primitive—with respect to the aesthetics of the lady's house. We priests are no different, I suspect."

"Nor are the corvid," Rika said. "It's the females that keep the nest tidy."

Rika had told Alfredo about her early adulthood in companionship with a genteel Patua' lady in the wealthy Victorian Heights neighborhood of Downtown Ledford. "Oh, I miss her, Jayzu! How we used to sip tea together."

"Well, perhaps one day you and Charlotte can drink tea together on the deck."

"Curtains," Rika said, aiming a wing at the window. "She'll need curtains, Jayzu. A lady likes her privacy, you know. And a rocking chair—a lady needs a rocking chair. And you must bring a stove, a cast-iron one. A lady can cook and keep herself warm with a cast-iron stove."

"Rika!" Alfredo said, laughing. "How will I haul a cast-iron stove here? They are quite heavy! I am not a muscle man!"

"Oh, pshaw!" Rika said, pushing at Alfredo with her wing. "Bring a small one, dearie! My lady's doorman took one up to her upstairs apartment with nothing but his two hands."

Alfredo turned to the tree house, jerked the door open and went inside. He took the bench and table out to the deck, but the box-bed could not be moved. "Bruthamax must have built the wall around it," he said. "That takes some planning!"

Several pots and pans sat on the shelf on the wall above the table, among them a cast-iron frying pan. When he grabbed the handle and slid it off the shelf, a folded piece of paper dropped to the floor. He picked it up, hoping it was part of Bruthamax's journal, and took it outside. He unfolded the paper; the disciplined penmanship bore no resemblance to Bruthamax's scrawl.

October 31, 1898

My Dear Nephew-

It is with great delight that I read your letters, which make me laugh and wish I could live in such paradise! I am grateful to the Good Lord that you remain in good health and spirits.

I received the manuscript. Thank you again for your work on behalf of the project. Without your efforts, and a handful of others, much knowledge would otherwise be lost.

May God bless you, and the Hozey family,

—Antoni

Alfredo's reread the letter, shaking his head in amazement. He stared into his thoughts for a few moments before folding it and putting it in his shirt pocket. *I cannot wait to call Thomas!*

He swept and scrubbed the tree house floor, bed, and shelves. Not a square inch of the interior had been left untouched. Such had been Rika's instructions, and not until he had scrubbed the bench and table would she allow him to put them back inside. All the while he cleaned, Alfredo could not get de la Torre's letter or its contents off his mind. Did de la Torre visit the island? Was *he himself Patua'*? It would explain a few things.

With the cleaning of the tree house complete, Alfredo packed his cleaning equipment and sat down on the deck. "Now, Jayzu, dearie,"

Rika said, joining him on the bench, "have you thought about Charlotte's wardrobe? She'll need clothing, you know."

Charlotte's Rosencranz garb seemed the perfect attire for the tree house, but she would only be coming with the clothes on her back. He had not given it a thought, actually, what she would otherwise need, living in a tree house in the middle of a wilderness forest.

"Perhaps you will help me, Rika," he said, feeling like a deer in headlights. "I know nothing of women's clothing."

"Indeed," Rika said, nodding. "Indeed. We'll make a list, Jayzu, you and I. Levis and sweaters should do. And shoes, and stockings. A nightie. And of course, unmentionables."

"Unmentionables?" Alfredo asked with raised eyebrows. "I am sure I do not know what that means, Rika."

The crow gave Alfredo a curious look and said, "Undies, dearie. You know, things that go underneath the outer clothing—underpants, a brassiere, garter belt—well I'm sure she won't be needing one of those!" Rika tittered behind her wing.

Alfredo blushed to his ear tips. The underneath of Charlotte's outer clothing. The unmentionables. It had been decades since he had lived with females. An image of his grandmother's enormous brassiere arose in his memory. He had taken it from the clothesline outside and was punished when his mother caught him firing melons over the fence with it.

But Charlotte was not shaped at all like his grandmother. She was thin and willowy and her breasts were not at all like melons. *More like peaches.* The thought of the body that lay underneath Charlotte's Rosencranz coveralls stirred regions of his body that had been asleep for decades.

"Uh, yes, unmentionables. I will give the list to one of the women parishioners at St. Sophia, to put together some clothes, including unmentionables."

He spent days at a time preparing the tree house for Charlotte and sleeping on the deck of the tree house at night. There was much work to do and little time. He refurbished the ramshackle outhouse

Bruthamax had built downstream from the tree house, installing a new wooden toilet seat and a small box to hold paper. *One day perhaps I can build Miss Charlotte her private chamber up in the tree house.*

The cistern was full, underneath the new wooden cover he had made weeks before. After he installed a piston pump that operated off an RV battery in the tree house, he filled the ten-gallon ceramic water crock he had packed in and hauled up to the treehouse. *One day I will bring my lady a sink. And a bathtub.*

He dragged a bale of hay up to the tree house and stuffed all the holes between the branches and vines. He plastered the entire interior except the wood floor, using a mixture of clay and gypsum plaster he brought in from Ledford on the Captain's boat. "It is good the tree house is small," he said one exhausted evening to Rika and Charlie.

But the job was done. Everything was ready for Charlotte.

FATHER PROVINCIAL THOMAS MAJEWSKI STARED out his office window. *Just a couple weeks ago, I was in paradise, and now I am in hell. My God, why have you forsaken me?* Even Snowbell had abandoned him in her near coma on a pillow next to the fireplace.

The gray sky oppressed him. The rainy day oppressed him. Washington DC oppressed him. His job oppressed him. He daydreamed about the island, with himself as its lone inhabitant wandering its dark forests that hid astonishing secrets like talking birds and extinct magical plants. At night, he dreamed of Stella's restless spirit haunting the labyrinths of his memories.

Stella's eyes, her sad eyes. Like today's weather—gray and full of tears. *If only I had known.* Majewski sighed and tried again to forgive himself for having tricked his sister so many years past. *But what would have become of her if I had not? Even I could not have left her in the woods by herself with winter coming. If only I had known another Patua' then. Like Alfredo—he could have talked to her, per-*

haps reasoned with her. He laughed at himself and his fantasies that events in the past could be changed.

If only I had known. The mantra of all the souls in hell.

Rain drizzled on the windowpane. *But why didn't we know? De la Torre knew a Patua' and left us all sorts of evidence.* He put another log on the fire, sat down in the armchair. Snowbell slept like the dead; not even a whisker moved. He took the faux *Treasure Island* from the end table and opened it. To review its inventory. Again.

The red sealing wax on Brother Maxmillian's letter caught his eye, and he examined it closely for the first time. A human hand stood out distinctly. *Good Lord! That fob on the lamp chain in Alfredo's cottage!* He imagined Brother Maxmillian pressing it into a blob of red wax, a crow standing nearby, waiting to post the letter. The idea of using crows as mail carriers amused him more now than it had before. *I wonder if de la Torre ever wrote back.*

A gust of wind rattled the window, and Majewski scowled at the endless storm. He picked up the folded letter from de la Torre's sister, and the color print of the Chapel of the Madonna della Strada fell out. For a brief second, he saw the chapel on Wilder Island nestled amid the dark green forest.

He examined the postmark. September 27, 1893, forty years after Brother Wilder built his hermit's chapel. He opened the letter and read the wispy script:

> *Greetings, My Dear Brother,*
>
> *The Chapel of the Madonna della Strata is absolutely gorgeous! Our guide told us that most of the old Roman churches had secret entrances into the labyrinth of passages in which the Church hid the early Christians during times of persecution. And so it was with the Madonna della Strata! From within the sacristy, we entered the catacombs and went down a*

steep and dark stone staircase. It was like stepping into a subterranean city, comprising many streets and alleys that went off this way and that. We could hardly contain your grandnephew!

Wish you were here,

Conchetta

"I was ordained at the Chapel of the Madonna della Strada in Rome," Majewski said to Snowbell, who woke up with a start. She yawned and stretched and came down from her perch on the hearth and leaped into his lap. "Built by St. Ignatius Loyola, as the Order he founded responded to the Protestant Reformation." Majewski stroked the cat in his lap, who attacked his hand. "Is that the connection, Your Highness? The reform of the Catholic Church, led by the Society of Jesus, and the large-scale disappearance of the Patua'?"

Snowbell turned an ear sideways and lowered her eyelids to half open. "So you really think the Order rounded up the Patua' and delivered them to the Pope for excommunication and possible execution?" he asked in mock surprise. The cat licked her front paw twice, rolled over onto her back, and offered him her soft underbelly.

"The Patua' would have been considered heretics, you know," Majewski said as he stroked her. "That's worse than simple insanity. Perhaps they were even burned as witches. Do you suppose the Order was part of that?"

"Miaw!" Snowbell protested and jumped off his lap.

"Oh, I quite agree, my Queen." Majewski leaned toward the fireplace, picked up the poker, and jabbed at the burning logs. "I was just playing the devil's advocate. More likely, the Jesuits led them into the catacombs, along with the Catholics, to protect them from the bigotries of religion."

He put another log on the fire and made himself a cup of tea. Hardly had he sat back into the armchair when Snowbell was back on his lap. He stared into the fire, sipping his tea. *What did de la Torre know? Connect the dots. The letter, the deed, the map, the will, the letter from his sister, the Madonna della Strada Chapel. The hermit's chapel.*

"De la Torre knew at least one Patua'," Majewski said, scratching the cat behind her ears. "And he wanted someone in the future to know him too. And that would not make any sense at all if Maxmillian were merely insane." Snowbell purred insistently. "But it would make sense that the Order had an interest in this peculiar race of humans. Perhaps even spiriting them off to a distant land for their own safety."

William's voice came through the intercom: "Alfredo Manzi, line one, Father."

"De la Torre wrote back!" Majewski exclaimed after Alfredo told him about the letter he found at the tree house. "That certainly suggests Brother Maxmillian wasn't a complete hermit. He obviously had some human contact."

"And," Alfredo said, "de la Torre refers to a manuscript; no crow could carry something that heavy all the way to Washington. Someone had to get it off the island and into the mail."

"What do you think this manuscript is about?" Majewski said. "Memoirs, perhaps?"

"At first, I had no idea," Alfredo said. "But then I remembered the last few pages of Bruthamax's journal. Have you read it yet? I e-mailed it to you right after you left."

"I did," Majewski said. "It was fascinating!"

"Look again at the pages at the very end," Alfredo said.

"Hang on a moment," Majewski said, upsetting Snowbell. He sat down at his computer and opened the file Alfredo had sent. "Okay, I'm looking at some cartoons of alien plants."

"I thought it was just doodling at first too," Alfredo said. "But now I am wondering if he was trying to write in Patua'."

"And you think the manuscript de la Torre is talking about is—" Majewski felt a rush of adrenaline.

"Is written in Patua'," Alfredo finished for him.

Majewski hung up the phone. *A written language of the crows! Imagine that!* Excitement kicked the weariness from his bones as he thought of the opportunity before him. *To translate the language of the crows! To leave this urban nightmare of the human spirit!*

Snowbell had taken up residence on her pillow on the hearth. With one last bored glance at him, she went to sleep. Majewski returned to the armchair and relaxed into the extra room left by his cat. Alfredo's words drifted into his awareness. *"The botanical lore of the Patua' is said to have been vast ..."*

Rain continued its relentless assault on the windows, amplifying the sensation of chill in the room. But in the armchair in front of the fire, the pleasantly rich hues of yellow and orange punctuated by an occasional flash of blue warmed him. His head nodded onto his chest.

"Follow me!" Stella whispered with a huge conspiratorial grin. She led him down a spiraling series of staircases and passageways through a network of caves excavated from the solid rock. A variety of sights, noises, and odors tantalized or repulsed as they tunneled back through time. Suddenly Stella grabbed his arm and pulled him off the stone staircase and into a dimly lit, roughly circular cavern, like the hub of wheel, where an astonishing number of passages met.

Alfredo Manzi lay upon the stone floor, and he ordained his prostrate body, reading from a book of runes. Candle smoke and incense briefly filled the air as he looked up at the white basilica of the Madonna del Rio. Bleached by sun and time, the tangled branches and the blue sky beyond made a grid through which a constant stream of black birds flowed, in and out.

We Are Small Alone

Minnie Braun watched the sky reflect the colors of the sunset from her balcony, after watching Henry take a butcher knife to the two paintings she had bought at Jade Matthews's art show.

"I'll not have this woman's work in my house!" he had raged, slicing through *Leave Me* as she watched, stone-faced. "She is my enemy! And as long as you're married to me, she is your enemy too, understand?" Henry plunged the knife into *Catching the Wind*, and Minnie grabbed her midsection as if it had penetrated her own guts. She ran up the stairs sobbing and closed herself in her bedroom.

She had no idea what had happened to *The Wilder Side*, the beautiful painting of the island she had outbid everyone at the auction for—only that it had never made it to the library. She had tried to call Father Alfredo to tell him—he always made her feel better—but she could not reach him. She had called him twice. Three times. But he hadn't returned her calls.

She gazed in despair out her window, at the dark trees of Wilder Island. *Henry will destroy that too. Is nothing safe from him?* When Floyd and Willy sailed down to her balcony, she cried out in happiness. "Oh, fellas, I'm so glad you're here! I'm feeling pretty low this evening." She looked over her shoulder, making sure her door was closed.

"We cannot have that, fair lady!" Floyd said.

"Indeed!" Willy agreed. "What makes you so blue, Miss Minnie?"

The two crows perched on the railing looked at her with such affection and sympathy, she nearly burst into tears. "Henry destroyed something I really loved," she said, trying to hold back the tears stinging her eyes. "Right in front of me." Minnie removed a hanky from her pocket and dabbed her tears.

"What a beast!" Floyd said. He put a wing out and rested it on her shoulder. "He didn't hurt you, did he, Miss Minnie? I'll peck his eyes out if he so much as lays a finger on you, let alone an ax."

Minnie laughed through her tears and said, "Thank you, Floyd! But it was a butcher knife. And Henry never touches me, so you need not worry about that. Which is not to say he hasn't found other ways to hurt me."

"I'm afraid I have to agree with Floyd," Willy said. "He is a beast." The brothers nodded to each other then turned back to her.

"He's obsessed," she said in a low voice. "He's like a crazy man over that island. The city as much as gave it to him, he says, so he's making all these plans to 'christen Ravenwood Resort.'" Minnie looked over her shoulder, checking that the door to her bedroom was still closed.

"Izzat so?" Floyd said. "The beast. What's 'christen mean?' Where's Ravenwood Resort?"

"On Wilder Island," Minnie said with a sigh. "Even though it isn't his to build on—at least not yet. He wants to park that riverboat he's been giving everyone rides on at the island, he says. And he's going to build casinos and shopping malls and hotels and, well, everything that Wilder Island is not. That's Ravenwood Resort."

"Yeah, yeah," Floyd said, nodding. "I remember now. Flapjack tables, roulette, and bingo."

"That's blackjack, Floyd," Willy said, rolling his eyes and shaking his head.

"Yes," Minnie said. "Blackjack, slot machines, roulette—all of that. He said the city condemned the island because it's a nuisance. 'A sewer of crows.' That's what he calls it."

"How very uncouth," Willy said. "In polite conversation, a gentleman should not invoke the sewer. Don't you agree, my brother?"

"The cad!" Floyd said as he gathered Minnie's hand in his wing. "To speak so in front of a lady so fair, I am shocked, nay, outraged!" He laid his head sideways on her hand.

"Thank you, Floyd," Minnie said, gently stroking his cheek with her free hand. "But now, listen. Henry is planning this picnic on the island—"

"Oh, goody!" Floyd said. He danced on the balcony railing and flapped his wings as he crowed, "We love a picnic! We a love picnic! When is it?"

"Floyd," Willy said, flapping his wings at his brother. "Please. Let Miss Minnie finish!"

"We don't love this picnic, Floyd," Minnie said. "Henry plans to do some very bad things to the island. But he needs a lot of other people's money to do it. That's what the picnic is for, so he can squeeze it out of his rich friends."

"I didn't know you could do that," Floyd said, tilting his head.

"Do what?" Minnie said, confused. She glanced back at her bedroom *door*.

"Squeeze orbs out of humans," Floyd said. "Where do they come out?"

"Crimony, Floyd," Willy said, cuffing his brother with a wing. "It's a figure of speech. Forgive him, Miss Minnie, but Floyd tends to take things literally."

"Oh, that's okay," Minnie said, laughing. "It's a pretty silly saying. Floyd, I meant that Henry will try very hard to convince people to give him money."

"Ohhhh," Floyd said, nodding thoughtfully. "I get it now. I thought you meant—"

"Floyd! Shush!" Willy said as he put a wing over his brother's beak.

Minnie looked over her shoulder, making sure, again, that her door was closed. She leaned closer to the crow brothers. "Henry's afraid to take the paddleboat to the island, so he invited his wealthy friends for a private ride on a helicopter for champagne breakfast."

"Champagne breakfast," Floyd said. "Yum!"

"A helicopter?" Willy asked. "You mean a whirly-bird? Them things are huge! Where will it land?"

"At the opposite end from the hermit's chapel," Minnie said. "I don't know where, other than he said they'll land on a beach or a sand

bar or something. He doesn't want to run into Father Manzi, he said."
She looked over her shoulder.

"He won't want to run into Charlie either," Floyd said to Willy.

"Absolutely not!" Willy agreed.

"Nosirreebob," Floyd shook his head emphatically.

"No way, Jose'!" Willy said.

"Under no circumstances!"

"He'd be real sorry."

"Might as well just throw himself off a cliff!"

"Sooner he should cover himself with honey and sit naked on an
ant hill!"

"Better he should shoot himself at sunrise every day for a week!"

"Or boil himself in oil!"

The two crows looked back at Minnie. "Nope, that'd be something he wouldn't want to do. Run into Charlie!"

Minnie could hardly contain her laughter. She loved Floyd and
Willy; they always cheered her up, no matter how terrible things
seemed. But she felt nervous that Henry would hear them.

"Shhh!" Minnie said, her forefinger across her lips.

"Sorry!" Floyd whispered.

Both crows hunkered down on the balcony railing. "When is this
shindig, Miss Minnie?" Willy asked in a low voice.

"A week from yesterday," she said. "Next Monday."

"Minerva!" Henry's voice permeated the house, vibrating walls
and windows.

"What was that?" Floyd said.

"Sounds like the man of the house has awakened," Willy said.

"Gotta go, gents," she said and blew them each a kiss.

"We ought not to miss this shindig, eh, brother?" Willy said with
an air of great dignity and sarcasm as they leaped off the balcony.

IN HIS ANCIENT TUPELO TREE, HIGH above the Woodman's Cemetery,
on the northern borders of the university, Starfire awaited his friend

Hookbeak. Before retiring within its sprawling branches, Starfire and his wife had raised a large number of young ravens, every year building a new nest not far from this very tree. He knew precisely how many children he had sired, and grandchildren. He even knew how many generations of great-grandchildren he had. Seven. Of course he could not come up with all their names, just their numbers.

As Chief Archivist, Starfire dealt in corvid genealogical data on a daily basis. It was a simple task to access the archival lattice; he could do it in his sleep. But he was not concerned with the names of his many descendants at the moment. Another fireball had ejected during Charlie's trance, and Starfire was flummoxed. He had created several Extermination Chants and went after the bugs that seemed to be eating the data. Charlie had struggled to speak as the lattice closed, and had said something that sounded like "ugs". *Did he mean to say "bugs"?*

The roar of the lawnmower on the other side of the cemetery distracted his thoughts. In spite of the noise, he appreciated mowing days for the evening buffet of chopped lizards, toads, insects, and other creatures that couldn't seem to get out of the way.

He watched his friend Hookbeak approach, admiring his wingspan and graceful glide down to the tupelo tree. The Aviar landed on the large branch near Starfire and folded his wings. The two old ravens greeted each other cordially.

"To what do I owe the honor of a visit, my friend?" Starfire asked. He knew the Aviar preferred to stay on his side of the river.

"There have been some complaints," Hookbeak said vaguely. He sharpened his beak on the branch near his feet.

"Complaints?" *Who? Does the Aviar somehow know of the mishap with the Keeper last week?*

"Yes, my friend, complaints," Hookbeak said. "But first, tell me about the damage to the lattice. Last time we talked, you suspected something was damaging it. 'Bugs', I believe was the term you used."

The lawnmower droned closer. Starfire could smell the gasoline engine exhaust co-mingled with fresh-cut grass. He nodded. "Bugs ate many holes in the lattice—mostly in areas where we store Patua' data. Bugs are why we did not find Jayzu in our database. I think."

"I see," Hookbeak said. "That is problematic. But you have killed the bugs, you say? Have you fixed the holes?"

"I thought the bugs were gone," Starfire said. "I thought I killed them all and left a systemic poison in case they come back. But, alas, I believe I have missed one."

It was no mean feat, killing the bugs. Starfire had been in a mildornia trance for an entire day with only a few novices to watch over him. Several times he had surfaced from the trance, gasping, "Not finished yet. Must go back." He beaked more mildornia berries, and though he felt he was dying of thirst, he did not drink.

After the extermination, he had fallen over stiff as a board. The novices told him later that they had been frightened he had died. But he was not dead, and the bugs were gone. Until Charlie's trance that ended with him struggling to say "bugs."

"I will run another Extermination Ritual," Starfire said. "After I am sure they are gone, I will continue repairing the damage they have done. It is very time-consuming to search the Keeper's memories for the Patua' data, and then to extract it and patch the holes the bugs made. Sometimes I don't find what I need very quickly, and the Keepers have to stay under longer."

"And is that dangerous?" Hookbeak asked.

Starfire looked deep into his friend's opaque black eyes. *Does he know?* "Not usually. Some do not tolerate such high doses of mildornia berries, it is true. But it is the only way I know to patch the holes."

He had screened the Keepers well, he had thought, experimenting with dosages of mildornia berries to filter out the Keepers for whom the deep trance might be fatal. *How did Beatrice get through the screening?* He had been grievously shocked when the young Keeper had fallen over stiff and dead as a doornail right at his feet. Before he had even searched her memories. *Such a tragic loss.*

The lawnmower droned nearby, like a giant cricket in the grass declaring the summertime temperature. "There are risks to the trance," Hookbeak said, eyeing the mower and its two riders. "We know that." He turned back to Starfire, his black eyes blazing in anger. "But to break into a corvid's private memory, Starfire? That is akin to stealing, is it not? I am quite uncomfortable with that scenario. This is a serious covenant you have broken."

Starfire sunk his head into a wing and pretended to scratch a sudden itch. How did the Aviar know he had wandered without permission through the Keeper's memories? The Keepers themselves did not know. It was true he had been warned. Severely warned. And he agreed it *was* a sacred trust he had violated, an unequivocal promise to the Keepers that their personal memories would be left private while their minds were open and unprotected.

Starfire had neutralized his guilt by continually reminding himself that what he had found was worth his minor rule bending. Besides, while he was only fixing holes in the archival lattice, he had found a few more Orbs of the Patua'.

"I am certain that the Keepers would all give permission for the searches," Starfire said, "but it is so very cumbersome and time-consuming to get it."

"Yes, that is true, Starfire. The Council founders deliberately made it difficult to obtain such permission—to prevent such violations as this one. I insist that you follow protocol."

"I do not have the time!" Starfire protested vehemently. "There are much greater issues I am attending to."

"What could be a greater issue for the Chief Archivist than keeping the Keepers of the Archival Lattice in good health?" Hookbeak asked. "That is, alive."

"You do not understand!" Starfire said. He hopped back and forth between two branches, grasping one for a few seconds before leaping back to the other. "We are running out of mildornia berries. Even before the bugs ate our data, I had none to spare."

Hookbeak blinked a few times and said, "What has that got to do with these invasions of yours, other than you're using large amounts of berries and killing your Keepers?"

Starfire stopped, gripping a branch tightly and glaring at Hook-beak. He tried to control the angry impatience that surged upward from his breast. *Calm yourself, raven. Anger kills reason.* He focused on the sound of the lawnmower as it traversed back and forth across the cemetery. He tried to visualize the pattern the mower always left in the grass and the smorgasbord of delectable dinner entrees.

"Quite by accident," Starfire said after composing himself, "during my searches, I have finally discovered the legendary Orbs of the Patua'."

"The Orbs of the Patua'?" Hookbeak said. "And these orbs—what relation do they bear upon your sacred oath?"

Starfire told the Aviar about the orb Jayzu found under Brutha-max's bones, describing in great detail the skilled craftsmanship of some unknown ancient Patua'. "And much to my surprise, another orb has turned up, nearly identical to Bruthamax's. Right in Ledford."

The lawnmower invaded the space in which Starfire's tupelo tree grew, capturing the attention of both ravens. A crow perched on the gas tank in front of the mower, while the operator steered it deftly around trees and tombstones. The noise was loud enough to prevent conversation, and the two ravens perched quietly until the mower moved on.

"And theses searches have revealed another potential Patua'," Starfire said, when the noise had diminished somewhat "of whom we knew nothing."

Hookbeak rose up on his thick legs and stretched, flapping his wings a few times before folding them back at his sides. His legs hurt. So did his wings. The lawnmower came into the small clearing underneath them. "Is the gardener Patua'?"

"No," Starfire said, "and he's deaf as a post. Julie just likes to ride the mower with him. She said she likes the smell of fresh-cut grass."

"And what do you think they are?" Hookbeak asked. "These orbs you risk so much for?"

"Seed pods," Starfire said without hesitation. "Mildornia seed pods!" A gust of wind blew through the branches, revealing the white ruff around his neck.

Hookbeak refolded his wings and said, "And how did you come to that conclusion? Have you broken one open? Were there mildornia seeds inside?"

"No," Starfire said. "I personally have never actually seen one of these orbs. But my hunch is that—"

"Your hunch?" Hookbeak shook his head in wonder. "You are risking lives for seeds? For 'potential' Patua'? My friend, what has happened to you?"

"You don't understand!" Starfire said impatiently. "We *need* mildornia berries!"

"I do understand that," the Aviar said calmly. "I know that the seeds are required for the trances. You have told me that more than once. And that the mildornia bushes used to thrive everywhere. And the last known bush, a hermaphrodite, grows on Cadeña-l'jadia."

A sense of profound weariness permeated his being. Suddenly life seemed severely complicated. *Ah, my Rosie, I shall leave all this soon and come join you, my love.* "I am trying to understand," Hookbeak continued, "why you have violated the sacred trust between the Council and the Keepers."

Starfire did not speak for a few moments. Hookbeak had watched his friend struggle with his passionate ambitions their entire adult lives. But never had he transgressed from the ethical boundaries set by the Council.

"Where is your conscience, Starfire?" he asked quietly. "You cannot continue this invasion of the Keepers' memories for any reason, no matter how lofty it seems. It is simply wrong, even if we are in desperate need of these seeds. Or discovering more Patua'. The Council will not sanction this."

Starfire shook his head as he strode back and forth on the branch. "The Council is myopic, Aviar! Can you not see what is at stake here? Our entire database, our entire history, our entire genealogy since the days of First Crow and First Raven will be lost—to say nothing of the Patua' data. For the love of the Egg, Hookbeak, these are perilous times! We cannot afford to adhere to ideology when our very survival is at stake."

"Do not think that I am unaware, Starfire," Hookbeak growled, "of what is at stake here. Am I not Aviar? It is my business to be aware, as I must make you aware of the dangerous winds you are flying in. Have you no regard for your Keepers?"

"I am careful," Starfire said sullenly.

"Not careful enough," Hookbeak said. He had been sorely disappointed in his friend, not so much that his experiment had been fatal to young Beatrice. *But why did he cover it up? Why did he not come tell me? Have I not been his loyal friend all these years?*

"There is no proof!" Starfire protested. "Even the Emplacement Ritual is sometimes fatal."

"And you refuse any remorse for the death of this innocent Keeper?" Hookbeak hopped onto the branch near Starfire. "I cannot continue to shelter you, Starfire, or your activities. One more mishap among the Keepers," he said, putting his beak into the other raven's face, "and I am going to blow the lid off this. Do I need to explain what will happen in that event?"

Starfire stepped backward under the Aviar's pressure but did not reply.

"The Council will strip you of your position as Chief Archivist," Hookbeak said, stepping toward Starfire and bearing down on him. "And your name will be blackened forever."

Starfire growled and flapped his wings. The Aviar backed off, and the two ravens stood eye-to-eye, searing the air between them with the charged particles of their anger. The leaves on all the branches of the tupelo tree suddenly rattled and quivered.

Hookbeak broke his stance first, shaking his head. "Have you gone mad, my friend?" he said quietly. "Too many mildornia trances, perhaps?"

"And if the database goes down," Starfire said, as their tempers cooled, "what will it matter if I have a good or bad name? Aviar, please, I beseech you, hear me! I do not know how else to save our database. At the small expense of my position in the archives, and even my good name among the corvid, I am willing to make this sacrifice."

"Did you ask the Keepers if they were willing to sacrifice their lives to your vanity before you volunteered them?" Hookbeak asked.

"This is not my vanity, Aviar," Starfire growled. "There is much at stake here, the preservation of all of our knowledge, history, and genealogy. Which is the more valuable? The rights of the individual Keeper to maintain memory privacy, or the rights of the entire corvid species for the past seventeen or so million years?"

"You call upon the dead?" Hookbeak asked incredulously, "to defend this mind invasion of yours? What rights do the dead have?"

"They have the right to be remembered," Starfire said. "Is not that why we ever constructed the archival lattice in the first place? To keep track of ourselves? Shall we allow millions of lives to be lost to this stubborn obedience to principles?"

"Shall we lose our moral compass over a database?" Hookbeak flapped his wings several times.

Charlie left Charlotte's windowsill at Rosencranz after their morning visit and flew across the river, across the university campus to Starfire's tree in the old Woodmen's Cemetery. Hookbeak was there with him, and the two old ravens seemed to be deep in a heated discussion—an argument from the looks of it. *Starfire seems angry! I wonder what they are arguing about?*

Charlie flew once around the tupelo tree, but as he started back toward Cadeña-l'jadia, Starfire called out, "Yo, Charlie!"

He turned around and sailed into the tree, settling on a branch near the two ravens. "Grawky! I hope I didn't interrupt anything important."

The two ravens looked at each other briefly. "Nothing that we have not been endlessly discussing," Hookbeak said wearily. "Grawky, Charlie."

"Indeed," Starfire said. "Perhaps we should thank you for the interruption. Otherwise the two of us could grow old and stiff and keel over right here in this tree, without solving a thing."

The two ravens looked at each other gravely for a moment, then cackled with laughter as they flapped their wings. Once they settled back down, Charlie told them what he had learned from Floyd and Willy. "And they said Henry Braun plans to land a helicopter on Cadeña-l'jadia."

"That would be the only way he could get there," Starfire said. "The river would never let him near."

Charlie nodded. "Jayzu and his friends are fighting him, but he has many orbs and is very powerful."

Starfire said, "That man is a menace, the very antithesis of the Patua'. We cannot allow him to gain control of Cadeña-l'jadia. We must stop him."

"But how?" Charlie asked. "We are just birds. Not even the humans seem to be able to stop him."

"We are small," Hookbeak said, "each of us. But together we form a multitude. Tomorrow we shall assemble the Great Corvid Council. We shall take a stand on Cadeña-l'jadia."

The Great Corvid convened on the roof of the hermit's chapel as the mid-afternoon shadows began to lengthen. Many more crows and ravens than councilors attended, and they perched all around—in the trees, the garden, and all over the marvelously rusty, sparkly contraption Jayzu had planted next to the pond.

"Greetings, Councilors!" the Aviar spoke from the apex of the chapel roof. "Greetings, corvids! Greetings, all birds of all feathers!" He turned slowly all the way around, his great wings unfurled as if to include everyone. "Thank you for flying in on such short notice. We face a grave threat."

"We?" Wingnut asked.

Charlie heard a wave of murmuring propagate through the trees all around him. "Who is that?" "That's Wingnut. He thinks he's going to be Aviar one day!"

"Yes, we," Hookbeak's voice rumbled. "We do not exist independently of the human sphere."

Wingnut folded his wings in displeasure but settled back on his branch. Charlie was glad he backed down. There was no time to argue.

"We must open our eyes to the uncomfortable truth," Hookbeak continued. "The events in the human world over the last century or two have encroached upon our otherwise idyllic existence, and we can no longer bury our heads under our wings and ignore the problem. We are losing our forests, our rivers, and streams to the inexorable march of human civilization across the landscape."

Hookbeak signaled Charlie to take the high perch next to him. "Tell all our corvid brethren of the threat to Cadeña-l'jadia," he said as the crow landed.

Charlie stood up as tall as he could, opened his wings, and called out as loudly as he could: "Cadeña-l'jadia is under siege as we speak. There is a plan afoot by the human, Henry Braun, to remove its forests and birds, and replace them with a human-built landscape of concrete and buildings."

Many of the birds gasped, and Fishgut called out, "Henry Braun?" The raven rose up on his roof branch near Charlie and shouted, "Henry Braun? You mean the Bunya? Have we such short memories, my corvids?" He unfolded his wings. "Is he not the same bunya who shaved the northern forests to nubbins?"

The birds snickered at the slur. "Bunya" meant "meat so rotten even a corvid would not eat it."

"Then he built the fish-canning factory," Fishgut said, "and the place now reeks of rotting fish. While I feed off the largesse of the Cannery, it is too much, and the landscape is spoiled. And it stinks. I would much prefer that the forest, my ancestral territory, had remained."

The older birds in the surrounding tree shouted angry epithets against the Bunya, recalling the destruction. The councilors maintained a slightly greater decorum, with only a few disapproving hisses.

"It was the Bunya's ancestor," Starfire spoke out, "who tore the forests down for the Cannery. The living Henry Braun, known among some of us as the Bunya, plans the same fate for our Cadeña-l'jadia."

"First Henry Bunya will purchase the island," Charlie continued, "and turn it into an amusement park for humans."

"Purchase?" asked Mikey. "As in purchase the branch?" He looked down at his feet.

"I thought he said purchase the island," Restarea said, blinking in confusion.

"Purchase? What is purchase?" O'Malley asked.

"Let us examine the word 'purchase,'" said Athanasius. "*Purchase* is derived from the Middle English *purchacen*, or as the Anglo-French would have said, *purchaser*. To purchase means to get a better grip on an object, as in 'grasp the branch with both claws for more purchase.'"

"Oh, that branch," Restarea said, nodding.

"What about the island?" Joshwa asked. "I thought we were talking about an island."

Walldrug said, "I thought purchase means, essentially, to own. In which case, I must ask: can anyone own that which he cannot carry off?"

Hookbeak motioned Charlie to continue. "Do not get sidetracked into these philosophical gopher holes, Charlie. Tell them about the threat to Cadeña-l'jadia."

Charlie nodded gratefully. He remembered when the Council first met Jayzu. *It's a wonder they can get anything said and done.* He hoped he was never called upon to be a councilor. "Henry the Bunya," he addressed the Council again, "has millions of orbs that he wants to give the humans in the city in exchange for the island. That's what I meant when I said he wants to purchase it."

Taken aback, many birds spoke at once: "Exchange orbs for the island?" "I cannot imagine!" "That is what purchase means?" "Millions of orbs!" "How many is a million?" "Imagine how big the nest would be to hold a million orbs!"

"What would anyone do with that many orbs?" Ziggy asked.

"Buy an island?" Joshwa said.

The councilors laughed raucously, including the Aviar.

"Seriously," Starfire said when the laughter had died down, "even among humans, ownership is a fairly abstract concept. But if anyone owns Cadeña-l'jadia, it is Charlie. His family has lived there since before there were any humans at all in this part of the world. Even humans regard that sometimes as legal ownership."

"However," Wingnut said, "humans do not consider that any other species has ownership over any fraction of the entire earth's surface."

"True enough," Hookbeak said. "But let us not exhaust ourselves trying to understand the human concepts of ownership. Let us return to the subject for which have convened. We all know that forest destruction hits us birds first, if not hardest. Remember when the Boonies were out in the middle of nowhere, Walldrug?"

"How could I forget?" the raven councilor cried out. "I watched my entire ancestral homeland devoured. Thousands of trees were shaved off the land to build a gigantic parking lot and a corn chip factory. Where there were trees, there is now only burning asphalt. They killed it all."

The birds in the trees surrounding the chapel had grown quiet. He knew some of the crows ate regularly at the corn chip factory. *Can we rise above our stomachs?*

"And Cadeña-l'jadia is next," the Aviar said, "unless we band together and stop the destruction. This is our sacred land, if not for the hundreds of corvid generations born here, but this was the home of the great Bruthamax, may his spirit forever walk this lonely isle. And Jayzu. Let us not forget Jayzu."

All of the birds within earshot of Hookbeak showed their approval by screeching and flapping their wings. Some called out, "Long live Jayzu!" "Bruthamax forever!" "Bruthamax will never die!"

"We have no more time," Hookbeak's strong voice cut through the noise. "We have waited long enough for the humans to come to their senses. We must stop talking and act. If we are going to prevent the Bunya's destruction of Cadeña-l'jadia, we must be proactive. We must act."

"And do what?" Wingnut asked. "Throw ourselves in front of the saws?"

Hookbeak said. "Saws?" He shook his head. "I was thinking we throw ourselves in front of the humans."

The councilors blinked in confusion and asked each other "What is he talking about?" "Is he serious?" "Throw ourselves in front of humans?"

"Follow me!" Hookbeak's voice rose above the private conversations, calling out to all the birds on the roof of the chapel as well as in the trees. He flapped his wings, lifting his great body above the trees. "Let us say no to the Bunya! A million birds taking a stand! We must all fly out and spread the word, starting today, to all birds in the land. We shall invite them all to the picnic on Cadeña-l'jadia. This land is ours. Now fly! Spread the word!"

Hookbeak led the way as he flew off shouting, "Calling all birds! All birds of all feathers! Picnic on Cadeña-l'jadia! Good eats! Take a stand against forest destruction! Take a stand against the Bunya!"

The councilors, Charlie, and a host of corvid volunteers flew far and wide, and they spoke to many birds across the land. Charlie sent off all the young crows on Cadeña-l'jadia to engage the birds beyond the timber mills, all the way to the northern border. He sent his sons JohnHenry and Edgar to carry the message Downtown, and to the Waterfront. More crows flew out across the river to the university, to the woods behind Russ and Jade's house. The airport ravens carried the word to the surrounding towns and countryside.

As the corvids spread the word, other birds heard the call and carried it into the wind for miles and miles around Cadeña-l'jadia. "Come ye! All birds of beak and feather, come to the picnic on Cadeña-l'jadia! Take a stand against the Bunya!"

Beak to beak, the word spread as the corvids raised the alarm from the cemetery to the timber mills, out east to the plains beyond Ledford, to the south all the way to MacKenzie. "Come all ye birds of all feathers! Join us and all our winged brethren for the Million Bird Stand on Cadeña-l'jadia!"

In a matter of one day, scores of birds over many hundreds of square miles took to the skies and headed to Cadeña-l'jadia. They arrived in multitudes, landing in trees, on the shorelines, and in the meadows, calling out, "Small alone, mighty together!"

The new bird sanctuary was jammed with birds, from the cliffs to the riverbanks. The sudden influx of such an enormous number of birds attracted the attention of the city as birds arrived continuously, hundreds and hundreds every hour. They assumed a swirling flight pattern above the treetops of the island as they searched for places to perch, stand, wade, or sit. The noise generated by many birds produced a low-decibel buzz that did not abate until nightfall, when the birds settled down in their roosts to sleep.

A reporter from the *Sentinel* ambushed Alfredo as he left his office in the Biology Department at the university. "Dr. Manzi," the reporter asked, "how do you explain the sudden arrival on Wilder Island of so many birds? Has your bird sanctuary become a nuisance, attracting too many of our avian friends?"

"A nuisance for whom?" Alfredo answered. "If you are asking is this odd, I would say it is very odd that so many birds of different species would suddenly show up in the same place. It is hard to know what to make of it, but I'm sure we will all find out soon enough." He smiled, edged past the reporter, and left the building whistling a popular tune from 1960s, a song about a blackbird.

—18—

The Million Bird Stand

Alfredo looked up from the papers he was grading at his table, distracted by the loud thump he had heard against the cottage wall. He put his pen down and went to the door and opened it to find a motionless crow lying on his doorstep.

"Grawky! JoEd," Jayzu said, smiling at the stunned crow on his step.

JoEd struggled to his feet. "Man, that was some *jaloosie!*" He smoothed his ruffled feathers back against his body. "It took me as soon as I left Downtown, Jayzu! It took me way up—higher than ever!"

"Are you all right?" Alfredo stooped down to see if the bird was injured.

"Oh, yeah! I'm fine." JoEd looked up at the sky. "But I wasn't even trying to ride a *jaloosie*. It just took me and dropped me here. I have come for the Million Bird Stand."

"As I suspected," Alfredo said. "Birds have been flying in from all over for the past two days."

He had watched a steady stream flying over the treetops. Many landed in the trees near the chapel, corvids mostly, to admire Bruthamax's worship nest. It was rather astonishing, that many birds. And how marvelous that so many different species came to gather in one place briefly, to make a stand against the destruction of Cadeñal'jadia!

An island this small could not support such a huge number of birds, even for a few days. Alfredo noticed many of them flew off the island in the morning, presumably to feed in the city of Ledford, in the surrounding fields and pastures, and along the riverbanks.

"I have been out spreading the word," JoEd said. "It's going everywhere, Jayzu, around and around, in wider circles all across the land." He dipped his beak several times in a puddle on the stone step.

"We cannot stop the Bunya without you," Alfredo said. "I am grateful for your help."

"I would be nowhere else," JoEd said. "We are small alone."

Alfredo watched him disappear into the forest as he flew off in the direction of the tree house. *For just this one day, I would like to be a crow. To be one of them when they take a stand against Henry Braun. The Bunya.*

"This is ours," Charlie had said when Alfredo asked if he could help with the Million Bird Stand. "You've already raised your voice. You have done much, Jayzu, to keep Cadeña-l'jadia the way it is. We know you are with us in spirit. It's our turn now."

JoEd found his parents perched on the rail around the deck of Bruthamax's tree house. As he approached, Rika nudged Charlie with her wing and said, "My Orbs! Husband! I think our son has come home!"

JoEd landed on the railing and put a wing out over his mother and said, "Hi ya, Weebs!" Rika pecked him lightly and spent a few moments grooming him until he squirmed away from her.

"Aw, Weebs!" he said, flapping his wings. "I'm not a hatchling anymore. I can clean my own feathers!"

"Your weebs is happy to see you," Charlie said. "As am I."

"It's good to be home, Zazu!" JoEd said. "I want to make a stand with you."

"Well, that is tomorrow," Rika said, nudging her son. "First you must tell us where you have been and what have you seen since you flew the nest. You look a bit thin. Have you been eating enough? Have you found a mate?"

JoEd thought of Shannon, the pretty little crow he had met on the roof of the *River Queen*. *She seemed to like me.* He wondered if he could find her again.

"I eat just fine, Weebs," JoEd said. "There's so much food in the city, it'd be hard not to eat well. And I'm still a bachelor."

"When it is time," Rika said, nodding, "she will come."

JoEd looked at his mother with great love. *She is so wise, my weebs.*

"I am in Keeper training," JoEd said. "Just like you, Zazu! I am a novice. Starfire says I take after you. 'You're a quick learner, just like your zazu'—that's what he said!"

"I'm proud of you, JoEd," Charlie said. "You have done well."

JoEd roosted for the night in his ancestral tree. He'd been all over since he left, intoxicated by the sight of the *River Queen* and Downtown. And the university! He thought he'd seen a huge chunk of the world after Antoine flew him around the university. But when he flew out to spread the word for the Million Bird Stand, he was staggered by the sheer size of it all. He flew for hours over strange landscapes without trees, huge lakes whose opposite shores he could not see, and off in the distance, mountains!

But it was good to be home.

HENRY STOOD AT THE WINDOW OF his office, scowling at the thousands of birds that swirled above Wilder Island. The picnic was tomorrow; everything was ready. "The last thing I need is a bunch of flying vermin in the air crapping all over the place," he growled to Jules Sackman. He wanted to throw his shoe at those two smirking crows in the tree outside his window.

He closed the window shade and took a seat in the huge leather armchair behind his desk. He fidgeted with the stapler and then the pens in the leather holder that matched his chair. He leaned back, swiveling away from the windows and toward the portraits of his ancestors. Henry the First's eyes bore down on him. *What is it? Have I forgotten something?*

"I wonder why so many of them suddenly flocked to the island in the last few days," Jules said, picking at a fingernail. "Almost like they knew something."

"You and my insane wife," Henry said, waving away the attorney.

"You think these stupid birdbrains are capable of thought? It's just a coincidence—probably some dead animal on the island they all want a bite of. That's all they know, Jules. They don't have thoughts, just urges. Eating, shitting, and screwing."

Henry the First nodded. "Don't let them stop you, Henry. It was the crows that took down my bridge, you know. Just like now—thousands upon thousands of them flying in at night, so no one saw. The next day, the bridge was no more."

"No filthy crow is going to stop me again!" Henry nearly shouted at Jules.

But what were all these birds doing here? If crows destroyed the trestle bridge, he shuddered to think what they could do to his picnic. He engaged briefly in a dark fantasy of thousands of crows bringing the helicopter down, loaded with his investors. And him.

He shook his head quickly a few times to dispel the gruesome image of bodies floating in the water and the helicopter lying on its side like a dead insect. He tried to focus his attention on the ceremony in the morning. He had dreamed of this day for years. He'd have an official ribbon-cutting and flag-planting, right on the banks of the island. He'd even commissioned a special flag of his family crest, in honor of reuniting the Brauns with their lost ancestral homeland.

"Tomorrow, the island will be mine!" Henry said, forcing a grand smile. "And I, Henry Braun the Fourth, shall turn it into a paradise. First I plant a flag, reclaiming the island for my family honor. Henry Braun Island—that's the new name."

Henry the First nodded and winked. "That's the spirit, boy!"

"Henry," Jules said, "you can't just summarily change the name like that. Wilder Island is on all the maps. And, the island isn't yours yet."

"A technicality!" Henry said, waving his hand at Jules. "What're they going to do, sue me?" He laughed bitterly. "And the name 'Wilder Island' was never official. It's my island; that makes it private property, and I can call it whatever I want."

"Yet the private property rights of others," Jules said, "doesn't apparently stop you from taking their land."

Henry the First frowned down upon Jules. "Whose side is he on? How is it you tolerate this insolence?"

"This whole eminent domain thing was your idea, Jules," Henry said, mopping sweat off his forehead.

"Don't whine, Henry."

He looked up at Henry the First.

"Just fire the leech."

AFTER BREAKFAST ON THE DAY of Henry the Bunya's picnic, all the birds on Cadeña-l'jadia, residents and visitors alike, convened at the edge of the forest near the tip of the island where he would land his helicopter. The noise was horrendous, as thousands and thousands of birds of all breeds and sizes flew in and found places to perch, sit, or stand. Every bush and rock held as many birds as could get a foothold. Younger trees bent to the ground under the weight of their bird load. Birds covered everything.

Charlie perched at the top of a dead tree whose leaves and smaller branches were long gone, a high point from which he would speak to the birds gathered below. He unfolded his wings and shouted, "Greetings, Birds of all Feathers!" He made a complete rotation on his perch, his strong mature voice flying out over the crowd as he repeated his salutation. "Greetings, Birds of all Feathers!"

He waited until the birds had mostly quieted down to continue. "Thank you for coming to the Million Bird Stand. In a few short hours, a small yet deadly invasion of the Bunya will begin. If we cannot stop them now, it will mean the end of Cadeña-l'jadia."

The birds squawked, hooted, cawed, honked, cheeped, quacked, trilled, and chirped their displeasure.

"But we are not just here to save Cadeña-l'jadia!" Charlie shouted. "The Earth beyond this little island is also a beautiful place and home to many more birds and many other creatures of all kingdoms! All creatures seem to know how to live here more or less peacefully.

All but one. Humans. And the Bunya is their king."

The birds again voiced their disapproval, some standing up and flapping their wings, some stamping around indignantly—though there was not much room, and everyone chattered at once. Charlie's voice somehow arched over the noise. "We can turn them back now, all of us. Though we are each small, together we form a multitude, a force to be reckoned with. We shall turn back this invasion, island by island, forest by forest, for however many tomorrows it shall take. Today, the multitude of us will just say no."

"What if they have guns?" a thrush asked in a reedy voice.

"We do not need to fear guns from this crowd," Charlie said. "They will not be armed with guns; they arm themselves with orbs. They think their orbs will protect them. But they are sorely mistaken. We will use the weapon of our guts and sheer multitudes to chase the Bunya off our island."

Charlie flapped his wings and shouted, "It is time! Let us now assume the position. Follow me!"

He swooped off his perch and flew low to the ground, leading a parade of walking, flying, and hopping birds. He dropped to the sand at the edge of the forest and shouted, "It is here we make our stand!"

As the birds arrived, he directed them into position. "We will create a barrier of birds. Yes, a solid wall of birds staring the Bunya down."

He knew most of the birds could not hear him, but those who did followed his instructions and began layering themselves into a solid wall of feathers, beaks, wings, and claws. "Larger birds on the bottom!" he shouted.

As the multitudes of birds arrived at the site, they followed the others, assuming their positions in the great wall. "One bird every half wingspan—in all directions," Charlie directed. "Find a perch in the trees, on the ground, on rocks, each other."

The wall of birds was enormous, comprising many species, many colors, many eyes. It was a marvelous spectacle. There were whole bevies of quail and dove, nides of pheasants, gaggles of geese, flushes of ducks, rafters of turkeys, sieges of herons, murders of crows, conspiracies of ravens, tidings of magpies, descents of woodpeckers, hosts of sparrows, charms of finches, exaltations of larks, wisps of snipes, kettles of hawks, parliaments of owls, and parties of jays. All within a wing's reach of one another, they formed a barrier of birds from the forest floor to its treetops.

Hookbeak and Starfire perched in a tree near the great wall of birds as Charlie spoke. "At my signal, we all take to the air, and we dump on him from above. The Bunya is our main target, but do not go out of your way to avoid hitting the others. Some of them are as guilty as he and, given the inspiration, would do exactly what Bunya wants to do. So, let it fly. Get some on everyone."

"Some what?" Floyd asked Willy. "Toxic waste? Hot wax? Fliers?"

"I believe he means excrement, brother," Willy replied.

"Ohhh," Floyd said, nodding. "I see." After a few seconds, he said, "Ours?"

"Who else's?" Willy said.

"Oh, goody," Floyd said gleefully. "I love a pasting!"

HENRY BRAUN LOOKED UP AT THE CLEAR blue sky from the deck of the *River Queen*. Not a bird in sight—a matter of great relief to him. No dull roar of bird noise came across the river. "Good riddance," he said with a growl. "And stay off my island!"

The *River Queen* pulled away from the dock with its cargo of Ledford's well-heeled elite, and headed across the river to the city boat landing where they would board the helicopter. Henry didn't dare try and take his beautiful *River Queen* to the island—not after what happened to his great-grandfather's trestle bridge. Thirty or so of Henry's guests sipped champagne and filled their plates at a buffet brunch on the promenade. While the boat paddled slowly past Wilder Island, the passengers enjoyed a marvelous feast that included grilled salmon, a mountain of jumbo shrimp, prime rib, quiche, a vast array of colorful fruit, and an exotic juice bar.

Originally he had planned to serve the feast on the island, but Jules had talked him out of it. "Come on, Henry!" he had said. "Think about it! Most people would prefer to dine on the decks of the *River Queen* than on the sandy banks of a deserted island. Remember, the island is full of crows; you don't want to create an attractive nuisance."

"Create an attractive nuisance?" Henry was sick of Jules. "Seems to me those blasted crows are the nuisance."

It was not an affair for children or spouses. This was not entertainment; it was business. The guest list was restricted to investors and influential politicos, including Henry Braun's long-time crony, the mayor. They were wealthy, all of them—except the newspaper people—otherwise they would not have been invited. A reporter from the *Sentinel* and his cameraman had been hired to publicize the event for Henry, and he magnanimously allowed them to indulge in the food but not the champagne.

After brunch, everyone disembarked from the *River Queen* and half, including Henry, boarded a large helicopter that waited in the parking lot. The helicopter took off almost immediately and bore down on the island like a dinosaur-size bird of prey. After disgorging its passengers, it returned to the dock for the second load.

Henry climbed out of the helicopter, strode up the bank, and stopped. The forest in front of him was dark and forbidding, and its stillness seemed uncanny. It unnerved him that he could not see very far into its shadows. This was his first time on Wilder Island, and he wanted to savor these first moments of almost owning it. But the forest repelled him. The profound silence bore down on him. He shook his fist and raged silently. *The day is coming, I promise, when I burn you down!*

Turning his back, Henry forced himself to override his fear. *At least those damn birds aren't still flying around overhead.* He climbed up to an elevated position on a rock and watched his guests make their way toward him. By the time they all arrived, Jules had finished setting up an easel to hold a set of colorful charts illustrating impressive returns on investments in Ravenwood Resort.

"My friends, at long last I fulfill a boyhood dream," Henry addressed the carefully chosen faithful, arms outstretched. "I've asked each of you here to witness this momentous occasion where I bring this island back into the fold of my family where it rightly belongs."

Henry gestured behind him as he spoke. "Many years ago, my ancestor Henry Braun the First was swindled out of his rightful ownership of this island by corrupt politicians and a railroad desperate to survive. Through the next four generations, each Henry Braun brought fortune and good times back into the family. But we have gnashed our teeth, waiting for the time to restore what is ours. This island. It is now that time. With great honor and pride, I plant my family flag on Henry Braun Island, as it shall be known from here onwards."

Unfurling the flag with the Braun family crest emblazoned in gold, Henry stuck the flagpole into the sand. Jules handed him a small sledgehammer; he smacked the top of the pole a few times and handed it back. Turning again to his guests, he threw his arms out and said, "Welcome to Braun Island, my friends. Upon this island we will build Ravenwood Resort."

The people before him remained silent. No applause, no cheering, no flag waving, no celebration. Henry's smile vanished and his neck hairs stood erect suddenly. He glanced over his shoulder at the forest and saw nothing but dark shadows woven into a patchy fabric of leaf and branch. Still, there was something not quite right about the scene.

He turned back to the investors, shoving his shaking hands into his pockets and licked his lips nervously. "I ask each and every one of you to join me in prosperity. Invest in Ravenwood Resort on Braun Island. Each of you has a prospectus and—"

No one was paying him the least attention. The investors looked past him into the forest, eyebrows raised incredulously. Henry stopped talking and turned slowly toward the trees. Perhaps it was the angle of the sun, but where a few minutes ago only a dark spooky forest stood, now thousands and thousands and thousands of eyes stared at him from within a great wall of feathers and beaks.

The birds remained motionless, but for the occasional blinking of an eye. Charlie suddenly flapped out to a rock adjacent to Henry Braun, fixing his blue eyes upon him.

"Well met, Bunya," Charlie greeted Henry politely, extending his wing in the traditional crow salutation.

Complete silence reigned over birds and humans. "In case you are wondering, Bunya, we are here to let you know that it is us, not your fellow humans that you will ultimately have to contend with. Your own species cannot stop you. We will." The crow turned toward the investors and said, "Best you all leave now, lest you become soiled."

No one moved. "Have it your way, then." Charlie leaped into the air above Henry and shouted, "Let it fly, birds of all feathers! Let it fly!"

The wall seemed to dissolve suddenly into an astonishing cloud of birds of all shapes and sizes. They flew toward Henry, a tiny target for so many birds, but in this they were adept. They had been practicing since dawn—a simple drill Charlie had devised, where they all circled and dumped in an intricate yet simple pattern.

The birds orbited Henry, and each took their turn diving and letting it fly. A thunderous noise of beating wings and ridicule from the beaks of the multitude accompanied the mass dumping.

"Your mother plucks your feathers!" yelled JoEd as he shat upon the Bunya's bald spot.

"You weren't hatched, you were laid!" Willy hollered as his load struck Henry's prominent nose.

"I wouldn't wear that suit to a dog fight!" a magpie yelled, her tuxedo markings clean and flawless as she dumped her load.

Not to be outdone, Floyd bombed Henry with his own repartee, "I've seen bigger peckers on chickadees!" *Splat!*

After whitewashing Henry's head, the birds moved on to other challenging territory: his suit coat, his trousers, his shoes. It took a long time for a million birds to dump their loads, and they did not hurry. The Bunya huddled near the rock upon which moments ago he stood in triumph, blubbering like a baby.

Starfire and Hookbeak flew out of their tree and took hold of the Bunya flag and pulled it out of the sand. They flew out over the river and dropped it in the water. "So long, Charlie!" Starfire yelled over his wing. The two old ravens parted company, as each headed for his respective tree in their respective cemeteries on either side of the river.

Once Henry had been thoroughly encased from head to toe, Charlie gave the signal for the birds to desist. "Birds of All Feathers, land in the sand!" The bombing suddenly abated as the birds dropped out of the sky. The entire tip of the island was covered with birds. Not a grain of sand could be seen from the river to the forest. "We don't want any of them to think about coming back," Charlie said. "Make it so there is no room for a human to stand."

The sudden shower of shit scattered Henry's guests all over the riverbank. No one escaped getting hit, but Henry bore virtually the complete brunt of the birds' fury. The investors had all abandoned him, clamoring over one another for a seat on the helicopter. The pilot jumped out and shoved half of them back, shouting, "I'll be back. Just stay right here. I'll be back."

Only faithful Jules stayed with Henry, waiting patiently for the birds to finish, but far enough away to avoid getting too badly pasted himself. The pelting finally stopped, but the sudden noise of that many birds crowing, quacking, honking, whistling, chirping, tweeting, clicking, and clacking all at once was hardly less fearsome. Henry ventured a quick peek. "Jules, where are you?" he cried out, digging his fists into his eyes like a lost little boy, smearing and grinding bird doo into his eyebrows.

"I'm right here, Henry. Come along now," Jules said, flicking a bit of birdshit off his sleeve. He handed Henry his handkerchief to wipe his eyes and escorted him to the helicopter. The birds closed in behind them.

"I can't let you aboard my 'copter all covered in crap like that, Mr. Braun," the pilot said, blocking Henry from climbing aboard. "You'll ruin my upholstery. Take off the shirt and slacks. Clean him up as much as you can," he said to Jules. "I'll be back."

The group of spattered yet well-heeled investors took off in the helicopter while Henry stripped down to his skivvies. The pilot returned for him and Jules after leaving the guests in the safe hands of their chauffeurs at the city boat landing. Henry climbed aboard and left Wilder Island forever.

Mission accomplished, a million birds headed home. All except for JoEd, who had promised his weebs he'd come back to the tree house for a few days. She had completely forgiven him, as mothers will do, for flying away to the *River Queen* and not coming home for days. But he wanted to spend a little time with her, before he left for good. And to say a proper good-bye.

"NEVER MIND!" SHOUTED THE *SENTINEL* headline the next morning, right above a photo of Henry Braun covered in bird droppings. The caption read: "Wilder Island birds just say no to Ravenwood Resort."

The whole front page, filled with news about Henry's precious island, made Minnie smile. She laughed at the pictures of Henry, remembering his cold rage when he came home from his picnic the previous day.

"Changed Our Minds!" headlined the article where the city revoked its condemnation of the island. *Oh, thank the Lord!* She heard Henry coming down the stairs and flipped the paper back. As he entered the kitchen, she set his perfectly cooled coffee on the table.

Henry scowled, and without touching the newspaper, he picked his coffee cup off the table and climbed the stairs to his office.

Minnie smiled and reread the lead article in the *Sentinel*, a humorous account of Henry's picnic, including photos of the birds in action. "As if they enjoyed it," the reporter wrote of the birds. "As if they enjoyed pelting the wealthiest man in the city with their excrement."

I enjoyed it too! Even if I did have to launder his stinky clothes afterward. It was worth it! Go, birds!

She wondered if Floyd and Willy had been there. *Would that I could have been a crow for that day!* She giggled into her coffee. Alfredo Manzi's name leaped out of the article at her.

"'Ganging up on and pelting,' says Dr. Alfredo Manzi, noted professor of ornithology at the university and pastor of the old hermit's chapel, "are not uncommon offensive tactics that many birds employ to drive off predators—the smaller birds, especially. I am most impressed at how this so-called attack harmed no one, yet completely conveyed the message, 'Hands off our island!' Everyone is washable. We humans should take lessons."

Minnie laughed to herself. *Oh, I love that man!*

Kate Herron's inside sources informed her that the mayor's office had been deluged with the Friends of Wilder Island postcards, with notes that read, "Save your job, Mr. Mayor! Save Wilder Island!" "No to Eminent Domain!" "Keep the island as is!" "No Casinos!"

"The city website shut down briefly," she told Alfredo on the phone. "Too many people tried to log on and voice an opinion. Three to one, the e-mails, faxes, phone calls, letters, and telegrams expressed support for keeping Wilder Island wild."

"God bless the people of Ledford!" Alfredo said.

"Well," Kate said, "we dodged a bullet, I think. If Henry had planned something other than a gambling casino, things may've turned out differently. Still, the birds had the final word. That should give the next guy pause."

Russ finished reading the *Sentinel* article aloud to Jade, and the phone rang. "Good morning, Russ!" Alfredo's warm voice said. "Have you two seen the morning paper?"

"We have!" Russ said, pushing the speaker button so Jade could hear. "I keep wondering if I'm dreaming. Is it true? Wilder Island is still ours?"

"Still ours," Alfredo said with a chuckle, "thanks to thousands of birds, our land trust, and the people of Ledford. Is it not marvelous! I am thinking it is only appropriate that we celebrate our victory here on the island."

"I'll second that thought!" Russ said. "The island is the only place to celebrate this. We deserve a party for all the work we did! This weekend? And maybe afterward I can show Jade around a bit? I want to get some more photos, and she's dying to see more of the island."

"Yes I am!" Jade cried out. "I'll paint while Russ hunts for the flower he'll name after me!"

"Of course," Alfredo said. "The island is your research and painting area; come and go as you please, both of you. I will call Sam and Kate, and Thomas too—he will be glad to hear this news. If you do not hear otherwise, please meet the Captain at the loading dock at nine on Saturday. I hope that is not too early?"

"Nope," Russ said. "We'll be there."

—19—

Conspiracy on the Fly

Alfredo put away the last of his nagging voices that made him hesitate. He loved Charlotte; there was no way he was going to leave her to languish among a wasteland of vacant stares. Or disappear forever within an ultra-secure state mental hospital. Sometimes one must do what is needed, he told his inner voices, though he felt like he was about to step off a cliff.

"We have no more time," he said to Charlie. "All the inmates are moving in two days. We cannot wait any longer. We must prepare Charlotte."

Alfredo drove to Rosencranz, and after he scribbled an illegible signature with his left hand on the visitor's log, he parked and entered the lobby. He introduced himself to Dora Lyn's weekend replacement, and asked to see Charlotte. The receptionist did not ask him to sign the visitor's log nor the release form to take her out of the building.

Sometimes the Lord speaks more softly than a burning bush.

As soon as Charlotte came through the patio doors, he whisked her off to the gazebo where Charlie was waiting. They ate lunch together at the wrought-iron table, from a picnic basket Alfredo had packed with cheese and bread that he had baked in his solar oven, a thermos of iced tea, and the cookies that Jade loved so much. Charlotte ate them as greedily as her daughter had, wondering how in the world food could taste so good.

After they finished eating, Alfredo took a pad of paper from his briefcase and made a sketch of the plan of the Rosencranz campus—the building, landscaping, driveway, the gazebo, and the fence. "Tomorrow," he said to Charlotte, "we will come here like we have been doing. But instead of going back to the hospital, Charlie and I are taking you away, to Cadeña-l'jadia."

"Tomorrow?" Charlotte's face broke into a smile and her gray eyes opened wide with excitement. "Really, Jayzu? Zero more days here?"

Alfredo nodded and she clasped her hands gently around Charlie and stood up. She held him above her head and danced around the gazebo singing, "Cadeña-l'jadia! Take me home! Cadeña-l'jadia!"

"I think she's ready," Charlie called out to Alfredo.

"Yes, she is." *And so am I.* Though he had never danced in his entire life, he wanted to take Charlotte in his arms and dance with her all around the gazebo.

Charlotte sat back down at the table and tucked the hairs that had escaped her braid behind her ears. "How far away is Cadeña-l'jadia, Jayzu?"

"Not too far," he said. "You'll walk a short way to the river, then travel by boat for a while, which will take you to Cadeña-l'jadia."

"And when we get there," Charlie said, "I'll take you to the tree house."

"Tomorrow," Alfredo said, "we will come here to the gazebo like we have been doing. But we will not stay here." He stood up and held out his hand. "Come. I will show you."

He led her out the back side of the gazebo all the way to the fence that surrounded the property. He dropped to the ground and motioned Charlotte to follow him. Without a moment hesitation, she flopped down on her stomach and shimmied along the grass after him.

Alfredo kept them low to the ground until they came to a right-angle turn in the fence. After he stopped, Charlotte crawled up next to him and he said, "Tomorrow, you will wiggle under the fence right here and come out into the woods on the other side. Charlie will be waiting."

"But, Jayzu," she said, smiling happily, "you will be there with me."

"No, Charlotte," he replied. "If I do not return, someone may notice we are both gone, and they will come looking for us."

"Oh," Charlotte said, and her smile vanished. She looked fearfully at the fence and the dark forest beyond and frowned.

"I'll be with you, Charlotte," Charlie said from his perch atop the fence above them. He dropped to the grass and put his wing on her arm. "It'll be like the old days, when we spent our days in the woods behind Mimi and Smitty's house."

Charlotte tilted her head slightly and frowned for a moment, murmuring, "Mimi?" Her face broke into a smile as a happy memory seemed to dawn and her smile returned.

"I will meet you later, Charlotte," Alfredo said. "At the tree house."

They crawled back to the gazebo on their stomachs, getting to their feet at the steps. They sat back down at the table and Charlie took his perch on the back of Charlotte's chair. Alfredo took her hands in his and said, "We have to get you out of here in broad daylight, Charlotte. So we need to be very careful. We have to trick them into thinking you are still here."

"Trick them," Charlotte said. The corners of her mouth turned up, and her eyes sparkled. "That is easy, Jayzu. They never pay any attention to me. They never hear a thing I tell them."

Alfredo recalled Dora Lyn's words during one of his earlier visits. "Charlotte don't give any trouble anymore. She fought like a wild cat when they first brought her in, but they broke her down. Anymore, she comes and goes as she pleases. Wherever inmates are allowed to go, of course."

"No one will notice your absence right away," Alfredo said to Charlotte. "While you and I are here in the gazebo" —she laughed as he mimed drinking tea— "a few crows will be creating a ruckus on the patio, to divert attention away from us as we slither away along the fence."

Charlotte giggled behind her hands. "Let us do it now, Jayzu!" she said. "I am ready!"

"Tomorrow," Alfredo said, patting her hand. "We are not ready today." He turned to Charlie. "Security is pretty lax, thank God."

God's hand, or habitual inattention? "There is a guard in the lobby occasionally, when he is not on the patio or making sure no one drives down the service road. And there's one at the guard house." He pointed up the road toward the gates. "There are three, maybe four, security cameras all around the building." He glanced up at Charlie. "Can we disable them somehow?"

"But of course," Charlie said. "My zhekkies will have them out of commission just before they throw a party on the patio, corvid style!"

Charlotte and Charlie said good-bye to each other, and the crow flew home to Cadeña-l'jadia. Alfredo escorted Charlotte back to the building and up to her room. She chatted happily all the way. "I cannot wait until tomorrow, Jayzu!"

"You must," he said, putting a forefinger to his lips. "And you must keep it a secret, Charlotte. You cannot tell anyone about our plan."

She nodded vigorously, her eyes shining with excitement. "Yes," she said as she solemnly put a finger to her lips. "I can keep a secret."

Her smile charmed him, the way the corners of her mouth turned up. And those gray eyes, completely without guile, yet somehow wickedly endearing.

"And who would hear me if I told?" she asked.

Alfredo drove back to Ledford, going over the details of Charlotte's escape in his mind. He had shut down the opposition, the voices that bullied him about laws and jail and reason. *She needs to leave Rosencranz. Who will get her out of there if I don't?*

The tree house was ready. He had cleaned it as well as any man could, but thanks to Rika and Minnie Braun, Charlotte would have a few more comforts. The tree house was stocked with some simple cookware, including a tea kettle, an abundance of nonperishable foods—rice, pasta, canned goods—and tea and coffee, a variety of utensils, including a can opener. There were curtains and bedclothes and towels, a rocking chair, a wood stove, two tea cups—"You'll be drinking tea with the lady, I reckon," Rika had said to him. Two of everything in fact—plates, bowls, spoons, forks.

"Today is the day, Captain," Alfredo said, as he stepped aboard the Captain's ferry at the inlet.

"Aye, Jayzu," the Captain said, turning his craft around to ferry them across the river to the boat landing. "I'll be waiting upriver for Miss Charlotte and Charlie. No need to worry none." He tipped his hat and pushed his boat back into the current.

Sam jumped out of his flesh-colored pick-up as the Captain pulled into the dock. "Does Kate know what we are doing?" Alfredo asked after he got in the passenger side.

Sam shrugged. "I told her I was driving you to Rosencranz to see Charlotte. Which is true."

Alfredo knew Kate wanted nothing to do with Charlotte's rescue. "I don't even want to know about it," she had said more than once. "And for the record, I strongly advise you against it."

"You don't have to do this, Sam," Alfredo said.

"Yes I do, Padre," Sam said and looked away for a few moments. "For my sister."

On the way to the asylum, Charlie flew above Sam's truck, followed by about sixty or so young crows, including JoEd, JohnHenry, Floyd and Willy. Near the entrance to the asylum, Sam pulled his truck off the road and behind a small group of trees.

"You guys ready for this?" Alfredo asked after the crows landed in the grass next to Sam's truck.

"We are," Charlie said. "I've been waiting for this day for twenty-five years, Jayzu. My zhekkies here," he gestured with his beak, "know the plan backward and forward."

"Pandemonium!" JohnHenry yelled.

"We are ready, Jayzu," JoEd cried out. "You can count on us!"

"All right then," Alfredo said. "Everyone knows what he has to do. Make it loud, zhekkies!"

"You betcha!" said Floyd as he stepped forward.

"Pandemonium, ho-o!" Willy shouted.

The crows flew into the nearby trees, and after Alfredo and Sam scrawled unreadable names on the weekend guard's log, Sam parked the truck in front of the building and cut the engine. Alfredo walked up the granite steps and into the lobby. He smiled broadly at the weekend receptionist, who again did not ask him to sign the visitor's log. *Thank you, Lord.*

He strode purposefully through the doors to the patio, sat down at a table near the rosebush hedge. He tapped his fingers on the tabletop and waited nervously for Charlotte. *Lord, stay with me now. Protect us and guide us safely back to the island.*

"Jayzu!"

He looked up at the sound of Charlotte's happy voice and rose from his chair as she approached. "Hello, Charlotte!" His anxiety dissipated, replaced by the certainty that he and Charlie were about to right a wrong.

"Jayzu," she said, putting her hands in his. "Is Charlie here?"

Alfredo nodded and said, "He is waiting for us at this gazebo. Now let us pretend we are coming back here. We do not want to attract any attention."

Charlotte held her finger to her lips and softly said, "Shhhh. Our secret."

He tucked her hand under his arm, and they left the patio through the lobby. "We will return in an hour or so," Alfredo said as they strolled past the receptionist desk and out the doors.

The sky had clouded over, and Alfredo frowned. *Please do not rain.* Charlotte skipped across the grass, after he told her to pretend it was the first day they had gone to the gazebo together. They sat down inside; Charlotte chattered while Alfredo looked nervously at his watch and then toward the building. A cloud of black smoke seemed to emerge from the trees beyond the hospital's excruciatingly manicured lawn. "The pandemonium has begun," he said quietly.

"And there is Charlie!" Charlotte cried, pointing to the crow on the fence.

"It is time, Charlotte," Alfredo said. "Let us go!"

From the trees outside the hospital grounds, JoEd watched Charlotte and Jayzu leave the patio and walk down the sidewalk toward the gazebo. About twenty people sat at the other tables. It was time.

"Nothing scary," JoEd told the young crows as they waited in the trees. "We don't want to reinforce their stereotypes about us. Just be silly. Act up. We're all experts at that!"

Alfredo and Charlotte walked up the step to the gazebo and he cried out, "Let 'er rip!" as he leaped from his branch into the sky.

From out of nowhere sixty-three crows suddenly burst into the grounds of the asylum, heading for the patio. The brigade of dozing patients in wheelchairs happened to face the stone wall encircling the patio. Old Rosie stood up and screamed something quite unintelligible as she pointed at the approaching black cloud. The old fellow shuffling behind his empty wheelchair turned his whole body sideways trying to lock up.

The crows descended on the patio. Screaming visitors, mobile patients, and doctors headed frantically for the doors. But the doors never came open, held shut by many bodies pressed up against them. The pile-up of flailing bodies fell back onto the patio. A few struggled to their feet and hopped over the stone wall encircling the patio and ran for the parking lot.

Crows were everywhere—on the tables, the chairs, the walls, the rosebushes, the trashcans, and the flagstone pavement. Hopping up onto tables and chairs, they made a great show of knocking over plastic water pitchers and creating a scene of utter chaos.

JoEd flew above the pandemonium barking out orders. "Disable the cameras! Sky Team, dive!"

Floyd, Willy, and JohnHenry took their positions at the three video cameras on the roof overlooking the patio and the hospital grounds. Floyd hopped onto one and looked straight into the lens, giving anyone monitoring it an enlarged view of an upside-down crow head. "Smile!" He waved his wings and plastered his eye against the camera lens. "I'm on *Candid Camera!*"

Willy grasped the wire that connected the camera to its power source, gave a firm tug, and ripped it from its connection. "Camera two down!" he called out as he headed to the video camera at the kitchen. Fledging at a drive-in movie theater had taught him many things about electricity and cameras.

JohnHenry perched with his tail feather fanned open and covering the lens. "Curtain's closed on camera three!" he shouted.

"Well done, dudes!" JoEd called out to the camera crows. He saw a white coat head for the door to the lobby. "Yo! Hosiah! Jedediah! Guard the doors!"

The pandemonium proceeded splendidly, and JoEd looked around for an opportunity to generate a little disorder of his own. "Mind if I join you, miss?" he asked a stupefied visitor frozen to her chair. "Thank you, don't mind if I do. The name's JoEd, what's yours?" He took a few sips of water from the pitcher on the table as she leaped out of his seat and ran screaming into the pile of bodies trying to get through the doors.

"Pretty birdies!" the patient she had abandoned said happily. She picked up the cup of water JoEd had just dipped his beak in and took a sip. "Share?" she said to no one in particular.

The crows made an absolute mess of the patio within minutes; there were overturned tables and chairs co-mingled with emptied plastic cups and pitchers of water and ice, a few books, sweaters, and baseball hats. The white coats screamed for help, and security guards yelled into their walkie-talkies for backup. A few patients continuously howled in terror, while others laughed with grotesque pleasure or cried like babies. Someone pulled the fire alarm, adding the appropriate harmony to the sound and fury on the patio.

Alfredo and Charlotte stepped out of the gazebo and onto the grass. Hand-in-hand, they walked the few steps to the fence and Alfredo dropped to the grass. With Charlotte behind him, they crawled in single file on their bellies until they came to the corner of the fence.

"Now under the fence, Charlotte!" Charlie called down.

"All the way through, Charlotte," Alfredo said as she shimmied under the fence. "Good! Now stand up and run!"

She dove under the fence, wriggling all the way through and popped to her feet on the other side. The front of her Rosencranz coveralls was covered in black soil.

The fire alarms went off at the building across the grass. Charlotte looked back toward Alfredo. "Jayzu?" she said.

"Go, Charlotte!" he said from the ground. "Go with Charlie! I will see you at the Treehouse! I promise. Now, go! Run like the wind."

"Come on, Charlotte!" Charlie called down to her as he took to the air. "Follow me, Charlotte!" He flew low enough in front of her that she could reach out and touch him if she wanted.

Alfredo watched Charlotte run into the woods with Charlie flying overhead until she disappeared. He waited at the fence for a few moments, listening to her laugh fade into the trees. *If all goes according to the plan, the Captain will be waiting for them at the river to take Charlotte home. To* Cadeña-l'jadia.

And if it does not...

He shimmied back to the gazebo, walked up the steps and out the other side, back toward the building. Cars screeched out of the parking and sped down the curvy driveway, past the guard shack and onwards to the highway. *Good, people are leaving. In all the chaos, who will miss Charlotte?* He heard sirens in the distance and quickened his pace. Undoubtedly, someone had called 911.

"What the devil is going on out there?" he said to the receptionist as he gestured with his head toward the mess on the patio. "Are we being invaded by crows?" He waved at the crow perched on the windowsill to the lobby, awaiting that signal.

"Oh, Dr. Robbins!" the receptionist cried out. "All of a sudden, a hundred crows dive-bombed everyone on the patio. They were all cawing and carrying on to beat the band. And then they started trying to drink the water from the cups on the table."

The pandemonium on the patio suddenly ended. En masse, the crows took flight and left the patio. Through the windows, Alfredo saw a few inmates wave and Miss Rosie weeping into her hands as the aides firmly escorted them into the patients' wing of the building.

The weekend receptionist giggled behind her hand. "People and crows were running everywhere, patients and visitors and people were leaving, and these crows were flying all around. You should've seen it a while ago, with all everyone screaming and trying to get off the patio!"

Alfredo forced himself to smile. "Well, I hope you get this sorted out and under control soon. Thank goodness my patient is safely back in her room."

"Well," she said, nodding, "things would've been a whole lot worse if I hadn't jumped up and locked the doors to the patio." She nodded toward the door. "Otherwise they would've all come in here! But they'll get everyone sorted out, though I wouldn't be a bit surprised if a few patients left in cars."

Charlotte wanted to kick off her shoes and skip through the forest barefoot, but Charlie kept urging her on. She had not run through the woods in so long, and her escape from Rosencranz took every drop of energy she had. There was no time to languish and marvel at the scenery flying by. She would sooner drop dead from running than go back.

She followed him through the woods, leaving the hospital far behind. Charlie let her rest briefly now and then, and drink from the tiny streams that crossed their path. Finally they came to a flowing river, and Charlie dropped down onto the grass into a small cove of fragrant trees. "We will wait here until the Captain comes with his boat," he said to Charlotte as she sat down on a fallen tree. "He'll take us all the way to Cadeña-l'jadia."

Charlotte leaned back against the tree trunk, closed her eyes and inhaled deeply. The aromas of the deep forest awakened memories of gathering leaves in the sun-dappled days with Charlie. She opened her eyes. "Have I ever been here, Charlie?"

"I don't know, Charlotte," he said. "I've never been here with you, if that's what you're asking. But you and I, we spent a lot of time in woods like this. You used to gather herbs and flowers, and I'd fly overhead scouting them for you."

Charlotte stood up and pinched a leaf off a low-hanging branch on the tree she had been sitting under. She crushed it in her palm and sniffed it. "Balsam poplar," she said, though she did not know where the words came from, or what they meant.

A gray-haired woman with red cheeks flashed through her thoughts and was gone. Charlotte had seen her many times since the graying ended, in other memories, and in her dreams. "I wish I could remember," she murmured, holding the crushed leaf up to her nose and breathing in its scent.

"You knew all the names of all the trees and flowers," Charlie said, "and you gathered baskets full."

"Why did I do that, Charlie?"

"You gave them all to your Mimi," he said. "You helped her make tea and other medicinal potions from them."

"Mimi?" Red cheeks, gray hair. A sad smile and blue eyes filled with tears flashed through her thoughts. "Mimi."

A bell sounded from the direction of the river and Charlie said, "There's the Captain, Charlotte." He rose up and unfolded his wings. "We're going home!"

A silvery forest with beautiful carved oars floated toward them and ground to a halt on the sandy bank. "Let's go," Charlie said. He flapped his wings a few times, lifting himself off the ground, and flew to the Captain's boat. He perched on the railing next to another crow and shouted out to Charlotte, "Come on! Follow me!"

She came out of the shadows of the trees, took the Captain's outstretched hand, and stepped aboard his marvelous boat—it seemed more like a tree with many birds flying through its tangled branches of wood and iron. Charlie introduced her to the Captain and to a young crow perched on his shoulder.

"We been waitin' a long time to meet ya, lass!" Sugarbabe hollered. "Ain't we, Cap'n?"

He grinned and winked at Charlotte. "That we have, Sugarbabe. Pleasure to have you aboard, Miss Charlotte."

She nodded and smiled at the crow, speechless with surprise. "Grawky!" she managed to say as she brushed her hand across Sugarbabe's outstretched wing. She turned to the Captain and studied him carefully; his great tattoo-covered arms seemed both flesh and wood as he powered his carved oar through the water. She felt the rhythm of the river through the Captain's motion and thought perhaps he had been wrought from both river and forest.

They traveled throughout the afternoon on the river, and Charlotte stared in astonishment at the sights and sounds of the world she had not seen in over two decades. She gasped at the huge city on either side of the river as the Captain rowed past the Waterfront.

"Look, Charlotte! Cadeña-l'jadia!" Charlie cried out.

"Is that the tree house?" she asked, pointing toward a domed roof. She smiled wildly, hoping that it was.

"Humans call it the hermit's chapel," Charlie said. "It is very old, and when Jayzu came to Cadeña-l'jadia, he fixed it all up like it was new."

"It's so beautiful, Charlie," she murmured.

The Captain steered the boat into a wide, shallow pool and brought them gently to a stop at the edge of the water. Charlotte laughed in delight at all the birds in the water, the air, on the cliffs at the edge of the pool, and in the branches of the trees that grew along the water's edge. A flock of loons screeched by over her head and landed out in the more open water, making waves and splashing each other.

The Captain helped Charlotte out of the boat, and she stepped onto Cadeña-l'jadia.

"Mighty obliged, Captain, my man," Charlie said as he lifted a wing in salute.

The Captain nodded and said, "I'll be going for Jayzu now." He pushed his boat back into the water and waved an oar as he rowed away.

Charlie stretched his wings, and Charlotte stretched her arms, reaching to the sky. "The tree house is this way," he said, pointing with a wing toward the island's interior.

Charlotte followed Charlie into the dense forest. The trees seemed to raise their overhanging branches, allowing them through what otherwise seemed to be an impenetrable wall of leaf and trunk. They stopped at an apple tree, whose fruit was dragging its branches nearly to the ground. "Bruthamax planted this tree," he said.

Charlotte picked two apples off the tree and gave one to Charlie. She laughed in sheer delight as she bit into it, and sweet juice gushed out all around, spraying her face.

After drinking from the small stream nearby, they continued on their way to the tree house. Charlotte picked her way among the marshes and bogs as if she could sense solid ground among the rocks and water amid sedges and rushes. Vaguely familiar odors tantalized her memory.

At last they stopped in a small clearing underneath a gigantic tree. "Is that your nest, Charlie?" she asked, pointing to the tree house roof.

"Yes, that's the tree house, your new home," Charlie said. "My nest is up above, in the branches."

As she looked closer, more features appeared—walls, windows, a door. There was even a spiral staircase leading up to the deck. Charlotte darted up the steps, laughing like a child, and as she poked her head through to the deck, a friendly voice called out, "Welcome home, Charlotte!"

A crow dropped to the deck from the branches above, followed by four young fledglings.

"Charlotte," Charlie said, opening a wing toward them, "this is my wife, Rika, and our children, Alfie and Rufie. They're twins. And Coal, and Lexy, and this is Buzzy, and over there is Burkie."

"Where is JoEd?" Rika asked. "Didn't he come back with you?"

"No," Charlie said. "But he'll be along shortly, I'm sure."

Charlotte dropped down to her knees, and the young crows all crowded in her lap. She laughed as they nibbled her fingers, her chin, her ears, her hair. After a few moments, they all ran to the other side of the deck, engaged in an instant game.

"And here is JoEd!" Charlie said as the young crow landed on the deck. "Many crows helped us get you out of Rosencranz, Charlotte, but it was JoEd who led the pandemonium on the patio!"

"Greetings, fair lady!" JoEd said, with a bow so low, his beak touched the deck.

Charlotte giggled as JoEd swished his feathers across her hand.

"Grawky, JoEd!" she said. "Thank you!"

"No greater pleasure shall I ever dream to have," the young crow said, "than to assist in the freeing of a lady so fair, with a heart so brave, from the cruel confines of so unjust an imprisonment."

Charlotte melted on the spot and took JoEd into her lap. Charlie and Rika looked at each other in complete shock at the eloquent speech coming from JoEd's beak. "I had no idea my son was such a romantic fellow!" Charlie said.

"There are many things you don't know about me," JoEd said from Charlotte's lap. "Many things."

"Jayzu!" Charlotte cried out as the priest poked his head through the hole in the deck. JoEd flew from her lap to the railing next to his parents.

Jayzu stepped onto the deck, and she leaped up and threw her arms around his neck. He hugged her warmly and said, "I see you made it safe and sound!"

He greeted Rika and Charlie and the *kreegans*, who all flocked around his feet, squawking and squeaking for his attention.

"Jayzu!" Charlotte said, "I rode on a boat that looked like a forest!"

"I have been on that boat many times," he said with a smile.

She took his hand and pulled him over to the bench at the edge of the deck. "And I ate a big golden apple off of a tree that Charlie said Bruthamax planted."

"An apple at this time of year?" Alfredo looked over at Charlie. "I thought we could only get apples in the fall."

"Bruthamax's apples don't know that," Charlie said.

Jayzu laughed again. Charlotte laughed too, at the sheer joy of being alive in this tree house with everything she needed and loved all around her.

Jayzu showed her the cistern nearby and how to get water from it. "I will keep the water jar in the tree house filled," he said. "But in case you run out while I am away, I want you to know how to get your own water."

Charlotte nodded and followed Jayzu in the other direction, downhill from the tree house. They came to a tiny rustic shack, and Jayzu said, "This is your toilet, Charlotte." He opened the door. "I am sorry I cannot provide you with more proper facilities, Charlotte, but—"

"Jayzu!" Charlotte said and put a finger over his lips. "This is good enough. I have been trapped in a stinky old building for a very long time, and I had to share the toilets with everyone else and walk down two hallways just to pee. The floor was always wet, so I had to put shoes on. And there were cameras."

He stared at her for a few moments and then laughed. She loved it when he laughed, the way his eyes crinkled up and his whole face seem to explode with mirth.

"Jayzu, I am very happy to be here with Charlie, and you, and Rika. And I can pee outside with no one watching!"

He laughed again and took her hand. "Let us go back and cook some supper," he said. "Shall we, Charlotte?" He tucked her hand under his arm, and they started back to the tree house.

"I do not know how to cook!" she said anxiously.

"But I do!" Jayzu said with a smile. "Let me teach you."

Charlie, Rika, and all the kreegans perched on the chairs and bed, the shelves, and the windowsills and watched as Jayzu and Charlotte cooked dinner together. Jayzu took the loaf of bread he had baked out of his pack, a few onions and garlic, and a fish he had caught from the river. He filleted it, putting the guts onto a small plate. "This we shall save for the kreegans," he said. He built a fire in the small wood stove and cooked the fish in a cast-iron frying pan.

Charlotte boiled some water and cooked the rice, according to Jayzu's instructions. She sliced the fresh tomato he had brought and prepared their plates—one for her, one for Jayzu, and a bowl for the crows.

They ate on the deck, sharing their meal with Charlie and his family, as well as a few birds that had flown by and detected the aroma of frying fish. "Delicious!" JoEd said after gobbling down a beak full of fish guts.

After Charlotte and Jayzu washed and dried the dishes, humans and crows sat or perched on the deck under the stars. It had been many years since Charlotte had been outside at night.

"So many stars," she murmured, looking up at the night sky. "I remember stars. Before the graying."

"There is Corvus, the constellation of the raven," Jayzu said as he pointed toward the southern sky. "Just four stars, see?"

Charlotte nodded and leaned against him. He was so warm and the stars so beautiful. It was hard to imagine that one day ago, she stared at the ceiling alone in her tiny room in a dark, cold building.

"Time for sleep, everyone!" Rika announced. "Come, Charlotte, it is time to dress for bed."

"Goodnight, Charlotte," Jayzu said. He held her hands and looked into her eyes, and then pulled her into his chest and hugged her.

"Goodnight, Jayzu," she said, snuggling into his chest. She loved the way he smelled. She wanted to stay there in his arms forever.

"I will be right out here on the deck," he said as he held her and stroked her hair. "If you wake up in the night and are scared, just call my name."

Charlie took the little ones up to the nest as Rika took Charlotte into the tree house and helped her find a nightgown in the box of clothes Jayzu brought. Charlotte brushed her teeth in the small basin next to the stove and said goodnight to Rika. She got under the soft covers and slipped into sleep.

Alfredo awoke suddenly. Stars twinkled brightly in the dark sky; dawn was still many hours away. He lay still listening to the sounds of the night, wondering if Charlotte slept peacefully. *Or did she wake in fear, not knowing where she is?* He threw his covers off and stood up. He stood outside the door of the tree house, listening for any sound coming from inside. *Should I go in and check on her?* He rejected that idea immediately. *That might frighten her out of her wits.*

He lay back down on the deck and pulled the covers back over himself. Stars peeked down at him between the leaves and branches overhead. He turned on his side. Corvus hovered low in the southern sky. He closed his eyes.

An unfamiliar darkness invaded Charlotte's sleep, and she awakened completely disoriented. There were no lights, no sound. She sat up and peered into the darkness. *Where am I?* Opening all her senses, she tried to instill in herself a sense of attachment; that was how she found her balance as the graying ended.

She focused awareness on her body, concentrating on sensation, any sensation. First, the feet. She could not detect her weight bearing down on her feet. *I am sitting.* She moved her hands around, palms down, feeling soft, smooth fabric. *I am in a bed. But it is not my bed.*

A rectangular patch of dark gray—or was it light black?—hovered above the floor. A cool breeze blew across her face. *Where am I?* She heard faint sounds coming from the gray rectangle—it seemed a lighter gray than before.

A black bird appeared in the window, silhouetted against the pale gray. "Good morning, Charlotte!" the bird said and flapped to the edge of the bed. "I hope you slept peacefully."

"Charlie!" Charlotte cried, suddenly flooded with the memory of the day before. *I am in the tree house!* "I am really here! I am not dreaming!"

Rika flew through the window, scolding Charlie. "For pity sakes, husband! Can you not let a lady even dress for the day before you barge in on her? Now shoo! Scoot! Go talk to Jayzu while I get Charlotte dressed."

Charlie obediently flew out the window, and Rika said, "He is just thrilled you are here, dearie! He just couldn't wait until you've done your ablutions. You know, your face, your hair. That's what my lady called it. Her morning ablutions."

"I am in a tree house!" she said, leaping out of bed gleefully. She looked out the window after Charlie.

"On Cadeña-l'jadia, dearie!" Rika said.

"Welcome to Cadeña-l'jadia!" That is what Charlie had said

when the Captain let them off his boat. Charlotte did not know where Cadeña-l'jadia was, and she had not asked. What did it matter? She was grateful to be away from the asylum and to be here in a tree house with her old friend Charlie. And Jayzu! What could be more perfect?

She remembered everything about her escape from Rosencranz—the run through the woods to the river, the almost unbearable noise and spectacle of the city they floated through, the heavenly smells and sounds of the forest, the water. And then Charlie took her from the river to the tree house, along a path in a forest so green and full of flowers, she could hardly believe it. *"Oh, the colors! Charlie! So beautiful!"*

"Where is Jayzu?" she asked.

"He's outside, dearie," Rika said. She hopped over to the bench against the wall. "Charlie and Jayzu are both outside. You must dress now, dearie. Here are some nice clothes you can change into. You'll be wanting long pants and sleeves for life here on the island."

Charlotte dressed herself from the box of clothes Jayzu had brought, delighted at the bright colors. "We all wore gray at the asylum," she said. "Everything was gray. And now the world is full of color! And music! So many birds singing so sweetly!" She closed her eyes, listening.

She splashed water on her face and undid her braid. After brushing it vigorously, she re-braided it. She opened the door and walked out onto the deck, where dozens of crows, magpies, jays, larks, and thrushes all chattered and screeched their versions of "Good morning, Charlotte!"

"Where is Jayzu?" she asked, looking all around the deck.

"I am here!" his voice said as he appeared through the hole in the deck. He leaped from the staircase to the deck and took Charlotte's hands into his. He looked into her eyes and asked, "Did you sleep well?"

"Like I was a rock," she said.

Jayzu laughed and bent down to greet the kreegans that had accumulated around his feet.

"A cup of tea, dearie?" Rika asked Charlotte. "Do you like tea?"

Charlotte nodded and said, "They gave me tea every morning."

"I will have a cup, please," Jayzu said as he stood up.

"Then let's make some tea, dearie," Rika said. "A cup for you, one for Jayzu, one for me." Charlotte followed her into the tree house. "Now take the kettle, dearie, and put some water in it."

Charlie appeared suddenly in the doorway, with Buzzy in tow. "I found him down by the sand bar. Hello, Charlotte!"

Charlotte spun around and reached out to touch his wing feathers. "Charlie!" she cried. "I am going to make tea with Rika!"

"Splendid!" Charlie said.

"You three wait out on the deck," Rika said, shooing Jayzu, Charlie, and Buzzy out the doorway. "Charlotte, that kettle won't boil on its own! You need to build a fire!"

Rika pointed to a box of matches on the shelf with her wing. "Now fetch the matches over to the stove. "That's good, now take some of these small pieces of wood and some paper and stuff it into the stove."

Charlotte followed Rika's instructions obediently, paper in the bottom, wood shavings on the top. She held the match to the paper. "Now feed the fire, dearie!" Rika instructed. "You want it to burn and not smother itself. That's good. Now shut that door, there, yes, dearie."

She stood up, and Rika pointed to the shelf above the table. "Get that tea down, will you please?"

Charlotte looked at the many cans of vegetables, beans and soup, boxes of rice and pasta, a bottle of cooking oil, and a jar of what she suspected might be peanut butter.

"Tea is in that blue can with all the flowers, right there," Rika said.

Charlotte opened the tin, and the aroma that emanated from it stirred a vague memory within her of forests, flowers, and sunshine. And the gray-haired woman with the red cheeks. Charlie said that is Mimi. But who is Mimi? So familiar, yet without attached memories.

"Oh! Hoy! The water is boiling, dearie!" Rika startled her back to the present. "Pick up the kettle and pour some water in the teapot, yes, just like that. A little sugar?" she pointed to a ceramic jar on the shelf. "Best to keep the top on that. No need to spill it, you know. None for me, though."

Jayzu appeared at the door, and Rika said, "Good on you, dearie. We're just needing another hand in here! Take the cups and what-not out to the bench, please. Charlotte, you take the teapot on out."

Charlotte picked up the kettle handle with a piece of quilted fabric and followed Jayzu whose hands were full of cups and the sugar.

"Ah!" Rika said after they'd all sat down to tea. She dipped her beak in the cup she shared with Charlie and took a sip, tilting her head back to swallow. "I used to sit with my lady on her balcony Downtown. We'd sip tea, just the two of us, and we'd watch the world go by."

"This is lovely, Charlotte," Jayzu said. "Thank you for the tea."

Charlotte and Jayzu ate the leftovers from the dinner he had cooked the night before. "I must go to my cottage," he said when they finished eating. "I have some visitors coming, and I must be there." She frowned, and he continued. "I will be back before dinner. Do not worry!"

Jayzu kissed her on the cheek and disappeared down the hole in the deck. Charlotte tidied up the treehouse; she folded her nightgown and made up her bed, washed and dried the tea cups and put them back up on the shelf.

Rika was gone when she went back outside to the deck, and so was Charlie. She reveled in the sunshine and the quiet loveliness of her surroundings. No bells, no one screaming. How exquisite to be alone with just the sounds of the cool, green forest.

It beckoned her, and she rose from the bench and went down the spiral steps to the ground. She looked toward the woods beyond the tree house, just across that little meadow. So close! And there was no fence to crawl under.

I am free.

—20—

Jadum *Wilderii*

Henry Braun became the laughing stock, not only of the investment community, but also of the Ledford community in general. Political cartoons in the Sentinel lampooned him; even his cronies couldn't help but get in on the fun. When he stepped into the bar at his club, someone called out, "Duck!" and another shouted, "Don't you mean, crow?" Everyone laughed. Henry's face turned bright red, and he turned on his heel and left.

"My hands were tied," the mayor sniveled when he demanded answers. "The people have spoken, Henry."

"It was not so much public opinion, Henry," his pal at Economic Development told him. "The city attorney told us the terms of the Friends of Wilder Island Land Trust make it impossible for Braun Enterprises to carry out its proposed Ravenwood Resort casino park."

Jules, you lying, incompetent, traitorous boob!

The investors all said no, too. "Wilder Island is for the birds," Whitey McDurbin told Henry. "Move on. Take your *River Queen* elsewhere and then call me." He hung up without even giving Henry the courtesy of a good-bye.

"It was an omen, Henry," Lloyd Roberts said. "Getting shit upon even before I see a prospectus speaks volumes. None for me, thanks."

The others didn't bother to return Henry's phone calls. He was enraged. "What the hell is this?" he shouted and slammed his hand down on his desk. "Gutless windbags! Why am I surrounded by cowards?"

He glanced sidelong at the portraits of the Henrys on the wall. All four stared vacantly back. Were they disappointed? Had he failed them? Henry the First was especially aloof; his hard mouth drawn into a straight line. His eyes went straight through Henry, making him feel as if he weren't even there.

"Screw 'em!" he said and got up from this desk. "Screw *you!*" he shouted at the portraits. "Screw everyone. Screw the whole god-damned world!"

He opened the wine cabinet and pulled out a random bottle. He opened it carefully, took a long gulp straight from the bottle, and poured himself a glass. Then another. And another until the bottle was empty.

Minnie heard Henry shouting from time to time and stomping around his office. When he didn't come down to the kitchen for breakfast, she brought a tray of food up to him.

"Leave me the hell alone!" he yelled at her from the other side of the door.

"I'll leave your sandwich and cookies on the floor," she said when he refused to let her in. When she brought dinner, the lunch tray had not moved. The bread on the ham sandwich had curled around the edges, and the lettuce was wilted.

"Henry?" She knocked. "Henry?" No sound came from behind the door. She piled the uneaten lunch onto the dinner tray and returned to the kitchen.

Henry had refused food for three days when Floyd and Willy showed up at the patio table in the backyard where Minnie ate breakfast alone. Delighted as always to see them, she hugged them close to her face.

"Well, we're right happy to see you too, ma'am," Willy said.

"Yep," Floyd said. "Long time no see, Miss Minnie!"

The two brothers perched on a chair that had been pushed all the way into the table. "'At's right," Willy drawled. "We just thought we'd drop by for a little visit, on account of we haven't been by since before the picnic. How're things?"

"Henry hasn't been the same since the picnic," Minnie said, looking fearfully up at his office window. "I'm afraid he's gone off his rocker." She removed her coffee cup from its saucer and put half a piece of French toast on it and pushed the plate toward the crows.

"You mean, like off in la-la land?" Floyd asked. "Or like in ax-murderer land?"

"Good Orb, Floyd," Willy said, whacking his brother with a wing-tip. "That's just crude. Can't you see the lady is in distress enough already?"

"Sorry, Miss Minnie," Floyd said, looking at the ground. "I just wanted to know—"

"It's okay, Floyd," Minnie said, patting his back. "To tell the truth, I am afraid he's heading toward the ax-murderer kind of crazy. Now please, help yourselves."

Floyd and Willy each beaked a generous chunk of French toast. Following the sound of a loud crash and a string of unintelligible non-sense laced with profanity, both crows and Minnie looked up at the open window above them.

"Sounds like he's having a tantrum," Willy said. "Like he's break-ing things." He dipped his toast in the small pool of maple syrup on the saucer.

"He's been doing that all day," Minnie said. She poured herself another cup of coffee from a silver carafe. "He started three days ago. I guess there was one joke too many."

"They're pretty funny," Floyd said, snickering. "The jokes, I mean."

Willy swatted Floyd again as the sounds of destruction contin-ued to pour forth from the upstairs window. "None of this is proba-bly funny to Miss Minnie, here," he said. "So think before you speak, brother!"

Floyd looked down and muttered an apology. He pecked at the French toast and chopped off a small chunk. He flipped it into the air, catching it on its way down and swallowing it in one gulp.

"Willy, you don't need to protect my feelings," Minnie said. "I'm not unhappy about the way things turned out. I mean that Henry didn't get the island and all. And the jokes are funny. But I'm afraid of him. I've never seen him like this."

She told the crows how the night before she had brought Hen-ry a sandwich and some milk. "He hadn't eaten since Tuesday," she said. "So, when I knocked on the door and he didn't answer, I just opened it and barged in." She put her hand to her chest and took a deep breath.

"The office was a mess—broken glass and paper strewn everywhere." She shook her head, remembering. "Henry didn't notice I came in the room, and I watched him take a poker from the fireplace and smash a big hole in his miniature Ravenwood Resort. And then he slammed the poker down on the pretty little *River Queen*, and it shattered into toothpicks. I was so shocked because he paid a fortune for it."

Minnie folded her arms against her chest and shivered. "And then he screamed, like his own bones had broken. And he looked up at the portraits of his ancestors, which he had sliced to ribbons. "Happy now?" he yelled and he shook his fist. And he started swinging the poker again and smashing the rest of it, the little train he loved so much. It was just horrible to watch." She buried her face in her hands.

"That," Floyd said, "sounds like a maniac."

"The man's off his rocker!" Willy said.

"Flipped his lid!" said Floyd.

"Lost his marbles!"

"Off the deep end!"

"Got a screw loose!"

"Cuckoo! Cuckoo! Cuckoo!" Floyd said, turning himself around in circles.

"He's just crazy," Minnie said, nodding. "I was so scared. I've never seen him so violent." She glanced up at Henry's office window again.

"Miss Minnie," Willy said, "you need to get out of here."

"That's right," agreed Floyd. "You should just go. There's no telling what he might do."

Minnie nodded and said, "I called Jules this morning. He's Henry's attorney and he took care of everything. I've got a bag packed inside. As soon as the ambulance gets here, I'm gone."

The brothers looked at each other and then back at Minnie. "Ambulance? Have you been harmed?" Floyd asked.

"Did that brute lay a hand on you?" Willy demanded.

"Oh, no." she shook her head adamantly. "Jules called an ambulance to come get Henry. Jules said Henry needs to dry out. I guess so—he's been on a four-day drunk. And Jules said they'll do a mental evaluation after he dries out to make sure he hasn't lost his mind."

She was grateful Jules had stepped in, his warm, calm voice telling her not to worry. "Just pack a bag and leave for a few days," he had said. "I'll get the house all cleaned up and Henry sorted out."

"Screw you!" Henry's enraged voice blared out the window. "And you! And you! And you!"

The sounds of breaking glass and splintering wood flowed out of the upstairs window, followed by a wave of incoherent swearing.

"He's at it again," Minnie sighed. "Beating things with the poker." She smiled wanly and stood up.

"Oh, Miss Minnie!" Floyd cried out. He walked across the table and put his wings around her waist. "I hope he doesn't hurt you!"

"You need to get out of here now," Willy said, joining his brother. "Don't wait for the ambulance."

Minnie stroked their backs. "I'll be gone soon, don't worry. I'm not planning on being here when they take Henry away. Jules has a taxi coming for me, so I must bid you both *adieu*."

"But where will you go, Miss Minnie?" Floyd asked.

"Will we ever see you again?" Willy asked.

Minnie was touched by their concern and affection. "Of course you'll see me again, fellas!" She stroked each bird gently. "I'm just going to visit my sister. I'll be back in a few days." She blew them each a kiss as she went into the house and closed the door.

Floyd and Willy flew up to the windowsill of Henry's office and peered in at the wild man inside. He had already ripped gaping holes into the portraits of his ancestors, and the crows watched him beat the canvasses off the wall. He looked up at the ceiling, screaming, "Are you happy now? Are you friggin' happy now?"

"I say," Floyd said. "The old chap truly seems to have gone away with the fairies."

"Right-o," agreed Willy. "Fully loaded and half-cocked."

"Oh, look," Floyd said, pointing a wing toward the driveway. "There goes Miss Minnie."

The two crows watched her run toward the gate, and the driver of the yellow cab get out and open the door for her. He put her bag in the trunk and sped off down the long driveway.

"Poor Minnie," Willy said. "Driven away. And not just by a taxi. Too bad."

Floyd shook his head and clucked. "She's such a charming woman. And always dressed to the nines."

"Damn you, friggin' crows!" Henry shouted and threw an empty wine bottle at Floyd and Willy on the windowsill. "Damn you!"

"I believe we are no longer needed here, brother," Floyd said as they dodged the projectile and took to the air. "Let us depart, shall we?"

"Let's," Willy said.

ALFREDO MET HIS FRIENDS AT THE inlet and escorted them up the path toward his cottage. "Majewski sends his regrets," he told them. "He got bumped from his flight and cannot make it." *Perhaps it is for the best, with Charlotte newly ensconced in the tree house. One day I will have to tell him about his sister. But not today.*

"Too bad!" Kate said. "It was Majewski who saved the island from Henry. Without him, we wouldn't be here celebrating anything."

"Or the birds," Jade said. The others looked at her in confusion. "The birds. Without them, we wouldn't be here either."

"In other words, the least deserving of all in this affair," Russ said with a laugh, "are those of us here partying?"

"Is that not always the way?" Alfredo said. He leaped across the small stream and waited for the others before continuing along the path. "But truly, we all brought this about. Majewski, the five of us, the people of Ledford, and the birds. It gives me great hope for the planet."

They arrived at Alfredo's cottage, and he opened the door. "Sit down, everyone," he said, gesturing toward the table. He looked at his watch. "We are officially celebrating."

"Wow!" Jade said as she slid into a chair next to the window. "You really put a feast together, Alfredo!"

The table was laden with food: sandwiches on three different types of bread, a large garden salad, and a bowl of fresh fruit. "Oh, just a few leftovers from the fridge," he said, waving away her compliment.

The others laughed, and Kate said, "In a pig's eye!"

"You don't have a fridge," Sam said.

Alfredo slapped his forehead and said, "I knew there was something we forgot when we built this place!" He looked at his watch. "Please help yourselves, my friends."

He sat down and stared out the window as his guests chatted happily while they piled food onto their plates. He felt anxious about Charlotte and her first day at the tree house. *I should not have left her alone.*

"That was an incredible thing they pulled off," Russ said. "How did all those birds know? Who told them to gang up on Henry like that? I mean, it's a feat of communication and organization that I for one didn't know birds were capable of. Were you involved, Alfredo?"

The sound of his name brought him back to the table. "They told themselves, actually," he said. "Though I would have been proud and honored to have been involved, this was completely a bird job." He glanced down at his watch.

"Kind of scary when you think about it," Jade said. "The way they all ganged up on Henry. "If all the animals could do that ..."

"It might give us pause," Kate said, narrowing her eyes and waving a pumpernickel sandwich at the others.

"Indeed," Alfredo said. "They do not really need us."

"Speaking of birds doing extraordinary things," Russ said, glancing casually at Alfredo. "There was an article in the paper this morning about a patient that went missing from the state mental hospital."

Kate frowned and Alfredo exchanged nervous glances with Sam as Russ continued, "Yeah, she just vanished, they said. It was funny though. The article said on the day of her disappearance, this huge flock of crows came down on the place and tore it up. They scared the bejesus out of a few inmates and staff."

"Really?" Alfredo said, hoping to sound sincere and surprised at the news. "They destroyed things?"

"From what the article said, they just kind of acted up," Russ said with a grin. "They knocked the plastic water pitchers off the tables, overturned chairs, and got into the trash cans. Everyone was on the patio trying to keep control of the patients and keep the crows out of the building. And she just walked away, they said."

"Who was she?" Kate said, looking straight at Alfredo without smiling.

Alfredo looked down at his watch. He felt exhausted and anxious, wishing there was no party and he was with Charlotte at the tree house. His discomfort grew by the moment and he could hardly sit still on his chair.

"They didn't say," Russ said. "All they said was she was not violent, and she couldn't speak English."

"How could a patient just disappear like that?" Jade asked. "You would think their security would be better than that."

Alfredo took a bite of the sandwich that had been sitting on his plate. He was relieved that the article had said she disappeared, as opposed to escaped. And that her name had not been published. Thanks to the weekend receptionist's forgetfulness, the name Dr. Robbins had not been left behind on the visitor's log.

"It's an old building," Russ said, helping himself to another sandwich. "The paper said they're moving to a new one next week. Security is one reason. But mostly, the building is just flat out too old. They couldn't upgrade the plumbing or the electrical."

Alfredo felt grateful to have gotten Charlotte out of the asylum before they moved her to the new facility. It had been laughably easy, and he wondered if he could have just walked out to the parking lot with her and driven her out. He looked at his watch. *I wonder if she is all right. Of course she is! Charlie and Rika are with her.*

"Well, funny you should mention the asylum," Kate said. "I heard that Henry Braun's been committed."

"Now there's some poetic justice," Sam said.

"No!" Jade said with her eyes opened wide. "Why?"

"They say he just lost it after the poo-bath the birds gave him," Kate said. "And he tore his house up."

"How'd you find that out?" Russ asked with a big grin. "Don't tell me a little bird told you?"

Kate threw her head back and laughed. "No, though I have a vast network of spies and informants, they're all humans, every one of them."

Though he was relieved that Kate had steered the conversation away from Charlotte, Alfredo felt a new burden of guilt bear down on him. *So that is why Minnie has been calling me. I should have returned her calls.*

He stood up from the table and took each of their plates to the kitchen area and returned with a plate of chocolate chip cookies and a carafe of coffee.

"Oh, I was hoping you'd baked cookies!" Jade said as she took one. "You could market these, you know. They're heavenly!"

Alfredo laughed and took a cookie off the plate. "Thanks, Jade! If I wash out as a priest—not at all a far-fetched scenario—and a college professor and scientist, I will consider that. Thanks for the testimonial!"

Once Majewski finds out I have his sister here, I will no doubt be cast out, perhaps arrested. If they can find me. Already the idea had germinated in his mind that he could disappear with Charlotte into the bogs and fens and forests of the island near the tree house.

"I'm afraid the world will never see these cookies," Russ said through a mouthful. "Alfredo's in danger of being signed on as a full-time, tenure track professor!"

"That's fabulous!" Kate said. "Congrats, Padre!"

Alfredo waved his hand at Russ. "The university wants to be our partner in research here, which in the long run will help our efforts to keep the island intact." His words slammed incongruously into his fantasy of vanishing in the wilderness with Charlotte. He felt confused, suddenly. And so very tired. He looked at his watch.

"Hooray for the U of M," Jade cried out, "and long live Wilder Island!"

"Thanks to all of your efforts," Alfredo said cheerfully, trying to shake off his weariness. He raised his coffee cup in salute.

"Thanks to all of *our* efforts," Kate said.

Five cups clanked together over the plate of cookies, and everyone cheered.

"One more," Sam said, turning to Kate. "Thanks to the Father Superior Majewski for bringing Kate to us, and most especially me." He raised his cup reverently to her.

"Aw, Sam," Kate said, blushing.

She loves him. Alfredo could see it in her eyes. And in his. Jade and Russ looked at each other like that. The old, familiar fog of isolation began to envelop him. *I wish I could love like that.* Charlotte's face appeared in his head, her gray eyes, so innocent and warm. A few strands of black hair blowing across her face. *I love her.* He felt his body respond suddenly, in a way he had not felt since graduate school. The tingling. The hardening he did not think himself capable of since then. He felt his face flush.

"So," Kate said with a grin, "when will you publish your research on the language of the crows?"

"Not any time soon," Alfredo laughed nervously. He moved his chair slightly. "I have only just begun to scratch the surface."

"Nonsense!" Russ said. "You're too modest! You carried on entire conversations with those crows on our table at the fair! Publish, man!"

Why does he keep pressuring me? I have no ambitions as a scholar.

But he smiled graciously and said, "And you exaggerate, Russ! I am many months from a publication, if ever. But how about you?

How is your tenure research coming?"

"I'm doing some field work today after we finish here," Russ said. "If that is all right?" He put a hand behind one ear. "I can't resist the siren call of the orchids!"

"And I'm going to sketch," Jade said. *"Wilder Island II* coming up!"

"Of course," Alfredo said. "The island is your research station and inspiration." He felt some anxiety about Russ and Jade out wandering around, with Charlotte in the tree house. *But she is far away from the bridge and the Boulders. There is no way she can find her way there without help.*

"Want to join us?" Jade asked. "Anyone?"

Sam shook his head. "I've got to get some work done in the studio. I got way behind because of the art fair. Not that I'm not complaining!"

"But another time, I'd love to," Kate said. "I've got some work waiting for me also,"

Alfredo hesitated a moment. *I really need to get back to the tree house. If I go with them, how will I gracefully excuse myself? But if I let them leave by themselves and they come back and I am not here ...*

"You two go on," he said. "I will catch up after I tidy up here." He hoped they would not find Bruthamax's bridge and cross the Boulders.

Russ and Jade left Alfredo's cottage and made their way through the forest. The early afternoon sun infused the woods with crisp clarity, revealing the most intimate details of leaf, twig, and trunk. "Alfredo seemed really nervous," Jade said as they walked. "Did you notice? He kept looking at his watch."

"When he wasn't staring out the window," Russ said. "Yeah, I did notice. Like he really wanted to be somewhere else."

"I wonder why?" Jade said. "He invited us; it's not like we barged in on him or anything."

Russ shrugged. "Who knows? He's a strange man."

Hand-in-hand they strolled through the woods, and from time

to time, they stopped while Russ pointed out and named the familiar as well as unusual plants that crossed their path. Suddenly the rustic footbridge bridge appeared through the vines and shrubs. "Wow!" Jade said. "This is pretty cool! Did Alfredo build this? Is it safe?"

"Yes it is safe," Russ said. "And no Alfredo didn't build it. But he told me about it. Brother Maxmillian Wilder did. Over a hundred years old, he said, and still sturdy."

They walked to the middle and looked down at the tumble of huge rectangular slabs of rock below them. The sound of water falling wafted up to them and Jade said, as she peered down into the rocks and trees. "I hear a waterfall, but I don't see and water."

"It flows under the rocks," Russ said, "and comes out on the other side of the island, where we built the sanctuary."

They crossed the bridge, holding on to ropes of twisted forest fibers. "Oh, look at that!" Jade cried out. She brushed past Russ to the platform where the bridge ended, down the rope ladder to the ground.

With Russ right behind her, she slipped between two trees, pushing the low-hanging branches aside. She stepped into a tiny clearing where the forest gave way to a pond surrounded by scores of tiny flowers. Jade skipped to the pond, dropped to her knees and brought handfuls of the cool water to her lips. "This is what heaven is," she said and wiped her mouth on her sleeve. "Cool, sweet water."

Russ drank from the pond and pointed to a tiny flower growing at the edge of the water. "It sure looks like a *Cypripedium reginae*, except for the color. I've never seen a blue one."

"Lovely!" Jade said after she flopped down on her stomach on the grass next to him. "What color are they usually?"

"Pink and white," he said. "You've seen 'em. They're known as Lady's Slippers, the state flower of Minnesota, though they've all but vanished from the face of the Earth. But I've never seen a blue one!"

"Crow's eye blue," Jade said. "They're the same blue as the crow's eyes!"

"Oh, look!" Russ said, grabbing her arm. "The *Arethusa bulbosa*, the Dragon's Mouth orchid. Unbelievable! This little beauty is extremely rare. But look!" He gestured with his arms. "It's everywhere!"

"Oh," Jade said, reluctantly pulling herself away from the *Cypripedium reginae,* "but the Lady's Slipper is so much sweeter!" She examined the *Arethusa bulbosa.* "Dragon's Mouth, eh? I never would have thought that, although I can see some resemblance to a tongue, and those little bitty yellow hairs must be the flames."

Russ had moved on to another flower. "Wow. This is a total score. A *Malaxis pclodusa,* aka the Bog Adders Mouth. It's a high-latitude orchid, almost unheard of here in the States. But here it is, right in my own backyard, so to speak."

"It sure is an ugly little thing," Jade said, bending down close to the wiry little plant with a thick stem. "I thought orchids were all beautiful. This one's all stem! Where's the flower?"

"Ah, but it's an exquisitely rare, ugly little thing," Russ said. "Who needs beauty? So commonplace! Rare is better! But no, my sweet, not all orchids are beautiful; some are really nasty looking. There's one that smells like rotten meat, in case you're also thinking all flowers smell nice."

"I was," Jade said with a shrug. "But I should have known."

Russ stood up. "This is just gobsmacking unbelievable. First the *Arethusa bulbosa,* which was rare enough, and now the *Malaxis palodusa!*" All around the glade, multitudes of pink, yellow, white, purple, and orange flowers grew in astonishing abundance. "I've never seen this many varieties of orchids in one place. I can't say I've ever even read about a place like this."

A spiky little plant with flowers of sticky, needle-shaped petals caught Jade's eye. She moved closer and saw a drop of clear fluid hanging on the end of each petal. "What's this one called, honey?"

"That's a *Drosera rotundifolia,*" Russ said after a quick look, "speaking of carnivorous plants. It traps insects with those little drops of stick-um." He touched one of the drops, pushed it against his thumb, and pulled his fingers apart to demonstrate its glue-like qualities. "The plant digests the insect as it struggles to get free."

"Eeuw!" Jade wrinkled her nose. "I think I'd rather be looking at the lovely Lady's Slipper—it'd make such a beautiful sketch. But maybe I'll draw that ugly one over there. Just for contrast"

"That's fine, honey," Russ said, and he disappeared from view among the flowers and long grasses. "Wait a minute!" she heard him exclaim. He fell to his belly and disappeared from her sight.

Not until he had examined whatever it was fully and described it in his field notebook in excruciating detail and taken several Polaroid photographs, as well as a gazillion digital pictures, would he allow the outside world to encroach upon his enchanted little world.

She took her sketchbook and a set of colored pencils out of her bag and sat down next to the Lady's Slipper. With quick, light strokes of a pencil, she blocked in the flower, its stem and leaves, and a few rough details of the surrounding cove.

Russ could hardly believe his eyes. A blue Cypripedium reginae! But there was something else unusual about this flower. It has two seed stems. Impossible! Orchids are monocots!

But there it was. A blue non-monocot *Cypripedium reginae*. And it grew in abundance in this little cove! Russ felt his pulse quicken. *Is this it? Have I found it? My Jadum wilderii?*

He took a mechanical pencil out of his pocket and his field notebook out of his pack and opened it to the first blank page. After noting the date and his location, he described the flower in full detail, from the base of its stem to the tips of the petals. He made a few sketches of the leaves, stem, and flowers, annotating each carefully with notes and labels. He took numerous photographs until the Polaroid was out of film and the card in his digital camera was full.

He knew it would be illegal to dig up a *Cypripedium reginae* plant. *But this isn't a Cypripedium reginae,* but he really wanted to see its root system. *There seems to be a viable population here. I don't think it would hurt anything. And I really need to get this into my lab.*

He rummaged in his pack for a small spade and carefully dug up one of the smaller plants, put it into a plastic sample bag and stowed it in his pack.

Alfredo escorted Sam and Kate to the inlet and waited with them for the Captain. After he saw them off, he returned to his cottage to change into clothes more suitable for a slog down to the tree house. As he opened the door, he saw his cell phone blinking, announcing a call had come in while he was gone. He listened to the incoming message:

"Ah, hello," Thomas Majewski's voice said. "It's Thomas. I, uh, I've received some very disturbing news concerning my sister. I'm catching a late afternoon flight out your way. I'll call when I land. Cheers."

Alfredo stood rooted to the floor for many moments, panicked thoughts racing through his head, the worst of which Charlotte would be returned to the brand-new, high-security state mental hospital. He saw himself alone in a prison cell.

Dear Lord, what have I wrought?

The orb swayed gently on the end of the lamp chain, attracting his attention and breaking his paralysis. He steadied it for a moment, then removed it and put it in his pocket. Just in case.

He tidied up the cottage as anxious thoughts gnawed at him. *Majewski will expect me to be here with him tonight, but I cannot leave Charlotte alone so soon.* He looked at his watch. 1:20. *I have time to run down to the tree house and visit with Charlotte, fix her some dinner and be back in time to meet Majewski at the docks.*

Or. His hands stopped drying the sandwich platter. *If I do not answer my phone when he calls ... he will no doubt get a hotel room in Ledford tonight and I won't have to deal with him until tomorrow.*

He turned his phone off and put it on the table. After throwing a few items in his backpack—some fruit and cookies left over from the party—he wrote a quick note:

Russ and Jade-
> *My apologies, but I got called away. I have arranged for the Captain to pick you up at the inlet at 4:00.*
> *AM*

He stuck it to the door with a small tack and called out to a group of young crows in a nearby tree. "Yo! JohnHenry! I need a favor, please. Find the Captain and tell him that I need him to please meet my guests at the inlet at four o'clock. Can you do that for me?"

"Yessir!" JohnHenry said and took to the air, his three brothers following close behind.

JADE FINISHED HER DRAWING OF THE blue Lady's Slipper and stood up to stretch. Russ sat in the same spot where she had seen him go down, hunched over the notebook on his lap. She looked at her watch and estimated he'd be so engrossed for the next half-hour at least. Time enough for a short walk. The cove and pond were bathed in sunlight, but as soon as she stepped through the two sentinel trees where she and Russ had entered the cove, she was in a dark forest of tall trees, so completely unlike the little cove. She looked back through the sentinel trees at Russ, still bent over his work surrounded by sunlight flowers.

The sound of falling water captured her attention, and she thought the bridge was just ahead of her. She peered over the edge of the boulder ravine, through the willows and rocks; the waterfall sound seemed to come from directly below her. She couldn't see water flowing, but supposed Russ had been right, as always. The water flowed under the rocks.

The boulder ravine cut the island in two, as if the river had chewed its way through from one side of the island to the other. *There really is no way across that. All those scrubby trees growing between those huge rocks—I'd never get around them.* She sat down in a sunny spot on a flat rock and admired the view with the music of the waterfall in her ears.

CHARLOTTE WALKED THROUGH THE FOREST ON ground that was sometimes spongy and sometimes firm. Birds sang all around her, and she heard their many conversations. Her neck hurt from looking up, and her face ached from a permanent smile. A few crows called out her name from the branches and she waved and called out, "Grawky!"

"I wonder where Jayzu's cottage is?" she said out loud.

A young crow dropped out of the branches and landed at her feet. "That way, Miss Charlotte!" He pointed a wing. "By and by, you'll come to a bridge. Jayzu's cottage is on the other side."

"Thank you!" she said, stooping down to bird level. "And what is your name, little one?"

"Zelda," she said.

"Grawky, Zelda," Charlotte said and brushed her hand across the crow's outstretched wing.

"Zelda!" a voice shouted from the trees above. "Come on!"

Zelda flew off and Charlotte continued walking in the direction the little crow had pointed. She walked around black water ponds rimmed with sedges and rushes, and a marsh where a few ducks quacked their surprise at seeing her.

Charlotte drifted through a patchwork of different shades and hues of yellow, blue, red, orange, and green. Everywhere she looked, a new wonder revealed itself. A spider web stretched across a forked branch, drops of dew from the morning still clinging to its threads. Hundreds of birds flew in and out of the tree branches, weaving a trail of songs through the leaves.

The sights and smells of the forest triggered fragments of memory from her life before Rosencranz. She saw herself gathering leaves and flowers and putting them in a basket. The gray-haired woman with red cheeks smiled as she took the basket and dumped it on a table. She sang as she sorted and arranged the leaves and flowers into small piles:

Oh, the summer time is coming
And the trees are sweetly blooming
And the wild mountain thyme
Grows around the purple heather

Charlotte stopped walking and listened for a few moments to the woman singing in her memory. *Mimi!* A rush of images crowded her thoughts and she stopped walking. Mimi smiled and said, *"Pick me some purple heather, lass?"*

Charlotte's voice sang out into the forest:

And we'll all go together
To pull wild mountain thyme
All around the blooming heather,
Will ye go, Lassie, go?

"And here it is, my love," Russ said as he stood up. *"Jadum Wilderii.* My ticket to tenure!"

But she was nowhere in sight. "Jade?" he called out. "Jade!" He strained to hear something through the chatter of the birds and the cacophony of insects. "Jade!"

He walked through the sentinel trees and stopped. A faint path led to the bridge. *Alfredo warned us about the swamps and bogs beyond the boulders. I hope she didn't go that way.* He took the path to the bridge, calling out her name every minute or so. "Jade!" *But where else would she have gone?*

The sound of the waterfall drew him away from the path, and he walked to the edge of the boulder-filled ravine. Jade's bag with her sketchbook and pencils lay on a flat rock before him. "Jade!" he called.

He picked up her sketchbook, hoping she had not tried to find the waterfall. *Jade's not exactly the adventuresome type,* he told himself. *I'm surprised she got this far away from me.* He cupped his hands around his mouth and yelled. "Jade!"

Nothing.

As if I could hear anything above the bird racket. He returned to the path, and when the old bridge appeared, he felt a strange certainty that she had crossed it and was on her way to Alfredo's cottage.

He climbed the steps spiraling around the tree trunk to the platform and stepped onto the bridge.

Jade luxuriated in the sensation of warm sun on her back. *This is why lizards like rocks. I could fall asleep here.* She looked at her watch and shook her head. *I'd better get back to Russ.* She hopped off the rock and after getting her bearing from the footbridge to her left, she turned right. *The little cove is just a few steps this way.*

The path took a strange turn and the forest closed in around her. She turned around to make sure she could still see the old bridge. It was gone. She couldn't hear the waterfall anymore either. And there was no sign of the sentinel trees or the sunny cove of flowers.

Everything looked the same, no matter which direction she looked. Nothing but leaf upon leaf, branch upon branch, like a kaleidoscope of green and brown all the way to eternity. She started to run back toward the bridge, but after a few steps the path disappeared, and she stopped. Nothing looked familiar. The ground was rocky in one place and slippery black mud in others.

She stopped and looked all around. "Where am I?"

"Where am I?" She heard her cry echo through the forest.

She looked up through the trees, trying to get a sense of direction from the sun, but no sunlight filtered down to the forest floor. She could only see patches of blue here and there.

She froze at the sound of someone singing, a strangely familiar voice singing a melancholy tune. *Who is that?* The singing came closer—a thin and silvery voice sang:

All around the purple heather
Will you go, Lassie, go?
We'll all go together,
Will you go, Lassie, go?

"Chloe?"

How can she be here? Am I dreaming? Chloe died five years ago. She slapped her face a couple of times ordering herself to wake up.

But the singing continued.

Will you go, Lassie, go?
And we'll all go together
To pull wild mountain thyme
All around the blooming heather,
Will you go, Lassie, go?

She rushed headlong into the thick forest toward the singing; the thorns and prickly branches of the undergrowth scratched her arms and face as she thrashed her way through. The singing compelled her forward, growing louder at each step.

All around the purple heather,
Will you go, Lassie, go?

Jade burst through the trees into a small sun-lit clearing. Right before her stood a tall, thin woman with a long black braid. But it was the eyes that arrested her. Eyes the color of the dawn.

✦✦✦

ALFREDO WALKED QUICKLY TOWARD THE Boulders, hoping to see Jade and Russ coming back. The bridge rocked and rolled as he trotted across, and he twirled himself down the spiral steps to the ground using only his hands. He sped down the vague path and slowed to a halt as he noticed Jade through two tall trees that stood side-by-side.

He crept up closer, keeping himself concealed. Jade's back was toward him, but he could see that she was sketching. *And there is Russ. I guess he found the blue orchids.* Jade looked back over her shoulder suddenly. He pulled himself into the shadow behind the tree.

When she turned back to her work, Alfredo snuck away, relieved that neither she nor Russ had seen him. *They are busy about their own concerns. And I need to get to Charlotte.* He felt a sudden urgency, almost panic to get to the tree house, though he knew Charlie and Rika were with her.

The panic remained as he sped through scrubby bog birch and fragrant myrtle, feeling the firm ground starting to go soft in places. He stepped in more than one black puddle or pond, cursing as he pulled his foot out of the muck. He tried to pay attention to the different greens and textures, but everything looked the same, yet unfamiliar. As if he had never come this way before.

He tripped on a tree root and slid face-first down a mud-covered slope into a pool of black water. He fished himself out, wiping black mud out of his eyes, and stumbled forward without being sure of where he was going. He stumbled over rock and sprawled onto his hands. Cursing, he picked himself up again and bushwhacked through the undergrowth, using his arms as scythes.

He arrived at the tree house, covered with black mud and blood, and he shot up the spiral steps onto the deck. "Where is Charlotte?" he asked, wildly looking around. "Where is she?"

Rika blinked at him. "She is gone, Jayzu. Gone for a walk in the woods, I reckon." She gestured with her wing.

"Why did you let her go?" he cried, his panic wilting into dread. He stared at her, wondering how she could remain so calm.

Rika blinked again and tilted her head to one side. "As if I could stop her, Jayzu. I had my wings full with the kreegans. I couldn't watch her too."

"I'm sorry, Rika," he said. His shoulders sagged, and he sat down on the bench with his head in his hands. *How could I leave her alone with only crows to look after her?*

After a few moments, he raked his hands through his hair and stood up. "I must find her."

He jumped over the railing around the deck, landing in the grass below. "Charlotte!" he shouted as he sped off into the trees. "Charlotte!"

The End

Book 1

GLOSSARY

Beezle (BEE-zull)—crap, excrement

Bunya (BUN-yuh)—rotten inedible food

Cadeña-l'jadia (caw-DANE-ya—la HADya)—'the land of swampy waters amid green forests and mists.'

Judavoid (JOOda-voyd)—a whippersnapper, a brat.

Kreegans (KREE-guns)—children

Weebs (WEEBZ)–Mother

Zazu (ZAH-zoo)–Father

Zhekkies (ZHEK kees) 'My boys,' 'my buddies'—male term for buddies, henchmen Note: pronounce 'zh' as in 'Dr Zhivago'

Zhurka (ZHURK-uh) – husband

Zwizhi (ZHWEE zhee)– wife

I hope you enjoyed my Ecofantasy-where humans and crows converse with one another, share friendship and common goals. My intention in *Corvus Rising* was to present a friendly and humorous way to think about the ecological problems we have created—as well as the solutions.I would love to know what you think, about the idea that humans can communicate with other species, and that we are not so very different from one another. Please feel an immense freedom to send me a note, write a review, pester me for Book 2

Please also visit my webpage:

http://www.authormarycsimmons.com

If you would like to be notified when Book 2 comes out please send an email request to:

The Book Midwife@gmail.com

Happy reading!